A War Apart

by

Barbara Whitaker

This is a work of fiction. Names, characters, places, and incidents are either the product of the author's imagination or are used fictitiously, and any resemblance to actual persons living or dead, business establishments, events, or locales, is entirely coincidental.

A War Apart

Contact Information: info@thewildrosepress.com

Cover Art by *The Wild Rose Press, Inc.*

The Wild Rose Press, Inc.
PO Box 708
Adams Basin, NY 14410-0708
Visit us at www.thewildrosepress.com

Publishing History
First Vintage Rose Edition, 2020
Trade Paperback ISBN 978-1-5092-3315-1
Digital ISBN 978-1-5092-3316-8

Published in the United States of America

Dedication

To my father, Vernon R. Knight,
who served in the Coastal Artillery near San Francisco;
to Frank Tower,
who served in the 30th Infantry Division,
fought with them
from the landing in France to the end of the war,
and spent much of his life insuring
that his division would be remembered;
to my father-in-law, Dewey Paul Whitaker,
who served in
the 276th Armored Field Artillery Battalion
and fought his way across Europe;
to all those who served in the military during WWII
and all the loved ones who waited back home;
and finally to my husband, Pat,
whose help researching the WWII era
has been invaluable.

Chapter 1

December 10, 1943

The bus lurched to a stop amid screeching brakes. Through the window a scene played out, one Rosemary had witnessed countless times before. A young woman flirted with a soldier, then he slipped his arm around her waist and led her into a nearby hotel.

Rosemary's wicked thoughts followed the couple as they disappeared through the door. She imagined how they looked at each other, how he touched her as he led her into a room where they would be alone, how his strong hands gently undressed her. The handsome stranger would pull her to him, lean down and cover her mouth with his in a mind-numbing kiss.

The bus jerked into motion and jarred Rosemary back to reality. Heat flushed her cheeks. She glanced around to see if anyone was watching her, reading her inappropriate thoughts.

No one noticed. Not Aggie next to her who blew out a puff of cigarette smoke and turned the page of her novel. Not the older man standing in the aisle staring straight ahead, a newspaper clutched in one hand while holding onto the strap with the other.

In a big city like San Francisco she could be anonymous. No one cared if she had inappropriate thoughts or did something she shouldn't. Back home in

Tennessee, where Rosemary grew up, everyone in her small town noticed everything everybody did. And they had plenty to say about it, too.

Her thoughts wandered again to the thousands of young men in uniform that filled the city waiting to go to war. They were lonely, starving for affection and facing possible death, so they grabbed any chance to enjoy life while they could.

The young woman was just giving a soldier a night to remember before he shipped out. And giving herself one, too.

Maybe that's what she should do. Yield to the temptation. Do something wild and wicked. Just once. Who would know?

Fatigue weighed on her shoulders. If she weren't so tired and lonely, she probably wouldn't have such wicked thoughts.

If Jack hadn't betrayed her…

The bus turned and headed up the hill.

Hard as she tried, she couldn't keep Jack out of her mind for long.

Damn him.

She'd followed her husband out here last year so they could be together, so they could be happy. But he'd destroyed it all…because of "her."

The last time she saw him they'd had a spectacular fight. He'd sworn he would file for divorce. Swore he loved the little tramp. Now all these months later Rosemary had resigned herself to the idea that she'd have to do it herself.

He would let her take the blame. Let her tell their families back home that theirs would be the first divorce ever in either family. Women weren't supposed to get divorces. They were supposed to stay with their man no matter what, be the good little wife who looked the other way when her husband strayed because she couldn't keep him satisfied.

Well, Rosemary couldn't do that. She wouldn't put up with being treated like that…cheated on and betrayed.

Yet part of her still halfway expected him to appear at her door with that disarming smile asking for forgiveness.

Another stupid daydream.

The bus stopped at the bottom of a narrow, wooden stairway that zigzagged its way up the steep hill, the last leg of her journey across town from the shipyard in Oakland, where she worked, to the three-story boardinghouse, where women who'd come to the city to work in the good-paying defense plants found refuge.

Aggie joined her. "I saw that pretty blue dress you loaned to Charlotte," Aggie commented.

Rosemary just smiled and nodded.

"You see," Aggie continued as they reached the halfway point. "This sailor asked me to go dancing. And my only good dress got ruined the last time I wore it."

"Ruined?" Rosemary asked. "How?"

"Oh, some jerk spilled a drink down my front. One of those green-colored froufrou ones. Anyway, the stain won't come out."

"So you want to wear my blue dress."

"Oh, could I?" Hope lit up Aggie's face.

"Sure. I'll be happy to let you wear it. Lord knows, I'm not going to."

"Don't you ever go out?"

Rosemary shook her head. “Not in a long time.” She didn’t dare mention her marital disarray. She’d taken care to keep the gory details to herself.

They reached the top and Rosemary paused to catch her breath. Her stomach grumbled. Even one of Mrs. Frey’s meals would taste heavenly tonight. No exciting evening with a handsome stranger for her.

“Can I come get it later?” Aggie asked as she pushed open the heavy door.

“Sure.” Rosemary longed to share in Aggie’s excitement. “It’ll look lovely on you. Bring out your blue eyes.”

They started to climb up even more stairs toward their third-floor rooms when their landlady called.

“Mrs. Hopkins?”

Rosemary peered over the banister halfway up the first flight. “Yes?”

“Something came for you.” The older woman pulled a yellow envelope from her apron pocket and held it out.

Rosemary hurried back down and met the woman at the foot of the steps.

“I’m sorry. It came earlier. I’ve been watching for you.” Mrs. Frey shoved the envelope toward Rosemary.

Black letters on the thin envelope said, “Western Union.” A telegram.

Her hands shook as she turned it over and slid her finger under the flap. One end ripped and she tried to straighten it.

No one sent a telegram unless it was urgent. What had happened?

She unfolded the thin sheet of paper and read.

Dear Mrs. Hopkins, The Army regrets to inform

you that your husband, Pfc. John R. Hopkins, was killed in a training accident on December 8, 1943. Letter with details to follow. Deepest sympathy, General Thurman T. Campbell, Commanding, Camp Roberts, California.

Her heart caught in her throat. *"...killed..."*

She couldn't breathe.

Mrs. Frey patted her on the back, mumbled something.

Rosemary's legs turned to jelly. She grabbed the banister and sank onto the step.

"Oh, Jack…Jack."

Chapter 2

"What do you mean, you're leaving?" Guy Nolan stared at his friend in disbelief.

"I have to meet Peg in half an hour, so we can catch our train."

"But can't you wait—at least another day?"

Guy's friend, Bill, snapped his suitcase closed.

"We could go out tonight. All of us. And then you could leave tomorrow."

"Sorry, ol' buddy." Bill shook his head. "Her parents are expecting us in San Diego. We're supposed to meet the family and all that."

Guy turned away to hide his disappointment. He'd counted on spending a few days with his friends. A final hurrah before going overseas.

Bill touched his shoulder. "I've gotta do this. Don't you see? She wants me to make a good impression."

Guy forced himself to smile as he faced his friend. "They can't help but like you. Everybody does." He stuffed his feelings deep down inside, alongside the hurt from his mother's cavalier attitude about his departure. He couldn't blame his friend.

"Thanks."

"So when's the happy occasion?"

"The wedding? We haven't set a date yet. Sometime in the spring, I think. Don't want to wait too long."

"Guess I'll have to miss it."

"Do you know where you're going?"

"Nope. All I know is that I have to report to Camp Atterbury. That's where the 30th Infantry is assembling to get ready to go overseas."

"Where's Camp Atterbury?"

"Indiana."

"I thought you said you were training on radios. Now they've got you in the infantry? That doesn't make sense."

"You don't understand how the Army works. I'm in the 230th Artillery, which is part of the 30th Division. I'll be helping to direct fire. Shouldn't be too bad."

"Do you think you'll be going to England or Australia?"

Guy laughed at his friend's persistence. "I told you. I don't know. They don't give out that kind of information."

"Well, I don't envy you either way."

Bill pulled a ring of keys out of his pocket and removed one. "Look, I feel bad leaving you like this." He handed Guy the key. "You can stay here. Long as you want. Just give the key to Mr. Tandy when you leave."

"I can't do that."

"Why not? No point in you paying for a hotel…if you can find one. You stay here."

"What about Louie?"

"Oh, I thought I told you. He moved out last week. Got a chance to move in with another guy. Said he'd better grab it while he could." Bill picked up his suitcase and looked around. "Louie said he figured me and Peg would want this place to ourselves. After we're married, I mean."

Guy nodded. What would he do now?

"Have you seen Julie?" Guy asked. "Talked to her?"

"You know she's engaged, right? To that Navy fellow." Bill gave him a hard look. "Don't get any ideas there. She probably won't even talk to you. Not after the way you two broke up."

Guy straightened and stuck his chin out a notch. "That wasn't my fault."

"Maybe not, but she doesn't see it that way. She's that stuck on the guy."

Despite Bill's advice, Guy made up his mind to go see Julie, just to apologize and let her know he was going overseas.

****

"I told you I didn't want to talk to you," Julie said as soon as she opened the door and saw him standing there.

"Just for a minute. I want to…"

"Go away and don't come back." She slammed the door in his face.

She didn't give him a chance to tell her about his overseas orders, or to apologize for being a jerk, or even congratulate her on her engagement.

He stood there on her doorstep debating whether to knock again. In the end he decided to leave rather than upset her any more.

What did he expect? For her to welcome him with open arms? Not after he'd taken a swing at a certain Navy lieutenant, now her fiancé. Didn't matter that the sailor had insulted Guy's mother. Julie hadn't heard that remark.

Bill had been right. He shouldn't have come.

From Julie's place Guy made his way through downtown San Francisco where he stopped at a bar he used to frequent, hoping to run into some old friends. All he found were strangers.

He ordered a beer and asked the bartender about people he knew. Everyone was either in the military or working. Not wanting to sit in a bar, alone, and get drunk, he finished his beer and headed back across the bridge to Bill's place.

Tomorrow, he'd go to the train station and get his ticket. The Army wouldn't mind if he showed up a few days early.

"Maybe there'll be someone on the train to talk to," Guy said to fill the silence after letting himself into the empty apartment. There'd been plenty of soldiers just like him either heading home on leave or reporting to new bases when he'd made the journey across country a short time ago.

He dropped onto the sofa and thought back over his visit home.

They'd all been happy enough to see him when he'd arrived. They'd even gathered together for a home-cooked meal in his honor. His older sister, Lorene, and her three, stair-step children had bemoaned her husband's absence in the Coast Guard. When his teenage sister, Harriet, criticized his plain uniform and suggested some medals to spruce it up, his mother had responded by saying how nice he looked in his uniform.

Guy smiled at the memory.

His mother had tried. Yet her constant references to Henry, with the Marines in the Pacific, had underscored what he'd always known. Henry was her favorite. Even Wilson, the eldest off in the Navy, had barely garnered a mention, so Guy never expected much of her attention. Yet he had always been the one she turned to when she needed something.

The family had returned to their everyday lives by the time he announced his plans to depart for Oakland a few days early to visit with friends. His mother hadn't objected. It was almost like he'd been home from the shipyard for a long weekend, as he'd done so many times before.

Even though she'd been busy making his teenage sister a prom dress, she'd torn herself away to prepare his favorite fried chicken and mashed potatoes for his last home-cooked meal.

"Come home safe, son," his mother had said, allowing him a rare hug. That had been enough for him to know she loved him.

Alone in Bill's apartment, he wished he had some of that chicken to eat. Instead he opened a can of soup for his supper before going to bed early.

Chapter 3

Rosemary lugged her heavy suitcase across the lobby of the Southern Pacific station and took her place in one of the ticket window lines.

Her mother's words echoed in her ears. "You have to come home immediately," she'd said. "What will people think if you are not here to bury him?"

Her mother always worried about what people thought. For as long as Rosemary could remember, her mother had feared something would rekindle the talk about her husband's untimely death. Rosemary's sudden marriage into one of the most respected families in town had given the small-town gossips plenty to talk about, including the questionable mental state of the Blackwoods.

Memories of that horrible day in the drug store brought back the humiliation and shame. She'd overheard the two old biddies speculating that scheming Rosemary Blackwood had forced Jack Hopkins to marry her by claiming she was pregnant. They said Rosemary had planned the whole thing, because otherwise no one would have ever married her. Their words still stung.

Now with Jack's death the talk would start up again. Talk about their marriage, about what she must have done to keep him on the string and make him marry her. And about how he died.

Well, she damn sure wouldn't give any of them the satisfaction of knowing what had happened in San Francisco. She wouldn't embarrass herself, much less her mother or Jack's parents, with the truth about how Jack had behaved so far away from home. The drinking, the anger, the ill-tempered moods, the despicable way he spoke to her, and especially not his betrayal.

No. She'd let his parents and the town keep their memories of the loveable, push-the-limits young man who tested his parents' patience yet who no one could stay upset with for long. They didn't need to know about the selfish, angry Jack who struggled to conform to what the Army expected of him.

She ran her finger over the smooth pearl on her earlobe.

Her Jack, who'd gone and gotten himself killed in a stupid accident, had become someone she barely recognized. His commander attempted to be kind in his letter, but Rosemary knew Jack, knew how reckless and impulsive he could be. So she had no problem envisioning what must have happened. His "I'll do it my way" attitude, just to show everyone that he could do something no one else could do, had ended badly. This time he'd paid the ultimate price for his bravado.

She moved forward and brushed aside a stray tear. She'd loved that bravado. Even if it did land him in another woman's arms.

Anger flared again. Damn him.

She looked around self-consciously to see if anyone noticed her warring emotions. A soldier in line behind her tipped his hat. She nodded but avoided meeting his gaze.

A man stepped away from the ticket window, leaving only one person in front of her.

She wanted to get this over with. Get on a train and start the arduous journey back, back into another world, to a world filled with relatives and neighbors she'd known all her life. Back to face Jack's parents, who'd loved him dearly, who'd never seen his faults. She'd never tell them what he'd done to her. Not now.

The man in front of her argued with the ticket agent over the availability of tickets.

Rosemary's mouth went dry. She never thought about not being able to get a ticket. She'd given up her room, packed or given away everything she owned, and journeyed across the bay to the train station. What would she do?

The customer paid for his ticket and moved aside. Rosemary stepped forward and faced the man behind the counter.

"May I help you?"

"I need a ticket to Kerrville, Tennessee." Her fingers squeezed the strap of her purse. "I need to get there as soon as possible."

The clerk grunted but held his tongue as he pulled out a book of timetables and flipped through its pages.

"Fastest would be to route you through Chicago. Then south."

"How long will it take?" she asked hopefully, maybe she'd misunderstood his conversation with the man in front of her.

He looked up and eyed her over his glasses. "It's just about forty hours to Chicago on the Zephyr. Another day or so going south."

"That's good. I told my mother I'd be there in three

or four days."

"Ma'am, that's travel time. Heading east cross country, the earliest civilian tickets we have available are for next Thursday, if they haven't already sold out."

"What?" she gasped. "But you don't understand. I have to get there." She gripped the counter with her free hand, holding on for dear life. "I can't stay here. I…I…" The words wouldn't come. She couldn't say it, yet she had to make him understand. "My husband…"

A man in uniform pushed his way to her side. "I have orders to report to Camp Atterbury, Indiana. And she's going home to stay with her sick mother, isn't that right, dear?"

Rosemary looked up into soft green eyes peering from beneath bushy brows. He nodded ever so slightly, and for some odd reason she instinctively trusted him.

"Aren't you supposed to give priority to the military?" he challenged.

The clerk looked from the soldier back to her. "Are you…together?"

She nodded emphatically, intentionally raising her left hand to expose the gold band. If she didn't go along with this man, she'd be waiting here for almost a week.

"Well, in that case," the clerk stammered. "Let me see."

The man searched his schedules. The sight of a uniform certainly changed his attitude.

"Let's see now, madam, do you want to accompany your husband all the way to Indiana? Then go south to Tennessee? Or would you mind parting ways a bit earlier? In Chicago?"

She looked up again into that kind, gently smiling face. A nice face. She prayed she could trust him.

"I, uh…" She pulled her gaze from the handsome man standing so close she could feel the heat radiating from his body and forced herself to look at the clerk. "Which way would get me there sooner?"

When the clerk's brow furrowed in a question, she quickly added, "I'm so worried about my mother…that I'll get there in time." The lying words rolled off her tongue so easily. Too easily. A flush burned her face.

A strong arm wrapped around her shoulder and pulled her into the scratchy wool of his dress uniform. She buried her face in his broad chest, not fighting the stranger's touch.

"She's just so worried, about her mother." He patted her shoulder. "And, of course, me shipping out and all."

"Yes, I quite understand."

The soldier's casual comment about shipping out stabbed her heart.

She pulled back and looked up. She wanted to ask him all kinds of questions. When? Where was he going? Overseas to fight?

"I'll need to see your orders."

"Sure." He placed his hands on her shoulders and set her away from him as if she were a fragile doll unable to move on her own. Never taking his eyes off her, he reached inside his jacket and pulled out a much-handled envelope and placed it on the counter.

The paper rattled as the clerk took his orders out and perused them. The soldier's gaze remained fixed on hers. His silent communication said for her to keep quiet and go along with the ruse. She could only nod. The answers would come soon enough.

"Very well." The clerk spoke, and the soldier

shifted his attention to retrieving his orders and listening to the vital information.

"You understand, there are no Pullmans available, not for some time."

The soldier nodded and she did, too. She had never expected such luxury.

"I can get you two tickets, leaving tomorrow…"

"Tomorrow," she gasped. "I…"

The clerk frowned. "There is nothing sooner."

The soldier placed his hand on her shoulder. "That's fine. Tomorrow will be fine."

She let out her breath. No use to complain. At least it wasn't next week.

"Leaving tomorrow," the clerk continued. "On the Zephyr to Chicago. From there you, ma'am, will take the Dixie Flyer to Tennessee. And you, sir, will travel to Indianapolis separately. Unless you would rather accompany the missus to Tennessee and then travel back north. I see that you have extra time before you have to report."

The soldier glanced at her and accurately interpreted her expression as a definite no.

He turned back to the ticket agent. "I think we'd better go our separate ways in Chicago. I don't want anything to happen to make me late reporting in."

Chapter 4

He picked up their bags and escorted her away from the ticket window to the far corner of the waiting area.

"Sorry to jump in like that, but you sounded kind of…desperate." She looked up at his words. "Was I right? About being desperate, I mean?"

"Yes." She nodded and looked away. Some unknown emotion distorted her delicate features. "I…uh…have to get home as soon as possible."

"Did I guess right? About your mother?"

"No, she's fine." Her head turned upward again and their gazes met. "Thank you for your help."

She fumbled in her purse and retrieved the cash to pay for her ticket. Something in him longed for her company, longed for the brief encounter to last just a little longer.

"Tell me how much I owe you."

He looked at the ticket and told her the amount.

When she'd counted out the money, she offered it to him. "Here's your money. You can give me my ticket now. And I won't bother you again."

She wanted to get rid of him. Give him the brush-off. But he wasn't ready to break the fragile connection they'd made. "Sure." He took her money. "Only problem is, they're made out to Mr. and Mrs."

Her mouth flew open "What! But…"

He hated lying to her, but something made him want to hang on to her as long as he could. "I know. But we're not married." He pulled his wallet from his pocket and slid the bills and both tickets into it. "Looks like we'll be traveling together, though."

A look of sheer panic marred her lovely face.

He reached out, to reassure her, but she jerked back from him.

Had he gone too far? Suddenly conscious of how his actions might look to her, he regretted being so flippant.

"Look," He rubbed his sweaty palm down the side of his uniform. "I didn't mean anything by it. I just wanted to help. Honest." Was she shaking? "I'm sorry if I frightened you. I didn't mean to."

She took a step to the side and sank down onto a bench as if her knees had gone weak. He sat beside her making sure to keep space between them.

"I saw you standing in line." He wouldn't tell her he'd chosen that line so he could stand near her. "And I saw your ring." She looked down and fingered the simple gold band. "So, I figured your husband was in the service…" He hesitated. "Going overseas, maybe." Her head jerked up and those incredibly pale blue eyes met his. "I wasn't trying to take advantage or anything. I just wanted to help a fellow serviceman's wife."

She nodded ever so slightly as her gaze returned to the ring.

After a long moment she whispered, "He's dead."

He wasn't sure he'd heard right. "Excuse me. What…?"

She turned to face him directly. "I said he's dead." Her voice broke on that last word, as she fought to maintain her composure.

His chest tightened. A widow. Her husband killed in action. He'd been flirting with a…a grieving widow.

"I'm sorry," he managed. "Where? The Pacific?" That would explain her being in California.

She shook her head. "No." Then, she pulled her purse into her lap and pulled out a crumpled handkerchief, swiping it beneath her nose while blinking furiously to keep the tears from overflowing onto her cheeks. "Nothing so glamorous."

He sat and listened.

"Jack always could do the craziest things." She dabbed at her nose again. "No. He was killed in a training accident. What was it the man said? Ammunition exploded unexpectedly. I think that's how they worded it. In the letter. He sort of implied that Jack died to protect the other soldiers."

She stopped then and looked directly at him. "That wasn't Jack. He wasn't the type to throw himself in harm's way to save someone else." Her words were bitter, unforgiving.

"Maybe he was," he said softly. "Maybe this time, he was."

Her face screwed up then. She buried it in her hands, clutching the damp cloth to her mouth to stifle the sobs. He scooted a little closer and slipped his arm around her slumped shoulders. She leaned into his embrace, her body wracked with sobs.

He hadn't expected this when he'd spotted the dark-haired beauty in the ticket area. He'd seen a pretty girl he thought might be fun to talk to. Standing behind her in line, he'd looked her over. The nice figure. The dark hair fashioned into one of those rolled hairdos like

Veronica Lake.

Then he'd spotted the ring.

Her demeanor had clearly indicated she was upset, and her reaction to the ticket agent had sent him jumping to her rescue before he had a clue what he was rescuing her from. Now he knew.

After a few minutes she settled down, pulled away, and blew her nose. He saw the apology coming, so he headed it off.

"You hungry?"

A hint of a smile broke through her teary eyes. She nodded.

"Well, let's see if we can't find some place to eat."

He stood and took her arm to help her up.

"By the way, I'm Guy Nolan."

"Rosemary Hopkins."

They shook, and as he released her hand, he added, "There's a little place just down the street."

Chapter 5

"The food here is both fast and tasty," Guy assured her as he pushed open the door to a little cafe crammed into the narrow space between two larger buildings. "At least it used to be."

The aroma of fresh coffee and fried food assailed her senses, and her stomach rumbled in response. She couldn't remember when she'd eaten last.

He steered her past several customers to a table near the back. It surprised her when he held her chair, like a perfect gentleman, before seating himself. Jack never did things like that.

A waitress appeared and plunked down two glasses of water. "Menu's there," she said, pointing to a handwritten list on a chalkboard hanging above the counter. "I'll give you a minute."

"The hamburgers are great. Nice and juicy," Guy said as he read the menu. "At least they used to be." He turned to face her. "Don't know about the soup."

"I wonder if they'd fix me some breakfast? Eggs and toast, I mean."

He tilted his head and looked at her, clearly asking a silent question.

"I didn't eat this morning," she explained, feeling herself blush. "I haven't eaten much since…"

He covered her cold hand with his warm one. "Sure. We can ask." She met his gaze and wondered how green eyes could be so soft and warm and understanding.

The waitress appeared out of nowhere. “Decide what you want?”

Guy looked up. “The lady would like to know if she could get some breakfast? Maybe eggs and toast?”

“Sure, hon. How do you want those eggs?”

“Two, scrambled with buttered toast.”

“You want sausage or bacon?”

“Uh…” She hadn’t thought of getting any meat.

“Give her the bacon. And make it two pieces of toast.” Guy met her gaze, smiling. “And some jam.”

“We’ve got strawberry and grape.”

“Oh, the strawberry would be wonderful.”

Guy grinned. How had he known?

“And bring me a big juicy hamburger with all the fixings.” He glanced her way. “Leave off the onions.”

The waitress didn’t look up from her pad. “You want fried potatoes with that?”

“Sure.”

“And drinks?”

He glanced back at Rosemary. “Coffee okay?”

She nodded.

“Two coffees it is.”

It amazed Rosemary how comfortable she was with this complete stranger. He’d just swooped in and taken charge of her life. And she’d let him.

“You’ll feel better once you’ve eaten.”

She nodded and self-consciously withdrew her hand from his grasp.

“I’m sorry,” he said. “I didn’t realize…” He glanced away. A tinge of pink brightened his ruddy complexion.

Despite his words, she had the distinct feeling that he'd known exactly what he'd been doing. But it didn't upset her. Much as her own natural caution warned her to be careful, she didn't feel in any way threatened by this man. On the contrary, he'd piqued her curiosity.

"Are you from San Francisco?"

He straightened. Had her question surprised him?

"No. I used to work here in Oakland though. My family lives out near Stockton."

"I heard you say you were shipping out. Have you been home to see your folks?"

"Yes. Visited them. Then I came into the city to see some friends."

"A girlfriend, maybe?"

His face reddened even more. "Yeah." His nervous laugh told her volumes.

"I'm sorry. I shouldn't have asked."

"Oh, it's okay." He met her gaze. "We broke up before I left for training. I just thought…well, anyway, she didn't want to see me."

Her heart went out to him. "I'm sorry."

His head tilted to one side. "You see, she's engaged to this other guy. And I'm happy for her." He shifted in his seat. "I really am. I just wanted to tell her that and that I'm going overseas." His voice trailed off at the end.

She understood. He'd wanted his ex-girlfriend to care, but she didn't.

"She probably didn't mean to be harsh. Maybe she thought her fiancé would be jealous."

He grinned. "She was probably afraid we'd have another…uh, altercation."

Her gut clenched at his mention of violence. The

reaction must have shown on her face because he instantly jumped to explain.

"That sounded bad, didn't it?"

She nodded, avoiding his gaze.

"It wasn't all that bad, honest." He hesitated before continuing. "Back when she and I were dating, we were in this club and this Navy guy started flirting with her. I didn't like him talking to her so I got a little hot under the collar and, well…he said something I didn't like."

She glanced up at the regret in his voice. He stared across the room, lost in the memory.

"One thing led to another and I ended up throwing a punch." He looked at her then. She met his gaze but drew back, unsure how to react.

His face twisted into a smirk. "I missed and he connected." He rubbed his chin as if it still stung from the blow. "She broke up with me that night and started dating him."

At that moment the waitress plunked down two mugs and poured them full of hot coffee. "You want cream and sugar?"

"Yes, please," Rosemary answered.

"No." He picked up the mug and took a sip of the steaming liquid.

They sat in silence as she fixed her coffee.

Finally, he spoke. "I wanted to apologize to her. Ask if we could be friends. But she told me to get lost and slammed the door before I could say anything."

"Maybe you disappointed her. Maybe she expected you to behave better than you did."

"I know. I was a heel. A real jerk." He clutched the hot mug in both hands as if he needed something to hold on to. "But how do I tell her I'm sorry if she won't even talk to me?"

"Maybe you should write her a letter. Apologize that way."

"How do I know she'd even read it?"

"You don't. But at least you will have tried."

The delightful fragrance of bacon arrived before the waitress placed the plate in front of her. Her stomach growled with anticipation. Without even looking up, she grabbed her fork and dug into the mound of scrambled eggs.

They ate in silence for several minutes until she came up for air, after she'd gobbled up half her food. Guy watched her, a smile crinkling his soft green eyes.

Embarrassed, she reached for the mug and took a swallow of coffee.

"It must be good, the way you're eating."

"Yes, it is. I guess I didn't realize how hungry I was."

He nodded and took another bite of his hamburger.

She bit into a slice of toast and made herself eat more slowly.

"So, what are you doing here in California?" he asked, toying with a fried potato with his fork. "You're not from here. I can tell from your accent. Was your husband stationed nearby?"

She met his gaze. "Yes. With the coastal artillery. He came out last year, and I followed him. I got a job at the shipyard. Then he got reassigned to the regular artillery, so they could send him overseas."

"He left and you stayed." He bit into the potato. "Why didn't you go home then?"

Rosemary could feel the anger roiling up from deep inside, engulfing her in its dark claws, Jack's betrayal still raw, still a gaping wound, unhealed.

"I…I didn't mean to pry."

His voice conveyed concern. Her face gave away too much of her emotions. She'd have to work on controlling her reactions. After all, when she went home there would be plenty of nosy people trying to find out all they could.

Guy could never imagine her horror at the thought of going home and telling her mother what had happened. Her mother had been through too much. She didn't deserve to have Rosemary's shame dumped on her. Rosemary had left home not just for herself but to protect her mother from the embarrassment and shame, not to mention what the gossip could do to her business.

This kind man didn't know. He had only asked out of curiosity, not malice.

She straightened her shoulders and drew a deep breath. He deserved an answer.

"We had separated. I didn't want to tell my mother or his family." She looked up and met his gaze, fearing the judgment she'd see there, yet needing him to understand. "I thought maybe if we were apart for a while…maybe we could…"

She started to say, "work things out," but in her heart she knew they wouldn't have. Jack wasn't the type to come crawling back, begging forgiveness. And she didn't know if she could have forgiven him. Now she'd never know.

"Kind of like me and my girlfriend, only worse. Splitting up a marriage must be tough." He shook his head and focused on the coffee mug in his hands.

He had no idea what it had been like. Nobody did. But he didn't question why. He simply accepted that there had been a good reason.

"Finish eating," he prodded after a few minutes. "It's getting cold."

Rosemary looked down at the plate of half-eaten food. She picked up a piece of toast and smeared jam on it. He raised his hand and the waitress appeared to refill their mugs.

"You said you worked at the shipyard. Which one?" The waitress moved on to another table.

"Moore's." She bit into the toast and marveled at the amazing taste of the strawberry jam.

"Moore's?"

She looked up, nodding. He had a strange half-smile on his face.

"That's where I worked."

Chapter 6

Guy couldn't believe that they had worked at the same place. He certainly would have noticed her. Even dressed in work clothes her beauty would have stood out anywhere.

"When were you at Moore's?"

Her face lit up and her gaze met his. Those blue eyes, pale and sparkling captivated him.

"I started last year. May or June. I can't remember exactly."

"That explains it."

"What?"

"Why I didn't meet you. I joined the service along about that time."

A smile spread across her entire face.

"What?" He grinned back at her.

She shook her head as she looked away. "Oh, nothing." Then her eyes cut back to his. "You just don't sound like you're from California."

"Oh." He'd been ribbed about his accent before. For some reason he'd never lost that Arkansas drawl, even though he'd been in California for years.

"Our family's originally from Arkansas. We came out here in '35 after Pop died."

"I'm sorry. I didn't mean to…"

He raised his hand to stop her apology. "Don't worry about it. It was a long time ago. Anyway, I guess

I still talk like I'm from back there."

"But you are. That's where you come from." She looked around. "A lot of people out here came from somewhere else."

The waitress slapped the bill down. "You want any more coffee?"

"No," he replied.

Rosemary shook her head.

"I guess we'd better finish up and get out of here."

She nodded and reached for the bill.

"Oh, no. I invited you, remember?"

"You don't have to pay for my food. I have money."

He couldn't help smiling at her protest. "I want to," he insisted.

On the street again, the familiar smells of salt water, fishing boats, and grime reminded him the docks weren't far away. Unlike the touristy Fisherman's Wharf in San Francisco, this was Oakland, the working-class side of the bay. He'd spent most of his time in this area, living and working, with only occasional trips into the more upscale and glamorous San Francisco. That's where Julie lived. And, as it turned out, she was out of his league, just as he'd feared from the beginning.

As they walked back toward the train station, he asked, "So, will you go back home tonight?"

She glanced up at him, those long lashes shadowing her eyes. "No. I can't. I gave up my room to another girl. Packed everything."

"Surely they'll let you stay another night."

"No. I'll just wait in the station."

"That'll be uncomfortable."

"I'm not going back." She stopped and stood there

on the sidewalk, her gaze locked on his.

He raised his hands in surrender. “All right. It’s your choice.”

She drew a deep breath and then sighed. “It’s just…they know. About Jack…that he’s…gone.” She looked away. “I can’t face them again. Tell them how stupid I’d been…again.”

“You’re not stupid. You couldn’t know how hard it was to get a ticket. The only way I knew is that I’ve just come across the country. I saw lots of people who couldn’t get on the train because the military took priority.”

“But I could have asked…” She shook her head as if trying to remove the memory. “I wanted to get away, as quick as I could. So I came across the bridge. Came all the way over here.”

“You live over in San Francisco?”

She nodded.

“But you said you worked over here, at Moore’s?”

She nodded again. “I went back and forth, every day.”

“But why? I’m sure you could have found somewhere to live over here in Oakland.”

She pursed her lips together and blinked. She was fighting tears. He’d pushed her too hard.

“I’m sorry. It’s none of my business.”

“No. It’s okay.”

They resumed walking slowly toward the station. After a few minutes she spoke again.

“When I first came here, I wasn’t working at Moore’s. Jack was stationed out at the Presidio, so I found a little apartment as close as I could. Most of the time Jack had to stay in the barracks out near the gun emplacements. When he could, he would come to the apartment." She glanced up at him as they walked. "So we could be together."

He nodded but said nothing, sensing her need to talk, to explain.

"After we…separated, I gave up the apartment and went to live in a boardinghouse nearby. I guess I still wanted to be…close enough…" Her voice trailed off.

He bit his lip to keep from speaking. She was clearly torn up about her husband, both his death and their separation. Much as he wanted to, he could offer no consolation to her.

After a few moments of silence broken only by their footsteps on the sidewalk, she spoke again.

"Truth is I don't want to go back, and I don't want to go home either." She sighed, and his heart broke for her.

"Why don't you want to go home?"

She looked up at him then. "Did you ever live in a small town?"

"Yes. Out where they grow vegetables. And back in Arkansas, my father ran a general store in a little town. Why?"

"Then you know how people talk in small towns. How they love to gossip about everyone."

He nodded.

"I hate gossip." Her lips flattened, and she closed her eyes as if she were holding something back.

They crossed at an intersection. He made himself stay quiet.

When they reached the opposite corner, she finally spoke. "I don't want anyone back home to know Jack and I had separated."

"You don't want them to talk, now that he is gone."

"Yes. No sense in telling it all now. He never filed any papers."

He took that in. Her husband had threatened to divorce her, not the other way around.

"His parents are already devastated. How can I tell them what happened? It would only hurt them more."

"I admire you for wanting to preserve his good name."

"And mine," she snapped.

She stopped and stared at him as if gauging his reaction.

"Because you had separated?"

She nodded. "They'll turn it around. Blame me." She started walking again.

"I'm sorry," he managed to say as he caught up with her.

"Some people will talk, no matter what. But he's gone, and I can at least try to preserve his memory for his family."

He wouldn't press her for the whole story.

At the main entrance to the train station, people hurried out, turning in either direction, crossing the street, hailing cabs, chatting with friends.

He and Rosemary stood back until they cleared away.

"You could get a hotel for the night," he suggested. "Although rooms are pretty scarce."

"Is that what you are going to do?"

"No. I'm staying with a friend." He paused. "Actually, I'm staying at a friend's place. He's gone, but he told me I could stay there."

A wild idea popped into his head. “You could stay there, too.”

Chapter 7

Rosemary couldn't meet his gaze, so she scanned the street while she searched her mind for a response. What did he mean? A simple offer of a place to stay, or was it more?

Two sailors, who'd come out of the train station, crossed the street to a bar where they spoke to two young women standing on the sidewalk. As they entered the bar, arm in arm, she thought of the many times she'd watched and wondered what it would be like to be free to talk to men on the street, to go out with them, and to discover what she wanted from a man.

She'd married her high school sweetheart, had never really known anyone but Jack. And once she'd come to California, she'd found out Jack had a cruel streak, that he hadn't wanted to marry her, hadn't wanted to be tied down. If she'd lived in a bigger place, if she'd had the opportunity to date other men, would she have chosen Jack? She'd never know.

Maybe, before she went back to Kerrville and buried herself in small town widowhood, maybe she could take a chance with this nice man, so kind and strong and handsome.

She straightened as she turned to face him. "I'll go with you…on one condition."

"What's that?"

"I want to sleep with you."

His mouth dropped open. His gaze darted from side to side. "Uh…I, uh…" He closed his mouth and drew in a deep breath. "I didn't mean…"

"I know." She struggled to keep from smiling. She'd never said anything so shocking in her life. His dark brows wrinkled into a frown. She had to explain. "Don't you see? I'll never have this opportunity again. When I go home, there won't ever be another chance to be free. To do something wild, and I don't know, exciting. And anonymous. We could do this, and no one would know. No one would care."

"What…what about your husband?"

"Jack?" She gritted her teeth to keep from screaming. "Jack cheated on me. In our own apartment. He didn't want me, not really. He wanted her."

He tugged her arm and guided her away from the doorway, away from the few people still milling around on the street in front of the station.

"Look, I wanted to help you. Get your ticket, cheer you up, talk to you. I never expected…anything…"

"I know. It's a crazy idea. I just…I feel like the whole world's gone crazy. You've got to go off to fight this war, and you might not come back. I have to go back there. Back to everybody watching me, even my mother. Watching everything I do, everyone I speak to. Talking behind my back." This time she grabbed his arm. "Don't you want to have one last fling before you ship out?"

Those soft green eyes stared at her. The wheels turned as he evaluated the situation. Jack would have jumped at the chance. This man, Guy, had to think about it.

"Look, if you don't want to, it's okay." She dropped her gaze to the sidewalk. "I know I'm a mess. Probably not the type of girl you go for…"

"You're beautiful."

Her head bobbed up, and again, she searched his face. Did he mean it? His lips softened into a faint smile, those eyes crinkled, and her insides melted.

He slid his arm around her shoulders. "What you need is some rest and someone to talk to." Then he gave her a little squeeze. "Come on. Let's get our bags. Then we'll go to Bill's place. It's not far."

Again, she followed his lead. She could talk to this nice, patient man, and she wouldn't have to worry about him judging her or making fun of her, like Jack had done.

Chapter 8

During the taxi ride, Guy remained silent. He didn't want to discuss her outrageous proposal in front of the driver, and thankfully, she didn't either.

The silence continued as they climbed the stairs. He fumbled with Bill's key and managed to unlock the door.

"Well, here it is," as he ushered her inside.

Rosemary took a few steps into the room. "It's cozy." She turned to face him. "Kinda like our old apartment, but…"

He couldn't read her thoughts, so he plunged ahead. "I lived here with Bill when I worked at Moore's." He walked across the room and pushed the screen back. "The kitchen's here, such as it is. There's not much here to eat. I can run down to the corner and get a few things."

She came up behind him and put her hand on his back. "Don't go. Not yet."

He turned. Her sweet smile made his heart pound. He needed to get himself under control.

"Sure." He glanced around. "We could sit. Talk a while." He pointed toward the couch.

Thankfully, she followed his direction and sat down. He joined her, wondering what to say. He'd never been in a situation like this before.

"Where's your friend? Working?"

"Uh…no. Bill's gone. Out of town." He searched for something to distract her. "He went with Peg, his girlfriend, to meet her folks." He spotted the radio, over near the window.

"Where does her family live?"

"San Diego." He got up and crossed the room. "Wanna listen to some music?" He glanced back at her.

"Sure."

He turned on the old set and waited. "It's gotta warm up."

"That's okay." She got up then and went over and opened the bedroom door. "When did Bill leave?"

Why was she looking in the bedroom? Was she already thinking about going to bed?

"Yesterday. I came by to see him just as he was going to meet Peg."

She faced him. "Did you stay here last night?"

"Yeah." He shifted his attention back to the crackling sounds of the radio and gently turned the knob to tune in some music.

"After you saw your girlfriend?"

"Ex-girlfriend. Yeah." He glanced over his shoulder as she roamed the room. "I went to a bar hoping to run into some old friends. They're all gone, and I didn't like drinking alone so I came back here."

"You could have picked up a girl."

He stood and faced her. "That's not my style."

"What is your style?"

"Well, I like to get to know someone, before…"

"Before you go to bed with them." She moved closer.

"Yeah." He turned back to the radio, and as soon as he touched the dial, orchestra music filled the room. He sighed. Maybe he could get her to sit and listen to the music for a while.

"That's nice." She stood right behind him. He turned, and she smiled that heart-stopping smile. "Let's dance."

****

He took her in his arms and moved with the music. She relaxed and leaned closer, enjoying the feel of his body close to hers.

Maybe this would be enough, spending time with this nice man who was clearly uncomfortable with her proposal. Even as the thoughts ran through her head, she knew dancing wouldn't be enough, not for her. Something had emboldened her. Some need to reach out and grab life before it passed her by.

Strange sensations engulfed her. Excitement, desire, and terror. Heat rose from deep within her gut, up her neck to her cheeks. She hid her face against his strong shoulder and pulled him closer. She didn't want to feel ashamed. Her desires were perfectly normal. She'd been married. She'd enjoyed sleeping with Jack. There was nothing wrong with that. Nothing shameful in wanting a man.

She and Jack had enjoyed each other…for a time…before…

No. She wouldn't think of those dark days.

She pulled back and looked up into Guy's soft, green eyes, eyes with lashes much too long for a man, and willed herself to stay in the moment.

He returned her gaze as if he were caught up in the same web of desire. Or did he just feel sorry for her?

She reached up and touched the shock of wavy, auburn hair a shade lighter than his thick brows. Those deep-set green eyes narrowed, but he said nothing. He just pulled her close again and turned her around the room with the beat of the music.

He wasn't as tall as Jack and not as intimidating. Yet he was solidly built with broad shoulders and strong hands. The wicked part of her longed to see beneath the uniform, run her fingers over his bare skin.

The song ended and he stepped back. She missed his warmth.

"How about something to drink?" He glanced toward the kitchen. "I could make some coffee."

She smiled. "No alcohol?"

He shook his head. "Nope. Bill never keeps any." He hesitated a minute. "If you want some…?"

"No. That's okay." She followed him to the tiny kitchen. "I'm not much of a drinker."

He grinned and her heart lurched. "Me neither."

He filled the coffee pot with water and measured out the coffee. Then he lit one of the two burners on the stove and placed the percolator on it.

As the water heated, he opened the cupboard above the stove. His long fingers wrapped easily around a mug and lifted it from its hook. He handed it to her, and his hand brushed against hers. Their gazes caught for a second before he twisted around to grab a second mug. Had he felt it, too? That tingle of connection.

"Not sure if there's any milk." He opened the small refrigerator and looked inside. "Hey, there is."

He pulled out a half-filled bottle of milk. "Hope this is okay for your coffee."

He remembered that she used cream and sugar.

"Yes. that's fine."

He brought the milk and a sugar bowl and put them

beside the mugs. "The coffee will be ready in a jiff."

"Sure." She reached for the chair, but he beat her to it and pulled it out for her.

Jack never did anything like that. Not the chair or the coffee. Instead he would have waited for her to do it all.

She looked up into his anxious face. "Do you cook, too?"

His expression softened. "Sure. I can take care of myself."

"Did your mother teach you?"

"Well, not exactly. I learned out of necessity. When I helped my dad, in the store back in Arkansas, we had a little hot plate, and I ended up being the one who made the coffee or warmed up something for us to eat."

She listened, fascinated by his story.

"Then later, out here, I worked a lot. After school, weekends. So, I had to fix my own food if I missed a meal."

"It sounds like you've been working for a long time."

"Oh, I didn't mind. I like staying busy."

He went to check on the coffee. "You want something to eat with it?" She heard him open the cupboard again. "Not sure what's here."

"I don't want anything. Just the coffee."

That wasn't true. She wanted so much more. Maybe more than he was willing to give. Yet she couldn't help the yearning for his arms around her again, safe in his warm embrace.

Chapter 9

They chatted about the shipyard as they drank their coffee. Amazingly, among the thousands of employees, there were people both had known. Their shared memories, even from different times, gave them a connection. He told her he'd worked in the electrical repair shop and helped repair naval ships after Pearl Harbor.

"I bet that was interesting work. A lot better than welding."

"I'm sure you did a great job. You women surprised a lot of the old-timers. They didn't think you could do the work."

She sat up straighter. "Yeah. We showed 'em." She looked at her hands. "It's rough on the nails, though. I gave up on manicures. Just a waste of time."

He took one of her hands in his. "You have nice, strong hands." He threaded his fingers with hers. "Besides, I like a woman who knows how to work…and how to play."

The pleasure of his touch warmed her. Maybe she could bring him around to her way of thinking. "I can work, that's for sure. It's the playing I've missed out on."

He smiled and nodded but didn't reply. Instead he let her hand go and stood.

She got to her feet and grabbed the cups.

"I can get those," he protested.

"I'll get them. You see if you can find another station with better music."

She put the cups in the sink and turned on the water while he found a different radio program.

"While you do that, I'll just go…" She moved toward the bathroom door.

Once alone she drew a deep breath. She hadn't changed her mind. She still wanted to do this, but she sensed his hesitation. What could she do to convince him?

He was so different from Jack. Her husband would have gone straight from the front door to the bed, no hesitation whatsoever. Guy was a gentler soul, which meant she had to turn the tables. She had to seduce him. She wouldn't force him to do anything he didn't want to do, but she could entice him.

She closed her eyes, remembering how he held her when they danced. She sensed his attraction to her…in the way he looked at her, touched her. What would he be like in bed?

Washing her hands, she looked in the mirror. She saw a grown woman, not the naive girl who'd married Jack. Maybe it hadn't turned out exactly like she thought, but she'd gotten out of Kerrville.

Before she went back there, to spend the rest of her life as the lonely war widow, there was one more thing she wanted.

She reached for the doorknob and the cold of the metal went straight to the pit of her stomach. She wanted Guy, but she didn't want any complications afterward. She would have to be extra careful.

Guy stood by the radio gazing out the window.

Soft music filled the room. When she approached, he turned. Instead of stopping at a socially acceptable distance, she moved closer, until his masculine scent filled her head and fueled her determination.

His face, only inches from hers, was tight with anticipation.

"Shall we dance?" She reached out for him.

He nodded. "Uh-huh."

She slid her arms around his neck, and he leaned toward her until their foreheads touched. Their gazes locked in some unspoken communication. His hands encircled her waist, their warmth penetrating the fabric of her dress. She sighed, her own tension relaxing into his body.

They swayed to the music. He shifted so that his cheek pressed against hers, his stubble scratchy against her smooth skin.

They didn't talk. They simply held each other and moved with the hypnotic rhythm.

Too soon the music changed. A faster beat, yet he held her tight and continued to move at the slower pace.

She turned her head so that her lips touched his cheek, then nibbled their way down to the tender skin below his strong jaw line. He shivered in reaction. Rumbling sounds of approval vibrated deep in his throat.

Pleased, she continued to explore. Her hand slid up the back of his head, the short, military haircut, like the soft bristles of a brush, stimulated the sensitive nerve endings in her fingertips.

She found his soft earlobe and stroked it while her lips brushed his cheek.

He answered swiftly as his lips joined hers, gentle

yet forceful, leaving no doubt that she'd aroused the desire he'd been so carefully holding back.

The fire between them took hold. Each tasted, explored, demanded.

She'd wanted this—to seduce him, draw him out of his shell. She hadn't expected the intensity he unleashed. His intoxicating desire gave her a heady sense of feminine power over this normally self-controlled male.

A man's voice barked an announcement. "That concludes our musical interlude for today. Tune in tomorrow…"

Guy jerked away. He drew a ragged breath and looked around until his gaze rested on the radio. She desperately hoped the spell had not been completely broken.

A new announcer's voice came over the radio. His words pierced through her desire-fogged thoughts like a bucket of cold water.

"The Japs inflict heavy losses on the Third Marine Division as our boys continue to slug their way through the jungles of Bougainville. The Japs stubbornly fight on, defending their positions."

Jack's words echoed in her head. "I hate those dirty Japs."

She pushed away and turned from Guy. The news story continued, and she listened, desperate to hear some indication that the Japanese could be defeated.

Guy touched her shoulder. "What's wrong?" he asked.

"I, uh…Jack…" She looked at him, into those green eyes, searching for the hint of gold she'd seen earlier. *Explain. Tell him.*

"Jack wanted to fight the Japanese. Get even for their sneak attack on us." She pointed to the radio still spewing war news. "That's why he joined up, right after Pearl Harbor. It was all he talked about. How he was going to go over there and kill Japs."

"I see." Guy nodded as if he was giving her permission to talk about it, about Jack.

"When he came out here," she waved her hand around to encompass all of California, "he was angry at being assigned to the Coastal Artillery. Wished he'd joined the Navy so he could ship out across the Pacific and fight the Japanese."

She sank into an overstuffed armchair, seeing only the past. Their little apartment, the only home they ever had, and Jack pacing the floor and ranting about how the Japanese were going to invade California.

Now that she'd opened the flood gate, the words spilled out.

"When he found out about the big guns and the danger of a Japanese invasion, he bragged about defending the coast with guns as big as the ones on a battleship."

Guy sat down beside her. "I remember the fear of an invasion in the months after Pearl Harbor. A naval officer told me they installed all kinds of secret obstacles to protect the entrance to the bay, in addition to the guns on the coast."

She nodded. "Jack's outfit patrolled the beaches carrying rifles. And they trained in hand-to-hand fighting so they'd be ready if the Japs came ashore."

"Did you get to go out there and see those big artillery pieces?"

"Oh, no. It's all restricted. All along the coast is

strictly off limits to civilians. Only military personnel."

"Why was he transferred?"

"When the Army decided that the Japanese weren't going to invade, they started pulling men from the coastal guns and sending them to regular artillery units."

"So it wasn't because of your break-up?"

"No." She thought back to when Jack told her he was being transferred. They'd argued, and her anger had kept her from asking many questions. "I think he said he volunteered to transfer, so maybe it did have something to do with his decision." She studied her hands, the broken nails she couldn't stop picking at.

"You can't hold yourself responsible for what happened to him."

"I know. It probably would have happened one way or another." It still didn't seem possible that she'd never see Jack again. "I just wish, for his parents' sake, that he'd died in combat instead of in some accident."

"He still died because of the war." He took her hands in his.

"I know."

"And you'll get his life insurance. That'll help you start a new life."

"Life insurance?" She hadn't thought of that.

"Sure. Every soldier takes out a policy. Just in case."

Jack's words sliced through her, just as they had that last day. "I love her, and I'm gonna marry her." He'd vowed that he would file for divorce, yet she'd never gotten any papers.

"What if he changed it? What if he made *her* the beneficiary?"

"Who?"

"Her. Miranda. The one I caught him with."

"Did he say he was going to change it?"

"No. But he could have." Her hands flew to her mouth. "Oh…."

"What's wrong?"

His warm hand rested on her shoulder. She wanted to collapse into his embrace.

"If he changed it, then they will find out what happened. His parents, my mother, everyone." She stared at him, shaking like a feather. "They'll know we broke up. They'll know he didn't want me."

Chapter 10

Guy wanted to help her, to comfort her. She was clearly upset about her husband's death, even if she did deny it. Like any young woman, she'd wanted her marriage to be a happy one. But it didn't always happen that way. A wartime marriage, or even a romance, was not a good idea. The war put too much pressure on everybody.

"Would it be so bad if they found out?" he asked. "Wouldn't it be better to tell the truth and get it over with?"

"No. I couldn't." She pulled back from him and wrapped her arms around her middle. "They'll blame me. They'll say I caused it, that I wasn't good enough for him."

"His family will be upset, sure. But they'll get over it."

"No, they won't. And my mother, she'll die of shame." She strode the few paces to the bedroom door then turned and came back.

He stood his ground. "Telling the truth is always better. Lies only cause more problems."

She stopped abruptly and faced him. "I'm not going to lie. Not exactly. I just won't tell them the whole story."

"It's the same thing."

Fear exploded across her face. "You're not the one

who has to face them." She turned away, running her hand through her hair. "You haven't been talked about all your life. You haven't been the favorite topic of those old biddies who love nothing more than to gossip about every mistake you made."

He had to find a way to calm her down.

He moved closer and put his arms around her, pulling her close. "It'll be okay." He stroked her back. "You're worrying about things that haven't even happened."

Her body relaxed a little. If he could distract her, he could get her mind off her dead husband and his betrayal.

"Where did you learn to dance?"

"What?" Her face pressed against his shoulder muffled her voice.

"You're a natural dancer. You have a feel for the music. Did you study dance?"

She emitted a little "humph" he hoped was a laugh. "We had a teacher that came around and gave lessons…in the community center, for two summers in a row when I was in grammar school. We learned to waltz and foxtrot and cha-cha. Even the Charleston." She looked up at him, a weak smile overtaking the tears. "I loved it."

"It shows." Glad he'd distracted her with a more pleasant memory. "You should do more of it."

She lowered her gaze, and long lashes covered her pale blue irises. "Jack didn't like to dance."

"Well, I love to dance." He gave her a little squeeze.

That brought her gaze up to his, with a hint of a teasing smile. "Jitterbug, right?"

He tried to hold back the grin spreading across his face. "Sure, I can jitterbug. But I love to waltz, too." He couldn't contain himself. "I guess you could say I taught myself by just getting out there and doing it."

He sat up straight, ready to jump to his feet. "I know a place we could go. To dance, I mean. Where they play all kinds of music, do all kinds of dancing, not just the jitterbug."

She sighed. "No. I don't want to go out anywhere." The sadness returned to her face.

"Then we can dance here. I'll teach you to jitterbug and you can teach me the Charleston."

"But the music…"

"I'll find something. I'm pretty good with radios. After all, that's what the Army trained me for."

"To find music on the radio?"

He nodded. "To find any station on the dial." He went over to the radio. "I used to bring in some good music stations." He turned the boxy apparatus around. "What I need to do is to extend the antenna."

She eased closer to watch him.

He took the back off and quickly found the internal antenna. Then he thought about what he could use to extend it. When he'd lived here, he'd rigged up an antenna on the roof for his ham radio, but for now a wire out the window should do the trick.

"Nose around and see if you can find some wire, something I can hook onto the internal antenna and stick out the window."

"You want me to search your friend's apartment?"

"Bill won't mind," he assured her. "You look around in the bedroom. I'll check the kitchen."

"Okay." She slowly made her way toward the

bedroom, while he opened the cabinet below the sink.

She returned in a few minutes and held up a wire coat hanger. “I found this.”

Guy laughed. “Nope. But I found something better.” He pulled a broken lamp out from behind some pots.

“It’s broken. Why would your friend keep that?”

“Knowing Bill, he kept it because his mother gave it to him.”

“But…” She fingered the broken glass base. “Why would he keep it after it got broken?”

“So he could tell his mother he still had it.”

“But it doesn’t work.”

He unwrapped the cord. “I can rig something up with this.”

She sat at the table and watched him work. With a knife for a screwdriver and some adhesive tape he found in the bathroom, he managed to hook up a wire about three feet long attached to the radio’s antenna. He raised the window just enough to poke the extension he’d made out where it hung down on the outside of the building.

“Now if it doesn’t short out, we should get a much stronger signal.”

While he worked on the radio, she pushed the sofa back a bit to make more space in the center of the room for them to dance.

Sure enough, in no time music flowed from the ungainly contraption.

He stepped to the center of the room and took her hand. “May I have this dance?”

Her eyes twinkled. “I’d be delighted.”

Pulling her into his arms, they glided into the one-two-three rhythm of the waltz. The combination of the music and the woman in his arms entranced him.

A loud knock on the door startled them both.

Chapter 11

Bill's landlord stood outside the door, frowning.

"Mr. Tandy. It's good to see you again."

"Guy," the older man nodded. "Bill said you'd be staying here a few days." The man continued before Guy could respond. "Mrs. Simmons, downstairs, says she saw you bring a woman in with you."

Guy opened his mouth, but the older man held up his hand. "Now, I remember you being a nice, quiet young man. And I told her I didn't think you'd be up to any shenanigans, but I said I'd stop by and see for myself."

At that Guy opened the door wide. "I'm glad you did."

Rosemary stood there smiling.

"Mr. Tandy, this is Mrs. Rosemary Hopkins. She's an old friend of mine. We worked together at Moore's." He silently willed Rosemary to agree with him.

"Rosemary, this is Mr. Tandy, Bill's landlord."

Mr. Tandy eyed her curiously but remained silent.

Rosemary stepped forward and offered her hand. When Mr. Tandy took it, she spoke. "It is so nice to meet you."

Her uneasy gaze shifted from the older man to Guy.

"Mrs. Hopkins...Rosemary, recently got word from the Army that her husband was killed in a training accident."

"Your husband?" Surprise registered on Mr. Tandy's face. "I'm very sorry, ma'am."

"Thank you." Rosemary's gaze dropped to the floor.

"I ran into Rosemary at the train station." Guy continued to explain. "She was trying to get a ticket to go home, but she couldn't get anything until tomorrow. All the hotels are booked solid, so I offered to let her stay here for the night."

"Yes, Guy's been very nice."

"When did your husband die?" Mr. Tandy directed his question to Rosemary, but his gaze locked on Guy.

"The telegram said December 8th. He was…" She drew a deep breath as if gathering her strength. "I hadn't seen him since he left for training. He'd been stationed out at the Presidio…on the guns…till they transferred him…to the regular artillery." Her voice faded with each word.

"He'd been with the Coastal Artillery," Guy jumped in. "You know, the big guns out on the coast protecting the entrance to the bay."

Mr. Tandy nodded. "I heard about those guns." The older man studied Rosemary as she fiddled with her earring.

"Rosemary came out here to join him and went to work at Moore's."

"Jack wanted to fight the Japanese." Her gaze met Mr. Tandy's. "He volunteered." Her voice caught. "But he didn't get the chance."

Mr. Tandy looked from Rosemary to Guy.

"There was an accident. With the ammunition," Guy stated.

"He got blown up!" Rosemary blurted out before turning away.

Guy eased closer to Mr. Tandy. "The music calms her when she gets upset. Kind of distracts her."

Mr. Tandy nodded. "I see."

She turned around, her face twisted. She wrung her hands and looked from one man to the other. "They're shipping his body home. I had to call his parents, tell them…" She pulled her crumpled handkerchief from her pocket. "They said I had to come home, to bury him. But when I went to get a ticket, I couldn't. If it hadn't been for Guy, I don't know what I would have done."

The radio crackled, interrupting her tale.

Guy went over to adjust it. "Wish I had my tools. I'd have it working fine."

Mr. Tandy followed him, glancing over his shoulder as Rosemary blew her nose. "I remember that big set you had when you lived here. What'd you call it?"

"A ham radio."

"What happened to it?"

"I've still got it. It's all packed up and stored at my mother's." Out of the corner of his eye he could see Rosemary. She'd moved across the room but still appeared distraught.

"That's what the Army trained me for," he continued. "A radio technician."

"That's perfect for you." The older man laughed. "Usually they put you in something you know nothing about, like the infantry."

Mr. Tandy turned to Rosemary, who stood wringing her handkerchief in her hands.

"Ma'am, it was nice to meet you. And I'm sorry about your husband."

Guy followed him to the door. Once in the hallway, the older man glanced back. "Shame a young girl like that losing her husband."

"Yes, it is." Then Guy remembered something. "Mr. Tandy, is Holt's still open? I thought I'd take her down there for something to eat."

"Sure. It's open. That's a good idea. Nice, homey place. Get her a good dinner."

Chapter 12

Rosemary sank into the sofa and stared at the wall. How had her life gotten so messed up? What was she doing?

She'd met a nice man who tried to help her. And she had tried to turn it into some kind of sexual encounter. What did that say about her?

Desperate. Lonely. Afraid. All that and more.

In truth, she didn't like herself very much right now.

Guy closed the door and turned to face her.

"I'm sorry," she said before he could speak.

"It's all right."

"No, it's not. I put you in a terribly awkward position. The people here…they're your friends. And I've come here and made them think badly of you." She looked toward the window, unable to face him. "I shouldn't have come here. I shouldn't have let you buy those tickets."

"Don't say that. If I hadn't…you would be stuck here for a week or more."

"And I would have sent a telegram to the Hopkinses and told them the truth, that I couldn't get a ticket. They would have understood. It's the war. It affects everything."

"And where would you have stayed?"

"I could have gone back to the boardinghouse.

Mrs. Frey would have squeezed me in somewhere."

He sat beside her. "I guess I shouldn't have interfered."

She turned to face him, and their gazes met. "Don't say that. Not that way. You are the kindest man I've ever met."

He smiled. "Don't be so sure. I saw a pretty girl I wanted to talk to." He broke the connection by looking away. "Pretty sad, don't you think? I lived here in Oakland for years, and I didn't have anyone to talk to or spend my last days at home with. They're all either gone or working or don't want anything to do with me."

She touched his arm. "I'm sure you have lots of friends. It's just bad timing."

"Yeah. Maybe." He looked at her again. "Just so you don't blame yourself for all of this. I'm just as much to blame as you are."

She looked down; her short, ragged nails seemed to represent her life.

"So, what now?"

He sighed. "Well, we can go get some dinner. There's a little place not far from here. They've got real good, homemade food. I used to eat there all the time."

"So they know you there?"

"Yes."

"And you want to take me there? Won't you have to explain all over again?"

"It's okay. We can tell the same story. That we knew each other at Moore's. We don't have to go into so much detail. They're always busy, so nobody will have time to ask questions."

"Are you sure?"

"Yes. I'm sure. Besides I'm getting hungry."

They walked the few blocks to the restaurant. He was right about the food. It made her homesick for her mother's cooking. For the first time she began to look forward to going home.

Thankfully, the new waitress didn't know Guy. The owner spoke to Guy when they came in, but he didn't have time to come over and ask questions.

During the meal Rosemary and Guy didn't talk much. He related a couple of stories about the place, but he kept it light.

They walked back to the apartment, a comfortable silence between them. A new sensation of contentment settled over her. Part of her wondered why now, why with this man? And part of her feared looking at it too closely or the spell would break, and she'd find it was all an illusion.

Back inside the apartment, she faced him.

"It's not going to happen, is it?"

"What?"

Had he forgotten her proposal? Was the idea so easy for him to put out of his mind?

"What I said earlier…about sleeping with you?"

"Oh, that." He turned away. After a long moment, he said, "Come over here and sit down."

He led her to the little dining table. She sat on one side and he sat across from her, obviously wanting to put something between them.

"You see, it's like this," he started. "You're in a bad place. Hurt. Afraid, even. So, I don't think you really knew what you were saying."

"I knew. I admit that it probably isn't a good idea. But I knew."

"Even so, you are too emotional. Your husband is

dead. And even though you and he were separated for —what? Six months?—he was still your husband."

She nodded. "It's been almost six months. Since I caught him with Miranda, and I packed up and left." She thought of the ugly scene and of her panic once she found herself on the street, alone, with no place to go.

"Did you see him during that time?"

"He'd drop off my mail every week or so. Sometimes we ran into each other, but mostly he avoided me."

"Didn't you try to talk to him?"

"I did. Once. We'd been separated about a month. I had cooled down some. At least I thought I had." She fingered the smooth pearl at her ear as she replayed that conversation. How she'd hoped for some kind of reconciliation.

"What did you talk about?"

"He told me not to tell anyone at home that we weren't living together. He knew me well enough to know I wouldn't want to admit we'd split up. He said he wanted to wait until it was all settled before we told them. That way nobody back home would interfere."

"Interfere? What did he mean?"

"He thought his parents would come out here. That they'd make him take me back. They're very strict Baptists. They don't believe in divorce." Her laugh came out in a huff. "What's funny is that they didn't approve of me. They didn't think I was good enough for him."

Guy shook his head.

"It doesn't matter now. He never filed the papers and now he's gone. There's no point in telling them…unless I have to."

"For your sake I hope you don't."

She got to her feet. "I'd like to take a bath. Then after a good soak, maybe I'll be relaxed enough to sleep."

He stood, too. "While you're doing that, I'll make sure the spare bed is made." He pointed toward the alcove behind the curtain. "I'll sleep out here and you can take the bedroom."

"I hope you don't mind. Sleeping out here, I mean."

"Not at all. I slept there for years. It'll feel like home."

Chapter 13

She made her way through the steel maze of a ship…looking for something.

She'd been welding, but she couldn't find the place. She went down a stairway to another level.

The light grew dimmer.

She searched for where she was supposed to be.

There were no workers. No sounds. Just echoing quiet and eerie shadows.

She hurried on, calling out.

Where was everyone? Why was it so dark?

There, ahead, a dim light.

She ran toward it.

A door loomed in front of her. A feeling of dread told her not to open it, but it pulled her, like a magnet. She had to see inside.

She flung open the door.

A man lay on the floor, face down. Somehow she knew who was lying there.

"Jack," she murmured.

She moved closer, knelt down and rolled him over.

Jack stared up at her. His eyes…empty…dead.

His mouth hung open. A mixture of vomit and blood covered his cheek, his chin, his neck. The stench took her breath.

She reached out…touched his cold hand.

And screamed.

****

Rosemary's scream jerked him out of the thin veil of restless sleep. He scrambled from his bed and ran into the bedroom.

In hysterics she wailed, "No, no, Jack, no."

He eased down beside her and gently spoke. "Rosemary. You're having a nightmare. It's all right. It's just a bad dream." He ventured to touch her, almost afraid he would frighten her even more. But she turned toward him. He slid his arm around her shaking shoulders. She pressed her face into his chest, and he pulled her close.

"Oh, Jack, Jack," she sobbed.

"It's Guy. You're here with me. Safe. You've had a bad dream. But you're safe now." He rubbed her back.

After a few minutes, she straightened and pulled away enough so she could look at him. Even in the darkness he could see the tears glistening in her long lashes.

"Guy?" she said, as if his name had finally sunk into her dream-addled brain.

He nodded. "It's Guy. Guy Nolan. You're here…in Bill's apartment. We're in Oakland, waiting to take the train."

She nodded her understanding, then looked around the room as if to verify his words. She reached up and brushed her hair back, still breathing hard.

"Do you want to talk about it?"

Her head jerked back around to reveal the torment in her face.

"The nightmare? Sometimes it helps to talk about it."

She shook her head ever so slightly.

"You screamed. You called out Jack's name."

She locked on his gaze, her eyes wild with emotion. Was it fear? Pain?

"Do you remember?"

"Jack's dead." The words came out in a harsh whisper. "He's dead."

"I know. You told me. He died in a training accident."

"Accident?"

"Remember? You got the telegram and the letter explaining what happened?"

She absorbed his words. "Accident. Training accident," she murmured.

"You're going home."

"No." The word erupted from her. Then she thrust herself against his chest, and he wrapped his arms around her.

He sat there holding her for what seemed like an eternity. Finally, she moved. She turned her head toward his face. Her kisses made their way up his neck until they reached his cheek, just a breath away from his lips.

"Make me forget," she whispered. "Make me feel alive. Please."

Before he could answer, her lips covered his and he lost his ability to think.

Her mouth devoured his, and heaven help him, he wanted it. Wanted her kisses and more. Much, much more.

Some nagging sense of conscience finally broke through. He pulled away from her, not only breaking the kiss but pushing her body away from his.

"We can't. You're too vulnerable."

"Please," she begged. "Don't leave me to that… that horrible vision of…" Her voice broke. And his heart twisted into a knot.

"But…" He tried to protest.

"Give me a memory. A live memory. Of a man." She caressed his arm. "Strong and full of life."

What could he say? What did she want from him? A substitute for her dead husband? Or did she want him? Guy Nolan.

"I'm not Jack."

"I know you're not. I don't want Jack. Jack's dead. Gone." Her grip tightened. "I want someone different. Someone strong and kind and…and alive. Someone who wants me." She kissed his cheek. "I want you."

He couldn't stop his body from responding to her. She was soft and warm and inviting. And here he sat on her bed, with only his skivvies between his growing desire and her sweet, willing body.

"I won't take advantage of you," he managed.

"You won't be. You'll be giving me a gift. One I can cherish for the rest of my life." She kissed him again, a hungry demanding kiss that cut through his arguments against anything. A kiss that left him groaning for more. Just as she wanted more from him.

"Don't you want something to remember on those cold, lonely nights surrounded by all those other soldiers? Soldiers who may never come back."

She ran her hand through his hair and trailed kisses along his jaw, finally reaching his tender earlobe. "For just tonight, let's both live. Live enough for a lifetime."

****

She desperately wanted to wipe out that vision of

Jack's lifeless body, covered in vomit, just like her father.

Jack…the lover who'd turned angry and mean. Who'd delighted in punishing her, in making her want him but only giving himself to her on his terms. Terms of violence and humiliation.

Guy was so different. So kind. So gentle. That's the memory she wanted. If she had to bury herself in Kerrville, the lonely widow tied to a dead husband, at least she could have this to remember. This one night.

If he'd only agree. This kind, honorable man.

He wanted her. She could feel his desire. She just had to overcome his conscience. His innate goodness.

So she showed him how much she wanted him. With kisses. With gentle caresses over his muscled arms, his magnificent chest, his strong bare legs.

He responded to her ministrations, devouring her mouth as she slid her fingers beneath the waistband of his shorts.

He pulled away then, and she feared she'd gone too far.

After staring into her eyes, she saw the decision made. His hands reached for the hem of her gown. He tugged it up, and she raised her arms to allow him to pull it over her head in one swoop.

He drank her in with his eyes. Her body pale and bare and longing for his touch.

She watched his face as his fingertips caressed her breast. First one, then the other.

"You're so beautiful," he whispered.

"So are you."

Their gazes met for mere seconds before their mouths touched.

Hands roamed each other's bodies, fanning the flames, both knowing only one way to extinguish them.

One last coherent thought emerged from her brain. "Protection."

Between kisses he murmured, "In my bag."

Unwilling to break the connection, he scooped her up into his arms and carried her out to the little sleeping alcove where his bag lay open on the built-in shelf. He fished inside the bag and came out with a package of condoms.

With quick, efficient movements he sheathed himself, barely missing a kiss.

"Thank you," she whispered.

From that point on, neither spoke, except with their bodies. She lost herself in the most sensual experience of her life, from this man who was willing to give her so much.

Chapter 14

Slowly she emerged from the soft clouds of sleep, gradually becoming aware of the warm body beside her.

Her fingers reached out, touched his flesh.

Her eyes opened. Guy lay curled around her in the little half bed in the alcove.

Memories flooded back as she watched him sleep. Memories of his touch, gentle but strong. Memories of how he'd driven her mad and how she'd loved it.

He'd given her what she wanted, what she needed. And he'd been perfect in every way.

He breathed, in and out, soft and sure and steady. She longed to reach out and touch his broad chest, run her fingers over his bare shoulder, down the arm draped across her body. Yet she knew if she touched him, he would awaken, and the magic spell would be broken.

A hint of light filtered through the curtained windows. It was early. Too early to get up. Too early to move from his warm embrace and face the cold reality. Let the dream last just a little longer.

He moved. His arm pulled her closer. Then those long lashes fluttered like butterfly wings. And just like that he awakened and broke the spell.

Those moss green eyes took her in as the smile lit up his face.

"Good morning."

Now she could touch him. Her fingers brushed his cheek. “Good morning.”

His smile widened, making deep creases that plumped up his cheeks and crinkled his eyes. He grasped her hand and pulled it to his lips. Their soft warmth sent a thrill through her entire body. Memories pushed her toward him until her lips met his. So soft. So perfect.

Within seconds that softness caught fire and gentleness morphed into strength. Nothing tentative. No hesitation. Only certainty. For now, for this brief time, they belonged to each other. In this magical cocoon where only the two of them existed, they came together again, creating more memories, memories for both to relish in the time to come.

****

He didn’t want to stop. Not ever. He wanted this time, this woman here in his arms, in his bed, forever.

Too soon light filled the room. They couldn’t languish in bed. They had a train to catch.

At least they’d be together. How long? Two more days. The time it took for a train to travel from California to Chicago. That’s all the time they had left.

The pain of anticipated separation cut through to his very soul. It shouldn’t be so hard to leave someone you just met. Could it really be only yesterday? She was part of him, like he’d known her forever, like they were meant to be together.

Did she feel it, too?

No. Not likely. She’d wanted a fling and he’d given it to her. He could tell himself that he’d been comforting her, but he’d be lying. He’d wanted her and she’d been willing.

She'd wanted, no needed, to block out the grief. Even if she couldn't see it, he could. Her anger at her dead husband. He'd cheated on her, left her, and then he'd gone and died before she had a chance to fully process everything that had gone before.

He remembered his anger toward his father when he died.

They could have kept the business going, the two of them. He'd had all kinds of ideas to make it work. But the strain of so many years had piled up on the older man's shoulders, the Depression when no one had anything, no money, no jobs, no crops. And instead of helping her husband, his mother had heaped more despair on his shoulders by telling him what a failure he was. So the old man had given up, had started the process of selling out. He'd never have gotten enough to pay off their debts. There just wasn't enough to sell. And all the money owed him by dirt-poor, starving people could never be collected, not in a million years.

Guy had watched his father die, piece by piece, day by day. So he hadn't realized how angry he was until his father collapsed, clutching his chest. Guy had screamed at him to get up, to stop, to not die. As if anything could have stopped the inevitable.

He remembered how people stared at his bloody fists. They said he'd pounded them on anything and everything.

So yes, he understood her anger and her hurt and her sense of being deserted by the one person who'd been her world.

He just didn't want to give her up. Not yet.

Would it hurt her if he died? Did their connection mean as much to her as it did to him?

He didn't want to hurt her. The timing was so bad. To meet just as he was leaving. To know he might not come back. He didn't know what awaited him across the ocean, but he did know that a war raged, a war that would get worse before it got better, a war in which a lot of men would die.

This time with her had been a gift. A beautiful, wonderful gift. Just as she said. It was nothing more. There could be nothing more. Not now. Not ever.

****

Rosemary emerged from the bathroom to find Guy stripping the bed.

He looked up. "I thought I'd get this done. I already stripped the little bed."

"Your friend…so he'll know we used both beds?"

He scooped up the used sheets. "Bill knows me. Knows I would change the beds after staying here. He won't think anything of it, if that's what you're worried about."

Worried. Did she look worried? The long tendrils of shame crept up into her body, bringing with it a tension, a fear almost.

"He didn't know about me, so…" Her mind began the journey down the rocky road of consequences.

"Oh, he'll know," Guy commented as he pushed past her and deposited his bundle atop a similar pile of sheets in a large laundry basket.

"The landlord."

"Yeah. Mr. Tandy will tell him." He met her gaze. "And don't forget Mrs. Simmons. She saw us come in."

"The resident gossip."

"That's her."

She hadn't noticed the door opposite the bathroom

that stood open revealing a closet. Guy must have pulled the laundry basket out of it. He grabbed clean sheets from a stack of linens on the shelves that lined the upper portion of the closet.

Rosemary took them from him. “I’ll do it.”

He let her take the sheets, but he followed her back into the bedroom. Together they quickly remade the bed.

She smoothed over the simple coverlet, trying to organize her thoughts and tamp down the swirling emotions that threatened to erupt.

“I don’t want anyone to know what we did.” The heat rose from her chest up her throat, almost choking her.

He came around the bed and pulled her into his arms. “We did nothing wrong. And it’s none of anybody’s business anyway.”

“What if someone finds out?” she asked. Tears pricked her eyes.

“They won’t. We’re just two friends. I gave you a place to stay for the night. Simple as that.”

“You won’t tell anyone.” She could hear the desperation in her own voice. “Promise me. You won’t tell anyone.”

He held her at arm’s length, his strong hands on her shoulders. “I promise. I won’t tell anyone.”

Those soft green eyes held only reassurance. He wasn’t lying. He’d keep their secret.

“I just…don’t…” She shook her head and pulled free. “If anyone back home ever found out.” She wrung her hands as she walked away from him. “Oh, God.” She whirled around to face him. “If they ever found out I did something like this, I’d never be able to face anyone. His parents. They'd blame me. Especially if they thought there was trouble between me and Jack. They'd say I drove him away."

She shook with emotion. That desperate fear she'd fought to keep at bay in the days after Jack left for his initial Army training threatened to creep back. His parents had known. His mother had looked at her with those narrowed eyes and flat lips, holding back the accusations she wanted to fling at Rosemary. The woman had held her tongue for her son's sake. She had allowed Rosemary into their home to live while Jack was in training. But now, with Jack gone, nothing would hold her back. Nothing would keep her from telling Rosemary exactly what she thought of her daughter-in-law.

Guy came close but he didn't touch her.

"No one will know," he said in that quiet, gentle voice. "No one but us."

She flung herself into his arms, needing desperately to feel his strength, his reassurance. She drew in a ragged breath and tried to regain her composure.

After a few moments he spoke. "We need to get going."

She pulled away and nodded. She swiped a stray tear from her cheek and ventured a smile. "It'll only take me a few minutes."

"Okay." He closed the closet and strode into the main room, calling back over his shoulder. "Be sure to look around. Wouldn't want to leave anything."

"I will."

She returned to the bedroom and gathered her remaining items. Her little bag of makeup sat on the dresser. She leaned down and stared into the mirror. Sunken eyes surrounded by dark shadows stared back. She took out the little box of loose powder and dabbed some around her eyes in a poor attempt to conceal them.

Jack used to say her face revealed her every thought and emotion. Maybe he'd just known her so well that he could predict her every thought.

Could everyone else read her as well? For months she had worked to hide her feelings behind a mask. She'd kept her plight from her co-workers. Only her landlady and her roommates knew she and Jack were separated. Thankfully they had never questioned Rosemary. That had meant a lot to a girl trying to find her way through uncharted territory.

She would wear that mask now, out into the street, onto the train. She'd play the role of a wife accompanying her soldier husband as if her life depended on it.

It wouldn't be hard to pretend to be married to Guy. After the night they'd spent together, a part of her wished they were. Even if she had to send him off to war, they'd been honest with each other, hadn't they? He'd understood and willingly given her what she needed. The least she could do was send him off believing someone cared.

Chapter 15

Guy returned Bill's key to Mr. Tandy and asked him to call a taxi for them. Then, carrying their luggage, he escorted Rosemary out to the street to wait.

Standing there, he thought about how he'd misled her about the tickets. After everything that had happened between them, guilt gnawed at his gut.

"Kerrville, Tennessee? Is that where your folks live?"

"Yes. It's between Nashville and Chattanooga." She met his gaze. "Why do you ask?"

There, she'd put her thoughts into words. And he had to answer.

"Well, when I write you, I need to know where you'll be." He wanted to stay in touch with her. And he didn't want to tell her about the tickets, not yet.

He reached in his pocket for the stub of a pencil he kept there, ignoring her startled look. "What's your address in Kerrville?"

"You can't write me." Her furious whisper was barely audible as she glanced back toward the apartment building. "Besides, that woman is watching us."

Guy turned to look. Sure enough Mrs. Simmons sat at her window. He touched his cap, smiled and nodded. The old woman nodded back.

The cab pulled to the curb, and Guy loaded their

bags while Rosemary got in.

Once inside the vehicle, he attempted to restart the conversation, or rather to actually get around to confessing, but she shushed him. She nodded toward the driver and gave him a look straight out of some mystery movie. Apparently, she didn't want anyone to overhear their conversation.

Okay. He'd wait. He didn't look forward to it anyway.

At the station they made their way to the platform, and as soon as the conductor gave the okay, they boarded the train and found seats in the near-deserted chair car.

"I hope you can sleep sitting up," Guy said.

She slid into the seat by the window. "I don't mind. Besides, it would be awkward." She glanced over her shoulder as if looking for the conductor. "In a Pullman, I mean."

"Yeah." He did know. Sharing a sleeping car would be awkward. He wasn't sure he could keep his hands off her in such an intimate setting.

He glanced around as a few passengers made their way down the aisle and took seats. He'd better speak up before it got too crowded, since she obviously didn't want others to overhear them.

"I have to confess something. The tickets," he hesitated, searching for the right words.

She looked at him with those big blue eyes. How could he have taken advantage of her? Was he more of a heel than even he thought?

"Here." He shoved the ticket in her direction. "They're not made out 'Mr. and Mrs.' I just said that so…so you would talk to me, so you wouldn't go away."

She examined the paper he'd thrust into her hands. Finally, she spoke. "I don't understand."

"Yesterday." Sweat popped out on his forehead. "You wanted your ticket so you could leave. And I didn't want you to. I wanted to talk to you, get to know you. So I said that."

"Oh."

He'd done it now. She would hate him for what he'd done. She'd be angry and wouldn't speak to him the whole trip.

"You really wanted to talk to me that bad?"

He met her gaze, astonished that she wasn't mad.

"Yes. You're beautiful. And you looked like you needed someone to talk to…as much as I did."

A hint of a smile crept over her face. "So you admit it? You needed someone to talk to, too."

He nodded. He could admit it to her, the only person who recognized his loneliness. How badly it hurt him to be all alone, leaving for an uncertain future. No family or friends to see him off. No one to care.

"So you understand? I didn't really mean to deceive you. Or take advantage of you. I just…"

"You just needed someone as much as I did."

A hint of pink tinged her cheeks and she looked away. He glanced around again, incredibly aware of her need for privacy. Then he slid his hand over and covered hers. She didn't look at him, but she didn't pull her hand away either.

After a few moments he spoke again, very softly. "I do want to write to you."

She glanced up then. "No. You can't," she whispered.

"Why? Can't we just be friends?"

"Don't you understand? People in Kerrville will think the worst if a man, a soldier, writes to me." She grasped his hand then and squeezed it. "Jack's mother would have a fit if I got a letter from a soldier. She never liked me, and I can only imagine how upset she is over Jack's death."

Her eyes darted around the car as if she expected someone to be spying on them. Thankfully, no one even noticed them.

"Don't you even want to know…"

She jerked around and pinned his gaze. "Of course, I want to know what happens to you. I don't want you to get hurt or…or…"

"Killed." He couldn't help finishing her sentence. He knew what could happen. There was no use beating around the bush.

She squeezed his hand with both of hers now. "Don't…don't say that. Don't even think that."

"But it's true."

He saw the jumble of thoughts warring within her. She was struggling with what she had to face when she got home. Something he couldn't even imagine. Just as she couldn't imagine what lay before him.

Their lives were so different. And they'd met at the wrong time, for both of them. It was no use. Their relationship, if you could even call it that, had been doomed from the start.

As the saying went, just two ships passing in the night. A brief encounter and both were gone, never to see each other again.

"It's all right," he told her. "I understand. I don't want to cause you any more problems."

"Thank you." She pressed her lips together and blinked furiously. Did she regret it? Could she care for him, even a little?

The conductor made his way down the aisle in the now crowded car announcing that the train would leave momentarily and for everyone to take their seats.

Quite a few military personnel, Army, Navy, Marines, and even a couple of Army nurses, filled the car. Guy saw a few civilians, but not many.

Soon the train pulled away from the platform and their journey began.

After the conductor checked their tickets, Rosemary leaned over and whispered, "When it's over, when you're safe, write me and let me know."

He turned so he could look her in the eye. "Are you sure?"

She nodded. "Yes. I'm sure. I want to know that you're all right."

"What if I'm not?"

She looked away then. "If I don't hear from you, I'll know…that you didn't make it."

She turned her attention to the scenery outside the window, which made it clear she didn't want to talk anymore.

He leaned back, stared at the ceiling and tried to relax. At least she cared enough to want to know if he lived or died. Maybe after the war, maybe then he could find her, and they could start over.

****

The steady rhythm of the train's clack-clack down the track lulled Rosemary into a fog of semi-sleep. She watched the towns and fields slip by in a blur, but none of it held her interest. Instead she reveled in the warmth of Guy's body close beside her and the comfortable silence between them.

Soon after the train left Oakland, he had pulled a paperback novel from his bag, an Old West adventure with a well-worn cover. Apparently, they shared a love of popular fiction.

He probably likes western movies, too. And Tarzan. What about gangsters or musicals?

She shuddered to think that she'd never know. They'd never get a chance to really get to know each other that well. He might never come back.

"I see you like to read?"

He looked up and met her gaze. "Yeah. I try to keep a book with me. Helps to pass the time."

She nodded her understanding. "I used to read a lot."

"You don't anymore?"

"Not for a while. Didn't have time when I was working."

"It's a great way to escape. That's why I like stuff like this." He held up the western novel. "It's light, fun. Nothing too heavy."

"So you won't think of where you are going?"

"Yeah. I guess." He looked down at his book.

Suddenly she needed to know more about what he would be doing.

"You said the Army trained you on radios. Does that mean you won't be out fighting the enemy?"

"I am trained to operate several kinds of radios and to do basic repairs," he explained. "And I'm assigned to the 230th Field Artillery. So, I'll be taking messages and relaying them to the Fire Direction Center who will then tell the guns when and where to fire."

“Oh. Artillery. Like Jack.”

“Yeah, I guess. Only he would have been firing the guns. I’ll be operating a radio.”

“You’ll still be in danger.”

“No more than anyone else in the artillery.”

That was exactly what she didn’t want to hear. He would be in danger. Just like Jack.

He must have read her thoughts. “Don’t worry about it. It’s not like I’ll be out there with the infantry. They’ve got their own radio men.”

She tried to find some comfort in his reassurances.

He patted her hand. “Thanks for worrying about me.”

She forced herself to smile and met his gaze. “I will pray for you.”

He nodded his thanks and then picked up his book and resumed reading. His calmness and his matter-of-fact way of explaining his role to her provided some reassurance that everything would work out—at least for him. Facing her own battlefield would be something entirely different.

Chapter 16

She made her way through the passage outside the restrooms. Since there weren't many women on the train, she hadn't had to wait, unlike the young uniformed men lined up for the men's room.

"Hi ya, doll," one of them said.

She ignored him and kept moving. Would she have flirted with the soldier if she hadn't met Guy?

Another tipped his hat, his come-hither smile clearly expressing his interest.

As she started down the aisle, the train hit a rough stretch of track. She grabbed hold of a seat back to keep from falling into a Marine's lap as the car swayed back and forth. Slowly, she made her way through the car, pausing to let a sailor by before continuing. That's when she caught sight of Guy, still reading, a newspaper this time

She'd always ignored the quiet types, considered them boring. A bad marriage to the most popular boy in school had changed her perspective. Now, quiet seemed good, preferable even.

She reached their seats before Guy looked up.

"Back already?" He stood so she could get past him to the window seat.

"Sure. No waiting for the ladies' room. But there's a line outside the men's. So be prepared."

"I know. I went earlier, remember."

She frowned as she settled into the seat.

"Maybe you don't. I think you were asleep."

He handed her a sandwich wrapped in waxed paper.

"What's this?"

"Baloney and cheese. Hope it's okay."

"But where did you get it?"

He had one, too. He reached down to the floor and retrieved two bottled drinks. "A vendor came by. I thought you might be getting hungry."

He held out the drinks for her to choose.

"The orange," she told him, still confused. "What about the dining car?"

He stopped unwrapping his sandwich. "We could go back there, if you want. I just remember on my way out the dining car was so crowded I had to wait a while to get a seat." He held up the sandwich. "After a couple of times I decided it wasn't worth it. The sandwiches are just as good, and there's always a vendor coming through selling something."

"I can't believe the train is so crowded." She looked at the sandwich and her stomach reacted. She gave him a quick smile. "Thanks for thinking about it."

He produced a bottle opener from his bag and pulled the cap off her drink. When he handed the cold bottle to her, she met his soft green gaze. His smile glowed, and she fought a strong urge to lean over and kiss him. Only hours before, in Bill's apartment, she could have. But not here.

"I'll take the orange if you'd rather have the cola."

She shook her head. "No. This is fine." Either he hadn't sensed what she had, or he hid his feelings better than she did.

As she ate, her thoughts returned to the self-examination she'd done in the ladies' room. She didn't want to be a coward. She wanted to be brave and face what was ahead with courage, not fear.

Guy admired her bravery for going to work in the shipyard. He knew what a hard time some of the men gave the women. Especially the ones actually working on the ships, like the welders and riveters and inspectors. She'd had to face down men several times when they tried to say her welds didn't meet the specifications. Every time they'd challenged her, the supervisor had, thankfully, backed her up. Gradually, but begrudgingly, the men had accepted her.

Facing her in-laws would require her to stand her ground and not give in to their accusations. After all, as Guy had pointed out, they didn't know what had gone on in California. As far as they knew, she and Jack had been happy.

And the one thing she knew about Jack. When he did write home, his letters would have been all rosy. He hadn't wanted his parents involved in their personal lives any more than she had, especially with his misbehaving.

The thought came to her, crystal clear. He'd known he was in the wrong. He hadn't wanted his parents to know because he'd known.

The thought somehow made facing them easier.

She would preserve their good memories of Jack. After all, he was their beloved son. She wouldn't take that away from them.

Her hand automatically went to caress the pearl earrings he'd given her. She would remember only the good times, when they'd been happy together.

She wouldn't be lying. She'd be withholding the truth to protect them. They'd lost their son. She wouldn't make it harder on them. No. She'd endure whatever they said, whatever they did, because they were grieving a terrible loss.

"I guess it was good. You really wolfed it down."

"Yes." She looked at the waxed paper wadded in her hand. She'd eaten the sandwich without really tasting it. "I'm sorry." She looked at him then. "I guess I was lost in my thoughts."

"Yeah. I know. It's okay. I do that sometimes, too."

"Thank you for being so kind. For understanding. You've done so much for me."

His face went blank for a second, and then the natural coloring that accentuated his cheekbones spread across his whole face. He jerked his gaze from hers and stared at the floor. "I…uh…haven't been the gentleman I should have been." He glanced up at her and then back to the floor.

She reached out and touched his hand. "You've been wonderful."

He met her gaze, then leaned closer and whispered, "I took advantage of you."

"No," she whispered back. "You comforted me. Gave me what I wanted. Don't ever feel bad about it. Promise me."

He blinked those long lashes several times and nodded. "Okay." He looked down again. "But…"

"No 'but,' " she interrupted him. Then she squeezed his hand. "If you can face where you are going, then I can be brave and face my in-laws and my mother. I couldn't say that before I met you."

He nodded, still not looking at her.

She waited, but he didn't say anymore. Still holding his hand, she looked out the window and watched the light fading on the passing scenery. Too soon they'd be in Chicago. Their time together would be over.

"I won't ever forget you," he said.

She looked around. He'd straightened and his expression again appeared calm and without emotion. But something in those green eyes spoke to her.

"I won't forget you either."

"And I won't write, not if you don't want me to." He squeezed her hand. "Until it's over. To let you know I'm alive."

Her heart thudded against her ribcage. He couldn't die. She couldn't even allow herself to think such a thing. "You'll make it. I know you will." She said the words to reassure herself as much as him.

His soft lips curved into a not-quite smile. "It's enough to know that you care whether I make it or not."

"I do. I really do."

"Excuse me."

They both looked up at the tall soldier standing in the aisle.

"Are you the one headed for Camp Atterbury?" He motioned over his shoulder. "The conductor told me there was another guy on the train going to the same place I'm going. Said it was the one with the pretty wife."

****

Guy stood and offered his hand. "I'm Guy Nolan. And yes, I'm on my way to Camp Atterbury."

"Amos Campbell."

The soldier looked past Guy.

"Uh, this is Rosemary."

"Ma'am," said Campbell, tipping his hat.

Rosemary nodded but didn't say anything. Guy let the soldier think they were married since that's what the conductor thought, yet she didn't look comfortable with it.

"Are you in the 30th?" Guy asked.

"Yup. 120th Regiment."

"I'm in the 230th Field Artillery as a radio operator."

"Good, good. Well, just wanted to meet you. Don't want to interrupt nothing. Just thought since we're goin' to the same place we might sort of go together."

"Sure," Guy agreed. He wasn't sure what to say. If he'd been traveling alone, he would have welcomed the company. But he wanted to spend as much time with Rosemary as possible.

His fellow soldier seemed to pick up on Guy's hesitation.

"Well, I'll be goin' back to the next car. Where my seat is. I was hoping somebody would get off so I could move closer and maybe we could talk some. Let me know, will ya? An' I'll move in here."

"I'll watch and let you know."

"Thanks." He leaned over to catch Rosemary's eye. "Nice to meet you, ma'am."

Rosemary nodded.

The soldier moved back down the aisle. Guy watched until he left the car.

"That was interesting," Rosemary said.

"Yeah. But it's not unusual. Lots of guys try to connect with other soldiers going to the same place."

"Comfort in numbers?"

"Something like that."

He waited a few minutes, but in good conscience, he had to say something.

"He assumed you were my wife, based on what the conductor said."

"I know."

"I should have corrected him, but I didn't. Do you mind?"

"It's okay."

He sensed her discomfort with their little deception.

"I'll straighten him out later. On the train to Camp Atterbury. Tell him we're just friends traveling together. He'll understand."

"You mean about the tickets?"

"Yeah. You don't have to travel much to know how these things work."

She looked out the window. Had he said something wrong?

"I'm sorry. I guess I shouldn't have said that."

"It's okay." She turned back to face him. "It's just that…all this…" Her gaze roamed the crowded car. "It's so different from when I traveled west."

"When was that?"

"In early '42. Jack joined up right after Pearl Harbor. As soon as I could, I joined him."

"Getting away from home, right?"

She nodded and blushed a little.

"It's funny 'cause I never wanted to leave home."

"Really."

"Well, I wanted to get out of the house. Get out where I had a little freedom without my mother wanting to know every little thing I did."

Those days seemed an eternity ago.

"After high school I went into San Francisco. I ended up getting a job at Moore's and living in Oakland."

"So you did leave home."

"It wasn't that far. At first I went home almost every weekend, until we started working so much overtime. Even then, I'd make it once a month."

He'd always sent money home to help support his mother and sister.

"You see, my oldest brother joined the Navy after Pop died," he continued. "We moved out west, then after the Japs attacked, my other brother, Henry, joined the Marines. That left me to support Mama and my little sister, Harriet."

"Your brothers didn't send money home?"

"Henry did. But what he sent wasn't as much as he'd given her when he was living at home and working in the cannery. After he joined up, Mama depended more on me."

"Your mother didn't work or earn any money?"

"Not Mama. She never worked outside the home. Back in Arkansas in the early days, Pop's store did pretty good. She had a cook and a housekeeper. She really came down in the world when business got so bad, and then Pop died. She just never got used to the idea of living on less."

"That's too bad." A hint of sarcasm told him she didn't have much sympathy for his mother. Before he could ask her about it, she continued.

"I guess it's hard for me to understand. You see, my father died when I was little, leaving my mother to raise the three of us. We moved into my grandmother's boardinghouse, and the two of them ran it for years. Mama still runs it on her own. She does all the cleaning and laundry and cooking. With only a hired girl to help."

Something compelled Guy to defend his mother. "My mother had it hard when Pop died. Everything had to be sold. We came out here to California to live, so Lorene and Ben could help mother and us kids. It's worked out, but she misses how things were before the Depression."

Guy thought of the conversation he'd had with his mother before he left. He'd given her his bank book and explained about the allotment.

"I'm increasing your allotment since I won't need as much money overseas," he had told her. "Take the extra money and put it in my bank account."

She'd been amazed that he'd been able to save so much money while working at the shipyard. He'd explained that with his nest egg, after the war, he planned to start up a little business of his own, maybe selling and repairing radios. By putting back a little each month he should have enough.

She'd been so pleased that he had saved for his future. She'd always said she wanted her children to have a better life and her approval meant a lot to him.

He'd basked in her praise. She rarely complimented him. Henry had always been her favorite, along with Harriet. So to have his mother say something nice about him warmed his heart.

When he told her that if she needed any money, for an emergency, she could take some out of his account, her face had lit up. She'd hugged him and thanked him for being so thoughtful and generous.

He'd quickly warned her that it was his money, his nest egg for the future, and she could only use it for emergencies. She'd drawn back a little but had reassured him that his money was safe with her.

Had he done the right thing? His mother had never been the best at handling money. He'd thought of his brother-in-law, who managed to keep his own household going, but every time his mother had needed money in the past, Ben had cried hard times. Guy and Ben got along okay, but Guy couldn't bring himself to trust Ben with his hard-earned money.

Of course, the money wouldn't matter if he didn't come back. That hard reality put everything in perspective.

Chapter 17

As the train rolled on through the night, the conductor dimmed the lights.

Rosemary dozed off, using Guy's shoulder as a pillow. He didn't mind. He liked the feel of her body so close to his. Thoughts of the night before filled his mind and stirred his body. It had been unbelievable.

Part of him wondered if it had really happened. Had this beautiful woman spent the night in his bed?

More rational thoughts told him the experience had been a double-edged sword. He'd benefited, yes. He'd enjoyed her lush, willing body. And the price to pay was his ache for her, along with the knowledge that she didn't want to hear from him, and he'd probably never see her again.

Before meeting Rosemary he'd longed for female companionship, to the point where he'd tortured himself by going to see Julie. It had been useless. He'd lost Julie. But he'd gone anyway, hoping somehow she'd take pity on him because he was going overseas, hoping she'd remember the good times they'd shared. If she'd remembered any of it, she hadn't acted like it. She'd said that she didn't want to see him.

Tomorrow Rosemary would tell him the same thing. She'd be nicer about it, but that didn't change the facts. When they parted in Chicago, Rosemary didn't want to see him or hear from him again.

That knowledge already hurt, even with her curled up beside him. He had only been someone to assuage her grief, not someone she could actually care for.

Maybe someday, when all this was over, he'd find someone. Maybe. If he was really, really lucky.

****

Something woke her. She stirred in her seat and straightened so she could look around.

Guy was gone.

She placed her hand on the seat. No warmth. He had been gone for a while.

And the train had stopped. Her gaze roamed the car. Everyone was quiet. Nothing seemed amiss.

A roar outside drew her attention. Something flashed by the window. She turned toward it and saw the blur of another train speeding by in the light of a half moon. Their train must have pulled onto a siding to allow another train to pass.

The noise became louder and the speeding train rocked the car back and forth. Not the steady rock from the normal motion of a train moving along the track. This was different, more side to side, and less regular.

Boxcars gave way to flatcars loaded with what looked like artillery pieces. Car after car passed the window.

Absorbed in the passing train, she didn't realize Guy had returned until the seat moved.

"I see you're awake," he commented.

She met his soft green gaze. One heavy brow arched in a question. Her gaze drifted down to his sensual lips. That's when she noticed. He'd shaved.

She fought the urge to reach up and caress his smooth face.

"The conductor says we won't be stopped here long. Just enough time for the freight to pass."

She nodded, trying to focus on his words.

He settled into the seat. "I thought while you were asleep, I'd go to the lavatory and clean up." He reached up and ran his fingers over his newly shaven jaw.

"Good idea." That sounded stupid but her brain didn't seem to want to function well enough to generate conversation.

"Almost cut myself when the train stopped." He looked over and smiled.

"Glad you didn't."

"Yeah." He looked away then as if he hadn't found what he was looking for.

They sat in silence for a few minutes.

Her attention returned to the passing train. Boxcars again. Anything could be aboard. Plates of raw steel. Crates filled with parts. Even ammunition for the guns she'd seen earlier. The trains today were not only loaded down with military personnel, but also with all kinds of war materials.

"I asked the conductor about getting off and stretching our legs."

"What?" Her head jerked around. "When?"

"He said we'd stop in a couple of hours in a town where they take on supplies. We'll be there a half an hour or so. Long enough for a short walk." He shook his head. "I don't know about you, but I'd really like to get off this train, even if it's only for a little while."

"Sure. That sounds nice."

He reached over and patted her hand. "Then it's a date."

She smiled. A date? Under the circumstances?

They'd spent the night together back in Oakland. A night she didn't dare think about for fear of losing control. Since that night they'd boarded this train pretending to be a married couple. At this point a date sounded a little out of place.

He must have read her mind. "We've got things a little out of order, don't we?"

She nodded, feeling the heat of a blush creeping up her neck.

She quickly looked around to make sure no one was watching them.

"It's okay. No one cares about us."

He was right. The passengers in the nearby seats were either sleeping or staring out the windows. A couple of seats up and across the aisle, two soldiers played cards exchanging just enough words to keep the game going.

The sailor and Marine in the seats directly across the aisle stirred from their slumber when the train jerked into motion. One sat up and looked around only to lean back and slide his hat over his face so he could continue his slumber.

When her gaze returned to Guy, he was watching her.

"Why are you so worried? We're just a normal couple traveling on a train. No one knows us and no one cares."

She dropped her gaze to her hands, automatically examining the many imperfections. She picked at a hangnail, her thoughts racing. How could she explain what seemed like a lifetime of vigilance?

"I guess my mother always worried about what everyone thought. She made me aware that people were watching, always. And talking."

"Did she think your lives were that interesting?"

She stiffened. "No. She was just very sensitive. She still is." No point in revealing the family scandal. He didn't need to know about that.

"Well, it looks like after living in San Francisco you'd have realized that everyone is busy with their own lives, and they don't have time to worry about yours."

"Maybe."

She had relished the anonymity of the city. People minded their own business. Never asked questions. Even Mrs. Frey had been close-mouthed about her separation from Jack. When Rosemary moved into the boardinghouse, she had to offer some explanation, so she'd told Mrs. Frey the truth. The older woman hadn't been the least bit shocked. She'd simply nodded her acceptance of Rosemary's story and then, to Rosemary's surprise, had offered to keep the information between just the two of them. Rosemary hadn't even had to ask. She'd wondered what Mrs. Frey had been through herself to be so understanding.

He reached over and lifted her chin, turning it so she faced him. "There's no one here but me and you."

She glanced past him.

"Ignore them. Like they're ignoring us."

His lips were so close and so tempting. As they got closer, she forgot everything else. There was only him, in the dark, kissing her.

Chapter 18

After a long day crossing the plains, talking and laughing with Rosemary, and then another night, the two of them alone in the dark, the train pulled into the Chicago station in the early hours of the morning.

The conductor came down the aisle a good half hour before their arrival, telling the passengers to be ready.

"You'd better wake your wife," he'd said to Guy.

He had referred to Rosemary as his wife before, and the idea had grown on Guy. What if she was his wife? He'd firmly put the idea of even a steady girlfriend out of his mind as he prepared himself for duty overseas. He'd told himself it wouldn't be fair to any girl to leave her behind with his future so uncertain. Now he wondered if he'd been right.

In training, other guys wrote to their girlfriends, and they read and reread letters from girls who loved them and worried about them. He had buried his envy beneath an "I know better" attitude. Now he begrudgingly admitted to himself how badly he'd wanted someone to care, someone other than his mother and siblings.

Then Rosemary had appeared, and their encounter had evolved from simply helping her get tickets to a complicated relationship full of lies and deception.

He'd benefited, he told himself. Even if all they

had were a few days of pretending, at least she'd given him memories he would cherish for the rest of his life. Memories of what might have been…in another time, another life.

This war had placed her in his path, created their shared sense of vulnerability and need, and within a few short hours this same war would separate them forever.

He laughed to himself as his perverse mind turned a biblical saying into an apt description of his situation. The war giveth and the war taketh away.

He roused Rosemary. Fatigue from the long trip slowed her movements as she straightened her clothes and gathered her things together.

Knowing what lay ahead of her, he reached out and folded her into his arms.

"Are you sure you don't want to stay the night here in Chicago? We could get a room…"

Her head shook back and forth against his shoulder. "No," came through clearly, despite being muffled.

He'd asked her during the night when he'd been unable to resist kissing her in the darkness. She'd turned him down then but hadn't denied him her kisses.

Her reasoning was sound. She couldn't delay her journey. And besides, the closer they came to her home in Tennessee the greater the chance they'd be seen by someone. She'd pointed out his new friend, Amos Campbell, who'd paid them several visits the previous day. Guy would have to tell his fellow soldier the truth or at least a portion of the truth. And they had no way of knowing who Campbell would tell.

In the huge Chicago terminal, they ate a hurried breakfast. Then, arm in arm, Guy escorted Rosemary to the platform where her train would depart. The two hours between trains ticked away so quickly that they barely reached the platform in time to board.

Guy faced her, not wanting to say goodbye.

"Well, this is it." She tilted her head up to meet his gaze and smiled cheerfully.

"You won't change your mind? Let me write to you?"

She shook her head. "No. I can't."

Someone bumped her and he pulled her closer, both to protect her and to hold onto her as long as he could.

Passengers were pouring from the train that had just arrived on the track on the opposite side of the platform. The crowd moved past them, surging toward the main terminal.

Boarding passengers pushed their way in the opposite direction.

The call, "All Aboard," rang out.

"I'd better go," she said.

"Can't I at least kiss you goodbye?"

She stared at him, her eyes shining with unshed tears.

She didn't want to leave him any more than he wanted to leave her.

When she nodded, his heart pounded as he leaned down and captured her mouth. She pulled him closer, her feelings clear in the urgency of her hungry lips.

Someone bumped into them, but he wasn't about to break this last-ever kiss. It wasn't just goodbye for now. For them it was goodbye forever. So as long as he held her, as long as he kissed her, she was still his.

****

Even as she kissed him, Rosemary knew she shouldn't be doing this. Much as she wanted to stay with this man, she couldn't.

But he tasted so good. And she'd never kiss him again. She'd never feel his body pressed against hers again. Despite the tears streaming down her face she couldn't stop, couldn't let go. As soon as she did, he would be gone. And a piece of her heart would go with him.

That sobering thought…that she'd fallen for this man, for Guy Nolan, a soldier going off to war, made her push away from him.

Even as she broke the kiss, he tried again with quick, light brushes of his lips against hers.

"I have to go," she whispered.

He met her gaze. "Not yet."

Her eyes darted past him into the crowd. "People are watching."

"Can't a man kiss his wife?" He captured her lips again.

"I'm not…" she managed to mutter against his mouth.

He stopped then. Their gazes met, and his wrenching pain spoke from the depths of those soft, green eyes.

"I'm sorry," she sobbed. "I didn't mean to hurt you."

His thumb swiped a tear from her cheek. "It's okay." He smiled. "You gave me more than I ever dreamed possible."

If she didn't go now, she never would. His pull was too strong.

She stretched up on her tiptoes and pecked his

cheek. "Goodbye."

Then she turned and ran for the steps up into the train car.

A man in the crowd caught her eye, a smile of recognition on his face.

She jerked her head around and climbed the steps without looking back. Her heart pounded and her hands shook as she clutched at the door handle and pushed herself into the car. Much as she wanted to lean down and peer out the window, she made herself stand still and at least look like she was trying to find a seat.

Tommy Pearson. It must have been. He'd been in uniform, but she'd know him anywhere. They'd gone all through school together. He'd been Jack's friend.

Her knees went weak.

He'd seen her kissing Guy.

Chapter 19

People whispered everywhere she looked. Did they know? Had Tommy Pearson called his mother and told her of seeing Rosemary kissing Guy on the platform in Chicago? Would word get back to her own mother? To Jack's parents?

The undertaker had insisted that Rosemary stand near the coffin to greet those people who came up to offer their condolences, but she couldn't concentrate on their words. Jack kept watching her. Everyone was watching her.

When she'd seen Jack for the first time, lying there in the casket, dressed in his uniform, looking as if he were just sleeping and would open his eyes and sit up at any moment, she'd panicked. Luckily her mother and Jack's parents had been on hand to hold her and keep her from running from the room. He looked so natural, with no visible injuries, just sleeping peacefully.

She'd hoped that this morning she would be better equipped to deal with his lifeless presence. She wasn't. She still wanted to rail at him for his cheating, for his drinking and all his hurtful words and misdeeds.

Now his gaze followed her, watched her, taunted her. Every time she glanced his way it seemed like he'd just closed his eyes so she wouldn't catch him watching. She imagined his face transforming into that disdainful smirk, the way he'd looked when she'd last seen him, when he'd vowed he didn't want her anymore, when he'd thrown his girlfriend in her face.

"Are you all right?" Mrs. Merriwether, the elderly lady who'd been Rosemary and Jack's high school science teacher, held Rosemary's hands in her cold, wrinkled ones. "You're shaking like a leaf."

"I…I'm all right." Avoiding facing her dead husband, Rosemary scanned the crowded room searching for Tommy Pearson's mother. "I just need to sit down."

She'd spent the whole trip from Chicago to Kerrville worrying that everyone in town would know about that kiss. No one would say anything to her. They would just stare at her and whisper behind her back.

"Mr. Hopkins," her former teacher called.

Rosemary didn't want her father-in-law, but she had no choice as he stepped to her side.

"She needs to sit down. She's too overwrought to stand up here."

"Thank you, Mrs. Merriwether. I'll take care of her."

Mr. Hopkins took Rosemary by the arm and led her to a small settee against the side wall. She dutifully sank down on the soft cushions.

"Thank you," she murmured, looking up into the face that could have been Jack with a few extra pounds and wrinkles.

"I'll get your mother to come over."

Mr. Hopkins treated her with the same coolness his wife had expressed when she'd arrived on their doorstep the prior afternoon, escorted by her uncle, James Greenlee, who had picked her up at the train station. Her mother-in-law had begun by complaining about how long it had taken for Rosemary to travel from California. She complained about the possibility of having to delay the funeral. She even complained that Rosemary had taken their son from them when everyone, including his parents, knew he had been the one who joined the army and that Rosemary had no influence in his decision.

Since being notified of his death, she had feared that, although his parents knew Jack had been the one who'd had the accident that caused his death, they would somehow blame her simply because they never approved of her.

From the moment she arrived it became clear that her fears were correct. They did blame her for Jack's death and for anything and everything else.

Those first few hours she'd been too exhausted to react to their barrage of blame. Showing them the telegram and letter she'd received didn't help to change their attitude. Then, without allowing her to rest, they'd insisted that she go with them to the funeral parlor and view Jack's body. Her uncle, sensing that she needed moral support, had gone to fetch her mother.

Her mother had been a blessing. She served as a go-between with her in-laws and provided Rosemary with some semblance of protection. Rosemary hoped her mother would insist that she come stay with her, but her mother made it plain that everyone expected Rosemary to stay with her in-laws.

After her initial panic attack upon seeing Jack's body, Rosemary had collapsed in sobs. The enormity of the situation finally hit her. Jack was really dead, and she was back in Kerrville. Back facing the very people she'd so desperately wanted to escape almost two years before.

Her mother eased down beside her on the settee and put her arm around her shoulders. "Now, now, dear. You'll get through this. I promise."

Rosemary looked up and nodded as she blew her nose on the damp handkerchief she'd kept crumpled in her hand. Her mother could be warm and comforting when she wanted to be. Someone appeared before them.

Rosemary's mother greeted the middle-aged woman, "Mrs. Pearson. So good of you to come."

Tommy's mother. Rosemary's stomach clenched so hard she almost doubled over.

The woman leaned down toward Rosemary. "I'm so sorry, my dear. Jack and Tommy were such good friends. Jack used to come over all the time."

Rosemary could only nod in response. She couldn't meet the woman's gaze.

"I know if my Tommy could be here, he would. I wrote him about Jack. He'll be so upset when he gets the letter."

"Thank you, Mrs. Pearson," Rosemary's mother said. "Tommy's in the Navy, isn't he?"

"Yes. Off in training…like Jack was."

Rosemary dropped her head. Her hands shook as she wiped her nose. Shame and humiliation threatened to suffocate her. What would this woman think? What would all of them think when Tommy told them he'd seen her kissing a soldier on the platform in Chicago?

Guy's image came to mind. That sweet, beautiful man off to fight…and maybe die. She'd never see him again, but that wouldn't matter to the gossips in this town. They'd crucify her.

Her mother patted her knee, and Mrs. Pearson

moved on. Rosemary couldn't let anyone know the real reason for her inner turmoil.

Grandmother Kerr took her mother's place at her side while her mother circulated among the many sympathetic townspeople who had come out on a dreary Sunday to pay their respects, not to her, or to Jack. They came for the Hopkins family and for her kinsfolk, the Greenlees and the Howells, all prominent families in this small town.

Rosemary made it through the endless morning and ate the sandwich her mother handed her, insisting she needed strength to get through the funeral.

Her mother was right. The preacher droned on, and Rosemary found her mind wandering. She stared at the now closed casket, grateful she didn't have to look at Jack. It occurred to her that she would never see his face again. At least not like that. There were photographs of him at his parents' house, but photos weren't the same.

At the close of the service her mother took her elbow and urged her forward. They followed Jack's parents out of the building and into the cold, where a gray overcast threatened rain.

She held tight to her emotions, afraid if she let go, the torrent of bitter anger would spew out of her mouth, and everyone would know how horrible her marriage had been.

In the car, her mother, who sat in the middle to separate her from Mrs. Hopkins, handed her a fresh handkerchief. She balled it in her fist and jammed it into her pocket. Mr. Hopkins rode in front. His height made his black felt hat brush the roof of the undertaker's automobile.

Outside, dreary, bare trees inched past as the procession crept up the steep hill to the cemetery.

The shivering cold kept many of the funeral goers from venturing up the hill to view the interment. Only family, close and extended, stood and watched as they lowered the coffin into the ground.

Numbness and a sense of surreal disbelief cocooned her against the cold wind.

Alone in this crowd of familiar souls, Rosemary said good-bye to her husband and to all her dreams of a life far away.

Chapter 20

Dreams interrupted Rosemary's rest twice during the night. Strange images with Jack the main character, talking to her, luring her into a strange and dangerous place, and in the last one chasing her through a maze of city streets into a blind alley.

She'd awakened from both dreams sweating and breathing hard. The reality of Jack's old room in the Hopkins' house calmed her down, and she soon drifted back to sleep. Her exhaustion won in the end.

When she finally awoke, light poured in from the cracks around the window shade. She looked at her wristwatch, the one her mother had given her for graduation, and discovered it was almost 10:30.

She never slept this late. Guilt niggled at her.

Don't be silly.

She had nowhere to be, and besides, she'd been through an ordeal.

She fumbled through her clothes and found a dress to put on. And then she eased down the stairs wondering where her in-laws were.

She found Mrs. Hopkins in the kitchen rolling out pie crust.

"There you are," Mrs. Hopkins said. She wiped her hands on her apron and went to the stove. "I saved you some breakfast." She lifted the napkin. "Although it may not be very good after sitting so long."

"It's fine," Rosemary quickly assured her. "I'm not very hungry. I would like some coffee, if there's any left."

"Certainly." Mrs. Hopkins set the plate on the table and nodded for Rosemary to sit. She then reached into the cabinet and retrieved a cup and saucer. In silence, she filled the cup with coffee.

Rosemary started to get up to get some milk.

"No, no," her mother-in-law patted her shoulder. "I remember. You take milk in your coffee."

The older woman set the bottle of milk on the table along with the sugar bowl. She didn't speak again until she'd returned to her pie crust.

"Did you sleep well?"

The question was polite and distant. "Yes, thank you."

She forced herself to eat the barely warm biscuits and eggs, to satisfy the rumbling in her stomach rather than her taste buds.

The hot, strong coffee jump-started her still-weary brain.

"I guess Mr. Hopkins is at school."

"Yes." Her mother-in-law paused. "In case you've forgotten, it is Monday. We wanted to have the funeral yesterday so that he could return to school today. The Christmas break starts Wednesday. He has a lot to do before then."

Rosemary remembered her high school days when Mr. Hopkins rode herd on the students and faculty. He hadn't been such a bad principal. His stern, no-nonsense demeanor had kept many a teenager in line.

He'd been less intimidating to his son, Jack, who'd loved to push the limits just to see what his father would do. Jack hadn't been a bad kid. In fact, he'd been a leader in their small school. He'd played center on the basketball team and first base on the school baseball team. And although his grades hadn't been the straight A's his parents wanted, he'd done a respectable job there, too.

Jack's choice of girlfriends had disappointed his parents the most. Rosemary was not their choice. They'd tried numerous times to break up the couple which, looking back, probably made Jack persist in seeing her. That's the way Jack was. Defiant. His parents pushed him one way, he went the other, just to show them he could.

Mr. Hopkins, the educator, wanted his son to go to college. He'd managed to get Jack into Middle Tennessee State College in Murfreesboro, but Jack defiantly rode the train home every weekend to see Rosemary.

Jack was her ticket out of Kerrville. She thought he'd continue in college and eventually graduate and leave their little Podunk hometown. She'd made up her mind to be at his side. And she'd accomplished her goal, just not the way she intended. She'd gotten pregnant.

For the most part, Jack had been an honorable man. He'd agreed to marry her. He hadn't been thrilled, but he knew what was expected of him. His parents had been as disappointed and as upset as her mother had been. But everyone had agreed to keep it quiet for as long as possible.

That had been the weekend Japan attacked Pearl Harbor. The shocking world events overshadowed their own situation.

The next week she and Jack drove down to Alabama and got married. Jack had joked that he might as well join the fight and that they could explain their hasty marriage as the result of war breaking out. Jack hadn't been joking. The day after their wedding he signed the papers to join the Army.

Afterwards, everyone acted surprised and put on a show of being happy for the couple. They even put on a little reception at the church.

Rosemary had hidden her anxiety about her condition behind her semblance of anxiety over Jack's impending military service. She'd had no idea what war meant, only that he would go away for training and eventually be stationed at some military base, maybe even sent overseas.

Had it really been only two years ago when she moved into the Hopkins home with Jack after their wedding?

Now, as Jack's widow, everyone expected her to live with his parents and for them to support her as Jack would have had he lived. Yet they were all miserable. Her in-laws could barely stand to look at her.

As they grieved the loss of their son, she hid her anger at Jack, disguising it as grief. Maybe it was grief, for Jack, for her hopes and dreams, for the life they could have had if he hadn't been such a jerk. Did Jack ever love her? She would never know.

"Harold said he'd come for Christmas. Lord knows Horace could use his company."

Ten years older than Jack, the staid, somber, younger version of their father had barely spoken to her at the funeral. Jack always said Harold was the perfect one, which left him free to have a good time.

"That will be nice," Rosemary commented.

She didn't look forward to Harold's visit. Despite the circumstances of their marriage, he'd been very vocal about his objections.

"He may bring his fiancé."

"He's engaged?"

"Well, if you'd bothered to write…anyway, I wrote and told Jack about it."

Her gut knotted into a ball. "Jack didn't tell me." She sipped her now cold coffee. "You know how Jack hated to write."

"Yes."

Mrs. Hopkins's tone sounded bitter.

"After he left for training, the twelve-hour shifts I worked barely gave me time to eat and sleep before I had to go back to work."

Her mother-in-law faced her. "You didn't even write to your mother. I know because I asked her. She promised to tell me when she heard from you, which was what? Twice in six months."

The woman's voice had escalated into a screech.

"I'm sorry," Rosemary mumbled. She couldn't tell her the real reason she hadn't written.

"You should be." Her voice broke then. Tears streamed down her face.

Rosemary stood and went to the woman, intending to comfort her. But her mother-in-law pulled away, swiped at her tears and turned back to the pie crust.

Rosemary watched her wrap the now thin dough around the rolling pin and transfer it to the waiting pie tin. She pressed it in place and then filled it with the apple mixture she'd already prepared.

"Is there anything I can do to help?"

"In the kitchen? As I recall, you have next to no culinary skills."

"I've learned some."

"Learning enough to avoid starving is very different from actually knowing how to cook." She glanced around at Rosemary. "I don't know how your mother managed to raise you and not teach you a thing."

A slap in the face wouldn't have hurt any more. Anger flared, but Rosemary gritted her teeth and did not respond. Instead she turned away.

She picked up her plate and coffee cup and placed them on the drainer by the sink. She returned the milk to the refrigerator and the sugar bowl to its place by the stove.

"I think I'll go for a walk," she said, as she left the room.

So it was going to be like this. She didn't think she could bear it. Not now, not after living on her own, not after all that had happened.

Chapter 21

Rosemary walked along the familiar streets of her hometown. War posters and meager Christmas decorations were the only changes.

As she stood on the corner waiting to cross, a truck with the Greenlee name printed on the side rolled by. Was her uncle's factory still making shoes or had they switched to war goods?

Distracted by the truck, she didn't notice the woman come up beside her.

"Rosemary, it's good to see you out and about."

"Mrs. Archer." Rosemary had no desire to talk to the biggest gossip in Kerrville.

"So sad about the Hopkins boy. Accident, was it?"

"Yes, ma'am." Rosemary wouldn't give the woman any details she could exaggerate and gloat over. At the funeral home the old biddy had been hanging around, and no doubt, whispering about people behind their backs.

"Well, it was too bad. I'd have thought the Army would have settled him down. But I guess, during wartime, we lose the young men, whether they're fighting or not."

Rosemary needed to get away from this woman, but as she politely nodded her farewell and started across the street, Mrs. Archer managed to stay by her side.

"For someone who'd been in some kind of a military accident, he certainly looked nice. All done up in his uniform. Everyone wondered what exactly happened to him."

What was she implying? That Jack's death hadn't been accidental?

"It was live ammunition. There was an explosion and he was…" She couldn't get the words out.

"Well, now, I didn't mean anything. It's just that he looked so natural and…well, untouched. And, well, some of us wondered."

"Yes. Isn't it amazing what the undertakers can do these days?" She had to get away before she exploded. "Good day," she muttered, as she turned from the old busybody and hurried up the street toward her mother's boardinghouse.

The cold wind penetrated her old coat. She hesitated on her mother's porch, shaking uncontrollably in the damp shadows. Rather than knocking and waiting for her mother to come, she grasped the knob and opened the door while knocking on the glass.

"Hello," she called. "Is anybody home?"

After hearing a faint, "In the kitchen," she closed the door behind her and made her way down the narrow hallway, absorbing the warmth and aroma of midday cooking.

Her mother stood over the worktable that ran down one wall of the long, narrow kitchen. She looked up as Rosemary stepped through the open doorway.

"I thought you'd come by," her mother commented, while her hands continued rolling out dough.

Rosemary couldn't help smiling at the irony.

"You're making pies."

The older woman stopped, and this time she perused her daughter as if she were trying to work out a puzzle.

Rosemary shrugged out of her coat. "Mrs. Hopkins was making a pie when I left." Much as she wanted to make some kind of humorous remark, she knew her mother well enough to keep her mouth shut.

"Making a pie. Humph!" The rolling pin went into motion again, with more vigor than before. "And here I am making a dozen."

Her mother worked hard, and she didn't mind letting everyone know it.

"How do you manage to still make pies with the sugar rationing?"

"My guests expect it. I pride myself at setting the best table in town." She stopped and glared at Rosemary. "Besides…after what happened…I had to do plenty to fill this house…"

"After what I did, you mean." Rosemary finished her thought.

Her mother returned to her work. "It took months just to get new people, ones who didn't care about the gossip. And even longer to thin out the deadbeats. I've got a waiting list again, and that means I can be picky who I rent to."

And now I've returned and stirred everything up again.

Familiar shame burned inside her. She couldn't deny the hardship she'd caused her mother. And she couldn't go back and change the past.

No point in arguing. Instead she'd return to safer ground.

"Where do you get the sugar? For the pies."

"I've modified my recipes to use honey."

"Of course. The beehives. Do you still tend them?"

"You don't think your grandmother would do it, do you? My mother has never touched one of those hives. She's always claimed to be terrified of being stung, but the truth is she doesn't want to get her hands dirty."

"Mother," Rosemary scolded. "That's not fair. Grandmother worked hard in her day. She raised you and your sisters, didn't she? And practically alone, too."

Her mother's hands never stopped as she reached for a pie tin and easily lifted the thin crust from the flour-covered table without breaking it and placed it in the pie tin. She then poured a mixture into the unbaked pie crust.

"Can I help you with something?" Rosemary couldn't just stand there watching her mother work.

The familiar nod toward the sink cued Rosemary to assume her previous duties of washing up. She pulled an apron from the hook and tied it around her waist. Soapy water and dirty pans her mother had already used filled the dish pan. The motions of washing dishes in this familiar sink came back as if she'd never left.

Her mother resumed rolling out dough for another crust.

"How many more are you going to make?" Rosemary asked over her shoulder.

"These two are the last for today."

Rosemary glanced across the room to the pie safe. Its doors stood open so the newly baked pies could cool. The smell of baking pies and the pie safe shelves loaded with the forbidden treats brought memories flooding back, of a busy warm kitchen and a house always filled to the brim with people. Not just family, but boarders, some like family and others total strangers.

She swallowed hard, knowing she was swallowing her pride.

"I wondered if you might let me move back in here, with you?"

Silence. Had she shocked her mother? The girl who'd always wanted to leave wanting to return.

"I thought maybe with Bobby gone I could move into his room." She turned to face her mother, drying her hands on a dish towel.

Her mother stilled. She stared straight ahead as if lost in memories.

"I don't know how long I can stand living there with the Hopkinses. You know they never liked me and now…well…now it's strange. The way they look at me."

How could she explain? It was her as much as them. Her guilt and her anger at Jack permeated every interaction with them. She could never tell them what had really happened. And even if she could, they wouldn't believe her. They'd always taken Jack's side. And she couldn't destroy their memories of him.

Without a word, her mother filled the second pie crust with custard and put both pies in the oven.

Finally, she straightened and turned to face Rosemary.

"Mr. and Mrs. Hopkins want you to live with them. You're their son's wife. Their dead son." Her words were cold, bitter even.

"They don't really. They're doing what they think

they're supposed to do." Rosemary wrung the dish towel around her hand. "All I am to them is a reminder of Jack. That Jack's dead. And I'm not."

Her mother drew a straight wooden chair from its place by the wall up to the table where she'd been working. She looked so tired and so much older than when Rosemary had left almost two years before.

Rosemary pulled a stool up to the table and sat across from her mother.

"Please, let me come home." Then a thought occurred to her. "You haven't rented out Bobby's room, have you?"

Her mother shook her head.

"Good. I didn't think you would. He'll need a place to stay when he comes home on leave. Don't worry about that. I'll stay with Grandmother then."

Her mother wouldn't meet her gaze. Her face betrayed her worry.

"I know you didn't want him to go into the Army, but he'll be fine." Her younger brother had always been a little different, and she'd always thought her mother had babied him too much.

"He's as bad as Jack about writing letters. I've only gotten one letter from him since he was drafted." She regretted saying the word as soon as it left her mouth. She could only imagine how her mother had cried when her baby boy left for the military.

"Surely he's written to you. He's such a dunce, but they'll make a man of him, you'll see."

Rage flared in her mother's eyes even as tears spilled down her cheeks. "No," she blurted. "They should never have taken him."

Rosemary's heart pounded. She'd never seen her

mother so upset.

She jumped up and went around the table to offer her mother comfort, but the older woman pushed her away, just like her mother-in-law had.

"What is it?" Rosemary asked. Her muddled brain couldn't figure out what was going on, why her mother was so disconcerted. "Has something happened?"

"I don't know," her mother managed to grit out.

"Did he write you?"

"Yes." She swiped a tear from her cheek. "And he's miserable. They're torturing him."

"I'm sure it's no different than what all the others go through."

"He should never have gone. They should never have taken him."

Her mother covered her face with her hands to hide the tears.

Rosemary hugged her mother then and wondered what her mother would do if something happened to her little brother.

Chapter 22

Christmas came and went for the men in Guy's company. Many had never been away from home on Christmas. Others, like Guy, were spending their second holiday with their buddies in the Army. *No big deal. Just another day.*

The brass had decided to delay the beginning of serious training until the new year, so they handed out passes into Indianapolis, rotating among the men during the two-week period covering Christmas and New Year's. Guy lucked out and got his leave over New Year's. He figured he could lose himself among the revelers.

He finished up KP and returned to the barracks where he sat on a bunk and watched a card game. His friend, Fletcher, lost the hand and asked Guy for money. Against his better judgment Guy loaned him five dollars.

Of course, Fletcher lost the five and asked for more.

"Do you think I'm a bank or something?" Guy grumbled. "I'm going on leave soon. If I loan you any more money, I won't have any for myself."

"Aw, come on, Guy. I'll win it back and more."

"I said no." Guy walked away, disappointed in his friend.

Another soldier who'd been watching the game

followed him. "That was a smart move."

Guy stopped and looked at the man, wondering what he wanted.

"I'm Louis Wilcox." He stuck out his hand to shake.

"Nolan. Guy Nolan." Guy shook the soldier's hand. "I saw you watching the game." He glanced over his shoulder to make sure they were out of earshot of the others. "You think it's rigged?"

"Yep. See the staff sergeant over there? That's Quince. He's always getting games going. And he always wins."

Guy eyed the sergeant. "I wondered if somebody was cheating. Fletcher has lost all his money and my five to boot. Nobody's that unlucky."

"Or that stupid," Wilcox added.

"That why you weren't playing?"

Wilcox nodded. "I learned the hard way. Lost a bundle last week. The stupid ones, like your friend Fletcher, keep coming back thinking they can win."

"I guess it's a good thing I don't like to play cards. I work too hard for my money to lose it that way."

"I agree." Wilcox grinned. "I heard you say you were going on leave soon. Over New Year's, maybe?"

"That's right. Heading to Indianapolis."

"So am I. Maybe we can go together."

"Sounds good to me."

At least he wouldn't be alone. He wanted to have some fun and not think about Rosemary. He couldn't forget her, but he'd like to not think about her every minute. And if he really got lucky, he might just meet someone else. Someone who wanted him, not some memory.

Chapter 23

Rosemary stood in front of the boardinghouse and studied the house across the street where she'd been born and where her grandmother now lived.

Kate Kerr was the strongest woman Rosemary knew. By sheer force of will the woman had raised her family and had endured endless trials in the process, yet she had never yielded. She'd taken every challenge head-on and singlehandedly kept everyone going.

That's what Grandmother Kerr did when Rosemary's father died. With three young children, Winnie Blackwood had been unable to deal with the simplest of problems. Everyone said that if it hadn't been for Grandmother Kerr, the Blackwood family would have fallen apart.

She had taken twelve-year-old Frances to hand by teaching her to sew and cook and generally make herself useful. Rosemary, only six at the time, did what chores she could, including watching after four-year-old Bobby to free up her mother to work.

Grandmother's strong faith and her practical sense gave her widowed daughter hope and purpose.

Rosemary vividly remembered the day she'd moved from that house into the big, barn-like boardinghouse with only her clothes and her beloved Anna doll. She hadn't understood the sense of loss, like they were leaving her father there in that old house, even though she'd been to his grave on the hill.

She climbed the steps to the porch, glancing around at the well-kept yard with its sprawling elm tree and the surrounding iron fence.

She only had to knock once. Grandmother opened the door, smiling in greeting.

"Rosemary, so good to see you." She stepped back. "Come in out of that cold wind."

Suddenly, in the presence of this formidable woman, Rosemary's insecurities surfaced. Had coming here been the right thing to do?

In the front sitting room, a warm fire burned in a black, pot-bellied stove. Shelves of books filled the back wall and an upright piano sat against the opposite one. Two overstuffed chairs sat before the three tall windows that formed the rounded front of the house, and beside one of them a basket overflowed with sewing.

"Did I interrupt?" Rosemary laid her coat on the piano bench.

"Oh, no, dear." Grandmother waved toward the other chair and resumed her seat by the sewing basket. "I was taking advantage of the light to get some of this done. But it can wait."

Rosemary forced a smile, still nervous in her grandmother's company. She hated to ask favors of anyone. She'd learned growing up to take care of herself, but this was different.

"How are you doing?" Grandmother's soft, sympathetic voice put Rosemary at ease. "All this must be hard for you. Losing Jack. Coming home…"

"Yes. It has been…it is difficult. That's actually why I've come." She could have bitten her tongue at her sudden bluntness. She hadn't meant to sound so desperate.

"What is it, Rosemary?"

She stood and walked over to the stove, holding out her cold hands to warm them. What could she say? She'd already started with bluntness, so she might as well continue. She turned back to face her grandmother.

"I can't live with Jack's parents any longer. I just can't."

"I see." Grandmother looked away and Rosemary could almost see the thoughts swirling.

Then she returned to Rosemary's gaze with that steel determination Rosemary remembered from her childhood. "Well, then. We must find you somewhere to live."

The older woman motioned for Rosemary to return to her seat.

"You've spoken with your mother, I surmise."

Rosemary nodded.

"No room there. I could have told you that. She's squeezed every room full and still has a list a mile long of potential tenants. I even thought about taking in one or two. But I lived too many years running a boardinghouse and, now that I don't have to, I'm enjoying the independence."

She smiled then. And Rosemary knew she would be all right.

"You'll move in here, with me. I'll enjoy your company."

"Thank you, Grandmother."

"And we'll find you something to do. You can't sit idle."

"What am I going to do in Kerrville?"

The old brow wrinkled into a frown. “That may be a challenge.”

“Before you suggest it, I don’t want to work for Uncle James.”

“But why? I’m sure he could find you something suitable.”

“I don’t want to be the family charity case. I was on my own in California. I can hold down a job. A real job. Not some make-work project to keep me busy.”

“Well, as much as James has going on, I’m sure you wouldn’t be doing anything superficial.”

“I’m sorry. I didn’t mean to sound ungrateful. It’s just…”

“I know, dear. This is a difficult time for you. You’ve lost your husband. Your future is uncertain at this point. I only want to help you.”

Rosemary cringed at the mention of Jack. Her feelings were conflicted. Coming back to Kerrville brought back memories of happier times when Jack had been her true love and the most exciting boy she knew. They’d had fun together, and she’d been naive enough to believe it would last.

That was the Jack she mourned. The Jack she’d lost over the months in California. The Jack who’d pulled away from her long before she’d found him in bed with Miranda. He’d discovered another world in the Army, in California, far away from his conventional family. And like so many young men far from home, he’d done things he would never have done at home. He may have been a rebellious teenager, but looking back, his parents and this town had kept him in check. Thousands of miles away there had been nothing to stop him, nothing but a wife that hung like a millstone around his neck.

Part of her understood what had happened to him. And part of her had believed that he would get all that wildness out of his system and come back to her. Yet there had been that niggling sense that he was glad to be rid of her. That eventually he would have kept his word and filed for divorce.

"Well, first things first." Her grandmother rose to her feet. "Let's see. Which room shall I put you in?"

Grandmother Kerr's words pulled Rosemary out of her thoughts and back to reality. "It doesn't matter."

She followed the older woman into the hallway.

"I've been using the front bedroom." She motioned toward the door across the hall, the room where her parents had slept those many years ago.

She opened the door into what they'd called the middle room, small with three doors and a window taking most of the wall space. An old Murphy bed stood against the remaining wall. Her grandmother's sewing machine sat in front of the window, open as if someone had just gotten up from their sewing.

Grandmother opened the door to the side room, built on to the house years before to accommodate her other grandmother. After that, the room had been reserved for Bobby. Frances and Rosemary had slept in the back room.

Rosemary stood in the doorway of the room she remembered the least of any in the house. They'd moved before her brother had gotten old enough to use it.

"It has the door leading to the back porch, so you can come and go as you please, without feeling like you are disturbing me."

Rosemary nodded.

"Of course, if you come through the front, you'll have to go through here," she waved to indicate the middle room. "I only use it when I'm sewing or when someone comes to stay."

"What about the back room?" Rosemary asked out of curiosity.

"Louise and Mary Ann are in there. Jim's gone to Michigan to work in one of those defense plants. Louise is staying here until he finds them some place to live."

"Oh, I didn't realize Aunt Louise was living with you. When did this happen?"

"Jim left right after Christmas. The people they're renting the farm to wanted to move in, so I told Louise to come stay with me."

"Won't it be too crowded with me barging in?"

"Nonsense. The room's just sitting here empty."

"What about Martha Sue?"

"After that soldier she married went overseas, she went off to live with his parents up near Knoxville."

Rosemary vaguely remembered her cousin's hasty marriage to a soldier she met at Camp Forrest the previous summer.

"If she comes for a visit, she can sleep on the Murphy bed," her grandmother continued. "I don't expect Louise to be here much longer. She's anxious to join Jim up north."

Rosemary walked around. The room was larger than she remembered, with sturdy old furniture. Without a fire in the little stove, the room was cold.

"I'll pay you rent," she insisted, turning to face her grandmother. "Whatever is the going rate. I want to pay my own way."

"Of course you do." Grandmother smiled. "You're my granddaughter, aren't you? That's what I'd do in your shoes."

Relief washed over Rosemary. "When can I move in?"

"Whenever you like."

Chapter 24

Her breaths came hard as she reached the top of the hill, a short distance from the entrance to the cemetery. Unable to face Jack's parents and tell them she was moving out, she'd gotten the idea of coming up here and talking it over with Jack. It's what she'd done years ago as a child with some problem she had to work out. She climbed the hill and talked to her father. It had seemed as silly then as it did now, but back then it had helped her. Maybe talking to Jack would help her now. She hoped so.

The day was warmer than when they'd buried him. Winds from the west carried rain clouds that threatened to release their burden at any moment. The scent and feel of the air, especially up high like this, spoke of rain.

Making her way to the mound of fresh dirt that marked Jack's grave, she kept an eye on the sky, hoping she'd recognize the subtle signals before the drops began to fall.

An old oak partially sheltered the Hopkins plot. A small metal placard engraved with his name marked Jack's grave. Mr. Hopkins told her when the headstone was ready, the family would come to see it put in place. For now, the small mound looked lonely, with arrangements of withered flowers from the funeral that lay askew where the wind had blown them over.

A little vase of violets, fresher than the rest, leaned to one side beside the placard. She reached down and straightened it.

"From your mother, no doubt." She spoke aloud to him as if that would break the ice in an awkward conversation.

A car passed on the road not far away. Self-conscious, Rosemary found a spot to sit where she could lean against a neighboring gravestone.

"I've come to talk to you, Jack. To try to work things out." She hesitated a minute, searching for words. "What happened to us? Why did everything fall apart?"

She picked up a small stone and rolled it around in her fingers. "I was so crazy about you. Didn't want to lose you. But I didn't mean to… You know I didn't." She tossed the stone away. "We both wanted to get away. Out of this town. And the war gave us an excuse to leave…together. Just the two of us."

"We were happy, weren't we, Jack? Those first few months. Out in California."

She stared at the mound of dirt, trying to imagine his face. How he'd smiled when she'd arrived. How he'd made love to her with such abandon, over and over.

"Was that all I was to you? Someone to go to bed with? Oh, I know. I enjoyed it, too. We had so much freedom. Even with the Army taking most of your time, when we were together, we were free."

She absentmindedly picked up a fistful of dirt and shifted it from one hand to the other, grinding it between her fingers.

"Me losing the baby after you left, is that what

ruined it all? You didn't seem to mind when I first got to California."

She thought back to the day she'd told him about the baby. He'd been shocked but quickly recovered. "What you mean is that we'll have to get married," he'd said, as if joking. But later, in California, he'd insinuated that she'd arranged it all, to make him marry her. And, once they were married, he implied she'd wanted to get rid of it.

She shivered at the memory of that terrible day.

Anguish roiled up so fast she couldn't contain the cry of soul-deep pain.

Flashes of memories bounced around in her brain. Waking up in the night, crying out in pain. Her mother-in-law hovering over her. The doctor's cold hands as he examined her. The whispers as Jack's parents stood by the door talking to the doctor.

No one had to tell her. She knew. It was gone.

She'd willingly sunk into the dull cloud of numbness. And the sense of being so totally alone.

"You were glad," she spat out toward the mound of dirt. "You didn't want it, so you were glad it was gone." Her chest heaved in angry sobs. "On the telephone you told me it would be better. That we could wait until after the war to start a family." Her fists pounded the earth. "You had no idea how horrible it was, how guilty it made me feel. And you didn't want to know."

Another car passed and she hid her face in her dirty hands.

After long moments she composed herself, drawing deep cleansing breaths.

"All that's done now. And all the other, too." She shook her head. "I just wish we could have talked about it. Resolved some of it. Instead of all that…stuff, hanging there, unfinished." The last time she saw him came to mind, and much as she tried to shove the memory aside, his angry face, his ugly words, pulsed through her brain.

The tears came then. Big deep sobs, as if the clouds had broken loose with a downpour. "I'm sorry," she blubbered. "I'm so sorry."

She didn't know how long she sat there. Her sobs subsided into a stream of tears that seemed to go on forever. Now that she'd let them loose, she wondered if they'd ever stop.

A hand touched her shoulder and she turned to look up into Jack's mother's face. A sense of shared sorrow connected them.

Rosemary got to her feet and found herself engulfed in a warm embrace. The tension that had built between them slowly dissolved into the acceptance of their shared grief. Only now she had to find a way to tell her mother-in-law that she was moving out. That she didn't want to live with them anymore.

The two rode in silence back down the hill. The rain started in earnest, pelting the windshield and blurring the passing town.

Her tears dried with the coming of the rain and Mrs. Hopkins' unexpected appearance. She weighed the words that she must inevitably speak. Should she wait until Mr. Hopkins came home for dinner? Or should she seize the moment and tell Mrs. Hopkins now?

They ran in through the back door into a warm kitchen that smelled of roasting chicken and spices.

Mrs. Hopkins grabbed a potholder and opened the oven to inspect the delicious-smelling food inside.

"You wash up. I have to go get Horace in a little while."

Rosemary took off her coat and walked through toward the dining room and the stairway beyond.

Mrs. Hopkins stopped her with a hand to her shoulder. "I'm glad…that we met up there. At Jack's grave. I think I understand better now."

Rosemary knew she didn't. There was no way she could understand. But at least she was reaching out, trying to make peace between them.

"I'm glad, too." Rosemary closed her eyes knowing she had to take the leap, now while her mother-in-law showed some sympathy for her. "I've decided to move in with my grandmother." Surprise flickered across the older woman's face. "It's for the best. You and Mr. Hopkins are not comfortable with me here, and I…"

"But we've just begun. You haven't been here long enough…"

"Yes. I have. I don't belong here." She looked away unable to watch the hurt in Mrs. Hopkins' face. "I have to find out for myself. What I want. Figure out what I'm going to do. I can't just stay here as Jack's widow. I don't even know how long I'll stay with Grandmother. I just know I can't stay here."

"When will you leave?" The cool reserve had returned.

"Tomorrow."

"So soon?"

Rosemary just nodded and turned away, to climb the stairs, to take the next step toward the unknown.

****

Her grandmother's house felt like home. The odd

arrangement of rooms seemed to match her thinking. Jumbled, yet somehow orderly, logical.

Rosemary made her way back to the kitchen to see if she could help with supper. After sleeping late and roaming around reacquainting herself with the house she'd lived in for her first seven years, she needed to make herself useful.

"Hello," she said to Mary Ann, who sat at the table munching on something.

Her ten-year-old cousin's head popped up. She smiled. "Hi."

Nora Kingsley stood in front of the stove. The tiny wisp of a woman turned to see who'd come in, and her beak-like nose snorted something disapproving.

"Miss Nora, is there something I can do to help?" Rosemary had learned years ago to ignore the older woman's bad moods. She'd worked for Grandmother Kerr as long as Rosemary could remember and yet she'd never changed one bit. She'd always had that wispy gray hair and grumpy attitude.

"I can manage," Miss Nora muttered, turning back to tend whatever she was cooking.

Rosemary glanced around. A handful of dirty pans and dishes sat in the sink.

"Well, while you are finishing supper, I'll just wash up these." She may never have learned to cook very well, but she'd spent plenty of time washing dishes. It was a chore that always needed to be done.

"Suit yourself," Miss Nora responded, which Rosemary knew to be the highest praise Miss Nora was likely to give.

After tying on an apron, Rosemary ran water into the sink.

"Mama said you lived in California."

"That's right."

"California's a long way away, isn't it?"

"Yes, it is. A very long way."

"Longer than Michigan?"

"Yes. Much longer. It took me three and a half days to come from California on the train."

"Wow." The little girl thought for a minute. "How long does it take to come from Michigan?"

"Probably only one long day on the train. It depends on how many stops you have to make."

"My daddy's in Michigan. Mama and me are going to Michigan to live."

"That's nice. Do you know when you're going?"

"Nope. Mama says Daddy will write and tell us."

Mary Ann turned her attention to Miss Nora. "Got any more of those leftover fried pies?"

"Hmpft," Miss Nora replied in her grumpiest tone. "Spoil your supper."

"Awww." Mary Ann turned away. "Can I at least have a drink of water?"

Miss Nora turned with her fist on her hip and glared at the child.

"I'll get it," Rosemary offered, trying to soothe the older woman. She dried her hands, reached up in the cupboard for a small glass, and filled it with cold water from the tap. "Here."

"Thank you," Mary Ann murmured.

At least Aunt Louise taught her good manners. At the same age, Rosemary doubted that she would have been so polite.

Mary Ann downed the contents of the glass and handed it back to Rosemary.

"Martha Sue is coming for a visit," the little girl announced.

"Is she?" Rosemary resumed her task. "When?"

"I don't know. Soon I think."

Rosemary made a mental note to ask Aunt Louise. She hadn't seen her cousin since she left Kerrville. It would be nice to visit with her and hear firsthand the story of her whirlwind romance with the Camp Forrest soldier.

Chapter 25

Guy glanced at his watch. Forty minutes before the next bus into town. He'd run late, thanks to being caught by Sergeant Billings. He'd missed Wilcox and his other friends along with the bus they were all taking into town. Now he'd have to spend half the night trying to find them or spend it on his own.

He sank down onto the bench to wait. No use crying over spilt milk. He'd just have to make the best of it. Going into town and getting away from this camp, even alone, was better than staying behind.

Since returning from his last leave, he'd craved company, craved something to do, something to keep his mind occupied. He knew why. So he wouldn't think of her. So he wouldn't remember.

Gloomy clouds hung low obscuring the winter sun. It wouldn't be dark for another hour. He reached inside his coat, unbuttoned his breast pocket, and pulled out his mother's letter. Maybe if he read it again it would make more sense.

He struggled to make out his mother's scrawling hand in the dim, half-light.

"*Your money didn't come. You said I'd get more money after you left but I didn't. I don't understand why you said you would send more money when you weren't going to. Henry's money came just like always. He may be off somewhere in the Pacific, but he sends me money like he promised."*

Best he could figure, she was complaining that the increased allotment had not started yet. The woman could always get so confused, especially when it came to business matters. She'd been a constant frustration to his father, never understanding that he had creditors to pay and he couldn't just give her the money he took in at the store.

Guy shook his head, remembering the conversation he'd had with her. He'd explained it as slowly and clearly as he could. Now it looked like he'd have to write and explain again.

He pushed aside her reference to Henry. Long ago he'd accepted that Henry was her favorite, that he could do no wrong, including joining the Marines. No. To hear his mother tell it, Henry would whip the Japs single-handed. Guy knew better. Both Henry and Wilson were in grave danger. Both were somewhere in the vast Pacific, and with censoring so strict, he didn't even know where.

"Nolan," someone called.

Guy looked up and saw Amos Campbell hurrying toward him followed by several other soldiers.

Guy stood just in time to grasp Campbell's extended hand.

"You ol' so and so. How've you been?" Campbell slapped him on the back grinning.

"Fine." Guy couldn't contain his smile. "How about you?"

"Couldn't be better." Campbell glanced over his shoulder. "Me 'n my buddies are headed into town."

Guy nodded to the three soldiers.

"You're not on your own, are you?" Campbell

asked.

"Yeah, kind of. Missed my bus."

"Well, you can join us. Always room for one more."

"Swell." It would be nice to hang out with Campbell. Maybe some of his friend's good humor would rub off on him.

"That a letter from that pretty wife of yours?"

"No." Guy glanced at the other men, afraid they'd heard Amos' remark. "You remember. I explained all that."

"Oh, yeah. I remember. On the train. You told me you two weren't married. You were just helping her out." Campbell's eyes twinkled with mischief.

"That's right. I just helped her get a ticket by saying she was my wife." Guy eased closer to Amos to ensure that their words were private. "We didn't actually tell anybody we were married. We just let them think we were."

"And you sure played your part." Campbell elbowed him in the ribs. "All that lovey-dovey stuff."

Heat flooded Guy's face. He tried to shake it off. "We're just friends."

"Sure, sure. And she's writing you, is she? As a friend?"

Guy held up the letter. "No. This is from my mother."

"Sure it is." Campbell winked.

"It is." Guy shoved the letter in Campbell's face so he could see the signature. "See?"

"Okay. Okay. So the letter is from your mother." Campbell put his arm around Guy's shoulder and leaned close. A whiff of whiskey confirmed Guy's suspicions. Campbell had already been hitting the bottle.

"You're still gonna write her, aren't you?" He'd lowered his voice to a conspiratorial whisper. "You're not gonna let a pretty little thing like that get away, are you?"

"We agreed we wouldn't write. Not until the war is over."

Campbell shook his head. "You're a fool. I'd write her every day, no matter what she said. I wouldn't take the chance that she'd forget about me."

Guy nodded. "Believe me I've thought about it."

"See. That's the spirit. Let her know how you feel."

How did he feel? His body ached for her. And his heart pounded at the thought of her smile. But his practical, down-to-earth conscience agreed with her. He was going off to war with no guarantee he'd come back. It wouldn't be fair to her. She'd already lost her husband, even if he was a cheating jerk. She didn't need to get attached to him and then lose him, too.

No. They'd made the right decision. And he'd respect her wishes. Even if it tore him apart inside.

Chapter 26

Rosemary sat in her grandmother's parlor, only half listening to her aunt and her cousins as they chattered away.

Since moving in, she'd been unable to gather her thoughts and think about anything for long. Instead she'd wanted to curl up in her bed and read one of her grandmother's old books. Anything that would draw her thoughts away from her life, from all she'd lost, from her hopeless future.

"Rosemary?"

Her grandmother's voice pulled her back to the conversation. "What? Oh, I'm sorry. What did you say?"

"Martha Sue asked you about your job…in San Francisco."

"Oh." She looked around until her gaze rested on her cousin. "I worked in a shipyard. Moore's. They built ships and repaired damaged ones."

"Did you work in the office?"

"No. No." When she first applied at Moore's they'd said most women wanted office work. "I don't type very well." She'd done horribly on the test they'd given her. Lucky for her what they needed were women to work on the ships.

"What did you do?"

"Most of the time I was welding." It certainly

hadn't been a very glamorous job. Dressed in dungarees with her hair tied up under a snood, she'd come home dirty and exhausted.

"So you didn't actually run any of the machines?" She paused but not long enough for Rosemary to respond. "Do you think you could operate equipment? If you were trained, I mean."

"I guess." What was her cousin talking about? A job?

Martha Sue grinned in a friendly conspiratorial way, telling Rosemary she knew she hadn't been listening to their earlier conversation. "As I was saying, I've been working at this defense plant, up near Knoxville, and they're always looking for workers. I'm operating a big machine." She blushed. "I can't really talk about it, but anyway, they have lots of women working there. And lots of different kinds of jobs."

"Near Knoxville?" That wasn't so far away. But too far to live here.

"Yeah. Actually, it's a ways out from Knoxville. They built this huge place out in the middle of nowhere. My father-in-law works there. On construction. Can you believe they're still building?" She glanced around at the all-female gathering.

"Must be something big. What do they make there?"

Martha Sue blushed again. She enjoyed being the center of attention.

"I had to swear I wouldn't say anything about it. About what I do or what goes on there. It's all top secret. You know, with the war and all, there could be spies listening anywhere." She glanced over her shoulder as if she thought someone might be hiding in the shadows.

"They were pretty strict in San Francisco, too. But working in a shipyard, well, everybody knows that shipyards build ships. So I never really thought about what other places did." Rosemary hadn't meant to express her thoughts out loud. Maybe she had spent too much time alone.

"Anyway, you ought to come and apply for a job. I'm sure they'd hire you."

Rosemary looked down at her ragged fingernails. Much as she wanted to leave this town and all its memories, she couldn't leave her mother. Not with her so upset about Bobby.

"You should think about it," her grandmother said.

Rosemary glanced up. "Sure. I'll think about it."

Later she retreated to her room. The fire had almost gone out and the room had chilled. She went over to the stove.

Embers came to life as she stirred them with the poker. Sparks flew. She retrieved a lump of coal from the coal scuttle and dropped it on the glowing red embers. More sparks flew. After watching the black mass sputter on the hot coals, she added a few more small pieces of coal to the fire.

She remained there, squatted in front of the little fire, and watched as the flames licked the edges of the dark shapes, mesmerizing her, transporting her thoughts to another place and time.

Guy's image, his smile, his touch. Where was he tonight? Had he gone overseas yet? Was he aboard a ship? In the middle of winter? The thought made her shiver.

"It's cold in here."

Startled by her grandmother's voice, she looked around.

"Did you let the fire go out? You mustn't do that this time of year. It'll take forever to warm the room."

Grandmother went to the back window and pulled down the shade. "That'll help a little." She turned to face Rosemary. "If it gets much colder, I'll get someone to tack a blanket or something over the windows. This room gets so much colder with the windows on both sides. That's one reason I don't use it as much."

Rosemary wondered why her grandmother had come to her room. It wasn't like her to come searching out drafts.

True to her character, the older woman turned to Rosemary. "I won't beat around the bush. You need to decide what you are going to do. You can't just mope around here forever."

"I've been helping Mother."

"I know. But your mother can manage perfectly well without you."

"She's upset about Bobby."

"Yes. She is. But the best thing for her to do is work. Stay busy. Right now, I am more concerned about you."

"Me? I'm all right."

"Are you? You've lost your husband. I understand grief. It's insidious. Gets hold of you and won't let go."

Rosemary looked away. When she thought of Jack, anger boiled up inside, anger at what he'd taken from her, anger at being deserted by him for another woman. The anger didn't feel like grief.

"Rosemary, you need something to do. Something to keep you busy, keep your mind as well as your body occupied."

"I'll try." She fought to contain her impatience as she faced her grandmother. The family matriarch meant well. She just didn't understand. "I don't want to go to Camp Forrest and apply for a job. I can't type, and I don't know if I can face…those men." Shame almost overcame her, and she struggled to maintain her composure.

"The soldiers, you mean?"

She nodded, fighting back the tears.

"That's understandable. The soldiers remind you of Jack."

Yes, she'd thought of Jack. But, worse, she feared she would search for Guy. He wasn't there, but she'd look anyway. Look for someone with his kind face, his laughing smile, his green eyes.

"This place Martha Sue works, maybe you should go there. It's not a military base. It's a defense plant. She says that a lot of the women live right there, in dormitories, and they've built a whole town."

"Mother needs me."

"Don't worry about your mother. I'm here. Delia's here. Frances isn't far away."

Rosemary had written to her sister Frances right after she'd returned. She'd told her about Jack, about the funeral, about how hard it had been coming home. Frances understood about losing their father. Her sister didn't know everything about that day, but they'd shared a common grief. And they'd looked after one another, at least until Frances graduated and left. By then Rosemary had thought she could take care of herself.

Now she longed to see her sister, longed for her

calming presence and reassurance that everything would be all right.

Her grandmother wandered around the room. “You go up to Knoxville with Martha Sue and find out about that job.”

Maybe her grandmother was right.

“From what Martha Sue says, even if they hire you, they never put anybody to work right away. So you ought to go on to Knoxville and apply. The sooner you go, the sooner they’ll put you to work.”

Rosemary meekly nodded her agreement.

“Now that that’s settled, I’ll leave you to your thoughts.” She walked toward the door. “That fire seems to have caught. It’s warming up in here.” At the door she turned back. “There’s more coal in the kitchen. You might want to get some before you go to bed. So the fire won’t go out in the night. The temperature has really dropped outside. That little stove will keep you warm, but it burns up the coal.”

“Are you staying up with Aunt Louise to greet the new year?”

Her grandmother emitted a little humph of a laugh. “Gracious, no. I need my sleep.”

Then she was gone, and the loss of her dominating presence left an emptiness. Rosemary’s grandmother knew her well. Knew she needed to get out of this town and its prying eyes and questioning faces. Knew she needed to stay busy, working. That’s how she’d dealt with Jack’s betrayal. She’d worked. Worked herself into exhaustion. Perhaps she did need to work, away from Kerrville, with strangers, somewhere she could start over, somewhere where her thoughts of Guy wouldn’t betray her.

Chapter 27

Rosemary sat near the front of the bus as they approached Oak Ridge. Numerous vehicles were ahead of them on the narrow rural road. Private cars and old farm trucks followed along behind big trucks hauling who knew what.

Soon the big trucks diverted onto another road and traffic slowed. The bus pulled off to the side and parked. The driver told everyone to stay in their seats. Out the window Rosemary saw armed soldiers stopping each vehicle and, one by one, inspecting the occupants' papers before waving the vehicle through the gate.

A soldier wearing an MP armband and a pistol on his hip boarded the bus and asked for each person's identification. All she had was the paperwork offering her a job. The soldier asked Rosemary and three others, also there to start work, to exit the bus.

At this point, Rosemary began to have misgivings. It had been bad enough waiting two weeks while they investigated her background. She'd feared the scandal over her marriage or Jack's death or even her brief encounter with Guy would be uncovered. She wouldn't have gotten the job and more talk would have ensued. She'd survived the investigation. Now she faced armed soldiers guarding a defense plant.

Another MP gave each of the new workers temporary badges to hang around their necks. Then he drove them to what he called the "Castle," a nondescript, two-story building beside a half-frozen dirt road.

"Watch your step," the soldier instructed.

She got out of the vehicle, and her foot sank into soft mud. She squawked in surprise. The MP grabbed her arm, lifted her out of the vile, squishy stuff and put her down on a wooden walkway.

"You'll get used to it," he chuckled.

Her shoe miraculously remained on her foot, covered in mud and probably ruined. A perfectly good shoe. If this was what she had to get used to, she wasn't sure how long this job would last.

"Thank you," she mumbled automatically.

He had already turned back to help the next person.

Despite the freezing weather, a sea of mud surrounded them. Not just between the newly constructed buildings but also alongside the roads and parking area. Wooden planks formed walkways that ran between buildings and beside the road.

"Does it ever dry up?" she asked the soldier.

"Sure," he grinned. "Then it turns to dust."

Inside the "Castle," a woman examined her paperwork. Another took her picture, and another gave her a stack of papers to fill out. She signed a number of legal documents including one that swore her to secrecy. The woman clearly explained to Rosemary that she could not talk to anyone about her work or about the site—Clinton Engineering Works and Oak Ridge. When she heard the penalty, twenty years in prison, she knew they were dead serious. Her hand shook so when she signed that particular paper she wondered if anyone would be able to read it at her trial for treason.

After she'd signed her life away, another woman ushered the new employees to what they called the "guest house" where they would stay until housing became available. The barracks-style quarters had less privacy than anywhere Rosemary had ever stayed.

The woman pointed to her bunk, where she would leave her things, and quickly ran through the basics of bathroom facilities, how she would sign in and out, where she would eat, and where she would catch the bus for her work assignment.

"How long will I have to stay here?" Rosemary asked.

"Depends. When a spot opens up in one of the women's dormitories you'll be notified. Until then, you stay here."

Rosemary wondered if Martha Sue could help get her into a dormitory.

The next morning, Rosemary traveled by bus to a training facility in a former local schoolhouse where she learned more about where she had come to work and the job she would do.

Of the thousands of workers at Clinton Engineering Works, most were civilians. The Military Police manned the gates, but there were also civilian police. Other military personnel worked on the site in various capacities. This disturbed her a bit because she hadn't wanted to work around soldiers. She hoped Martha Sue was right when she said she'd be working with women.

When Rosemary asked if they would be given a tour of the facilities, she quickly learned that simply asking such a question might get her fired. The woman in charge made it clear that employees only went where their specific badge allowed them to go. The designation on the badge would allow them to enter their work area and the common facilities, like the stores or the recreation hall, but nowhere else.

Several days later Rosemary reported to the enormous K-25 plant.

The physically and mentally demanding work was exactly what Rosemary needed. Instead of welding on a ship, she inspected pipes of various sizes and shapes for leaks. Like at the shipyard, after arriving at the plant, she changed into coveralls, tied her hair up and covered it.

An overhead crane brought pipes to her workstation where she stood with her leak tester. She had no idea what the pipes were for, only that they could not leak, not even a little, tiny bit. At first, a middle-aged woman named Patricia stood beside her and trained her, emphasizing the precise requirements.

Her cousin, Martha Sue, had said she ran a big machine. From the little information Martha Sue could share about her job, it sounded boring to Rosemary. Sitting all day watching gauges would have put her to sleep. She hoped inspecting pipes would prove to be more interesting.

A week later, she ran into Martha Sue by accident at the cafeteria where they were both getting their supper after a long workday. Rosemary explained that she hadn't wanted to jeopardize her job by asking any more questions, even if it meant she didn't see her cousin. Martha Sue claimed she'd been to the "Castle" twice asking about Rosemary. She'd learned that Rosemary had been hired but little else.

"Sure wish I could get into permanent housing. I'm sick of the barracks."

Martha Sue laughed. "I'll see if I can get you into my dorm. There's always somebody leaving for some reason."

Either Martha Sue's inquiries worked or Rosemary got lucky, because within a few days Rosemary moved into the dormitory next to the one Martha Sue lived in.

****

Rosemary stood outside the cafeteria shivering as she waited for Martha Sue. She pulled her coat tight around her and faced away from the biting wind. The low, gray clouds threatened to drizzle rain, or if the temperature dropped any more, sleet.

"Come on," she muttered to herself. "I'm not standing out here much longer."

"Did you say something?"

Rosemary turned to face a soldier, bundled in an overcoat and looking lost. She smiled at the stranger before she could stop herself.

"No. Nothing important."

The side of his mouth went up slightly as if he were trying to return her smile but didn't really mean it. He glanced around. "This must be the cafeteria."

He hadn't asked a question, but his words carried a tone of uncertainty.

"Yeah." She waved toward the door. "Go on in."

"I'm sorry, Rosemary." Martha Sue came running up trailed by two other girls.

Rosemary held up her hand. "Inside." She turned toward the door assuming the others would follow.

Near the coat rack, the soldier had shed his coat and stood scanning the room, as if looking for someone. The fog on his glasses insured he wouldn't see much.

By the time she'd unbundled and hung up her

things, he'd taken out a handkerchief and was cleaning his lenses.

She stepped closer to him. "That's an unusual patch."

He put his glasses back on and looked down at the red and blue patch on his uniform. "It's for 'Old Hickory.' The 30th Infantry Division."

"Did the infantry invade?" one of Martha Sue's friends queried.

He looked from Rosemary to the others standing nearby. "Uh, no. I just left them. I was reassigned to here." He looked around again. "Wherever here is."

Rosemary laughed, maybe for the first time since she arrived. "I know the feeling." She glanced over her shoulder at the lengthening line. "Come on. Join us for supper."

He smiled then. "Thanks."

"But don't get any ideas," Martha Sue chimed in. "We're just being friendly to the new kid."

He nodded and followed the four girls into the waiting line. He introduced himself as Lt. Virgil Rushing, and each girl rattled off her name in turn.

Once they filled their plates and found a table to crowd around, Rosemary took the opportunity to ask the question that had been burning inside her. "Did you mention the 30th Infantry Division?"

He nodded and finished chewing a bite of roll. "Yeah. We were in Boston getting ready to ship out when this officer showed up with orders for me to report here."

"I used to know someone in the 30th." Rosemary tamped down her reaction, afraid to ask about Guy. Her heart pounded in her ears, drowning out the dull roar of conversation in the crowded cafeteria.

"Why'd they do that? Order you to come here, I mean?" Martha Sue's friend Suzy asked.

"My degree in chemical engineering."

"Well at least you didn't have to go overseas. My husband is over there. In England. He's a cook, so I'm hoping that will keep him safe."

"I don't know. The cooks have to take hot food out to the men in the field. At least they did when we were on maneuvers."

"Don't tell her that. She worries too much now."

"I guess you had a lot of friends in the 30th," Rosemary ventured.

"Yeah. Great bunch of guys." He took a bite and tried to smile as he chewed.

Rosemary's mind raced. She couldn't just ask him if he knew Guy. She'd have to ease around to it.

"I guess you'll be writing some of them. Keeping in touch?"

"Sure. I'll keep up with a few. Guys in training get pretty close."

"You're an officer, aren't you?" Molly asked.

"Second lieutenant."

"Silly girl. You see all these soldiers around here and yet you don't know the first thing about them," Suzy said.

Molly smiled, not the least bit offended. "All I know is that they're soldiers. I don't know how to tell the difference between their uniforms."

"For one thing, you pay attention to these patches on their sleeves and whether they have stripes or these little gold bars." Martha Sue pointed to Virgil's lieutenant's bars.

"Or oak leaves or birds," Virgil added. "I'm a lowly second lieutenant. There are probably plenty of captains and majors and colonels around here."

Molly shrugged and the others just laughed.

When they settled down, Rosemary resumed her questions. "I suppose you're staying in the guest house."

Virgil nodded.

"I stayed there for a while. I guess we all did at one time."

"There's not a BOQ here. That's Bachelor Officers' Quarters. So they said that I'd have to stay there until they could get me into the officers' barracks." He shrugged. "Doesn't seem to be many options in housing around here."

"Tell us about it. We're living in an overcrowded dormitory."

"They keep building housing, but I think they're hiring faster than they're building."

When the group finished eating, Virgil thanked them for being so friendly. "You've all made my first night here much nicer than I expected it to be."

They donned their coats preparing to venture out into the cold again. Rosemary hung back.

"Maybe we'll see you here again."

"I hope so."

"I'm Rosemary. Rosemary Hopkins. You'll remember me, I hope."

"I'll definitely remember you."

Rosemary joined the girls. She hoped she hadn't been too friendly. She didn't want him to get the wrong idea. She just wanted information from him.

Martha Sue took her by the arm.

"So, you like this guy Virgil."

"No," Rosemary insisted. Then she met her cousin's gaze. "Well, maybe a little bit. He's interesting."

"Uh-huh. I thought so."

"I'm not looking for a boyfriend. Not now. Maybe not ever. He's just interesting to talk to. More interesting than you girls."

"That's 'cause he's a man."

Rosemary shook her head and pulled her arm free. She walked on ahead of the others, their giggles trailing behind her.

They didn't understand and they never would because she wasn't about to tell anyone anything about Guy Nolan. Not now. Not ever.

Because she couldn't keep him out of her thoughts.

Chapter 28

The truth of what he'd done sank into his gut like lead. He'd joined the Army on an impulse. To show everyone he could and would. Now, waiting in line to board the ship, loaded down with all his gear, snow spitting from the low, gray clouds, he wished he'd stayed in Oakland, installing wiring on ships.

Maybe the hangover he'd had for the last two days had brought on these feelings of regret. The division had been at Camp Myles Standish for almost two weeks, and the one pass he'd gotten to Boston had turned into a drinking contest. The girls they'd picked up hadn't interested him. They'd only reminded him of his lousy luck with women. First Julie, then Rosemary. So he'd spent his time drinking, challenging himself to see just how much he could put away.

Ha! The joke had been on him. Again. He'd passed out, or so his friends had said. Next morning when the sergeant woke him, his body ached like he'd been run over by a train.

Then the orders had come. "Pack your gear. We're shipping out."

"Coffee, soldier?" The young woman's smiling face looked down from the Red Cross stand.

He nodded and she handed him a steaming cup. Another woman held out a plate of doughnuts, but he waved them away. The coffee would warm him up, but his stomach couldn't take the weight of even one doughnut.

Curly grabbed two. "I'll take his since he don't want it."

Guy forced a smile. Curly was one of those guys who could eat anytime.

As they inched forward in the shelter of the shed that covered the dock, Curly elbowed him.

"Sure you don't want it?"

"No. You eat it. I'm not much on doughnuts."

He sipped on the strong coffee, hoping it would stop the shivers running through his body.

"You ever been on a ship?" Curly asked, still chewing.

"Sure. Lots of times." Of course they'd all been in dry dock. He'd never been to sea.

"I never have. Sure hope I don't get sick."

Guy turned to look at him. How could he munch on doughnuts and fear getting seasick at the same time?

"Did you ever get seasick?"

"No." Guy turned away and took another sip of coffee. He wondered if he'd get sick on the voyage. After the hangover, he wouldn't be surprised. With his luck he'd be sick all the way across the Atlantic.

The gray steel wall of the ship's side loomed closer.

You've been on a ship before. This one's no different than the ones you worked on back in Oakland.

He'd climbed on and off those ships lots of times. Safely in dry dock. Not heading across the North Atlantic in the dead of winter.

The military converted the *SS Argentina* to transport troops. Thc big liner had made lots of trips across the ocean. Her crew was experienced, even in wartime. And they'd be in a big convoy with Navy escorts. So the German U-boats had little chance of hitting them.

The more he thought about it the more he realized that he feared Mother Nature more than the Germans. He'd heard tales of ships sinking in storms on the North Atlantic. Not to mention icebergs. No one had forgotten the tragedy of the *Titanic* even though it had sunk before he was born.

On board he followed other members of the 230th Field Artillery toward the stern. They went down so many stairways that he wondered if they'd be traveling on the very bottom of the ship. Turned out he was almost right. Only one deck up from the bottom, their bunks were stacked four high with tight aisles in between the rows. He managed to grab a middle bunk and Curly climbed in above him.

As he stowed his gear a sergeant roamed around instructing the men to sling their helmets by their bed to use in case they got seasick.

Guy looked over at Curly, who grinned. "Don't worry. I won't miss."

The bunks filled up quickly. Guy located several friendly faces. Somehow being with these men he knew, that he'd trained with and partied with, reassured him. They were in this together. Sink or swim.

He chuckled at his own little joke. From way down here there'd be no swimming if they were hit. And best he could figure they were pretty close to the stern so any propeller-following torpedo would land right in their laps.

Neither he nor Curly had to resort to using their

slung helmets. Once recovered from his hangover Guy quickly gained his sea legs and easily maneuvered the ship for their twice daily meals and once daily exercise sessions on deck. His life vest became standard wardrobe and abandon-ship drills kept them on their toes.

Fears of bad storms and German submarines proved unfounded. After eleven days at sea they sighted the coast, their secret destination, Scotland. From there they loaded onto a crowded train and traveled south to their base in England.

****

Rosemary's shift changed. She worked through the night and slept in the daytime. Since their schedules conflicted, she could no longer meet Martha Sue in the cafeteria for supper. Rosemary must have been on a different shift from Lt. Virgil Rushing, too, because she didn't see him in the cafeteria.

She had intended to pump the lieutenant for information about the 30th Division, but since she had no idea where he worked or his schedule, it was impossible. And at Clinton Engineering Works, you didn't ask any questions about another person's job or share any information about your own. That was a sure-fire way to get canned.

So Rosemary scanned the face of every soldier she saw, hoping to see him somewhere. She even went so far as to ask some of the military personnel if they knew Lt. Rushing. So far she had found no one who did.

In the meantime, she made the most of her life in Oak Ridge. She joined others as they stood in line at the store to purchase the most basic things like soap and toothpaste. As for clothing, she quickly learned that the selection on site was extremely limited. She missed the shopping in San Francisco. There had been plenty of shops within walking distance of where she lived, and when she got lonely, she had strolled around window shopping and occasionally buying something that caught her eye.

While standing in line, she met Drucilla Hawkins, who talked about shopping in Knoxville on her day off. This new friend offered to take Rosemary along on her next foray into town.

Drucilla was married to a Navy pilot serving somewhere in the Pacific, and she lived in a nearby dormitory. Not only did the two women share an interest in shopping, they both relished a good movie. Drucilla invited Rosemary to join her one afternoon at the movie theater, where she delighted in both the film and the company.

The women at Oak Ridge tended to hang around in small groups of friends who shared common interests or similar backgrounds. Talk focused on families, past experiences, and hobbies. Since Rosemary had never really had any hobbies except reading, she found herself trying new things.

She went with a group of girls to the bowling alley on her day off and had a blast. Going out with married women whose spouses were stationed elsewhere gave Rosemary a sense of freedom. They didn't treat her differently because she was a war widow. And they didn't chase after men. They just enjoyed each other's company.

She'd almost forgotten about Lt. Rushing when she

ran into him outside the recreation center.

Chapter 29

June 8, 1944

"Are you sure those girls will be there?"

"Yeah. They'll be there."

Guy listened to George and Curly argue. He'd agreed to go with them into High Wycombe because they needed a third man for the girls they'd met. An opportunity to get out of the barracks and socialize with friendly English girls would provide the distraction he needed.

Outside the barracks loud whistles blew. The door burst open and Sgt. Smith hurried in.

"Listen up. Everyone."

They all turned to face him.

"We've got forty-five minutes to be packed and loaded on trucks to pull out."

Everyone just stared impatiently. Another practice run.

He strode further into the barracks.

"Move. Pack your gear. Trucks will be here in thirty."

"Again, Sarge?" George pointed toward Guy and Curly. "We've got passes to High Wycombe."

Sgt. Smith stopped in front of George. "Get a move on." His hard gaze scanned the men waiting in anticipation. "You know the drill." The tone of his voice made it clear that it didn't matter if this was another practice run or not. He expected them to follow orders.

Tension ran high. Two days ago, they'd gotten word that the cross-channel invasion of France had started. Relieved that the much-awaited invasion had begun, they anxiously waited for orders to come down that the 30th Infantry Division would join in the fight.

Was this it? Or just another impromptu practice run?

Leave to High Wycombe forgotten, Guy grabbed his half-packed duffel bag and started mentally inventorying his clothing and equipment.

"There ain't no way the whole division is gonna be ready in forty-five minutes," Curly complained. "No matter how often we practice."

Sgt. Smith must have heard his comment. "It's not the whole division. It's just us."

Guy's head went up. He and a dozen others stared at the sergeant as he continued.

"The 230th has been assigned to the 29th Division. They're already in France and they need our guns. This is no dry run." He glanced around again. "So, dress for combat. Pack your duffels and be ready to load the guns when the trucks get here."

With that he turned on his heel and left.

Guy and Curly exchanged glances.

"Wow!" Curly shook his head. "Didn't think it'd be like this."

Guy pulled the half-written letter to Rosemary out of his pocket, ripped it into pieces, and walked over to the trash can. He couldn't mail it anyway. Might as well ditch it now.

Much as he'd like to let her know what was going on, the bitter truth was that she didn't want to know. The letters were just a way for him to cope with his situation, create the illusion that someone cared where he was and what happened to him. Every time he tore up a letter, he reminded himself that she didn't want to know. She had a family and a whole other life in Tennessee. And she didn't want him to be any part of it.

They traveled all day by truck along roads lined with English people who seemed to know where the trucks were taking them. Evening closed in as they approached the docks and parked along the roadside. The drizzling rain didn't stop the process of waterproofing the vehicles and guns with the help of service troops. Word spread that they were high priority. That meant they'd be loaded on ships as soon as possible.

Nerves strung too tight thwarted Guy's attempts to sleep. He blamed the rain and dampness when he started shaking. To get his circulation going, he got up and circled the truck. Would morning ever come?

Before daylight they moved again, down a steep incline that led to the docks. The busy harbor came into view as the sky lightened. With no road signs along the way he could only guess from the size of the harbor and the number of ships that they were in Southampton.

The battalion loaded onto two ships called LSTs, short for Landing Ship, Tank. Battery C ended up on an English ship. Guy had responsibility for their radio equipment, so he stayed with the truck to ensure that it was loaded securely.

He asked the English sailor if he knew where they were going.

"Omaha Beach," the Limey replied. He must have noticed Guy's confusion, so he added. "In Normandy. One of the invasion beaches. We took the 29th over three days ago." He looked up from the lines he'd just secured. "Guess you guys are replacing the artillery that got blown up."

"Blown up?"

"Yeah. On the beach." He scratched his head. "Lotta stuff gettin' blown up on that beach. Men and equipment."

A chill ran down Guy's spine. "How bad…?"

"Real bad. At least it was the first day. It's better now. On the beach anyway. Can't say about further inland."

How many were dead? The whole 29th Division had landed with all their artillery. And enough guns had been destroyed that they needed the 230th.

"You staying here?"

Guy's head jerked up. "Uh. No."

He made his way to where the other soldiers were gathered. Whispered comments buzzed through the confined space.

Curly shouldered his way toward Guy.

"Did you hear? About the landing?"

Guy nodded.

"Sounds like the first day was a nightmare."

Guy nodded again. "Yeah."

"Glad we didn't have to go in then." Curly lit a cigarette with shaking hands. "You think we'll make it across on this tub?"

Guy straightened his shoulders and looked around. "We'll make it across okay. It's what's waiting for us on the other side that I'm worried about."

****

June 10, 1944

The ship shuddered as it slid up onto the beach. Guy climbed up a ladder where, from his limited vantage point, he saw water surrounding them. They'd have to wade in through the surf.

The men waited for word to disembark. Stomachs, nauseated by the ship's violent motion while crossing the channel, now settled. Nerves did not.

Barrage balloons floated overhead, tethered in place to prevent enemy aircraft from getting too close to the busy ant hill on the beach. The water around them churned with vessels of all sizes.

His gaze shifted to the beach. That's when he saw them. Bodies bobbed against the metal obstructions that protruded from the water.

He shuddered.

The sound of artillery fire in the distance pulled his gaze from the gruesome sight. He tried to judge the distance to the firing guns based on the sound but before he could figure it out a nearby destroyer let loose its guns in a deafening thunder.

That meant that although the Americans had made it off the beach, the beachhead was still so narrow that the naval guns could easily bombard the enemy.

Reality hit him from every direction. Naval gunfire. Distant artillery shells exploding. Dead bodies in the water. An ungodly amount of material being unloaded, and thousands of men pouring onto the beach. He was here and there was no going back.

Curly and several others joined him on deck. A series of explosions nearby turned everyone's attention to a cargo ship as it sank not two hundred yards away.

"U-boats," Curly muttered.

"That weren't no U-boat. They're sinking them ships to make a harbor, so's more ships can be unloaded." Guy and Curly exchanged glances. The Englishman spoke with authority, so they had to assume he knew what he was talking about.

"How many trips have you made?" Curly asked.

"This'n makes three. And I ain't seen no sign of no U-boat yet." He rubbed his chin. "That ain't to say they're not out there. I just ain't seen 'em."

Guy scanned the water. "Glad they left us alone."

"If I was you," the Englishman continued. "I'd be more worried about the Germans on shore." He waved toward the land, where smoke billowed from exploding shells.

Guy nodded, acknowledging the man's words. U-boats were the least of their worries now.

By the time the huge doors at the front of the awkwardly shaped ship opened, the tide had receded, and they were able to walk onto the beach barely getting their feet wet. Guy climbed onto the truck carrying the radio equipment before they drove across the sand to the road that wound its way up the hill and off the beach.

Out of the back of the truck he saw ships on the water as far as the eye could see. LSTs rested on the beach amid a myriad of metal obstacles and unloaded men and vehicles while the beach masters directed traffic with their megaphones. He could have been watching a film on a wide, panoramic screen, but this was real. The images would be forever imbedded in his memory.

More waiting in a staging area grated on Guy's

nerves. Hurry up and wait. That phrase could sum up his Army experience.

The partial remains of a concrete structure, maybe a pillbox, stood off to the right of the road. On the other side someone had strung white tape. He climbed down and walked toward the front of the truck.

Someone yelled at him, “Hey, watch where you walk. Mines.” That’s when he saw the skull and crossbones sign beside the tape. Evidently the engineers had marked the mine field and moved on to more pressing matters. Eventually someone would clear it.

As he stood waiting by the truck, the breeze off the ocean ebbed and they were engulfed in the most horrible odor he’d ever smelled.

He looked up at the driver. “You smell that?”

“God, yeah. It’s awful.”

The stench grew worse. Guy covered his mouth and nose as best he could. He made his way back and climbed into the covered truck, hoping it would provide some protection. They’d trained for gas and this smelled nothing like that, but he decided to put on his gas mask just in case.

When they moved forward along the road, they discovered the grisly source of the smell. Dead bodies. They were lined up along the road beyond the mine field. A handful of men dug with shovels or examined the lifeless figures.

Guy turned away from the sight, proof of the price already paid to gain this narrow strip of land. He steeled himself against the death and violence that lay ahead.

Chapter 30

Adrenaline ran high as the battery set up the guns and prepared to fire their first rounds in the hedgerow country near Chantilly.

Guy worked furiously, with shaking hands, to finish setting up the radio. George's entrenching tool flung dirt into the air nearby. In only a few minutes, fear of flying shrapnel had inspired him to dig almost a foot.

Another shell exploded nearby.

Guy froze. Despite his innate desire to flatten himself on the ground, Sgt. Smith's words echoed in his ears.

"Get the Fire Direction Center up and running—*now*. Foxholes can wait until after our guns start firing."

That meant ignore the incoming Jerry fire and focus on the task at hand.

A voice crackled through the device. "Able calling Fire Leader. Over." Guy grabbed the receiver and answered.

Within minutes calls came in from Batteries A and B and the Forward Observer. George came up for air and Guy gave him the thumbs up. They were up and ready.

Guy relayed coordinates to the guns and they soon heard the sweet sound of outgoing artillery. Theirs. All their training had paid off.

Once the radio was in place, Guy shifted his attention to helping George finish their foxhole.

The two men took turns digging and manning the radio. During a lull in radio traffic, George took a break and grabbed some rations.

"Is this what you expected?" George asked, waving his hand in the air.

"You mean combat?"

George nodded and took another bite.

"I guess. It's not much different than training."

"Yeah." George rolled his eyes. "Except for the live ammo."

A distant droning drew Guy's gaze skyward. It grew louder. An airplane. A German airplane. Guy dove for the foxhole. He landed on top of George, who had had the same idea.

A bomb exploded nearby, then another. Guy grabbed his helmet and ducked.

After only a few minutes the blasts stopped. Guy and George looked around. The radio was intact.

Other men extended their heads to see if it was safe to come out of their hiding places.

That's when the machine gun bullets sprayed the ground.

The German pilot, having dropped his bombs, now returned to strafe the guns and the men who fired them.

Somewhere an anti-aircraft gun fired. Then another.

The plane disappeared beyond the horizon.

"You okay?" George asked.

"Yeah. I guess." Guy crawled out and got to his feet, glad to be alive.

Nighttime brought additional attacks from the air

with flares dropped from above to illuminate targets in the darkness. Adding to their misery, rifle fire from unseen snipers kept men low to the ground. Soldiers fired into the night at unknown targets, sometimes their own men and sometimes a farmer's cow.

The men of the 230th had tasted combat for the first time. Guy wondered how long it would take to get used to it. They'd all have to learn to do their jobs despite the danger or they'd be of no use at all.

After several days firing in support of the 29th and moving forward to new positions, elements of the 120th Regiment of the 30th Infantry Division joined up with the men of the 230th. Control of the unit passed back to their old division.

Guy saw Amos Campbell briefly, but before the friends could talk much, a sergeant yelled for Campbell to "come on."

Every few days the artillery location changed. Setting up and digging foxholes became routine, as did the specter of death and destruction all around them.

When the familiar call of "hot chow" rang out, Guy punched George in the shoulder. The other man looked up from the radio and shoved the earphone from one ear.

"I'll get your supper. Where's your kit?"

"In the hole." George slid the earpiece back and started writing on the pad before him.

A fire mission call. Something that couldn't be ignored.

Guy and George took turns manning the radio. Calls could come in at any time. Some could be handled with only one gun. Others needed them all.

Guy dug under a blanket in the foxhole the two

shared and found George's mess kit. He took it along with his own over to the kitchen truck where the cooks were dishing out hot food.

"Always know we can find C Battery by the dead cow," the cook remarked with a smirk.

They'd heard the same joke from cooks before, not to mention the communications boys and the mail clerks. Guy wondered if the CO picked these spots intentionally as his idea of a joke. Or maybe he thought it would get them used to the stench of death. In that case, it was working. The smell didn't bother him nearly as much as it had at first.

He returned to the radio tent and placed George's food-filled mess kit down beside the radio.

"Did they call for much fire?" They had learned that if the infantry up ahead called for more fire and more often, it meant more intense fighting.

"Naw," George replied. "What about coffee?"

Guy set his own plate down. "I'll get it." He headed back to the kitchen truck with a metal cup in each hand.

Guy got in the coffee line right behind Curly.

"Did you fix that radio I found?" Curly asked.

"I told you I couldn't fix that piece of junk."

"It seems to me that if you are going to open a business fixing radios, you ought to be able to fix that one."

"And how am I supposed to do that? The tubes are all busted. And I'm not about to take the tubes out of the company radio to fix a broken-down piece of junk like that."

Curly burst out laughing, along with two of his friends standing nearby.

Heat rose as Guy gritted his teeth. He didn't like Curly getting his kicks at Guy's expense.

"Lighten up, Nolan." Curly slapped him on the back.

Guy shook his head and held out the cups for the cook to fill. He forced a smile for Curly's sake and turned to go back to the radio tent before Curly started up on something else.

Bam!

An explosion blasted the earth not a hundred feet away.

Guy hit the dirt. Hot coffee flew in all directions.

"Incoming," someone yelled as another blast threw debris into the air.

Soil laced with shrapnel rained down, pelting Guy's body.

He grabbed his helmet to hold it in place.

A few seconds passed. He looked around anticipating the next blast. Emboldened by the silence, he scrambled to his feet and made a dash for the radio tent.

Another explosion hit near where the kitchen truck had been moments before. He couldn't blame them for making a run for it.

"Get in the hole," George yelled just as another round exploded almost on top of the last one.

Guy dove headfirst into the nearby foxhole. He felt, rather than saw, George's legs beneath him.

Within seconds another explosion landed much closer.

The bulky radio toppled from its table as the tent partially collapsed from the force of the blast.

"Mortar," George screamed. "Got to be."

Guy nodded. "They're right on top of us."

They huddled together in the shallow hole. They had to stay put and wait until it stopped, until the infantry or one of their tanks either destroyed the mortar or forced them to withdraw. Or until one of those shells landed on top of them and ended it all.

Chapter 31

July 22, 1944

Rosemary looked up from her mending when Minnie came in with an armload of clean laundry and dumped everything on her bed.

"I washed those socks you loaned me."

"Put them in my drawer. The second one." Rosemary focused her attention on finishing the delicate job of repairing a nylon stocking that had pulled loose at the toe. She wanted to wear them, her last pair, on her date with Virgil.

Minnie wagged something in front of her. Rosemary glanced up and froze.

A bundle of envelopes. From her drawer.

Shame spread through her body like poison, burning up from her gut, and spreading fire across her face.

"I…I…" Humiliation kept her brain from devising some plausible lie. Some reason she would have envelopes addressed to the Acme Insurance Company.

"I see you got a stack of these, too."

What? Had Minnie said "too?"

Her roommate turned to her own dresser and pulled out the bottom drawer. After digging underneath the clothes, her hand emerged holding an identical bundle of envelopes.

"Here's mine."

"You…you have them, too?"

Minnie nodded. She handed one bundle to Rosemary and tossed the other one onto the bed beside her clean laundry. She then plopped down almost on top of them.

"Yeah. Two guys in suits gave them to me right after I arrived. Told me if I saw anything or heard anything suspicious, I was to write it down and mail it in one of these envelopes."

Rosemary's body relaxed just a tad. Yet she couldn't shake the feeling she'd been caught in a compromising situation and publicly humiliated.

"I guess they did the same with you?"

Rosemary nodded. She remembered the deadly serious expressions on their faces as the two men told her that it was vital to the war effort and to the security of Oak Ridge and Clinton Engineering Works that she report any suspicious activity, regardless of how trivial it seemed to her.

"I never liked the idea of spying on my friends. I mean, I don't think I could turn anyone in, not unless they did something really bad." Minnie fingered the envelopes as if she were counting them.

"Me either," Rosemary added. "I've still got all of mine."

Minnie met her gaze. "Kind of scary, though. Knowing everyone is watching you all the time."

Rosemary nodded again and looked away. She knew. Everybody had watched her all her life. She'd thought it was just in Kerrville and maybe other small towns. In San Francisco she hadn't thought much about anybody watching her.

She'd come here hoping it would be like in California. New place. New people. And everybody would accept you as you were and how you treated others.

Then those men had given her the envelopes and asked her to spy on the people she'd just met. Her new friends. She'd looked at everyone differently after that. Wondered what they were really thinking, who they really were.

Now she realized she'd been doing just what they wanted her to do. Spying on her friends. Even though she'd never reported anyone, she'd been watching them.

Minnie got up and put her envelopes back in her bottom drawer. Then she put her laundry away.

The need to talk overrode her sense of reticence. "Minnie, have you ever been gossiped about?"

Her roommate turned, a quizzical look on her face. "I guess. I mean, hasn't everybody at one time or another?" She came over and sat on the bed opposite Rosemary. "Why do you ask?"

"I…" Rosemary wasn't sure how to start. "Back home, in Kerrville, it felt like everyone in town was talking about me."

"Why?"

"Oh, I don't know. Because of me and Jack." She didn't want to confess all to Minnie, but maybe she could talk about part of it. "You see, we got married when the war broke out. After Pearl Harbor."

"That's not unusual. Lots of people did."

Rosemary nodded. "I know." How could she explain. "His parents weren't so happy about it, even though we'd been dating for a while. I don't think anybody in town thought I was good enough for him."

"You shouldn't worry about that. It's what he thought that counts."

"I know. And he wanted to marry me. He did." She'd better stop before she said too much. "Anyway. It seemed like everyone was talking about us."

Minnie stood. "We'd better get dressed. The boys will be here soon."

Rosemary quickly finished her darning and pulled out her new dress. She'd bought it in Knoxville on her last shopping trip with Drucilla.

"I hope it's not too hot. Dancing outside sounds fun, but if it turns muggy it could get miserable."

"Yeah, I know. I'm hoping for a nice breeze down from the mountains."

Rosemary enjoyed Virgil's company, especially since he corresponded with friends in the 30th Division. She could pump him for information about where they were and how the war was going, and, in doing so, she learned a little bit about Guy.

Despite her efforts to put Guy out of her thoughts, he cropped up on a regular basis.

Maybe tonight she'd find out more. If Virgil had heard from his friend and if he could decipher enough from the heavily censored letter, he could tell her where they were. She had a couple of maps that had been published in the newspaper. They were vague at best, but sometimes they showed the Army number or referred to a General. Virgil was an expert at deciphering the least little tidbit and explaining to her what it meant.

A pang of guilt gnawed her insides. She had more interest in the information Virgil provided than the man himself. She hoped her interest didn't give him the wrong impression.

Tonight she would reiterate to him that she didn't want a romantic relationship, not now and possibly not ever.

Chapter 32

The air hung in a heavy, moist veil. Sweat trickled down between her breasts and she fought the urge to rub her dress against her chest to dry it. That would only cause the dampness to show through the thin cloth. Thank goodness she'd thought to wear pads under her arms or there would have been huge damp circles around her armpits.

"Would you get me a drink?" she asked Virgil as they left the crowded dance floor.

"Certainly."

He looked cool and collected, as usual.

"On second thought, I'll go with you. Maybe it will be cooler if we get away from all these people."

Virgil wasn't much of a dancer. He danced with her a couple of times, yet he'd been perfectly fine when she danced with someone else. If it hadn't been so hot, she would have loved the chance to cut loose and enjoy herself.

Virgil grabbed two cups of cool punch.

"Have you gotten another letter from your friend overseas?" she asked.

"Nope. From the news accounts I'd say he's too busy to write."

"Busy fighting, you mean?"

"Yep." He gulped down his remaining drink.

Rosemary spotted her cousin, Martha Sue, in a

tête-à-tête with a handsome young civilian. Rosemary had seen them dancing earlier. Time to get an introduction.

“Excuse me a minute.” She veered away from Virgil and approached Martha Sue.

“Hi, cousin. Aren’t you going to introduce me to your friend?”

“Oh!” Martha Sue looked around, startled to see Rosemary. “Uh, sure.”

The man stepped forward and extended his hand. “Wallace Monroe, at your service.” The words rolled from his tongue in a deep southern drawl and the smile on his face said “southern charm” from ear to ear.

Rosemary took his hand. “Rosemary Hopkins. I’m Martha Sue’s cousin.”

“So I gathered.” He shifted his smiling gaze back to Martha Sue. “Are all the women in your family so lovely?”

Martha Sue’s face flushed a rosy pink.

Something about this man’s smooth manner sent alarm bells ringing loudly in Rosemary’s ears. “Of course, we are. Aren’t we, cuz?”

While Martha Sue fumbled for words, Rosemary charged ahead. “Martha Sue, wouldn’t you like to accompany me to the ladies’ room?” She hoped her little head gesture got it across to Martha Sue that she needed to see her.

“Well, uh, I…”

“Go right ahead, ladies. Take your time. I’ll be waiting right here.”

Rosemary flashed a smile his way and grabbed Martha Sue by the arm. They passed Virgil. “We’ll be back in a minute.”

A few steps away Martha Sue finally found her tongue. “What do you want?”

“You brought your bag and I didn’t.” Rosemary pointed toward the little leather purse dangling from Martha Sue’s arm. “I shouldn’t have worn these stockings. I’m burning up.”

“And you want me to stuff them in my purse?”

“Just till we get back to the dorm.”

Apparently, Martha Sue didn’t like the idea.

They picked their way carefully along the wooden boards that passed for a sidewalk. When they reached the designated ladies’ room, Rosemary removed the offending garments.

“Who is this Wallace fellow?”

“Oh, isn’t he handsome?”

“Sure, he’s okay. But who is he? When did you meet him?”

“His name is Wallace Monroe, but he said to call him Wally. And he’s from Alabama. Near Montgomery, I think he said. His family’s got a big place down there. Old southern money.”

“Did he tell you that?”

“Well, not exactly. He told me some things about his home. The house and land and all. He’s got a big ol’ diamond pinky ring. So I just figured that he’s loaded.”

“He knows you’re married, doesn’t he?”

“Of course. I told him about Stanley being overseas.”

“And that didn’t bother him one bit.”

“That’s right. He said we could just be friends.”

“Martha Sue Aldridge, you better watch your step.”

“And who are you to say anything?”

“I’m your cousin, and your mother would want me

to watch out for you."

"Yeah. My cousin who got married to the most eligible man in Kerrville and ran off to California the first chance she got. Everybody in town knew why you married him, or rather, why he married you."

Rosemary's already hot skin got even hotter. She imagined steam escaping from her ears. How dare this little backwoods farm girl say anything about her marriage.

"Look who's talking. I heard you married the first soldier who asked you. Just so you wouldn't have to go off to Detroit with your mother."

Now Martha Sue's temper flared. "How dare you say such a thing? I'll have you know that Stan and I fell in love."

"In a week's time?"

"More like two weeks. But what does that matter? We loved each other and we got married."

"Then why are you hanging around with this Wallace fellow?"

Tears glistened in Martha Sue's eyes. "Because he's nice to me. He likes me. He's a handsome, rich man who likes me. Is that a crime?"

"Depends. If he's who he says he is and if he just wants to be friends with a married woman, well then, I guess it might be okay."

She finished rolling up her stockings and stuffed them into Martha Sue's bag.

"You just be careful, okay? Something about him I don't like."

"You're just jealous 'cause he's way more handsome than Virgil."

Rosemary laughed at that. What did she care? She

wanted nothing more from Virgil than a friend and a comfortable date.

They walked toward the tennis courts that had been converted to a dance floor for the night.

"Maybe you should think more about Stan. After all, he is your husband."

Martha Sue stopped abruptly and faced her. Their gazes met. "The thing is, about Stan, I mean…" She hesitated and glanced away, toward the crowd. "Stan's folks are poor. Dirt poor."

She turned back to Rosemary. "When I went to stay with them, I couldn't believe it. They live in this little shack down a dirt road in the middle of nowhere. They don't even own the shack. They rent it from some farmer. And his father, well, he came to pick me up in this old trap of a truck. A logging truck. He uses it to cut logs in the woods and haul them to a sawmill. Right now he's working here for one of the construction contractors and says he's making more money than he has ever seen."

"That doesn't mean that Stan won't make something of himself."

"Oh, his father has plans for him and Stan to buy a little piece of land and farm it."

"There's nothing wrong with that. Your father's a farmer."

"Yeah. And the land's been in our family for generations. Besides, I made up my mind I wanted to get away from the farm. Go to some big city."

Rosemary sighed and gazed down to where the men waited for them. "You and Stan can work that out when he gets back. You never know what might happen."

"Yeah. He might get killed."

The heavy air hung between them. Rosemary thought of Jack and all the big dreams she'd had. None of them worked out. Maybe she had no right to tell Martha Sue anything. Maybe Martha Sue deserved to have a little fun. Hadn't she wanted some fun? Wanted to experience outrageous behavior before she came back home? Who was she to judge?

Chapter 33

On July 23rd, word came of a massive attack planned for the next morning. The guns of the 230th moved into position behind the 120th Regiment of the 30th Infantry, ready to follow when the infantry attacked. The Air Corps bombers would blast the enemy first and destroy their defensive positions, making it easier on the infantry.

For now, they waited.

In the dim light of pre-dawn, George offered Guy a cigarette.

"Sure." He took the smoke and tapped it on his knee. George leaned in and let Guy light it from the glowing end of his cigarette to conserve matches and to avoid the inevitable reprimand if they let a flash of light show in the darkness.

The two sat in silence in the shallow foxhole they'd got in the habit of digging every time they stopped.

"I saw you got some mail," George commented. "Anything interesting?"

Guy touched the letters he'd stuck inside his shirt, one from Henry and one from his mother. The mail had arrived the night before, only a short time before they moved up, so he'd only had time to quickly glance through them.

"Got a letter from my brother. He's with the Marines 'somewhere in the Pacific.' "

"Your other brother is in the Navy, right?"

"Yeah. Wilson's on a ship in the Pacific somewhere. But the letter is from Henry, the Marine."

"Wouldn't want to be him. Landing on those little islands. Fighting Japs in the jungle. No, sir. Not for me."

Guy chuckled to himself. "I'm not sure that fighting Germans in France is any better."

Before they'd come to France, Guy had tried to keep track of the military action around the globe. He heard that the Americans took Rome right before the cross-channel invasion of France. And he'd seen a *Stars & Stripes* article that described something called a "turkey shoot" where U.S. Navy planes shot down numerous Japanese aircraft near some chain of islands. But nothing told him anything about his brothers.

"So what'd he have to say?"

Guy glanced at his friend. He'd never seen George reading mail. Didn't he have any family?

"He says he's on a ship in the Pacific heading for some unknown island. I guess that's all he can say." Guy would have liked to read through Henry's letter again, but the pre-dawn didn't provide enough light.

"He said something about meeting a girl. A nurse. Sounds like she made quite an impression."

"American?"

"Yeah."

"Where'd he meet an American nurse? Did he get shot?"

"Not that I know of."

It amazed Guy that his brother could fall for a girl in the middle of the Pacific. Henry's words about the woman sounded eerily similar to his thoughts about

Rosemary.

But Guy couldn't tell anyone about her. He'd promised.

The sky lightened as dawn broke.

Lieutenant Ballentine strode through the men checking on them like an old hen counting her chicks.

"You boys all right?" Lt. Ballentine asked.

"Yes, sir," Guy and George answered in unison.

"Won't be long now." He looked up into the sky toward the northwest where a distant roar sounded. The lieutenant straightened, then turned on his heel and headed back toward 230th headquarters.

Within minutes the roar became almost deafening. Bombers appeared just above the horizon. Lots of planes on a path to fly directly over them.

They'd studied pictures of aircraft, so they easily identified the planes as B-25 medium bombers. Not as big as the "heavies" but big enough.

The planes flew low, lower than the formations they'd seen in England.

"I'd sure hate to be those Jerries," George shouted as the lead planes came right overhead.

Guy looked up and saw the bombs inside open bomb bay doors.

Objects fell from the planes.

Guy blinked, hoping his imagination was playing tricks on him.

An explosion nearby sent him down into the hole.

Another. And another.

"Those damn bastards are bombing us," George screamed.

"What the hell?" The bombers were supposed to bomb the Germans who had to be half a mile ahead, on the other side of the road.

Guy looked up between explosions. The worst of it seemed to be hitting up ahead where the infantry waited to start the attack. Those guys were in shallow holes like the one he and George clung to. Nothing that could withstand a plastering like they were getting.

The planes continued overhead, and bombs continued to fall for what seemed like an eternity. Finally, the explosions stopped but the planes continued, with their now ominous roar, for maybe a half hour.

An officer he didn't know jogged by, checking on men and equipment.

A cry for medic came from somewhere to the right.

"Hey, Lieutenant. How bad is it?" Guy called to the officer who'd stopped to talk to some men not far away.

"Don't know yet. I'm trying to find out who's hurt."

"Why'd those bastards bomb us?" George shouted.

"I don't know, soldier. That's something I want to find out myself." The officer's voice betrayed his barely contained anger.

The lieutenant moved on. Guy stared at George. Both nodded, silently conveying to the other that he wasn't hurt. Neither spoke. Instead they sat in shocked silence waiting for orders.

Despite the friendly-fire bombing, and another plastering the following day, the attack proceeded. The 230th supported the 30th Infantry as they fought furiously for the next week to break the German lines around Tessy-Sur-Vire.

Chapter 34

August 2, 1944

Word came down the line like wildfire. The 30th was being pulled back. Out of combat. To rest after being in the fight for fifty-two days.

Guy watched the infantry file into the rest area. Tired, filthy, unshaven. These men had been through the wringer, but they'd survived.

He heard comments of "Let someone else get shot at for a while," and "Just let me sleep without those big guns pounding in my ears."

The soldiers lined up at the shower points and peeled off their mud-caked, blood-soaked uniforms. One by one they showered, dressed in new clothes, and emerged looking like new men. Yet their eyes betrayed them. They'd been through hell and even a few days rest would not change the fact that they had to go back. Back to fighting and back to dying.

The artillery men watched and waited. The infantry deserved to go first. There would be plenty of time for them to shower and change later.

Guy examined each tired, dirty face, looking for his friend, Amos Campbell. He'd last seen Amos weeks ago, before the mass attack across the Perrier road, before the disastrous bombing. Amos had sought him out one evening while the chow truck was doling out food, and they'd talked for a while.

After so much fighting, he hoped Amos had survived.

Guy approached one of the men dressed in a clean, new uniform. He offered the man a cigarette. "Which regiment are you with?"

"120th." He took the smoke, a questioning look on his face.

Guy offered a light from his prized Zippo. "I thought so. I've got a friend in the 120th. G Company. Name's Amos Campbell." Guy paused to light his own. "You wouldn't know him, would you?"

"Campbell?" The man shook his head. "Naw. Can't say as I do." He looked toward the men still lined up to take their showers. "G Company ought to be back there somewhere."

Guy nodded. "Thanks."

He wandered among the men waiting to shower. A few nodded in greeting. He stopped by one of the friendlier-looking men and asked about G Company.

"Those boys over there. That's George Company." He pointed to a group gathered under a tree. Some sat on the ground, patiently waiting. Others milled around talking.

As Guy approached the group, he heard a familiar voice.

"Nolan. You ol' son of a gun. What are you doing here?"

"Looking for you."

The two shook vigorously, matching grins spread across their faces.

Finally, Guy spoke. "I didn't know if you were still alive."

"Oh, they can't kill me. I'm too lucky for that."

"Or too smart."

Amos' face grew serious. "It takes pure luck to stay alive out there. You never know where it's gonna come from next."

Guy nodded, unsure what to say.

"So how's life back with the big guns?" Campbell's smile returned.

"Oh, we stay pretty busy. You guys keep calling for fire and we keep pouring it on."

"And believe me, we appreciate it."

Campbell introduced Guy to several of his friends, explaining that they'd met on the train on the way to Camp Atterbury.

"By the way," Campbell asked after they'd talked for a while. "How's that pretty girl of yours?"

Guy shook his head. "I told you all about that. She's not my girl and we agreed not to write. So I don't know how she is. Or even where she is."

"Big mistake. Girl like that you gotta hang on to." He placed his hand on Guy's shoulder and leaned close. "Now listen to your ol' friend Amos. You write that girl and tell her you can't stop thinking about her."

Heat rose to Guy's face. How could Amos know him so well? He didn't dare tell Amos he'd been writing her and then tearing up the letters.

"See. I knew it. You think about her. And you want to see her when you get back. So you need to tell her."

"What if I don't make it back?"

"Don't think that way." Amos hesitated then. A dark shadow crossed his friend's face. Guy wanted to ask but decided to let it lie. Campbell would talk about it when he got ready.

Instead, Guy brought the conversation back to Rosemary. "I made her a promise. And I intend to keep it." He shifted his gaze away from Amos. Her soft voice still played in his head. "She had her reasons."

"Maybe so. But out here a guy needs someone to think about. Needs to believe she cares whether he comes back or not."

"You never mentioned having a girl back home."

"That's 'cause I don't," he barked back.

"So she dumped you."

Amos hung his head. "Yeah." He stared off into the distance. "Sally's her name. She didn't want to wait. Said she wanted her freedom. So she could date other fellows."

"That's too bad."

"Too bad for her." Amos stubbornly raised his chin. "She'll be missing out on a real good thing."

Guy smiled. "Yes. She will. She couldn't find one better than you."

"She writes me, though. Every now and then. Asks how I'm doing."

"That's good." Guy wondered if Rosemary would write him just to check on him. Would that be enough? He wasn't sure.

After a while, Guy made his way back to C Battery.

"Hey, Nolan. The captain's looking for you."

"Okay." Guy nodded his thanks. "Where'd they set up the command post?"

Curious as to why he'd been summoned, he followed the directions to a farmhouse where a hand-made sign clearly read "230th FA CP."

Inside he told the clerk his name and waited until

the captain was free. Further inside he heard voices deep in discussion, but he couldn't make out what they were saying.

"Send back that radio man."

The Pfc. motioned for Guy to go back, but not into the room where the meeting was being held. Instead he went into a side room, being used as an office of sorts.

The captain sat in a straight wooden chair at a small table with papers spread haphazardly. The officer waved for Guy to enter the room.

When Guy saluted, the captain gave an obligatory salute in response. "At ease, soldier."

Guy stood waiting to hear what the captain had to say.

"I understand you're a radio man…uh." He picked up a piece of paper. "Nolan."

"Yes, sir."

"Good." He met Guy's gaze with his cold, steel-blue eyes. "I'm assigning you to Lt. Barry, the Forward Observer."

"Sir?" Guy tried to control his reaction.

"His radio man was wounded. More seriously than they originally thought. So Barry needs someone to operate the radio." He looked back down at his paperwork. "Whenever we get orders to move out, you'll go with Barry."

"Yes, sir." Guy's mind raced. He'd never worked with an FO before, but he knew enough from training that it meant he'd be out on the front lines with the rifle companies.

"Check with Swanson on your way out. He'll tell you where to find Barry."

And just like that he was dismissed. Given a new,

dangerous assignment and then dismissed like it meant nothing.

****

August 5, 1944

The Jeep bounced its way up the rough track toward the high ground of Hill 314. Lt. Barry told Guy that they had orders to locate the 1st Infantry Division's Forward Observer and take over his position.

In consolation for having their promised two-week rest period shortened, the 30th relieved the 1st Division's occupation of a quiet hilltop so it could further pursue the Germans. From this position the 30th could sit and rest and observe any enemy activity down below.

At the high point on this end of the hill they found the FO from the 1st Division's artillery ready to leave.

"Quiet spot. Hate to leave it," the FO commented.

Lt. Barry took out his binoculars and gazed across the broad valley beyond the hill. "Have you observed any enemy movement?"

"Next to nothing."

Lt. Barry called back to Guy and the other two men in the Jeep. "Okay, boys. Let's get unloaded."

Guy and a tall man called Langford unloaded the radio and batteries while Holly, the driver, unloaded the rest of their gear. The 1st Division crew disappeared down the rough track they'd driven up.

The observation position was near a road that ran along the crest of the hill with the town of Mortain down the hill to their rear.

Guy carried the bulky radio and Langford brought the heavy battery to the crest where Lt. Barry stood looking through his binoculars and studying the terrain.

"Where do you want the radio?"

He lowered his binoculars and looked around. "Close by." He waved his hand toward a clump of small trees on his right. "Over there. We'll have a little protection."

"What about this stuff?" Holly's hands were full of canteens, packs and bedrolls.

"Find a spot to dig in, nearby." Lt. Barry glanced around. "Probably be hard digging in this rocky terrain."

"We'll dig in the radio, too," Guy suggested. "To protect it."

"Good idea," the lieutenant responded.

The three noncoms went to work while Lt. Barry continued to study the terrain beyond the hill. He made notes on his map.

Guy was curious about what the lieutenant saw. As the new man in the group he hesitated to ask many questions. Yet as he and Langford worked, he couldn't resist.

"What's he doing?" Guy asked.

"Marking coordinates. When we get the radio set up, we'll call them in. Then if we need some fire power all he has to do is give them the pre-arranged code."

Guy was familiar with the codes the Forward Observers set up. He'd just never seen the work from this end.

"Guess he's just being cautious." Guy didn't want to think about being shot at. "I mean, we're not expecting to have to call in any fire missions. We're just observing, right?"

Langford laughed. "You never know."

Guy regretted saying anything. It revealed his

greenness and his nervousness at being this close to enemy territory. As the new guy, he should keep his mouth shut and his eyes open.

They'd moved over to help Holly improve on foxholes the 1st Division boys had started when a communications team showed up running wires between command posts and the rear.

Holly stopped digging and joined Lt. Barry.

"Who all's up on this hill?" Holly asked before the officer could speak.

"K Company's back that way." The signal corpsman jerked his thumb over his shoulder indicating where they'd come from. "And G's supposed to be further down the road."

"What about Easy Company? They were supposed to take the high ground, too," Lt. Barry asked.

The other man spoke this time. "They're even further down. There's another team running wire to them."

"Who's closest?"

"K. Their CP is not too far back. Hundred yards, maybe. Through the trees."

The lieutenant turned to Holly. "Go back along the wire and make contact with the commander of K Company. Tell him where we are. Then head back."

Holly grinned. "Yes, sir."

The driver gave Guy and Langford a salute as he strode off in the opposite direction from the wire crew, clearly glad to get out of the digging job. When Guy hit a big rock, he wished he'd been sent to contact K Company instead of Holly.

At least with G Company nearby, Amos Campbell might be on the hill, and Guy would see his friend.

Maybe knowing someone in the infantry would loosen up Holly and Langford. So far they'd treated him decently, but they'd kept their distance, waiting for Guy to prove he knew what he was doing and could handle being out in front.

By the time Holly returned they'd broken out their rations and were preparing to settle in for the night. Satisfied that nothing was going on out beyond the hill, Lt. Barry joined them.

"What kept you so long?" the lieutenant asked Holly.

"Just talking to some of the guys in K Company. I looked around while I was over that way. To see if there was any other position we could use."

Guy wondered if Holly was sucking up to the lieutenant or just being helpful.

"Did you find anything?" Lt. Barry asked between bites.

"Not much. There's one spot we could use. But it ain't as good as here."

Holly sat down and dug into his own meal.

"Well, keep it in mind. Just in case."

In case of what? Guy wondered. Why would they move? With no enemy activity down below and the rest of the division spread out all around them, why would they leave this spot? Their roadblocks should stop the enemy if the retreating Germans did decide to mount a delaying action to let the rest get away. The troops below should be able to handle that.

Darkness descended. Surrounded by only night sounds, Guy lay in the foxhole he shared with Holly and tried to sleep. The immovable rock had become his pillow with smaller ones poking him in other places.

Guy hadn't expected to sleep, but he must have dozed off when something startled him awake.

Lt. Barry stood on the highest point gazing through his binoculars.

Then he heard it. The rumble of motors and the clinking of metal treads on the paved road below.

Langford moved to Lt. Barry's side. "What is it?"

"Tanks. Moving along the road to our left." The officer looked around toward Guy. "Get the radio fired up."

Just then the sounds of artillery shells streaked through the sky above them, quickly followed by a series of explosions down below.

"Looks like that other FO is one step ahead of us," Langford remarked.

Lt. Barry scanned the terrain. "That's okay. There are plenty of targets."

Chapter 35

August 8, 1944

Before dawn, artillery pounded them again.

Guy protected the radio as best he could, crouched in the shallow hole. After three days he should have been used to the explosions, should have expected the attack that would follow. Yet each detonation shocked him, made him wonder if he was in the middle of a horrible nightmare and couldn't wake up.

The attacks started in the early morning hours of August 6th. Lt. Barry watched through binoculars as German tanks, mobile artillery, and infantry poured down the roads in front of the hill in what must have been a massive counterattack on the American positions. As the sun rose, sounds of battle came from all directions.

Germans attacked the roadblocks below, crashed through them, and then assaulted the men positioned on the hill. Strong resistance kept the enemy at bay. With each new attack, more of the defenders fell or disbursed into the woods to regroup.

Sometime in the first two days, the men of Company G pulled back from their original positions to consolidate with Company K. When the Germans attacked from the direction of Mortain, they realized the enemy had gotten behind them. Attempts to contact the

120th Command Post in Mortain failed. The telephone wires had been cut. The CP didn't answer their radio either. The men on the hill were on their own, except for the FO's radio contact with the 230th Artillery behind the lines.

The combined companies set up a roadblock on the road that came up from Mortain, crossed the crest of the hill and went back down toward the east in hopes of stopping the German attacks from Mortain. The company commanders on the hill agreed that the high ground must be held and ordered their men to establish a perimeter on all sides to fight off any attempt by the Germans to take the hill.

Lt. Barry and the forward observer on the other end of the hill called in artillery fire when they saw any movement below. This rain of explosives stopped the Germans every time they attacked.

By some miracle the GIs succeeded. The high ground remained in American hands for now. They just had to hold out until they were reinforced.

When the artillery barrage let up, Lt. Barry resumed his position. With binoculars trained on the roads below, he called out coordinates for fire missions. The lieutenant's directions were relayed by Langford to Guy and Guy repeated the instructions into the radio microphone. The 230th Artillery battalion acknowledged each request, and within moments shells sailed overhead. Barry would acknowledge the hit or call for adjustments which again were relayed through Guy and his radio to the 230th.

An enemy artillery shell exploded directly in front of Lt. Barry. Everyone hit the dirt.

Another shell sailed overhead. Debris rained down

from a few yards behind them.

Guy grasped his helmet and covered the radio with his body as two more shells exploded almost on top of them.

Lt. Barry called out between explosions. “Let’s get the hell out of here before they blow us off the hill.”

Langford scrambled down to Guy. The two huddled together as another shell hit. Both fumbled to disconnect the radio from the batteries. Combined, they were too heavy for one man to carry. Langford lifted the battery and took off behind Lt. Barry.

Holly grabbed two carbines and a canteen. “Go on,” he yelled.

Guy hoisted the radio up and slid his arm through a strap that allowed him to carry it on his back. Frantically feeling for the other strap, he took a step in the direction Lt. Barry had taken.

The world exploded around him.

He landed hard. The weight of the radio slammed into his shoulder.

When he opened his eyes, the world spun and rocked like a crazy carnival ride. A loud, shrill buzzing rang in his head.

He squeezed his eyes shut and dug his fingers into the rocky soil as if holding on would stop the spinning.

Something shook him. Instinctively, he clutched at the earth. After a few seconds he ventured to open his eyes again.

The green shapes of trees with blue sky beyond.

He tried to move. Gasped for air. Something grabbed his hand.

Holly appeared above him.

His lips were moving but Guy couldn’t hear

anything. It was like a giant motor running next to his head.

He blinked.

The sound gradually moved away from him.

Holly shoved the weight off him and then pulled on his arm.

Guy gritted his teeth and with tremendous effort pulled his left shoulder up. The rest of his body seemed to follow until he found himself on his hands and knees gasping for breath.

The explosions had stopped. An eerie thick smoke hung around them.

Lt. Barry appeared. He barked questions. Or maybe orders. Guy only heard bits and pieces.

"Radio…Langford…hit…"

Someone pulled Guy to his feet. He looked around while staggering to maintain his balance.

The radio lay in the dirt a few feet away. A piece of metal protruded from the smashed-in side.

Guy stumbled over to it and bent down for a closer look. The case was split, and the inside glittered with broken glass. The tubes. Without them the radio wouldn't work.

"That thing saved your life," Holly said over his shoulder, in a muffled voice that told Guy his hearing had returned.

"Yeah. I guess." Guy couldn't quite think what to do next.

Lt. Barry appeared beside them. "Can you fix it?"

Guy shook his head but stopped when it felt like it would come off. He put his hand up to steady it only to find something wet and sticky behind his ear.

The lieutenant stepped closer. "Well?"

"It's busted," Guy said. "Need a new one."

"Shit!"

"What do we do, Lieutenant?" Holly's voice almost squeaked.

"Get another damned radio. That's what."

Two soldiers appeared.

"You the FO?" one asked.

"Yeah. That's me." Lt. Barry shifted his attention to the newcomers. "What'd ya want?"

"Sgt. Becker said they need an artillery strike. Krauts are attacking the roadblock."

"See that?" Lt. Barry screamed. "That's our radio. It's busted. We can't call anybody."

The soldier gawked at the officer. "Sir?"

"Go back and tell your sergeant we can't call the artillery. Not till we get another radio up here."

"Yes, sir." The man bobbed his head and turned to join his companion, who stood well back. Both men quickly disappeared into the trees.

Lt. Barry turned back to Guy and Holly. "Okay. Let's round up Langford." He looked around. "Holly, you go get him. He should be over there somewhere."

"Yes, sir."

After Holly disappeared, Guy squatted down to inspect the radio a little closer. The shrapnel had ripped into the most vital portion of the box where tubes and wires came together. What wasn't broken was melted into a tangled mass.

"Any hope?" The lieutenant's tone had softened.

"No. It's useless." Guy looked up. "You think we can get through? Get another one?"

Lt. Barry looked off into the distance. Small arms fire sounded to their right. Larger guns pounded the hillside to the south.

"I don't know."

Holly and Langford appeared.

"Holly, you and Nolan get back to the Jeep. See if you can get through to headquarters and get us another radio."

Holly looked at Guy and then back at the lieutenant. "You think we can get to them? The CP hasn't answered since last night."

"They've probably moved back."

Lt. Barry motioned for all of them to move into the nearby trees.

"Langford and I will look for another spot. The Jerrys have this one bracketed." He glanced around as if trying to decide which way to go while he fished a map out of his jacket.

Still feeling weak, Guy leaned against the trunk of a tree.

He watched the other three as if he were observing actors on a stage. Their jerky movements and shaking hands revealed their nervousness or maybe their fear. Three days on this hill, under attack. Now, with the radio busted, their only means of contact with the outside world had been destroyed. Of course, they were all jumpy.

"The rest of the division is northwest. Head that way and see if you can break through. The Germans are spread thin. And our guys are bound to be pushing in this direction."

"What if we don't make it through?" Guy asked.

"Then Langford and I will just have to fight with the infantry."

Guy didn't like their odds. But the lieutenant had

given them orders. They'd either break through the German lines or get killed trying.

He should have stayed back with the guns, where it was safe.

After making their way to the hidden Jeep, Guy and Holly broke out some rations and hurriedly ate. Holly bandaged the cut on Guy's head. Then they loaded up with ammo and climbed aboard.

"You ready?" Holly asked.

Guy patted his loaded carbine and nodded. He remembered a western movie with two cowboys riding out to fight the Indians. In the movie they'd both been killed.

Is that what's going to happen to me? Is this my last hurrah?

Holly barreled the Jeep downhill, dodging trees. Maybe the Germans would stay on the roads. Maybe they would slip right through.

A machine gun rat-a-tat-tatted.

The windshield shattered.

Holly jerked the wheel.

The Jeep careened sideways and flipped over.

Guy flew through the air and landed hard, his carbine still in his hands.

The German machine gun let loose on the Jeep again. Bullets pinged and ricocheted.

Holly belly-crawled from underneath just before it caught fire.

Guy stumbled forward enough to grab a dazed Holly by the arm and pull him away from the burning vehicle.

A shot whizzed by, too close for comfort.

"Get up," Guy yelled. "We gotta get out of here."

Holly struggled to get his feet under him.

Guy turned toward the Jeep and fired two quick shots into the woods beyond. Then he grabbed Holly's arm and ran back the way they'd come.

Shots rang out from behind them. The Krauts were close. Too damn close.

Guy scanned the hillside for cover. Just a few feet uphill and to the right a tree lay where an artillery shell must have felled it.

"There." He pointed his weapon toward the fallen log as he sprinted toward it.

Holly followed.

Guy jumped and crash-landed behind the fallen tree. His head spun around. Holly dove through the air as rifle fire exploded around them.

Guy jerked his carbine up and returned fire.

The German was only a few yards away.

Guy's third shot hit him. The man fell.

For a split second Guy stopped, aware he'd killed the man. A bullet hit the log, sending splinters flying.

Guy returned fire.

A second German fell.

Guy dared to breathe.

He didn't see another German.

"Come on, Holly. Let's get out of here." Guy tugged at his friend's arm, but the man didn't respond. "Holly?"

He pushed Holly over onto his side. Bright red blood soaked his chest and the ground below him. His eyes stared into nothingness.

Guy turned back toward the two dead Germans. He thought he saw movement in the trees beyond.

Gripping the carbine to his chest, he stood and ran

like the devil himself was chasing him. He darted into a patch of bushes, moved sideways, then climbed again.

Shots rang out from below. They were farther away now.

He kept moving until he crashed through some bushes and into two men. It took a second to register that they were Americans. They both raised their guns, but, luckily for Guy, they didn't shoot him.

Much as he wanted to collapse at their feet, when one of them said, "Come on," he willingly followed, toward the protection of his own kind.

Chapter 36

Guy huddled in the shallow foxhole cradling his carbine and trying to ignore the men's casual talk.

He still saw Holly staring into nothingness, covered in his own blood. Not to mention the Germans he'd shot.

He was a soldier, and this was a war, but he'd never killed anyone before. Until the last few days he'd been safe, back with the artillery.

Sure, they'd occasionally had sniper fire nearby. They'd been bombed by the Luftwaffe and shelled by artillery. But this was different. He'd seen their faces. Seen them fall. And Holly. He'd seen Holly.

A commotion pulled him out of himself. A patrol had come in. They were talking to the K Company lieutenant. From the snatches he could make out, it sounded like the Jerries were close. They were as determined to take the hill as the Americans were to hold it.

The lieutenant called to another man. Guy surveyed the group that had gathered around the officer.

One man looked familiar. Campbell. His friend.

Guy climbed out of the hole and eased toward the group of men. Just as he reached them Campbell turned and recognition bloomed across his face.

"Nolan?"

Guy shrugged. "Lost our radio. Guess I'm in the

infantry now."

Campbell nodded. "Sorry to hear it. We need the artillery. They've been protecting us from the Krauts."

"I know."

Campbell introduced Guy to the others.

"Where's your lieutenant?" one asked.

"Oh, he's around here somewhere. Probably on high ground with his binoculars."

"What's the point?"

"Hard for him to face the facts. The radio's gone and that means we're no use for anything but firing our rifles." Guy held up his carbine.

"Is that all you've got?" Campbell queried.

"Yep. It's what we're issued. We're not usually out here doing what you guys do."

"I'll keep a lookout for a real rifle."

"Thanks."

The men settled in for the night. All of them knew to expect another attack. They just didn't know where it would come from.

Later that night, they fought off another German assault with the help of friendly artillery shells called in by the only remaining FO on the hill.

Guy, Langford, and Lt. Barry remained with Company K, fighting alongside them when needed. Guy and Amos checked on each other regularly, the two friends each relying on the other to keep going.

Something inside Guy had changed. He had fought back despite the fear of being killed. He'd defended himself and his comrades. A sense of inevitability settled over him. He could die on this hill.

If he didn't die here, then he'd die somewhere along the line before it was over. He kept telling himself that it wouldn't be now. It would come, but not now. Now he had to fight. For himself and for his buddies.

****

"That set of luggage came in handy," Drucilla laughed. "Even if it does weigh a ton."

"I can't believe we stuffed everything into this one suitcase." Rosemary took the heavy case from Drucilla and gave her the smaller one.

"At least we don't have to walk too far."

"Just so I don't drop it in the mud." Rosemary glanced around. "The storm that came through last night must have dumped as much rain here as it did in Knoxville."

The two friends had spent all day yesterday shopping in Knoxville. They'd been so tired they'd spent the night and come back to Oak Ridge on one of the morning busses.

As they passed the shopping plaza, a familiar face appeared.

"Hello, ladies."

"Hello, Virgil," Rosemary responded, unsure what to say to her soldier friend.

"Have you been on a trip?" he asked, eyeing the suitcase.

"Yes," Rosemary replied. "To Knoxville."

Virgil nodded. His gaze shifted to Drucilla.

"Oh, uh…" Rosemary set the heavy bag down. "This is Drucilla Hawkins. Drucilla, this is Lt. Virgil Rushing."

Drucilla shifted the small case to her other hand so she could offer to shake. "Nice to meet you."

Virgil politely tipped his hat and shook her hand.

"The pleasure is all mine."

"Polite. I like that." Drucilla nodded her approval to Rosemary.

Virgil turned to Rosemary. "I guess that's why you didn't return my call."

Rosemary frowned. What was he talking about?

"I left a message at your dormitory for you to call me," he explained.

"What about?"

He smiled. "I wanted to ask you out. For tonight. How does dinner and a movie sound?"

Rosemary's mouth dropped open. She and Virgil had been out a few times, but she'd decided to back off before he got too friendly.

"I don't think so. I'm really tired." She glanced at Drucilla for help.

"You wouldn't believe the day we put in yesterday. Why, I bet we walked over every square inch of Knoxville."

Gratitude welled up. At first Rosemary had hesitated to share much about her personal life with her new friend. But now she was glad she'd opened up and talked to her about her hesitation in getting involved in another romantic relationship after losing Jack. She had refrained from telling her about Guy. That was a little too personal.

"And my shift is changing so I have to be out early in the morning."

"I thought it was about time for your shift change. That's why I thought it would be a good time for us to get together." Virgil looked from Rosemary to Drucilla and back. "I didn't realize you had other plans."

"Oh, we've been planning this trip to Knoxville for

weeks. Haven't we, Rosemary?"

"Yes. We have."

Virgil's face lit up. "Then maybe we should plan to get together. How about next week? We could go ahead and set a date now. That way…"

Rosemary shook her head. "No, Virgil. Not now." She reached down and picked up the heavy suitcase. "I told you before. I don't want to get involved right now. Not with you or anyone."

His face fell but he remained silent.

"I'm sorry," Rosemary murmured as she walked away from him.

"It was nice to meet you," Drucilla said, following Rosemary toward the dormitory.

They walked in silence until they reached the building.

"I hate to be like that. But he just doesn't get it."

"Oh, I've got a feeling he'll try again. Something about the way he looks at you."

"Well, I'm not interested. At least not now."

"Don't turn your back completely. He's not bad behind those glasses. And he's very polite."

"I know."

"After a while, you might want someone to take you out. Show you a good time, even if you don't want to get serious."

Rosemary sighed. She knew her friend was right. She needed to keep her options open. Jack was gone. And Guy might never come back. And he might not be interested even if he did make it back safe.

Chapter 37

August 10, 1944

By the fifth day on the hill, their supplies had dwindled to nothing. Guy counted his ammo and, like all the others, prayed it would not run out.

Reinforcements were on the way, so the rumor had it. The remaining FO, on the other end of the hill, still had a working radio. He still called in artillery strikes to keep the Germans from gaining the vital high ground. And the remaining men, surrounded by the enemy, waited for their fellow GIs to fight their way in to relieve the exhausted troops.

Their water ran low, and the rations they'd brought with them had long since been eaten. Medics tended the wounded with whatever they could piece together.

Knowing the desperate situation on the hill, Guy's artillery battalion fired shells filled with medical supplies. The well-intended idea proved totally impractical. All the supplies inside the recovered shells were smashed and ruined by the concussion.

To replenish their water, someone found a well at farmhouse part way down the hill, but the Germans had guns on the place and fired at any movement. Volunteers made the perilous journey with canteens slung over their shoulders and rifles at the ready for the fire fight that came with each trip to get water.

Yesterday two men were wounded making the journey. Today Guy volunteered.

"I'll go," he told the K Company lieutenant organizing the mission. "I'm not as experienced firing my weapon, but I can carry the canteens."

As they neared the farmhouse, German bullets pierced the air, hitting the ground ahead of them. One at a time, they dashed across the open ground to the safety of the house. Getting to the well was tricky. Depending on the German's position, he either had a clear shot or only an angled one.

Their ace in the hole was an ex-baseball player who was a dead shot with a grenade. The man belly-crawled into position to watch for the enemy's muzzle flash. When Jerry fired, the ball player threw a grenade right in his lap.

When the grenade exploded, Guy and another soldier rushed to the well and dumped the canteens in. Guy held onto the straps as the canteens sank into the shallow water in what was more like a walled-up spring than the deep well he imagined.

He poked each canteen down under the water. His buddy pulled up two or three full canteens at a time and screwed the caps on tight while Guy made sure the others were filling.

When all the canteens were full and secured, Guy signaled to the other two GIs to lay down covering fire. Guy and his friend sprinted for the safety of the tree line followed closely by the firing soldiers.

The whole operation took about ten minutes.

Breathing hard from the exertion and the excitement of completing his mission, Guy reveled in his accomplishment. He'd proven his worth. In a bad situation he'd carried his own weight. Even if he died tomorrow, in this moment he'd done his part to keep them all alive.

He helped distribute the filled canteens, finally giving one to the medic overseeing the wounded. The morphine was long gone, bandages, too. Without relief soon, many would die. The medic welcomed the gift of fresh water that would provide a little comfort to the wounded.

Guy gave a couple of men drinks from his own canteen, careful to conserve what water he had. One man lay to the side, pale as a ghost. Guy started toward him with the canteen.

The medic stopped him. "He's gutshot. Can't give him any water."

"But…" Guy could see the man's parched lips.

"He's bleeding inside," the medic whispered, shaking his head. "Water'll only make it worse."

Guy gulped and swallowed hard to keep his stomach from turning wrong side out. He hadn't eaten since yesterday so nothing would have come up, yet bile boiled up in his throat, making him turn away. The poor man was dying a slow death, and nothing could be done to help him.

Guy walked back toward his own foxhole. His hands shook as he stowed his canteen with what was left of his gear. The dying man's face burned in his memory. Guy didn't want to know his name. Didn't want to know if he lived or died. For now, Guy just wanted to be alive. He refused to think about dying. Not now. Not today.

He forced his thoughts to home, to what might be happening back in the States. As usual, Rosemary's face filled his mind's eye. Her smile, even her tears. What was she doing? Had she found work in that small town she came from? Did she ever think of him? He hoped so. Even if she didn't want to think about him, he hoped she did. Hoped she prayed for him.

He pulled the crumpled letter from inside his shirt. He'd written it two days ago on his last scrap of paper. He read through it for the umpteenth time. Somehow writing the letters, even without mailing them, brought him closer to her. Let him pretend she cared whether he lived or died. Maybe she didn't, but he could pretend.

Sometime later Campbell appeared.

"Lieutenant Shockly wants us to find Lt. Barry."

"What? Is he missing?"

"Don't know. Nobody's seen him in a while. He may be up there." He gestured toward the high ground where the FO could have found a spot to observe enemy movements below.

Guy pulled himself up and grabbed the rifle he'd inherited from a soldier who hadn't made it. "He won't let go, even with no radio. He still thinks he can make some kind of difference by watching the enemy."

It didn't take long to find Lt. Barry. After relaying his orders to return to the CP, the officer reluctantly followed. They climbed down and headed back to K Company's camp.

The whistle of incoming artillery pierced the air. Guy hit the dirt, digging in with his fingernails.

Explosions shook the earth beneath him.

Soil and debris rained down.

A few feet away Campbell and Lt. Barry crouched beneath an overhanging rock. It looked safer than where Guy lay in the opcn.

He pulled his knees up under him and crawled in their direction.

Another explosion picked him up and sent him sailing through the air.

The next thing he knew Campbell knelt over him shouting, “Nolan, Nolan.”

“Amos,” Guy whispered. “Cover. Get to cover.”

Amos glanced over his shoulder to Lt. Barry. “Help me get him up.”

Guy tried to get his feet under him. He could barely move. His side hurt like hell. Must have landed on something.

With the help of the two men, Guy found himself upright.

“Can you walk?”

Guy’s gaze locked on Amos, struggling to understand his muffled voice, and nodded.

With one on each side of him, they started walking. Pain stabbed through his midsection. He slumped over. His ragged shirt was wet with blood. His blood.

“I…I’ve been hit.”

“We know. We’ll get you to the medic.”

Chapter 38

Guy lay in a shallow trench dug into the rocky soil alongside the other wounded. The medic put a makeshift bandage on his side, complaining as he worked that he had no supplies.

"Don't have any morphine. For the pain." The man shrugged as he said it.

Guy reassured him he didn't need it.

"Humph. Wait till the shock wears off. It'll burn like hell and throb with every beat of your heart. Then you'll wish I still had some morphine."

"Gee, thanks." Guy could have done without that little pep talk.

"Good thing is," the medic went on, "the hot metal seared the wound. So there's not much bleeding, at least…"

Guy caught his eye. He understood. Not much bleeding on the outside didn't mean it wasn't bleeding on the inside.

Another wounded soldier called out, and with a quick pat of reassurance, the medic moved on to another patient.

Guy glanced around at all the wounded men. What would happen to them if the Germans took the hill? Would they end up in a German hospital? As a prisoner? Or would they simply dispose of the wounded?

If relief didn't show up soon, everyone left alive would be prisoners.

He pushed the thought from his mind. No point in worrying about that. Right now, he had to focus on staying alive.

He shifted slightly and searing pain shot through his middle. Damn medic was right.

As it subsided and he could breathe again, he fumbled around with his hand until he found the rock underneath him. He flung it away with his last bit of strength and sighed deeply.

Got to get my mind off the pain. Think of something else.

Rosemary. She always came to mind when he wanted to get away. Warning himself to avoid things he couldn't afford to think about, his mind settled on memories of their train ride. That long journey across the country.

They'd kept up the pretense of being man and wife so the conductor wouldn't give them a hard time. He could have put them off for providing false information. Then they would have been stuck out in the hinterland. At the time Guy had thought it wouldn't have been a bad thing. After all, it would have given him more time to spend with her. Even if it would have made her crazy desperate.

He thought of her mood swings, of the deep hurt she kept locked down tight yet just beneath the surface, coloring everything she did. Her husband hadn't just died. He'd nearly destroyed her. Guy's gut told him her husband had treated her badly before their breakup. She was too hurt and humiliated to talk about it, so Guy would never know all of it.

He did know the jerk had cheated on her. How horrible it must have been for her to find her husband in bed with another woman. In her bed. The bed they shared as man and wife.

Guy had met some selfish bastards in the Army. Men who only thought of themselves and never considered who they might hurt as they bullied their way through life.

Had Julie thought he was like that? Regret welled up from deep inside. Rosemary had suggested he write to Julie, to apologize and to explain. Right now, he couldn't think of any explanation that justified his taking a swing at the officer. Guy had been hurt and threatened, so he'd acted on his emotions without thinking about the consequences. And he'd been wrong.

He drew a deep, cleansing breath only to have pain answer, deep throbbing pain that made him wonder how long he would lay there, bleeding inside. Maybe bleeding to death.

He jerked his mind back and promised himself that when he got out of here…yes, when, not if…he'd write to Julie and he'd apologize. Like Rosemary said, even if she didn't accept his apology, he would feel better about it.

Exhaustion must have overtaken him because when he awoke it was dark. The medic hovered over him.

"Just checkin' on you."

"I'm still alive, if that's what you're wondering."

Even in the darkness he could see the white of the medic's teeth as he grinned. "Good to know."

"Any word on relief?" The same question everyone had been asking for days.

"Not any I've heard." He reached down and lifted

Guy's head so that his lips touched the edge of a canteen. Cool, welcome water seeped into his dry mouth.

"Thought you weren't supposed to give water to someone who's gutshot."

"You were hit in the side. Not the gut. Besides you're getting pretty dry. Got to keep your fluids up."

"You think I'm bleeding, inside?"

The medic put the cap back on the canteen and put it down. He placed his hand on Guy's side. Even the gentle touch increased the throbbing, and Guy gritted his teeth to keep from crying out.

"If you're bleedin', it ain't bad."

Guy could only nod.

"Too bad I don't have some morphine for you." The medic got to his feet. "I'll check on you again later."

He then disappeared into the darkness.

Guy listened to the distant sound of small arms fire and wondered what the Germans were doing.

Probably waiting until morning for their final push.

****

Guy drifted in and out with only the loud noises of mortar or artillery shells bringing him fully awake. Night receded and daylight brought movement around him. Medics brought more wounded to join those on the ground nearby.

Would it ever end?

The sun warmed his body and he drifted off again.

Commotion brought him quickly to his senses.

Someone leaned down. "We're going to get you out of here."

Soon strong arms lifted him onto a stretcher. Two

stretcher bearers carried him to the road where they loaded him onto a Jeep alongside two other wounded men.

We've been relieved. That's what's happened. We're getting out of here.

Even the bumpy ride down the hill with the resultant pain didn't dampen his cheer. He would see a real doctor in a real hospital where they could fix him.

They halted near a damaged building. Men scurried to get him off the Jeep and inside where a doctor examined him.

"You'll need surgery," the doctor said matter-of-factly. He motioned to someone nearby and then moved on to the next battered soldier.

An aide appeared.

"I'm gonna give you a shot of morphine. That should hold you until they can operate."

"Will it knock me out?" Guy asked as the man took his right arm and poked a needle into it.

Guy jerked his head around to watch what they were doing to his arm. He heard the first one say, "Shouldn't…" Then a slight stabbing in his throbbing side.

"Be still," the other man ordered. He must have immobilized his arm. The next thing Guy knew a bag of clear fluid hung above him. They moved him to another part of the room, presumably to await surgery.

After a while, the fluid and the shot did the trick. The pain subsided, and he craved a cigarette. He glanced around to see if he could catch someone's attention.

Near the door he spotted a familiar face. Amos Campbell. His friend spoke to someone, then made his way between the stretchers to Guy.

Amos grinned. “Thought I’d come check on you before we headed out.”

“Glad you did,” Guy answered, a grin spreading across his own face.

“Told you you’d make it, didn’t I?”

“You sure did.”

Amos reached inside his shirt and pulled out a crumpled piece of paper.

“I found this. When you were hit. Must have fallen out of your pocket.”

He handed Guy the letter to Rosemary.

“I glanced at it,” Amos said sheepishly. “Started to read it and then decided I’d better not.”

“Thanks,” Guy murmured as he fingered the wrinkled paper.

“You ought to write that girl, for real. Instead of tearing ’em up.”

“I promised I wouldn’t.”

“It’s a dumb promise, if you ask me.” Amos pulled his helmet off and scratched his head. “Anyway, I wanted to give that back and make sure you were okay before we pulled out.”

That got Guy’s attention. “Pull out? When?”

“Today. We’re already off the hill. The Germans have pulled back. Looks like they’re in full retreat and we’re gonna be on their tails.”

Guy nodded. “Good.”

He glanced around then, back to his friend. “How about a cigarette before you go?”

Amos laughed. Then he unfastened a pouch at his waist and pulled out a pack of cigarettes. “We just got these with our supplies.” He placed the pack in Guy’s free hand. “Keep ’em. I’ll get some more.”

“Thanks.” Guy fumbled, one-handed, trying to open the pack.

“Here. Let me.” Amos took the pack, opened it, and got a cigarette out. He lit it and then stuck it between Guy’s lips. As Guy took a deep drag, Amos picked up the letter and stuffed it into Guy’s breast pocket. “Don’t want to lose that.”

An aide stepped to the foot of Guy’s stretcher. “Sorry, fellows.”

“Looks like they want me to leave.”

“Amos,” Guy called.

Campbell met his gaze.

“Thanks. And take care of yourself.”

Campbell grinned. “Will do.”

Guy puffed on his cigarette as another man appeared at his head. They lifted him up and deposited him on a table where a masked surgeon waited.

Chapter 39

Rosemary returned from her shower with a damp towel around her head. She reveled in the comfort of her new robe, a pale blue chenille she purchased in Knoxville, something just for herself.

She hadn't decided if Drucilla was a good influence on her by encouraging her to enjoy a little of her hard-earned money, or if her shopping expert friend just wanted someone else's money to spend.

Either way the comfy robe boosted her spirits.

Minnie strolled into the room and dropped onto her bed. "I brought your mail up."

"Thanks."

Rosemary shuffled through the envelopes. One bulky one from her mother. A small, thin envelope from Frances and a bigger one with the familiar logo of the department store in Knoxville. No doubt they wanted her to return and buy something else.

She ran her fingernail under the flap of the letter from her mother, wondering what she'd stuffed inside.

A single sheet of paper was wrapped around another letter, a strange one with a military-looking return address. Her heart started pounding as her mind raced.

No, he wouldn't. He'd promised.

She quickly scanned her mother's words.

This came for you. Looks like it's from someone

overseas. Don't know who you'd know in the Army unless it is some friend of Jack's. Decided to send it on to you.

Good news from Bobby. He's going to get leave to come home. Can't wait to see him. I'll let you know when so you can come see him.

Write when you can.

Mother

Rosemary stared at the envelope. Wherever it had come from it had been roughly handled. The name scribbled in the corner looked like "Campbell," which would be Amos Campbell, the soldier she and Guy met on the train. This couldn't be good.

Her stomach knotted up.

She gripped the fragile paper with shaking hands. She didn't want to open it, not if it was like the thin, yellow envelope that held the telegram, not if it delivered the same bad news.

"Are you okay? You're as pale as a ghost."

Rosemary only nodded. If she tried to speak, she might break down. She might not be able to open it and read the inevitable news it held.

She turned away from Minnie toward her dresser and fumbled to get the drawer open. The towel tumbled from her head and cold, damp hair fell around her face and shoulders.

She shuffled through the drawer with much too much force. Finally, she uncovered the little manicure kit containing fingernail scissors. As if opening some precious package, she cut through the edge of the envelope. The scissors tumbled back into the drawer as her shaking fingers pulled the folded letter from its hiding place. The pages seemed to unfold themselves.

She blinked back tears threatening to overflow.

Rosemary,

I'm writing to let you know that Guy was wounded...

Wounded. That means he's not dead. She struggled to breathe, to calm herself so she could read the letter. Her lips spread into a smile.

Rosemary,

I'm writing to let you know that Guy was wounded. He won't write you because he promised you he wouldn't. So, I'm letting you know. He got hit with shrapnel. It's not too bad now that he's at the field hospital. I made sure to check on him before we pulled out. He'll be out of the fight for a while, but the doc said after a few weeks he should be okay and back in it.

He would be mad if he knew I was writing you. But after I read a little of the letter he wrote to you, I had to let you know. He's been writing letters to you since we shipped out. Only he tears them up. He's really stuck on you. It's dumb to me that you made him promise not to write.

What you ought to do is write him a letter and let him know that you care whether he lives or dies. From what he told me, his family doesn't care if he comes back or not. I don't know what I'd do if I didn't get mail from home. Even my ex-girlfriend writes to me. I know she's seeing other guys, but it's nice that she still thinks of me. With what we are going through over here letters really mean a lot.

I am including Guy's address. You can do what you want, but if you are the nice girl I think you are, you will write him a letter.

Yours truly,

Amos Campbell

The relief that had spread through her as soon as she read the word "wounded," now morphed into worry. Guy had been writing to her. Amos said he was stuck on her. She hadn't wanted that. She'd wanted him to forget her or at least look back on their brief encounter as just a pleasant experience before he went overseas. Just a girl doing something nice for a soldier facing possible death.

Of course, she'd struggled to put her own feelings aside. She'd hoped that her thoughts of Guy would fade over time. That she'd meet new people and get busy working and stop thinking of him. It hadn't happened, not yet anyway.

Now she knew he thought of her, too. And he'd been wounded bad enough to put him in the hospital for a while.

"You're awfully quiet over there," Minnie commented. "Not bad news, I hope."

Rosemary plastered a smile on her face and turned to her roommate. "Just a letter from Mother. Some good news about my brother. And…" She held up Amos' letter. "A soldier I met on the train coming from California wrote me."

"Mmm." Minnie focused on painting her toenails. "Is he good-looking?"

"Okay, I guess. A little too friendly, if you know what I mean."

"Yep."

Rosemary turned back to the dresser, took her brush, and began to pull it through her damp hair. She'd have to decide whether to write to Guy or not. Before, she'd been so sure. Now she wondered if she'd made the right decision.

****

She jarred awake. "No."

The image of Guy lying on the ground in a pool of blood was still vivid and real.

She swung her feet onto the floor, clutching the thin quilt in her fist.

It was a dream. Just a dream. It wasn't real. It didn't happen.

Her thoughts raced as she drew deep breaths. Amos' letter said he'd been wounded. That he would be okay. Just a few days in the hospital.

"You okay over there?" Minnie mumbled. She'd rolled over to face Rosemary in the dark. A faint light from the hallway illuminated her friend's shape in the inky atmosphere of the tiny dormitory room. Rosemary could have reached out and touched her friend on the nearby bed, but she didn't.

She couldn't share the intimate dream with anyone. They'd been making love. She remembered that much. Then something had pulled him away, away to be shot right before her eyes.

"I'm fine. Just a bad dream. You go on back to sleep."

"Okay. If you're sure."

Rosemary heard Minnie repositioning herself on the bed, probably rolling over to face the wall, like she usually did when she went to sleep.

Despite telling herself she needed to go back to sleep, too, she knew she wouldn't. She couldn't sleep with the images still imprinted on her brain.

She pulled the cover up over her, neatly tucking herself in, and forced her thoughts to Amos Campbell.

She pictured the soldier she'd met on the train as she ran his words through her mind again.

Guy had been wounded by shrapnel. Probably from artillery fire. Amos had seen him before they took him away to a hospital. They told him Guy would be okay.

She tried to imagine what that meant. Tried to picture Guy in a nice, clean, orderly hospital with nurses to care for him. Far away from the fighting. Safe.

Except Amos had said that Guy would be "back in it." Those were his exact words.

Those words had scared her, more than she could have imagined. She'd tried to think of Guy as far away but relatively safe sitting in a tent operating a radio. Now she knew that wasn't true. Guy wasn't safe. He was in a war zone where he could be killed, where artillery shells could explode.

Jack had been in the artillery. He had been killed by an exploding shell.

Her hands gripped the edge of the quilt. Her throat tightened as she tried in vain to hold her emotions inside. Violent sobs shook her body. She covered her mouth to muffle the sound so she wouldn't wake Minnie again.

Eventually, she pulled herself together. How would she explain why she was so upset? She could lie. Say she'd dreamt about Jack. She'd done that before, but it left her feeling guilty. Part of her wanted to acknowledge Guy and her feelings for him. But that would mean explaining how they met and what had happened between them in the brief time they were together. She couldn't even explain it to herself.

She knew enough to know how others would judge

her for sleeping with a soldier she barely knew. No one would understand how it had happened. No one could know her feelings at that time. Betrayed, abandoned, left to face her mother and Jack's parents alone and unable to tell them the truth about Jack.

She hadn't thought about the consequences. That she would actually care for Guy. That she would fear for him.

Her thoughts circled back to the letter from Amos Campbell. She didn't have to read it again to see the words floating in the dark. He'd said Guy was writing letters to her. Had been since they shipped out. Guy would write to her and then destroy the letters.

Amos must have been there when Guy was hit. He'd found one of those letters. And he'd read part of it. He said that's when he decided to write to Rosemary, to tell her how much Guy loved her. That's what he'd written in the letter, the letter Guy never intended to mail because she had made him promise not to write to her. Amos knew about the promise, too. That's why he wrote and asked her to write to Guy. He said Guy needed to know someone cared. That he rarely heard from his family in California.

Rosemary remembered the way he'd talked about his mother. The longing in his voice when he spoke of her had told her more than what he said. He'd wanted his mother to care as much about him as she did about his brother. To worry about him and fear he might be killed. Rosemary understood about mothers having a favorite child and not being that favorite. It hurt deeply.

She knew the answer before she actually formed the thought. She would write to him. Because she did care whether he lived or died. She wanted him to live.

And she wanted him to be whole, not some broken wretch like her father had been when he returned from the Great War.

Tears slid out of the corners of her eyes and into her hair. She swiped them away with her hands. She wouldn't let herself think of her father. Not now. Not ever. She'd think of Guy. Of his sweet, handsome face. Of his gentle touch. Of his kisses.

Her body ached for him. She wouldn't sleep. Maybe not for the rest of the night. Instead she'd let her mind focus on him and what she'd say in her letter.

Chapter 40

September 1944

His side still hurt some, but he was tired of doing nothing.

He'd been sitting around for over a month in the small French town where the Army had set up a temporary hospital. Instead of being sent back to England to recuperate, he'd been relegated to a chateau surrounded by tents. Once his side began to heal, he'd spent long hours lounging around playing cards, reading, and waiting for orders. Finally, they'd come.

After a bumpy ride on the back of a two-and-a-half-ton truck, Guy arrived in the replacement depot.

A group of soldiers mingled around the building where he was directed to report. Inside, after standing in the typical Army line for half an hour, he took his turn.

The sergeant scanned his paperwork and put it in one of the piles on the desk. "You're temporarily assigned to Company B. Report to Sergeant Warner. You'll find his HQ down the street."

Guy sensed his dismissal. He'd been in the Army long enough to know he'd better speak up for himself or he'd be shuffled around indefinitely.

"Sergeant, I'd like to be sent back to my outfit. The 230th Field Artillery Battalion of the 30th Infantry

Division."

The sergeant met his gaze, clearly unhappy with anyone who held up his line. "You would, would you?"

"Yes, Sergeant." Guy knew he had to observe military courtesy even when stepping way out of line with his request. "Just send me back to the 230th and I'll be out of your hair. Simple as that."

"Simple? You think that would be simple? Do you know how many men we've got here to process?"

"No." Maybe he hadn't used the right approach with the sergeant. "But I'm sure you'd like to get one, namely me, off your list." He smiled at the disgruntled noncom and thought he saw the man's face soften just a bit. "I'm a radio operator for the artillery. I guess you saw that on my papers." He swallowed and plunged ahead. "I landed with the 230th. And I got wounded at Mortain on the hill with the forward observer." The sergeant jerked his paperwork off the stack. "I just want to get back to my buddies in the 230th."

"Look, soldier. We've got a lot of guys who want to get back to their old outfits. Only their old outfits are all the way across France. I don't even know where the 30th Division is right now." He pressed his lips together and shook his head. "Just do like I said and report to Company B. We'll sort it out as best we can."

"Thank you, Sergeant."

Guy walked away with a sense of relief. He'd find Company B's Headquarters and report like he'd been told. In the meantime, he'd have to have faith that the sergeant and the Army's personnel department would sort it out and get him on his way.

****

After almost a week and numerous attempts to get

someone to listen to him, Guy would have climbed the walls, if there had been any walls.

The men of Company B lived in 8x8 tents set up in a small field just outside the village. They slept on cots, not in foxholes. They ate hot chow and enjoyed actual showers, but nobody wanted to stay here.

Most, like Guy, had recovered from wounds and were anxious to get back to their units.

He sat down beside Abernathy, who'd survived an encounter with a mine field. "You heard anything?"

"Naw. Not a word." The Iowa man lit a cigarette and offered Guy one.

Guy declined with a shake of his head. "I swear. If I knew how to find the 230th, I'd hitch a ride and just go, orders or no orders."

"Yeah. I know what you mean. I can't find out anything around here. I think the *Stars & Stripes* knows more about the war than these guys do, and it's three weeks old."

"You'd think they'd be in a hurry to get us back to fighting the Germans instead of sitting around here doing nothing." Memories of Mortain and the Germans he'd shot pushed him to his feet with the need to move. Much as he wanted to get out of this place, he didn't ever want to be in that situation again.

"Hey, look." Abernathy doused his smoke in the dirt and jumped up.

Sergeant Warner approached with papers in hand.

"Nolan, your orders came through."

Finally. He took the papers from Sergeant Warner. "Thank you, Sergeant."

"What about me?" Abernathy asked.

"Sorry, Corporal. No orders for you, yet."

Guy read over the document in his hand. Radio Operator, 276th Armored Field Artillery Battalion.

"Wait a minute. This isn't right. I'm supposed to go back to the 230th."

"We had a request for a radio operator." Sergeant Warner's gaze bore into Guy. "And you're it."

"But I don't know anything about this outfit." He looked down at the paper again. "What the hell does Armored Field Artillery mean?"

"It's a mobile unit. Track mounted 105s."

"Track mounted?"

"You mean like tanks," the Iowan asked.

"That's right. Like tanks. But with a 105mm Howitzer mounted on 'em."

Guy shook his head. "This can't be right. I'm supposed to go back to my unit. The 230th Field Artillery."

"There's a war on, soldier. You go where you're sent." Sgt. Warner turned to leave, then stopped and looked back. "You leave first thing in the morning. 0600."

Guy's heart sank. Since being taken off the hill, he'd been surrounded by strangers, first in the hospital, then in the recuperation center, and now in the replacement depot. All that time he'd expected to return to the familiar faces of the 230th. Looked like the Army had other ideas. They were sending him off to another unit with another bunch of strangers.

On the hill he'd come to understand the bond formed between men in combat. He'd already known Amos and Langford, and it hadn't taken long to get to know the others as they fought side by side to survive. Now he'd never see any of them again.

As he packed his meager belongings into his duffel bag and waited for morning, he resolved to make the best of it in this new outfit, the 276th.

If these guns were like tanks, then that meant they'd be out front with the tanks. He'd be fighting for his life again. Maybe not with the FO. He prayed not with the FO again. From now on he'd be happy to stay in the background relaying messages rather than being out front directing fire.

****

At the bus terminal, Rosemary mingled with the other workers who wore the K-25 badges like hers.

She didn't expect to be this nervous about changing jobs. After all, she would be in the same plant, just in another area. Before, when she'd come from the Wheat school where she trained, everything had been different. There she'd had to learn the routine of badges, of changing into work pants and tying her hair up. Everything had been new. Yet now the butterflies in her stomach were worse than before.

A girl from the leak test line gave a friendly nod.

That's what she would miss the most, the camaraderie with the other girls who'd worked close by doing the same thing, leak-testing pipe welds. She'd even miss the millwrights who controlled the ceiling-mounted cranes, who'd call her Rosie when they deposited a huge pipe at her station. This new job would be different.

The enormity of the K-25 plant defied her imagination. There were miles and miles of pipes. No wonder the thought of having to go out into that vast, open building and inspect the pipes already in place intimidated her.

"Rosemary," a familiar voice called.

She looked around just as a breathless Martha Sue reached her side.

"Did you hear? About Drucilla?"

"No. What about her?"

"She got a telegram. You know, one of those telegrams."

Rosemary's gut clenched into a knot. "Are you sure?"

Martha Sue nodded. "Missing in action."

Rosemary looked toward the bus coming to a halt in front of them. "I've got to go to work. Where is she?"

"She's still here. In the dorm. Don't know if she will stay or go home."

"I'll go see her when I get off."

The line pushed them forward toward the bus. "I'm sure she needs someone to talk to. Someone who understands."

In the early light of dawn, the security guard flashed his light from Martha Sue's face down to her Y-12 badge. He spoke in a polite but authoritative tone. "Sorry, Miss. This is the wrong bus. Your stop's over there."

He pointed toward the Y-12 workers clustered beneath their designated sign.

Martha Sue flashed him a smile. "Oh, right." She shoved her way back through the K-25 workers and made a dash for a place in line to board the approaching bus.

By then, the guard had compared Rosemary's face to her K-25 badge and motioned for her to board the bus. Murmuring and shuffling accompanied Rosemary as she and her fellow K-25 workers squeezed into an old trolley converted from use in the world's fair to the ever-expanding Oak Ridge bus system. There may not have been a charge to ride to your designated workplace, but that didn't mean the ride was comfortable.

Instead of observing the continuous construction along the route, from new dormitories going up to trailers being hauled up dirt roads newly carved into a hillside, her thoughts were on Drucilla. At least the telegram had said "missing in action" instead of "killed." Maybe there was some hope.

Rosemary knew better than most how Drucilla must feel. Devastated. Lost. Even with a hint of hope the term "missing" gave, Drucilla should prepare for the worst.

Right after her shift she would go to Drucilla's dorm. Maybe she could help her friend cope with this terrible news.

Before she knew it, the bus stopped in front of the entrance to the K-25 plant. She'd forgotten all about her new job.

She glanced up at the billowy white clouds against a brightening sky one last time before entering the artificial light of the industrial building.

Her new supervisor began his practiced spiel explaining her duties. At least she'd be earning a few cents more per hour. More money to squirrel away for her uncertain future.

The war made everyone's future uncertain.

Chapter 41

When Guy climbed down from the ammo truck he'd ridden to 276th AFA headquarters, loud voices drew him toward a group of men. French mixed with heavily accented English came from French soldiers arguing with a GI whose deep southern drawl made him almost as hard to understand.

"What's all this?" Guy asked a soldier standing on the edge of the crowd.

"Aw, that Frenchy says Hap insulted his country and the French army." The man glanced at Guy as if he recognized him as a newcomer for the first time. "You been around many of these Frenchmen?"

Guy shook his head. "No."

"Arrogant bunch. Especially the tankers. And the officers."

"It is their country."

The soldier turned to face Guy. "You're new, aren't you?"

"Yes." Unable to determine the soldier's rank, Guy continued. "I'm Guy Nolan. Supposed to report to 276th headquarters."

"Over there." The soldier pointed toward a house not far away.

The crowd grew, especially on the Frenchman's side. Angry comments had Guy expecting fists to fly any minute.

"Why's the French Army here anyway?"

"'Cause Patton attached us to their Armored outfit."

As the shoving started in earnest, Guy and the other soldier backed away to avoid being drawn into the impending fight.

"By the way, I'm Eddie." He turned toward the headquarters and quickened his pace.

Guy followed.

An officer emerged from the house and strode toward the belligerent crowd. Another hurried out behind him. Guy recognized their insignia, a captain and a lieutenant colonel, but now was not the time to snap to attention and salute. He just stood back and watched the officers wade into the soldiers, shouting orders.

They soon separated the nationalities and quieted them down.

He watched in fascination as the lt. colonel addressed the French contingent, sending them back to their tents while he talked to a French officer.

Still standing nearby, Eddie spoke again. "The Frenchies are all fired up to take Metz. But Patton hasn't turned them loose yet. Says there's not enough supplies for an all-out push."

"What outfit is that?"

"Second Free French Armored Division. Supposed to be a crack tank outfit."

"And the 276th is part of their division?" Guy struggled to understand the set-up.

"Naw. We're non-divisional. We go where Third Army sends us. Sure wish they'd send us to another division. This here's not working too good."

Guy glanced back at headquarters, thinking he'd better check in. But his curiosity about his new outfit spurred questions.

"How long has the 276th been in France?"

"We landed back in August. Took a while to make our way across France." He looked over at the still milling crowd of GIs. "You here to replace Berkowski?"

The question surprised Guy. "I don't know. Who's he?"

"Radio man. Broke his leg when his Jeep ran off the road and hit a mine."

"Well, I'm a radio man, so I guess so."

"Glad to have you." Eddie grinned. "Don't let this little ruckus give you the wrong idea. This is a good outfit. Great bunch of guys."

Guy hoped Eddie was right about the 276th because, with the realities of war, he doubted he could transfer out if he didn't like the situation.

****

Rosemary held Drucilla and let her cry.

A few days after the telegram, her friend received a letter from her husband's commanding officer. Where the telegram had simply said "missing in action," the letter went into more detail about what had happened to him.

"Did the letter say where he went down?"

Drucilla pulled away. "Not exactly. They can't say too much." She blew her nose and stood.

"But he was flying near an island, right? Wouldn't that make it more likely that he made it to shore?"

"Don't you understand?" Drucilla lashed out. "He's gone. They looked for him. They couldn't even find the plane."

"Didn't someone see him get hit? I mean, he wasn't out there alone. Surely someone saw something."

"I don't know." Drucilla ran her hand through her hair. "They go out in groups, but that doesn't mean they stay together. Not when they are fighting with other planes. Japanese planes. For all I know the others could have been shot down, too."

Rosemary remembered how upset she'd been. All the questions she'd had. She wouldn't leave Drucilla to wrestle with it alone, like she had had to.

"What exactly did the letter say?"

Drucilla jerked a piece of paper from her dresser. "It says that his plane was shot down and "after an extensive search they did not find either the wreckage or the pilot." She waved the paper in front of Rosemary. "They concluded that Ronald J. Hawkins had been killed in action."

"So it's official."

"No. Not without a body." She sank down on the bed again. "Oh, Rosemary. I can't even bury him. He's out there somewhere in that vast ocean. Lost."

Rosemary fought tears of her own. At least she'd been able to bury Jack. She'd been able to say goodbye. Poor Drucilla.

She touched her friend's shoulder. "I don't know what to say."

"It's all right." Their watery gazes met. "Thank you for being here. It helps so much."

Rosemary nodded and thought of how much Guy had helped her. Not just with her grief. He'd helped her to see how terribly Jack had treated her. She'd almost convinced herself that their breakup had been her fault. Then Guy had been so gentle and kind. He'd treated her like a loving husband should have.

If she hadn't met Guy, she might never have gotten over Jack's death.

The thought startled her. Had she really gotten over it? The familiar ache told her she hadn't. Not yet. But she'd accepted it.

Drucilla's loss brought back the terrible pain she'd experienced. The loss of Jack, of their marriage, of a life they would never have. It still made her heart ache. Yet time had created a distance that allowed her to look back with some objectivity. She never wanted to go through anything like that again, but she'd survived.

Drucilla was still struggling with accepting the reality of what had happened. She had to face the fact that her husband was never coming home. Just like Rosemary had had to face Jack's death.

Guy had helped her so much. And she would never forget the gift of showing her what it was like to be with a gentle, loving man rather than a selfish boy. That memory helped her let go of her dream of a life with Jack.

She hoped she could help Drucilla deal with the loss of her husband, if only by being a loving friend who would be there when she needed someone to talk to.

Chapter 42

October 14, 1944

Guy stared at the letter in his hand, disgusted. Why did his mother always sound like the world was coming to an end and only money would fix it?

"Bad news from home?" His new friend, Tony Valachi, asked.

"Oh, I don't know. The way my mother says things, I'm never sure if it's a crisis or just some passing something that'll blow over before she gets my reply."

"Mothers. Like wives. They get upset over everything."

"I understand her worry about my brother Henry. He was wounded. But she says he is in Australia, in a hospital, so it's not like she hasn't heard from him."

"Maybe it's a good thing. In a hospital is better than dead, no?"

Guy nodded, then looked at the letter again. Henry had stopped sending money home to her. Knowing Henry, he planned to spend his money living it up in Australia. And, of course, the favorite son could do no wrong. Instead of complaining to Henry, she implied that Guy should send more.

Despite his frustration he felt responsible for her. Years ago, before his death, his father had asked him to take care of his mother because his father knew Guy was the only one she could really depend on. So Guy had delayed joining the military. He might still be working in the shipyard if his mother and two sisters hadn't needled him about joining up. The last straw had been when his mother called him a coward. That hurt.

Out of sheer stubbornness he'd chosen the Army rather than following his brothers into the Navy or the Marines.

He sighed. He'd have to write her back, tell her she could have more of his money to make up for Henry's selfishness. But he'd emphasize that she should continue to put part of the money in his savings account, his nest egg for the future.

Lieutenant Blanton entered the tent. "Nolan, get on the horn to Third Army. I need to know exactly where "Ol' blood and guts" wants us to go. Seems the French got different orders."

Tony quickly got busy fixing the damaged radio he'd been working on. An expert at looking busy, Tony managed to avoid the officers' attention, at least most of the time.

The call to Patton's Third Army Headquarters proved interesting. After only a month on the line their orders were to pull back, to billet in some French village.

Guy didn't complain. He'd seen enough combat.

As soon as Lieutenant Blanton left, Tony headed out to the kitchen truck to grab a bite to eat. He didn't offer to bring Guy anything or to spell him on the radio so he could go eat. Guy shook his head. Good thing he wasn't hungry.

A soldier he didn't know entered the radio tent.

"Are you Nolan, Guy Nolan?"

Guy looked the stranger over before answering. "Who wants to know?"

"I'm George Noah, from C Battery. Uh..." He hesitated. "I guess the clerk got your mail in with mine, by mistake, mind you."

When Guy didn't answer, the man asked, "You are Nolan, aren't you?"

Guy nodded.

The soldier handed Guy a letter. "It's yours, isn't it?"

Guy stared at the envelope. It bore his name, and it was addressed to the 230th Field Artillery. But that address had been marked out and his new one written beside it in a different hand.

"Yeah. Looks like it."

His gaze shifted to the upper left-hand corner where "R. Hopkins" followed by an address in Tennessee glared back at him.

His heart skipped a beat.

Guy forced himself to look up at the soldier. "Thanks."

His pulse raced with anticipation. His hands shook. He couldn't believe she'd written to him. She'd actually written. After all the fuss she'd made about not writing. Had something happened to change her mind?

Guy made sure Noah had left the tent before he slid his finger under the flap.

Praying that no one would come in to see his reaction, he took out the single page. His hands shook as he skimmed through her words.

Dear Guy,

Amos Campbell wrote to me and told me you had

been wounded. He said you would live. Which is wonderful, except he also said that you would recover and return to the fight. I guess that's good, too, except it means you are not out of danger.

I want you to know that I think about you and I worry about you. I do care what happens to you. I hope you know that.

My request that you not write to me was to avoid me having to explain a correspondence with a soldier so soon after Jack's death. I hoped you understood. Thank you for honoring my request.

Since I am no longer in Kerrville, it's okay for you to write to me here. If you still want to. I'm working at a defense plant and living in a dormitory. My cousin works here too. She's the only one here from home to spread gossip but I don't think she will.

I couldn't stand it at home. There was no real work I could do, and you know what I said about his parents. I couldn't stay with them, so I moved in with my grandmother. She encouraged me to take this job and I'm glad she did. This place is bustling with activity. Lots of younger people all working for the war effort. I've never seen anything like it. A new town built in the middle of nowhere. I can't tell you much about it, but it is important to the war effort.

Stay well and safe. I will write again soon.

Yours truly,

Rosemary

He fought the tears that threatened to overflow down his cheeks. She'd written to him. She'd actually written to him.

He swiped the back of his hand across his eyes as his thoughts raced. He'd have to thank Amos, if he ever saw him again.

He chuckled to himself. He should be extremely angry at his friend for writing to her. But he couldn't be mad at Amos. Not when this letter was the result.

Amos must not have told her about the letters Guy wrote to her and then destroyed. Or maybe he did, and she was too polite to mention them.

None of that mattered because she'd written to him. And she'd given him permission to write to her.

Incredible!

Rosemary cared. She'd said it. On paper. And she said he could write to her.

He wanted to jump for joy. Let the others think he was crazy. Maybe he was. She might just be being nice. Or maybe, just maybe, she cared for him, too.

Trying to rein in his emotions, he read the letter again.

Chapter 43

Martha Sue was waiting at the entrance to Rosemary's dormitory. They went upstairs to her room. Then Rosemary asked her cousin, "What's going on?" Martha Sue rarely came by for a visit these days.

"Thanksgiving's coming up." Martha Sue avoided making eye contact as she moved around the small room.

"What about it?" Rosemary hadn't thought much about the holidays. "It's weeks away."

"I've got plans. To go home with a friend, to Asheville, North Carolina."

"Oh." Rosemary sensed more than just a visit with a friend, but she held her tongue.

"Mama and Mary Ann have gone to Michigan." She paused and met Rosemary's gaze. "Mama said I should spend the holidays with Grandmother. But the thing is…I don't want to."

"You'd rather go to Asheville…with a friend."

"Exactly." Martha Sue's face brightened.

"This friend wouldn't happen to be Wally, would it?"

Telltale red crept up Martha Sue's neck until her cheeks blossomed. That told Rosemary all she needed to know.

Her cousin quickly recovered her composure. With her chin up in defiance, she explained, "I'm going with a girlfriend."

"I know you better than that." Rosemary sat down on the bed and drew a deep breath. "I thought you stopped seeing him."

"Not exactly," Martha Sue replied softly.

When Rosemary shook her head, her cousin offered more. "He's really nice. And I really, really like him."

"Martha Sue, you're married. You can't go off with another man." How could her cousin do something so stupid? So downright immoral. Rosemary eased closer and lowered her voice. "What if Stanley finds out?"

"He won't. We've been very careful."

"Your father-in-law works here. What if he hears about it? Or sees you two together?"

Fire shot from her cousin's eyes. "Stop it. Nobody's going to find out unless you tell them."

"Me?" Rosemary shook her head. "They won't hear it from me."

"How do I know that?"

She couldn't bear the thought of a scandal, even one involving her cousin. That's why she'd tried so hard to keep anyone in Kerrville from finding out about her troubles with Jack. And she couldn't bear the thought of the gossips getting wind of her relationship with Guy.

"I promise. I won't tell anybody."

Martha Sue eased over to stand by Rosemary's dresser. She ran her finger across the surface until it rested atop an envelope.

Guy's letter. It had arrived yesterday, and she'd hurriedly read it over again this morning before leaving for work. Apparently, she forgot to put it away.

Fighting panic, Rosemary stifled the urge to go over and snatch up the letter before Martha Sue could react. Maybe her cousin wouldn't realize that it was from a soldier overseas or how important it was to her.

But Martha Sue didn't pick up the letter. Instead, she turned and faced Rosemary with a sly smile.

"Remember when I went home before Mama left for Detroit?"

Rosemary nodded, unsure where this was going.

"I ran into an old schoolmate, Tommy Pearson. You remember him, don't you?"

Oh, God! What had he told her?

"He was home on leave," Martha Sue continued. "And he told me this extraordinary story, about seeing you in the Chicago train station." She waited for Rosemary's reaction before continuing.

Rosemary refused to meet her eyes, much less respond.

"He said he waved, but you didn't wave back. I wonder why?"

What could Rosemary say? She dared not admit anything, not to Martha Sue. The girl could twist something perfectly innocent into a torrid affair. And her relationship with Guy was anything but innocent.

"Tommy said he saw you kissing a soldier." Her eyebrows raised, expressing her satisfaction in having caught Rosemary in an embarrassing position. "I don't suppose it was the same soldier who wrote that letter?" Her voice dripped with pleasure as she pointed toward the envelope on the dresser.

Rosemary drew a ragged breath. "It's not what you think."

"And what exactly do I think? That you were carrying on with a soldier when Jack wasn't even cold in his grave? And you have the nerve to criticize me."

"You don't understand. It wasn't like that."

"It doesn't matter, does it? It's what it looks like."

"I know it looks bad." Stick to the truth as much as you can. Just don't say too much. "He's just a soldier I met in the train station, in California. We rode the train to Chicago." Memories flooded back making her heart thud in her chest. "He was going overseas so he asked me to kiss him goodbye, for luck."

"You know what? I don't really care. All I care about is going off on this trip with Wally."

"I won't tell anybody. I promise."

"Oh, you'll do more than not tell. You'll cover for me. I want you to tell Grandmother that you know my friend. Jane's her name. Jane Ferguson. Tell her that you know all about my going home with her for a visit. You're going to make sure nobody in Kerrville suspects anything about me and Wally."

Rosemary nodded.

"And if you don't, then I'm going to tell Aunt Winnie what Tommy told me."

"I'll cover for you…in Kerrville. But what about here? What if somebody here tells your father-in-law?"

"You'd better hope that doesn't happen…'cause if it does, your dirty little secret will become public knowledge, here and at home."

"I don't have any 'dirty' secret. I met a soldier on the train. I gave him a kiss goodbye. That's all."

"Don't forget the letters. Writing to a soldier overseas is…oh, I don't know…so noble, so innocent."

"That's right."

"Then you won't mind me reading it." Like lightning, she snatched up the letter.

Rosemary jumped to her feet. "Give it back. It's none of your business."

The sly smile returned. "Just as I thought." She handed Rosemary the letter. "Pretty hot, huh?"

Rosemary didn't dare respond or she might completely lose her temper with her dear cousin.

"I always wondered about the rumors when you and Jack got married."

"What are you talking about?"

"Oh, just that you made Jack marry you. Something about a child that you conveniently lost after you had him hooked."

The shame gripped Rosemary's insides until she couldn't breathe. It crept up from deep within and threatened to choke her. She couldn't speak. She turned away unable to face Martha Sue.

"So the rumor is true." Her cousin's voice dripped with satisfaction. "And if that's true, then it will be easy to get people to believe that you were seeing another man while Jack was off in training."

Fury finally gave Rosemary back her voice. She whirled around. "Go ahead. Have your little affair. I don't want to have anything to do with it. Not one thing."

"Oh yes, you will. You'll tell Grandmother I went home with a girlfriend, just like I said."

Chapter 44

Late October, 1944

"Mail call."

Guy never hurried to mail call before he got the letter from Rosemary. Now he raced toward Pfc. Clark, who stood in front of HQ handing out letters and packages.

The clerk soon reached the bottom of the bag. Nothing for Guy. At least not this time.

After that first letter from Rosemary, he hadn't gotten another, even though he'd written to her twice. He hoped she hadn't changed her mind about writing to him. She had sounded reluctant to begin a correspondence.

Or it could be the slow mail. He hadn't heard from his mother in a while either. She was the only one who wrote to him with any regularity. She probably hadn't liked the tone of his last two letters where he had cautioned her to keep putting a portion of his money away for his return.

"Nolan, I've been looking for you." Lt. Jones approached.

Guy recognized the reconnaissance officer, but he didn't know the man that well. This couldn't be good. "Sir?"

"They tell me you have some experience working

with a forward observer?"

"Yes, sir." He couldn't lie to the man. "Limited experience."

"Well, I need someone. Mortimer was wounded the last time out."

Guy didn't respond. He knew about the German counter-offensive at Landroff. Jones and his men had been in the thick of the fighting and Guy had relayed their messages to the battalion commander. At the time he'd thanked God he hadn't been out there with them.

The last thing he wanted was to go out with another forward observer. Mortain had taught him that. But what could he do? If he was given a direct order, he had to obey.

Jones' gaze took in the HQ area where several men still loitered, then shot to a nearby gun as it fired a round at some distant target. When his gaze returned to meet Guy's, he said, "I'll have you transferred to 'A' Battery. We'll work out the details after that."

The officer walked away without another word.

Guy blew out the breath he'd been holding.

"Great."

He reached into his pocket and pulled out the letter to Rosemary he'd started. Might as well finish it. And include his change of address. Instead of HQ, he'd be in "A" Battery with more new faces. At least he knew some of the men and officers, so it wasn't like his last reassignment.

Around the side of the building, he squatted against the wall. After reading through what he'd already written, he added a few lines about being reassigned. Much as he wanted to say that he'd be going up front, returning to danger, he didn't. No. He wouldn't lay it out for her. Let her worry about vague dangers, not real ones.

He folded the finished letter, addressed the envelope, and put it in the clerk's box inside the building to await censoring.

As soon as he stepped outside, the whistle of a different kind of incoming "mail" sent him diving to the ground.

A shell exploded about 100 feet away, sending shrapnel and debris flying through the air.

Another explosion hit a little further away, near "A" Battery's positions.

The Jerries had spotted the guns. He hoped they didn't realize the command post was so close.

He scrambled back inside the stone building. Several others had the same idea.

Inside an officer yelled into a phone. "Find that damn Kraut position."

"They've bracketed "A" Battery," Guy told a sergeant.

"Don't you think we know that?" the sergeant barked. "They're already moving."

Transferring to one of the gun batteries meant he would be closer to the action. And going out with a forward observer meant he'd be with the infantry, on the front lines. And if the recent battle around Landroff was any indication, it meant hot and heavy fighting.

Memories of Mortain made his stomach churn. He never wanted to be surrounded, not ever again. But he'd do what he had to do.

And now he had more reason than ever to want to live. Rosemary. If there was even a chance of capturing her heart, then he had to survive and go back to her.

****

"Halt!"

Four German soldiers stood only thirty feet away, their weapons aimed at Guy.

Gripping his rifle, Guy stood his ground.

"Surrender," he yelled, with as much authority as he could muster.

Behind him, Stavely, the driver, grabbed his weapon and jumped out of the half-track.

"Hands up." Stavely backed Guy's bluff.

"*Lass ihre Waffen fallen*," the lead German shouted while motioning with his gun.

The Germans looked scared too. Yet they stood there facing the two Americans ready to fight.

"No way I'm gonna be taken prisoner," Guy muttered just loud enough for Stavely to hear. "They'll have to kill me first."

"I'm with you."

Guy wanted to glance over and thank Stavely for his support, but he didn't dare take his eyes off the antsy enemy soldiers.

"Surrender," he shouted. "You can't escape. There are other Americans not far away."

Fact was, they were out ahead searching for a good observation post. Lt. Jones had climbed the hill and left Guy and Stavely behind with the half-track. Jones was the only nearby American "reinforcements."

The Germans talked among themselves while keeping their guns trained on the Americans they apparently hadn't expected to stumble upon.

It was probably a patrol sent out by a larger body. How far back were the rest of them?

Guy took a chance and motioned with his arm.

"Come on, we'll take good care of you. And you'll be out of the war. Safe."

"They don't understand a word you're saying."

"They understand enough."

The lead German took a step forward.

Guy raised his gun, ready to fire.

A voice crackled over the radio as Lt. Jones called in.

The Germans stiffened. They looked at each other and then at the two Americans.

"Shit!" Stavely moved toward the half-track.

"Be still. If we don't answer, he'll know something's wrong."

"Yeah, but he won't get here soon enough to help if they start shooting."

"Like I said before, I'm not going to be a prisoner. I'd rather be shot."

"Great. A gung-ho radio man. Just what I need."

"Surrender," Guy shouted again. "Germany *kaput*."

The silence spread between them like a cloud charged with electricity. Despite the cold, sweat trickled down the side of Guy's face. He fought the urge to reach up and wipe it away. Any movement might serve as a signal to fire.

Something rattled the bushes on the hill to their left. He and Stavely knew it had to be Lt. Jones coming back. The Germans didn't know what or who it was. They tensed, their rifles at the ready.

Seconds passed. Guy's heart pounded in his ears.

"*Gib auf, bevor ich schiesse*."

Lt. Jones' order startled the Germans. He stood on the hill above and behind them.

Almost immediately, the enemy soldiers lowered

their weapons to the ground and raised their hands.

"*Hände auf Köpfe*," Lt. Jones barked again.

The Germans put their hands on their heads.

Stavely ran forward to retrieve the enemy weapons. Guy followed more slowly, his gun still aimed at the four men to insure they didn't try anything.

With the prisoners loaded in the half-track, they drove back to "A" Battery's position.

Guy sat up on top with his gun on the Germans. "How did you know?" he asked Lt. Jones, who sat behind him.

"When you didn't answer, I figured something was up. Saw them from up above, so I worked my way around behind them."

"Sure glad you did," Stavely said.

"I'm pretty sure they would have surrendered anyway. If they had been going to shoot, they would have done it right away. Not hesitated."

Guy studied the men's faces. They were tired and dirty, just like the Americans. Regular German Army soldiers hoping to survive the war. Now they would. And someday they'd go home. After this was over.

Lt. Jones turned the prisoners over to the intelligence officer at headquarters for interrogation. Afterward, they'd be sent back to a POW pen.

Guy would have liked to talk to them. Find out what they thought of the war. But they spoke little English and his German was limited to the few words they'd been taught in training.

The thought occurred to him that if he were captured, his mother would be notified but Rosemary would never know what happened to him.

He approached Lt. Jones.

"Lieutenant, will you do me a favor?"

"What is it, Nolan?"

"Will you write someone for me? If I get killed or taken prisoner?"

"Of course, soldier. I can do that."

Chapter 45

Rosemary rehearsed the story she planned to tell about Martha Sue's visit with her friend in North Carolina as the bus followed the twisting turns into Kerrville. She'd stick close to the truth and remain vague on details. Maybe talk of Bobby would dominate the conversation, or even an update on her cousin who had been wounded in France.

The bus pulled up in front of Smitty's Cafe and the driver announced, "End of the line." Workers returning from Camp Forest pushed their way into the aisle and out into the near dark of early evening.

Rosemary stood and pulled her small overnight case from the rack. She was the last one to disembark.

A man came toward her from the cafe. "Rosemary."

"Mr. Hopkins," she exclaimed. He touched the brim of his hat.

Had he been waiting for her? If so, why? "It's good to see you."

"And you." He glanced down at her case and extended his hand. "May I?"

"Of course." She surrendered her luggage to him.

"I came over to meet the last bus, assuming you would be on it."

"That was nice of you, but unnecessary." She turned toward Main Street.

"I know," he said. "I'll walk you home."

"I'm staying with my grandmother," she said, although he already knew that, just like he knew which bus she would be on. "I thought I'd stop in and see Mother first."

"I'm sure she'll be happy to see you."

She sensed that he had something on his mind, but she couldn't very well ask him. It wouldn't be polite.

After crossing at the intersection, she couldn't stand the silence.

"I planned to come by to see you and Mrs. Hopkins while I'm home."

"I'm glad," he stated.

"I'll only be here three days. Then I have to get back to work."

Silent moments passed.

"Mrs. Hopkins and I want you to come over Friday evening for dinner, that is, if you don't have other plans."

"I'd like that." It saved her having to call and arrange a time to go over, and it saved her the embarrassment of having to turn them down for Thanksgiving dinner.

"We took it for granted that you would be eating with your mother and grandmother tomorrow. But we wanted to make sure that you set aside some time to spend with us."

"I wouldn't come home without coming by to see you. I hope you know that." She scanned the sidewalk ahead. "Is Harold coming?"

"No. He couldn't get away. We're hoping he'll be here for Christmas."

She nodded. "Good."

Jack's rather stiff older brother didn't approve of her, and she didn't care for him either.

An awkward silence hung between them. Rosemary concentrated on the sidewalk, knowing she had to be careful of the cracks and glad she didn't have to worry about mud.

"We appreciate your letters." Her father-in-law's voice came out of the darkness.

"Yes, well, I'm sorry I haven't written more. I seem to stay so busy. Working so much." She'd made herself write to them, driven by guilt at not writing from California.

"You didn't write anything about your job. Just that it is similar to what you did at the shipyard."

"Yes, that's right." She hesitated, not wanting to say too much but also not wanting Mr. Hopkins to think she was hiding anything. "Like I told you before, we aren't supposed to say anything about where we work or what we do. I had to sign a bunch of papers swearing I wouldn't talk about it." She turned so she could see his face. "You do understand, don't you?"

His forehead wrinkled into a frown. "Not even what you do? Camp Forest isn't that secretive."

"Well, all I can tell you is that at the shipyard I was welding. And at Clinton Engineering Works I do something similar but not exactly the same." She glanced up to see if he expected more. "I'm just one little person in a very big operation. A big, secret defense plant with guards at the gates and people watching your every move."

"Sounds intriguing."

"No. It's just hard work and long hours."

"And you live right there at the plant?"

"Yes. In a big dormitory." She wished she could tell him more. "I can't even talk to my roommate about my job and she can't tell me about hers."

"That's quite strange."

"What's strange is being home. Back in this small town where you can hardly tell there's a war on at all."

They'd reached her mother's porch. The boardinghouse glowed with lights in almost every window.

"Thanks for walking me home. And thanks for the dinner invitation." She didn't really want him to come inside. She could imagine the chaos as all the boarders gathered for dinner.

"We look forward to having you." He tipped his hat. "Come around six."

She watched him disappear into the night. Except for the physical resemblance, the man was nothing like Jack. The older man's natural serious demeanor now seemed to be even more somber. Perhaps it was facing the holidays without his younger son.

"Who was that?" Her mother stood in the open doorway.

"Mr. Hopkins. He met me at Smitty's and walked me home." She hugged her mother before being pulled into the over-warm house.

The aromas of food as well as the warmth assailed her senses. She shrugged out of her heavy coat.

Rosemary hurried to catch up to her mother as she strode down the hallway and into the dining room. Many of the boarders were already seated and called greetings to her.

"You can sit at Mr. Simpleton's place. He's gone to Guthrie to visit his relatives."

After dinner Rosemary helped her mother wash up the dishes before gathering her things to cross the street to her grandmother's.

"Is that all you brought?" her mother asked as Rosemary picked up her small case.

"I have to go back on Sunday to start a night shift Sunday night. I didn't think I would need much. I can wear what I'm wearing on the bus back."

"I suppose." Her mother eyed the case, so Rosemary held it up for her to get a better look.

"I bought it in Knoxville. I got a bigger one, too. They match."

"Looks expensive."

Rosemary knew where her mother was going. "I got a really good deal on the set." She needed to get away from her mother before she said something she shouldn't.

"You are saving some money, aren't you? This war won't go on forever and these good jobs will disappear once the war's over."

"I'm saving my money, Mother. I just went to Knoxville shopping with a friend, and I decided to buy me some things. Is that all right?"

"Of course, it's all right. You are a grown woman. You can do as you please."

Yes, I can.

Rosemary crossed the dark street and climbed the stairs to her grandmother's porch.

I can do anything I please.

****

Rosemary quite enjoyed the sensible, quiet dinner with her in-laws after the heavy meal the day before. Thankfully, her mother and grandmother had accepted

Martha Sue's supposed trip to North Carolina with few questions.

Mr. Hopkins led her to the living room while his wife brought the coffee tray.

"Make yourself comfortable." He waved toward the overstuffed chair in the corner by the fire.

"Oh, I couldn't take Mrs. Hopkins' chair."

"How many times must we tell you to call us Dad and Mother?"

"I'm sorry." A blush rose from her throat to her cheeks. They'd probably told her a dozen times, but she just couldn't get it in her head.

"It takes time," he said.

Rosemary eased down into the chair he'd indicated. "I guess it's just that Papa died when I was young, so I haven't had a man…a father figure in my life for a long time. And, well, between my mother and grandmother, it just seems strange to call someone else 'Mother.' "

"Then perhaps you should call me Felicia. Would that be easier?" Mrs. Hopkins set the large tray on a low table in front of the sofa.

"I don't know, but I guess I can try…Felicia."

"See, that wasn't so hard." She looked up at her husband who got the message and sat down beside her.

"And I suppose you could call me Horace."

He didn't sound at all enthusiastic, so Rosemary quickly replied, "No. I think I'll try Dad for a while."

That seemed to please him, so she made a mental note to try very hard to remember.

After Felicia had poured each of them a cup of coffee, her in-laws exchanged a look that told Rosemary they had something they wanted to talk to her about but were reluctant to start.

She sipped the hot liquid and patiently waited.

"Rosemary," Mr. Hopkins started.

"Yes, Dad." She smiled at him and, although he seemed pleased, he also looked nervous.

"A while back, we had a visitor."

"Oh?"

"Her name was Miranda Baxter."

Rosemary almost dropped the coffee cup in her lap. Her hands shook violently as she eased it down on the table. She focused on the cup, unable to look at either of them and unable to speak.

"I gather you know her…or at least who she is." Felicia's voice quivered.

"Yes, well, I suppose that makes things a bit easier," Dad stated in his take-charge, principal's tone.

Rosemary looked up. The pain in their faces pulled her together enough to speak. "I'm sorry you had to find out about her."

"We need to know if the story she told us is true."

Rosemary wanted to sink through the floor. She couldn't relive it, not again, not when she'd tried so hard to forgive Jack and move on with her life.

Finally, she managed to say, "What did she tell you?"

Dad recounted the story. Miranda told them Rosemary had been a terrible wife to Jack. He'd fallen in love with Miranda and had left Rosemary. He planned to get a divorce, but Rosemary wouldn't have it. When he was reassigned, Miranda went with him. She said that it broke her heart when he died.

She also said that she didn't have any money, so she wasn't able to come to the funeral. She'd worked and saved her money to be able to come to Kerrville and visit his grave. She also wanted to meet his parents to tell them what happened.

When Dad stopped, they waited for Rosemary to say something.

Felicia discreetly wiped away a tear.

"I loved Jack. And I tried to be a good wife to him." She stopped and took a deep breath. "He didn't like me working. But he was gone so much, on duty. I had to have something to do. When he got time off, he wanted to go out and have a good time. I couldn't always go. Sometimes I was just too tired." She stopped again. "I've tried to figure out what went wrong. What I did." She looked at each of their faces. "I tried. I really did."

"I'm sure you did," Felicia responded.

That little bit of sympathy and understanding went a long way. It gave Rosemary the courage to continue.

"I don't know when he started seeing Miranda. Probably on a weekend when he had a pass, and I had to work. Anyway, I didn't know about it, until…"

She stopped. She couldn't tell his parents that she had caught them in bed together, in their apartment. She couldn't tell them about the hurt or the anger.

She drew in a deep breath to calm her nerves. "Anyway, I found out about them and I left."

"You left?" Dad questioned her story.

"Yes. I told him I couldn't live with him cheating on me."

He glanced at his wife.

"She said he left you."

Rosemary shook her head. "No." She struggled to explain. "I…I packed my things and left." She looked at him. "I stayed with a friend from work. A girlfriend. And then found a place to stay, in a nearby boardinghouse.

"I thought maybe if he cooled off, if he thought about it, that I wouldn't put up with it, that he would come back. Would want me. Would want to get back together."

"But he didn't." Felicia spoke this time. The resignation in her voice told her that the woman understood more than Rosemary ever imagined.

"No."

"Miranda wants his life insurance money." Mr. Hopkins said the words in a flat, matter-of-fact way.

"But she can't…"

His hand went up. "That's what we told her. The money went to you as his beneficiary. Jack never changed it, so we told her that there was nothing we could do."

Rosemary looked down at her hands clasped tightly in her lap. "I thought maybe since he didn't change it…"

"The fact is that he didn't." Mr. Hopkins stood up and walked around the room. Rosemary had seen that look before, when he'd gotten frustrated at Jack's antics. "He could have, but he didn't."

"She said she'd make trouble if she didn't get the money," Felicia said.

"There's nothing she can do," Mr. Hopkins insisted.

"She can cause trouble for Rosemary, and I won't have it."

Felicia's anger surprised Rosemary. She knew her mother-in-law had accepted that she loved Jack and truly grieved for him. But Felicia had become her strongest ally.

"She's not going to cause any trouble," he insisted.

Rosemary thought of her mother. Another scandal would hurt her deeply. She might even lose boarders, again.

"I still have the money. If that's what she wants, then…"

"No. We will not pay her a penny." Mr. Hopkins sank down on the sofa beside his wife. "We have engaged an attorney to deal with her."

Rosemary's mouth flew open. She didn't know how to respond.

"He's in Nashville. We wouldn't use anyone local. He says he will handle it."

"What…what should I do?"

"Don't talk to her," Felicia replied.

"We didn't want to get you involved, but the lawyer insisted. You are Jack's wife, and the beneficiary of his life insurance, so you must agree to have him represent you also."

"Of course. Whatever you say."

"He gave us some papers for you to sign. That is, if you are willing. You could choose to stay completely out of it. We would understand."

"Oh, no, no. I'll sign the papers. And I'll trust you to handle it."

Mr. Hopkins went to his desk and retrieved a large brown envelope. She signed the papers where he indicated, and he put them back where they had been.

"I'll take these to him next week."

He sounded relieved, as if a burden had been lifted from his shoulders.

“Perhaps it is a good thing that place you work has such tight security.”

“Do you think she’d try to bother Rosemary where she works?”

“You know what she was like when she was here. I wouldn’t put anything past her.”

Chapter 46

December 25, 1944

Guy and Lenny huddled inside the half-track to keep warm. They had moved the big radio into the cab with them to preserve the batteries. Then they'd tied down the tarp to keep their other supplies out of the wind and blowing snow that piled up against anything that didn't move.

"I'm gonna write my congressman about not having any heat in this vehicle." Lenny had complained for days.

"Lotta good that'll do."

"I've already complained to the CO."

"And anybody else who would listen."

Lenny shot him an evil eye. "I tell you, my ten-year-old Studebaker has a heater that will get so hot you have to roll down the windows. You'd think they could put some heaters in these vehicles. They're brand new."

"Maybe they didn't think we'd be here this long. Remember how everyone said after we invaded the continent it'd only be a few months and we'd be heading home."

"Yeah. What a load of crap."

Nearby guns blasted away toward targets far out of sight, supposedly near Bastogne where the Krauts had our boys surrounded.

With access to the radio, Guy knew more about what was going on than most of the men. But it still wasn't much.

The German counter-offensive had started over a week ago. Guy had relayed enough frantic messages to know it was something really big, big enough to shake up the brass.

The Krauts had come through the Ardennes Forest, rough terrain in good weather. In winter it seemed ludicrous that they'd even try. And yet, they'd surprised the Americans and had pushed through their lines and far beyond.

The 276th had been 200 miles south, near Metz. But good ol' Georgie Patton had seized the opportunity and ordered them to march north, through bad weather, along narrow mountain roads covered in snow and ice. The way Guy heard it, Patton had bragged that he would come to the rescue and stop the Germans in their tracks.

The order had come down to the 276th to pack up and be ready to leave by midnight on the twentieth. For seventeen hours straight, the unit convoyed north into Luxembourg before stopping for a few hours' rest. From there they pushed on to positions further north where their guns could fire on the Germans plowing through Luxembourg and Belgium.

So here they were, on Christmas day, delivering presents, in the form of artillery shells, to the Germans. Alongside the 215th Field Artillery Battalion with their 155mm howitzers, the 808th Tank Destroyer Battalion, and assault guns from the 42nd and 2nd Cavalry Squadrons, the 276th fired thousands of rounds. With all that fire power the Americans should have destroyed the German army. Yet Hitler's fanatics continued their attack.

Guy and Lenny feared they might freeze to death before morning. Their winter clothes weren't warm enough for the polar temperatures, and despite wearing two pairs of socks, Guy couldn't feel his feet. Yet they did have some kind of shelter from the elements, unlike those poor doughboys huddled in foxholes or behind mounds of snow.

Orders forbidding fires meant they couldn't warm food, much less thaw themselves out. They couldn't even light a K-ration box to melt some snow and warm up the lousy coffee powder included in the packaged meals.

Snuggling the extra radio batteries under their coats, Guy and Lenny hoped to keep them warm enough to stay operable. The one thing they had to be thankful for was that the Germans weren't pounding them, yet.

The radio squawked to life. Guy answered, his gloved hands moving slowly as he flexed his fingers to get the circulation going.

"Get Lieutenant Shaffer," he told Lenny.

Within a few minutes the lieutenant opened the door and stuck his head in. "What is it?"

"Second Cav, sir. They want to talk to you about new orders."

The officer squeezed into their little home and got on the radio. He scribbled notes, then signed off and handed the paper to Guy.

"Contact A & B batteries. Have them fire on these coordinates. And tell C to stand by."

"Yes, sir."

The lieutenant started to leave, then hesitated. “Did you two get your turkey dinners?”

Guy’s stomach responded before he could. “No, sir.”

The officer shook his head. “Sorry, boys.” He looked from Guy to Lenny. “Get those messages sent. Then get over to the service battery and get some chow.”

“Sir, where’d the turkey come from?” asked Lenny.

“General Patton. He sent down orders that all his men should have turkey dinners for Christmas. I don’t know how hot it’ll be, but it’s definitely better than C-rations.”

“Wow!” Guy exclaimed after the officer departed. “Real food.”

“Yeah. Good thing they called for him on the radio or we might not’ve gotten any Christmas dinner.”

Guy’s family back in California would be gathered at his mother’s house exchanging gifts and enjoying homemade food. And Rosemary. Where was she? Back home in Kerrville with her family or working in that defense plant she said went round the clock?

He told Lenny to go get the food for both of them while he took care of the messages. “And try to get back before the coffee gets cold,” he called after his friend.

Between messages he reminded himself to be happy he was still alive, that they hadn’t frozen to death. For someone who’d always lived in relatively warm locales, this freezing cold really got to him. And to think it was only December. What would January and February be like?

Lenny returned with the food and, like the lieutenant said, it was better than C-rations, but not much. It was cold and only served to remind them of what they were missing back home.

It hadn't been too bad when they were moving. As long as they were going somewhere, anywhere, they weren't retreating. Maybe the Germans hadn't quit, like everybody thought they would, but they hadn't beat the Allies, either.

****

December 26, 1944

Rosemary wasn't used to drinking. Even the 3.2 beer made her head buzz. But no one in the lively group noticed. Several men were sipping on "hooch" someone acquired from an undisclosed source, and they were far more intoxicated than Rosemary.

Virgil had invited her to join his friends for a holiday party. Howard and his wife Dorothy lived in the cozy two-bedroom, prefabricated house on what was referred to as "snob" hill. In Oak Ridge, only the higher-ups who were married and had families qualified for such exclusive housing, which made her wonder about Howard's responsibilities at the top-secret project.

Speculating about someone's job could be dangerous, but she couldn't help it. Although Virgil had simply said he worked with Howard, she sensed that he actually worked for Howard. The way Virgil and the others deferred to the man, he must hold some position of authority despite the fact that they were all about the same age.

Gloria, one of the other girls, fed the record player from a stack of records. "I picked this one up today," she announced.

Soothing strains of orchestra music filled the room, followed by a woman's full soprano voice that evoked a strange, exotic mood.

"That bastard Hitler really pulled a fast one." The man's loud comment pulled Rosemary away from the music.

"Yeah, I've been trying to figure out what happened." Virgil's voice slurred just enough to tell Rosemary that he'd had enough of the moonshine. She'd made it plain to him that she didn't like it when he drank too much.

She'd given in to the temptation of having a steady beau after months of persistence on his part. She liked him more than anyone else she'd met at Oak Ridge, and they'd come to an understanding. Nothing serious. Just a little fun. And she had made it very clear that meant limiting physical contact to an occasional kiss or hug. Nothing more. She'd learned her lesson.

She eased closer so she could listen to the talk of war.

They had one of those maps the newspaper printed up to show how the war was going in various parts of the world spread out on the dining table. On this one, bold arrows representing the opposing armies overlaid Europe. A crooked line depicted the front.

"I still don't understand why the paper is calling it the "Battle of the Bulge," Dorothy commented.

"Yeah," another girl chimed in. "It sounds so…I don't know…rude or vulgar. Like someone fighting the middle-aged spread."

Virgil pointed to a spot on the map. "See that. How the line curves out here?" He looked up and caught

Rosemary's gaze. "That's the bulge."

"I still don't get it. The front has never been a straight line."

"No, but..." Howard leaned in and pointed to another spot to the east of the line. "Only a few days ago it was back here."

"Do you think Hitler's going for Antwerp?" another man asked.

Virgil straightened and adjusted his glasses. "That's the logical target, from where this thing started."

"How did it all change so fast? I thought we had the Germans on the run...back to Germany."

"We did. But somehow they managed to mass their troops somewhere in here." Virgil pointed to a spot behind the word "Ardennes." "That's a forest. Rough terrain. Not somewhere anyone would expect an attack."

"What do you mean?"

"It's like they attacked through the Smoky Mountains. In the wintertime, no less."

"Oh." Dorothy studied the map. "Can't we stop them?"

"Sure. We're trying to." Howard put his hand on his wife's shoulder to reassure her. Rosemary envied the couple's affectionate relationship.

"My old outfit, the 30th, is up here somewhere." Virgil pointed to the map again. "And Patton's down here, pushing them from the southern side of the bulge."

Rosemary's ears pricked up. Guy said he was in Patton's army. Reassigned after being wounded. Was he fighting in this new, enormous battle?

"The newspaper said our planes can't fly, 'cause of the weather."

"Yeah. That's got to be making it rough on our boys."

Rosemary glanced out the window. Was Guy out in the freezing cold? And being shot at?

"Hey, I thought we were here for a party." Gloria started another record, this one a more upbeat tune. She pulled her boyfriend, a bespectacled man named Tom, onto the makeshift dance floor in the middle of the living room.

"Gloria's right." Dorothy nudged her husband, who responding by pulling her close and swinging easily into dance mode.

Virgil appeared at Rosemary's elbow. "Care to dance?"

She took his hand, happy to be with a man who'd learned to enjoy dancing. Although still no expert, he'd come a long way. As he swung her around, deftly dodging the couch, she remembered another man and another dance on a makeshift dance floor.

Had it been a year…since she'd danced with Guy? Since Jack's death? What would happen in the next year? Would the war be over? Would Guy survive it?

The music slowed, and Virgil held her close as they swayed to the rhythm.

She couldn't lose anyone else. Virgil was here and safe from the horrors of war. He obviously cared about her. But she'd kept him at a distance. Refused to be anything more than good friends. She'd even warned him she would date other men, if someone asked her.

Was she so afraid of losing someone else? Like her father or Jack? Death was so final, so painful. She couldn't imagine enduring it again. Yet Jack had taught her that there were other kinds of loss, kinds that hurt just as bad. And if she opened herself up, allowed herself to care, then she could get hurt again. Virgil didn't have to get killed to hurt her. If she let him, he could hurt her simply by rejecting her. And she was determined never to let that happen again.

Just like she was determined not to care too much about Guy and what might happen to him. She'd promised herself that she would never let herself care about anyone like that again.

"Why so sad?" The song had ended, and Virgil led her toward the kitchen.

"Oh, I don't know. The holidays, I guess."

"Don't you like the holidays?"

"In a way I do. In another way I don't."

"Well, I don't understand. I love the holidays, from Thanksgiving to Christmas to New Year's."

"But you didn't try to get off so you could go home."

"I'd jump at the chance to go home this time of year. Only it would take so long to get there and back. I'd need at least two weeks. No way was I getting that."

They sat in two kitchen chairs watching the others dance. He leaned in closer. "I know. I'll get you another drink to cheer you up."

She shook her head. "I don't want any. Besides, drinking won't cheer anyone up."

He shrugged. "Then what's wrong?"

"It's just…the last few years…Christmases have been…well, different."

"How so?"

"Well, in '41 Jack and I had just gotten married,

and we knew he was leaving for training after the first of the year. It was exciting and a bit scary." She drew imaginary circles on the table with her finger as the memories swirled in her head. "Then in '42 we were in California. Just the two of us." A bit of a smile crept across her face. "Neither of us had ever been away from home for Christmas before. Jack got drunk." Her smile faded. "Then last Christmas…"

She stopped herself. How could she tell him how miserable she'd been? Virgil didn't know everything that had happened in California, just that Jack had been killed. She wasn't about to go into it now.

He lifted her chin up so she could look into his eyes. "This year's different. You're here with me. And by next year this crazy war will be over."

"Are you sure?" She dropped her gaze to the table where she'd drawn those imaginary circles. "Some people said it would be over this year."

"Yeah, I know." That reminder brought down his cheery mood. He covered her hand with one of his and raised his glass with the other. "Here's to victory, whenever it comes."

She met his gaze then and forced a smile. "Whenever it comes."

Chapter 47

February 6, 1945

Guy climbed to the second floor of the abandoned house. Lt. Jones joined him.

"Do you see a way to get to the attic?" the officer asked.

"I'll look around. See what I can find."

Lt. Jones went through an open doorway into a bedroom. The window faced east, just what they needed.

Guy checked the other rooms. Nothing.

"Can't see over the trees," Lt. Jones commented. "Did you find anything?"

Guy jerked open a door that looked like a closet. Inside, a narrow stairway led upward into blackness.

"Bingo!"

Lt. Jones came over. "That's it." He hesitated a moment. "You get up there. I'll get Stavely."

Guy nodded, then entered the dark, narrow space. He crawled up the steps, swiping at the cobwebs as he went.

His head bumped into the ceiling. After feeling around, he found the latch, unhooked it, and opened the trap door into the attic.

The faintest hint of light shone through the darkness. Guy hauled himself up, wishing he'd brought a flashlight.

His eyes soon adjusted to the lack of light so he could make out odd shapes around him.

Typical attic full of junk.

On either end of the gabled roof, tiny slits of sunlight told him there were windows, the ones they'd seen from the ground below.

He oriented himself and then made his way toward the one he thought faced east.

"Ow!" He banged his shin on something. He shoved it aside and moved a little more cautiously.

He pulled at the wooden shutters nailed over the window until his freezing hands ached. With one last tug, they gave way.

Sunlight flooded through the dirty pane, blinding him for a moment.

Behind him he heard Lt. Jones clambering up the stairs.

"Watch your step," Guy called to the officer.

He could barely see through the filthy glass.

"Move."

Guy turned to see the officer with a chair in his hands. Lt. Jones plunged the leg through the window. Glass shattered and flew in all directions. He hit it twice more to clear the remaining shards.

"Now we can see." Lt. Jones peered out the opening. "Perfect." Then he extracted his binoculars from their case and took a closer look at the opposite ridge.

Peering over the officer's shoulder, Guy saw the dragon's teeth lining the distant hillside. He could make out a couple of structures he guessed were pillboxes.

They were looking at the famous Siegfried Line.

Or at least a small piece of it, the part that stretched across the path of the 80th Division's planned attack.

January had been a slugfest, first in snow and freezing rain and then in mud. Slowly, the Americans had pushed the Germans back to their border.

He'd learned to survive the cold that made his body ache constantly and his feet go numb. As a result, he'd promised himself if he ever got home, he'd never be cold again. That dream of someplace warm and Rosemary in his arms kept him going.

"You and Stavely get the radio. Set it up on the second floor. Then send Stavely up here. He can relay the coordinates down to you."

"Yes, sir."

Guy and Lenny lugged the heavy radio and battery pack up to the second floor. Guy set it up in the bedroom by the window that faced west, to optimize the signal back to the gun battery. Once he made contact, Lenny started calling down the numbers that would translate into targets for the guns.

The three of them worked for over an hour sending coordinates for pre-planned targets.

"Let's get something to eat," Lt. Jones said. "Then I want to go south a ways. See if I can find another spot to use."

Guy followed the other two down to the Jeep, shaking his head. Jones never quit. Never let them rest. The attack would come at dawn. Then all hell would break loose all around them.

Guy took a long drink from his canteen while Lenny unpacked the C Rations.

Remembering Mortain and their lack of food and water, Guy spoke up. "We'd better find some water if we're going to be here a while."

"You're right," Lt. Jones agreed. "You stay here and look around. We'll go check out the other spot."

"Are we staying here for the night?"

"Looks like the best place to me. When the shelling starts in the morning, we can correct fire from the attic."

Guy grabbed his weapon before they drove off. He grinned at his new toy. A grease gun. He'd gotten it off a tanker who showed him how to use it. Now he had enough firepower to defend himself if he had to. He prayed he'd never be in a position where he needed it. But, out on his own like this, he'd be an easy target for a Kraut patrol.

He'd better nose around and find them a water supply, then get upstairs out of sight.

He found a well near the back of the house. He filled his canteen and then reconnoitered the area, just to be sure, before climbing the stairs to the second-floor bedroom.

Taking advantage of a few quiet moments, Guy pulled out the paperback he'd stuffed inside his shirt. Opening it, he slipped out the snapshot of Rosemary. So beautiful, even in this casual photo her friend made. Her pale blue eyes didn't really show up in black and white, but the image was good enough to bring her face into his mind's eye in vivid color.

He unfolded her letter and read through it again, even though he'd practically memorized her words.

"My friend, Drucilla, made this of me so I could send it to you as part of your Christmas package. When we go to Knoxville again, she promised to take me to a photographer where I can have a nice one made. Not

sure how long it will take. Hope you enjoy the book. I remember you reading that western on the train and thought you might like this one."

The colorful cover of the paperback, *Riders of the Purple Sage*, by Zane Grey, looked out of place on the worn, dirty wood floor. He usually picked up dime novels, not written as well as this.

Her package, along with almost a month's worth of mail, had caught up with them in mid-January when they were dug into foot-deep snow and pounding the Germans with artillery fire. When he saw the photo of her, his emotions had almost gotten the best of him. He'd huddled in his foxhole staring at her picture. Later, he'd read the novel in short snatches whenever he could. In the last few days, he'd started through it for the second time, marveling at her insight into what he would like.

He debated whether he wanted to read some more of the book or write to Rosemary. He didn't think he'd brought any blank paper, so he decided to read a few pages while he still had enough light.

The sound of a Jeep outside made him jump to his feet. He slid the photo and letter into the book like a bookmark and stuck it inside his shirt for safekeeping. He'd read some more later if he got the chance.

With the attack coming in the morning, he wouldn't get more than an hour or two of sleep. They'd take turns standing watch, but they all had to stay alert. If the Jerries got wind of the coming attack, they might just attack first.

****

March 1, 1945

Rosemary climbed the steps to her second-floor

dormitory room, tired and hungry. She needed a shower, but she'd promised to meet Drucilla in the cafeteria for a hot meal.

Her friend kept up the outward appearance of cheerfulness, but Rosemary saw the grief eating away beneath the surface. Her husband was still officially missing and presumed dead after his plane went down in October. Yet Drucilla clung to the hope that he'd been picked up by the Japanese and held prisoner.

In the hallway, men workers were carrying beds and generally causing commotion.

"What's going on?" she asked a girl standing in a doorway watching.

"They're adding extra beds. Didn't you see the notice? Every room on this floor will now have three girls instead of two."

Rosemary squeezed by a man trying to get a mattress through a doorway.

When she entered her room, her heart sank. In place of Minnie's single bed stood a bunk bed. Minnie's bed clothes were piled on the bottom bunk. The top one was bare except for a stack of folded sheets, courtesy of Roane-Anderson, the landlord.

Roane-Anderson ran everything in Oak Ridge, from bus lines to housing. They even decided what retail vendors could set up shop and what recreational facilities were available. Laundry, hospital, cafeterias, they controlled everything that affected her life except her job.

Rosemary shut the door behind her and locked it. She took out a dress she'd worn to supper the night before, pulled off the dirty one and slipped into the cleaner dress. She glanced in the mirror and stopped long enough to pin up the loose ends and smear on some lipstick before grabbing her coat. Again, she made her way past the workmen and curious onlookers, down the stairs, and out into the early evening.

She'd deal with the new roommate later. Right now, she needed something to eat.

When Rosemary got within sight of the cafeteria, Martha Sue came running up, giggling. "Rosemary, you'll never guess," she gushed. "Wally wants to take me to New York. Can you believe it?"

"Why would you want to go to New York?" Rosemary asked.

"Well, wouldn't anybody? Besides, it'll be with Wally. Doesn't it sound romantic?"

"I told you a long time ago what I thought of your carrying on with him. So don't tell me anymore. I don't want to know about it."

Martha Sue took her arm and leaned in conspiratorially. "Can I tell you a secret?"

Rosemary stopped and looked her cousin in the eye. "No. I don't want to know any of your secrets."

She noticed a middle-aged man standing nearby. As if on cue, he stepped forward.

"Mrs. Aldridge?"

Martha Sue looked blank for a moment before responding, "Yes?"

"May I speak with you? Privately?"

"I was just going," Rosemary said, hoping she could get away from her cousin.

Martha Sue caught her arm. "No. Stay." Then she turned to the man. "Who are you anyway? And what do you want?"

The man flashed his identification badge. "I'm Ed

Bailey." He looked from Martha Sue to Rosemary as if trying to decide how much to say. At Oak Ridge most people didn't ask questions beyond "Where are you from?"

He glanced around. "Can we go somewhere a little more private?"

"Sure. How about over there?" Martha Sue pointed to a spot in the shadow of a nearby building.

He nodded and then held his hand out directing them to go first.

Martha Sue glanced at Rosemary. "Come on. You're going, too. I don't trust this guy."

Once out of earshot of others, a clearly irate Martha Sue asked, "Okay. What's up? What's this all about?"

"I am Wallace Monroe's supervisor. I've come to advise you to stop seeing him…immediately."

"What? Stop seeing Wally. Just like that? Why should I?"

"For your own good, Mrs. Aldridge." The man was dead serious.

"Martha Sue, I think you better listen to him," Rosemary said.

"Why? Because you never liked Wally?"

"No. Because this sounds serious and you don't want to get into trouble."

"You should listen to your friend," the man added.

Martha Sue turned to him. "Why? What's wrong? Is Wally in trouble or something?"

"I can't say any more than I have. I shouldn't even be talking to you." He glanced around again.

Rosemary followed his gaze. Was anybody watching them?

"Just do as I say. Don't see him again. Don't call him or talk to him." He looked over his shoulder and then walked past them, crossed the street, and melted into the crowd outside the cafeteria.

"Well, I never." Martha Sue stood watching him.

"It sounds serious. Really serious."

"But Wally wouldn't do anything…well, not anything real bad."

"You probably don't know what he's been up to. And you don't want to. If he's in trouble, you don't want to be any part of it."

They resumed their walk toward the cafeteria.

Finally, Martha Sue spoke. "This place is so strange."

"What do you mean?"

"Last week, they took one of the guys where I work out of the plant. These men, they just came in, right to his workstation, and took him out."

"Where did they take him?"

"That's just it. Nobody knows. He just disappeared. Never came back." She paused. "Someone said security took him."

"Everybody watches everybody around here." Rosemary thought of the men who'd given her the envelopes when she first arrived. How many other people had envelopes like those?

"Yeah." Martha Sue stopped abruptly. "Oh, Rosemary. Do you think Wally is in real trouble?"

"I don't know. Sure sounds like it." She touched her cousin's arm. "If not for your sake, for the family's sake, please stay away from him, like the man said."

Martha Sue nodded. She didn't promise, but at least she was thinking about it.

They'd been lectured from the beginning that this place was top secret and that they could get in serious trouble if they talked about anything. And by serious, they meant jail time.

"My friend, Ada, got a little tipsy at one of the dances. She started running her mouth, asking a lot of questions. Her date took her home. Later she told me the security people came to see her. They told her in no uncertain terms that she'd better stop asking questions or she'd lose her job. Maybe more."

Rosemary waited for her cousin to reply before continuing. "So, you'd better do what the man said. Or you'll be out of a job."

Martha Sue stuck her chin up defiantly as she walked. "Maybe Wally's worth it. Maybe I don't care about this old job."

"And maybe you don't care about your husband, or his family, much less your family. Aunt Louise would be mortified if you ran off to New York with him and lost your job."

"Oh, Mother's such a ninny."

Rosemary stopped. "Fine. If that's the way you think, then you can stay away from me. I don't want any part of any of it."

"What?"

"You heard me." Rosemary turned and hurried away. She had her own troubles. She didn't need to take on Martha Sue's.

For now, she would try to help Drucilla work through her grief.

Chapter 48

Rosemary's new roommate added a new level of tension to her life. She and Minnie had gotten along swell, and thanks to their rotating work schedules, each had some time to themselves in their shared room. With Aggie Carlson in the mix, no one had the room to themselves.

Aggie came from northern Michigan. She'd traveled south when her fiancé was in training at Ft. Oglethorpe, Georgia. Both of them liked the warmer climate so, when he went overseas, she decided to find work nearby. Somehow, she'd heard of the Clinton Engineering Works and took the job because she would be able to live in on-site housing.

Rosemary and Minnie didn't have a chance to voice their complaints about the crowded room. Aggie did it for them. She complained about everything, from the lack of closet space to the distance to the bathroom to the rules about no cooking in the rooms.

At first Rosemary tried to be helpful with suggestions for ways Aggie could adapt to her new living situation. But it soon became evident that Aggie had her opinion and her way of doing things. It seemed to both Rosemary and Minnie that nothing suited Aggie, so they stopped trying to be helpful.

Rosemary took to reading in the lounge downstairs or she trekked to the nearby bowling alley with a book in hand. The noisy alley had a cheerful atmosphere that appealed to her.

One evening a group of soldiers came in and took a lane nearby. One in particular reminded her of Jack. Something about the way he moved, the way he interacted with the other soldiers.

The familiar ache filled her chest. Yet this time it wasn't as intense. It was more of a sadness as she wondered where they would be if he'd lived. Would he have gone overseas? Would she have come here to work, or would she have stayed in San Francisco? What would their future have looked like?

When she thought about the future, she wasn't sure what she wanted anymore. She knew she didn't want to continue living in a tiny dormitory room with two other girls. And she didn't want to go back to Kerrville and live with her mother or her grandmother.

She didn't mind the work, but after the war, her job would go to a man. She'd heard enough comments by her male coworkers to understand that fact. No, they wouldn't want women inspecting pipes after the war.

Everyone expected a young woman like her to get married and raise a family. Problem was Rosemary wasn't sure that was what she wanted. After her marriage to Jack, her miscarriage, and his betrayal, she feared trying again.

Maybe after the war was over, she'd go to Knoxville or Nashville and start over. Maybe something would come along. For now, she barely had time to think much less make plans.

****

"I hoped I'd find you here." Virgil stood over her, smiling. With all the noise in the bowling alley, she hadn't heard him approach.

"Hello." She slipped her bookmark into place and closed her book. She'd been dodging him for weeks, using every excuse she could think of to avoid him.

He slid into the seat across from her and settled his elbows on the table. "Still hiding from your new roommate?"

His comment startled Rosemary until she remembered telling one of his friends a few days before. "Yeah. Just can't take her nagging. I've put in for a transfer to another room, but they say it's near impossible."

"Suppose I told you that I know of the perfect room for you?"

Rosemary's suspicions perked up. She met his gaze. "What do you mean?"

"I mean that a friend of mine and his wife are looking for someone to move into their spare room. And you were the first one I thought of."

"What…" She ran his words through her brain. "Who's looking for someone?"

"Ida and Steve Winston. You met them at the holiday party. Remember?"

"I met so many people that night. I don't really remember."

"She's a blonde, nice looking, from California. He's darker. Okay guy. Kinda funny."

Rosemary fought the urge to roll her eyes. She'd never figure out who they were from Virgil's descriptions.

"Okay. I'm sure I'd remember if I met them again. So, what's this about them having a spare room?"

"Well, they live in a house up on the Ridge."

"A house?" Rosemary wondered who these people were and how they rated living in an actual house. Only the higher-ups lived in houses.

"Yeah. Somehow they qualified for one early on, even though they don't have any children. Now Roane-Anderson is telling them that they either have to find a roommate for the spare room or move out."

Rosemary nodded. Leave it to Roane-Anderson to mess with people's lives. "Yeah, I understand. Just like them moving extra people into the dorm rooms."

"This place is growing so fast they can't find places to put everybody."

"You'd think some of them could live in Clinton? Or even in Knoxville?"

"Have you ever seen the stream of cars coming into this place?"

She nodded again. "When we went to Knoxville shopping, I couldn't believe all the traffic on these crooked country roads." She wanted to add that this place sure must be making something big, but she knew better than to make any such remark. Someone might overhear and she might get in trouble.

"Shall I tell Ida you're interested? Steve's leaving it up to her to decide on who lives with them."

She hesitated. These were Virgil's friends, which meant she'd see more of him. Yet, she'd actually toyed with the idea of quitting just to get away from Aggie. Virgil's idea sounded like a Godsend. Surely she could manage their relationship, especially if she had her own room.

"Sure, I'll talk to her. It might be nice to live in a house and have a little privacy."

"Swell. I'll set it up."

"Tell them I can't pay much more than I'm paying now. I'm not one of those high paid management types, you know."

"I know. You can work that out with them. I just know they're desperate to find someone, so they won't have to move."

She wondered how long they'd been looking. Maybe the wife didn't want one of his friends moving in. She couldn't blame her. With the odd hours everyone worked around here, the wife probably preferred having a woman around rather than another man.

Chapter 49

March 6, 1945

"Climb aboard the lead M-7 and keep me posted," Lt. Jones ordered Guy as the 4th Armored Division resumed their march.

Guy grabbed a walkie-talkie and, as ordered, scrambled aboard just before the armored gun jerked into forward motion.

Their days had become hectic. In February they had remained in the same positions for days while their guns pounded multiple targets, but, since the first of March, the 276th had been on the move. Assigned to the 4th Armored Division's Combat Command A, they pushed northeast toward the Rhine in one of the famous armored division's breakthrough pushes.

"Keep your eyes peeled for Germans," the gun commander, Sgt. Bill Nussbaum, advised.

"You expecting snipers?" Guy asked.

"Snipers, *panzerfausts*, or anything else they could throw at us."

That didn't ease Guy's mind. Moving so fast in a long convoy like this, the Krauts could easily fire on them and then run.

They drove through villages that American artillery had shelled only days before, which gave Guy a good look at the destructive power of 105mm and 155mm shells.

"What if they want to surrender?"

The sergeant shrugged. "Not our problem."

"We wouldn't just by-pass them, would we?"

"The 4th will take care of them. They'll leave a detail to guard them until the infantry catches up."

An explosion ahead brought the M-7 to a halt.

Guy listened to the report coming in on the onboard radio. A tank up ahead ran over a mine. Blew off a track.

"They'll push it to the side so the crew can fix it. We'll go around."

"What if there are more mines?" Guy asked.

"Probably are. If the Krauts buried one, they buried several alongside the road covering their retreat." The sergeant smiled. "Don't worry. The guys up front'll watch for 'em. That's why we try to stay in the tracks of the tank in front of us."

Guy nodded.

Soon they were back underway, through more villages turned to rubble and roads in rough but passable condition.

Guy was amazed at how quickly an armored column could travel. How far could they go without refueling? A hundred miles or more? By early afternoon they were closing in on their destination—Coblenz. Beyond the city the mighty Rhine River created a more formidable barrier than the Siegfried Line, protecting the inner fortress of Germany.

White sheets hung from the windows of many buildings as a symbol of surrender. Few people were visible, and those who were stared at the column of vehicles with a mixture of sadness and anger.

Up ahead Guy heard a shrill whistle and catcalls from the men on the lead tank. Two buxom, blonde women stood in a doorway, smiling and waving. The men on the M-7 added to the raucous fun as they drew nearer the flirting females.

All eyes were on the women, including Guy's.

Bullets whizzed by their heads, accompanied by the cracking sound of machine-gun fire.

Guy hit the metal deck. Shots pinged off the armor. Someone cried out.

Returning fire from the onboard 50-caliber machine gun spewed forth in deafening bursts.

Guy covered his ears and craned his neck upward to see where the enemy fire was coming from.

Rounds plastered the second floor of the building opposite where the women had stood. Had they been a decoy?

The tank behind them swiveled its turret and let loose a thunderous blast.

The second floor of the offending structure exploded.

Machine-gun fire continued from more than one direction.

A second blast from the tank brought the entire second floor crashing down.

Then silence.

Guy looked around. The women were gone.

A man, only inches from Guy, held tight to his bleeding arm while another soldier wrapped a bandage around it.

"Is he hurt bad?" Guy asked.

"Naw. Just a scratch."

The soldier's gaze went to the rear, so Guy turned

to follow it.

Infantry soldiers ran toward them from somewhere back down the line, their weapons ready. They swarmed around either side, going house to house in search of any additional hostiles.

The M-7 jerked. The column moved forward again.

"Shouldn't we stop…until we know it's safe?" Guy asked.

The gun commander replied, "No. The infantry will flush them out. Our orders are to proceed to the Rhine." He motioned toward the leading tanks. "We'll push on through. Let the ones behind mop up."

Guy didn't like it. He'd been out ahead before but only scouting for observation positions. Never had he been just three vehicles back from the lead tank driving into enemy territory in plain sight, way out ahead of everybody else.

"Guess that's why they call it "spearhead."

The sergeant patted him on the shoulder and grinned. "Don't worry. This is what these guys do. We're lucky to be along for the ride."

Guy nodded. They'd been lucky that Kraut with the machine gun didn't kill them all. But he didn't feel lucky to be here. While the bullets were flying, his training and instincts had kicked in. Now the fear crept back into his soul. His eyes darted from one building to the next, half expecting another burst of fire.

Not today, he repeated to himself. Not today.

Chapter 50

Her fork pierced a potato boiling in the pot, which told Rosemary that they were ready to drain and mash. She put a lid on the pan and set it aside.

She would mash them as soon as Ida and Steve got home.

The table was set, and everything was ready to put on the table.

Rosemary sighed and allowed herself to ease down into one of the straight wooden chairs. She'd missed cooking. Not that she was very good, but she could make a simple meal like this.

She'd almost forgotten the luxury of living in a real house with a real kitchen. Not since the tiny apartment she and Jack had rented in San Francisco had she had a kitchen to cook in.

Back then she'd dreamed of the day when they'd have their own house, a home full of love and children.

Now she was afraid to dream. Afraid to wish for something that could be snatched away.

Her finger ran across the chip on the plate before her. It brought back memories, not of Jack and their little place, but of the night she'd spent in Oakland…with Guy…in his friend's apartment.

She had no illusions about her relationship with Guy. It had been one fleeting moment in time, when both of them had been lonely and desperate for companionship.

They might be exchanging letters now, to keep his spirits up while he faced life-threatening danger. But reality would come soon enough. The war would be over, he'd come back, and both their lives would go back to normal.

What was normal for her? Not living in Kerrville. She had no idea what she'd do.

The door pushed open, bringing with it a chill breeze.

Rosemary stood as Ida hurried in, lowering her umbrella. Steve followed and quickly shut the door before the dampness could overcome the heat generated by the warm stove.

"Supper's done," Rosemary announced to her housemates. "I just have to mash the potatoes and get everything on the table."

"Oh, Rosemary. You're a dear," Ida cried.

"Smells fabulous." Steve smiled his approval as he shrugged out of his coat.

"You two wash up while I get it all ready."

Ida beamed. "Rosemary, you've outdone yourself."

"It's nothing. Just a simple meal."

"But so much work."

"Not really. I enjoyed it. Having a real kitchen to cook in and all."

By the time Steve and Ida returned, she had everything on the table.

"You two sit down," Steve said. "I'm starving."

"I just need to fill the glasses," Rosemary said.

"I'll get them. You sit." Ida filled each glass from the tap and set one in front of her husband, who grabbed it and took a long drink.

Rosemary watched as her landlords dug into the hot food. Neither complained.

Steve took a second helping of potatoes, having devoured his first. "You'll have to show Ida how to mash potatoes. She can't seem to get the hang of it." He smiled and winked at his wife as he spoke.

Ida smiled back. "Maybe not, but you still eat them."

"I know better than to complain."

Rosemary liked them. They seemed genuinely happy together and they'd welcomed her into their home. She hoped someday to have something similar.

"Virgil asked about you," Steve announced.

"We'll have to ask him over for a meal. Don't you think so?"

Ida looked at her, expecting an answer, as if it were up to Rosemary to decide. "I don't know. If you like."

Ida put her fork down. "He really likes you, you know. I thought you liked him."

Rosemary met her gaze. "I do. I like him." Then she glanced away. How could she explain that she didn't like him in the way they thought? Not romantically.

"Okay then. Just figure out when we're all off at the same time, and we'll have him over for dinner." Steve caught his wife's gaze and some silent communication went on between them.

"You have my schedule, unless they want me to work extra hours." Rosemary returned her attention to her food and forced herself to eat. She had to go in to work later so she needed her nourishment. She'd think about Virgil another time.

When they'd finished, Rosemary started stacking

up the dishes.

"Don't you dare," Ida said. "You cooked, so it's only right that I should clean up."

"I don't mind, really."

"Nonsense. You have to get ready for work."

Rosemary nodded. Despite her dislike for the night shift, she didn't have a choice. At the K-25 plant they rotated shifts so every other week she worked a different shift. In the dormitory she'd had trouble sleeping in the daytime, where some activity was going on all the time. Today, in this quiet house, she'd actually slept.

"Virgil's a great guy," Ida said. "And he's got a great future ahead of him."

Rosemary knew that Virgil worked with Steve. And although she didn't know exactly what he did, she knew he did something highly technical. He'd been pulled out of the infantry because of his education. And his circle of friends seemed to know a lot more about what went on at Oak Ridge than any of the girls she'd met. Was that what Ida meant? About Virgil's future?

"He'd make a great husband for the right girl," Ida continued.

"I'm not looking for a husband right now." Rosemary wanted to make her position clear.

"You will be, some day. I'm just saying that you should keep him in mind."

Rosemary forced herself to smile and nod to her new friend. "I'd better get ready for work."

As she dressed, she tried to think of Virgil. She pictured him as a husband, a lover, but another face encroached on her thoughts. Guy. For some reason she couldn't get Guy out of her mind.

It was useless. He might not make it back. He might come back all messed up, unable to function in a normal life, like her father.

She pushed the thoughts away and forced herself to focus on getting to work, on trudging through the rain and mud to the bus stop.

The only downside to living with Steve and Ida was that no board sidewalks had been built on the winding streets lined with single family homes. So she made her way down the hill to the main street in her trusty boots. She stood at the bus stop, under a streetlight, in the rain. It would be daylight when she got off. Maybe by then the rain would have stopped, and the sun would be shining.

The damp chill penetrated her dungarees below her raincoat and above the mud-covered rain boots. She'd elected to wear the pants instead of putting on a dress to trudge through the rain and mud. No one would see her if she came straight home after work.

The local bus pulled to a stop. She climbed aboard for the short trip to the central bus shelter where she'd get her bus out to the K-25 plant site. She didn't worry about tracking mud onto the bus because there was no way to avoid it. Until it stopped raining and the sun shone for a while, mud covered everything and everyone.

For now, she just wanted to work, to eat, and to sleep. And a little less mud.

****

March 24, 1945

Guy paced back and forth beside the Jeep. He didn't dare go far. Not when the Rhine River ran only a hundred yards ahead. He couldn't seem to settle down.

Since early March, the 276th had fought their way south with the 4th Armored Division clearing out German resistance west of the Rhine. They'd fired thousands of rounds while moving from one position to another. With little need for the radio out ahead, Guy had spent most of his time with the gun battery. And the constant pounding of the guns had worn his nerves to a frazzle.

Rumors filtered down the line that General Patton had ordered the engineers to build a pontoon bridge across the Rhine. The debate among the men shifted from when to where the Americans would cross.

Officially they were already across, further north at Remagen, where the Krauts failed to destroy a railroad bridge before the American Army arrived. Capturing an intact bridge across the Rhine was a major coup for the Allies.

General Patton was not one to be outdone. He'd build his own bridge.

To protect the engineers on the river, the guns of the 276th had fired all day and into the night. So no one had slept.

The M-7 ahead pulled forward, so Guy scrambled aboard the Jeep just as Lenny put it in gear.

Guy stood up when the river came in sight.

"Man. Look at that. I didn't expect it to be so big," Guy said.

"Yeah. They say it's swift, too. Not like the Moselle."

Guy laughed. "You're right about that. Can't imagine trying to wade across this one."

He thought of the many rivers and streams they'd crossed as they pushed their way across Europe. By far, this was the biggest.

"You better sit down," Lenny called as he wrestled the Jeep down the bank already worn into ruts by the tanks and trucks and assorted vehicles that had gone before them.

"I'm okay. I'm holding on." Guy held tight to the windshield. "I wanna see this." The breeze off the water calmed him and brought to mind forgotten images of San Francisco Bay.

Lenny maneuvered in the long line onto the bridge. The vehicle bounced on the treads, and Guy grabbed the seat back to steady himself.

Better sit down.

Before he could sit, something hit the Jeep from the rear, jarring him so hard he lost his balance.

He clutched the seat as his weight shifted sideways, wrenching his leg. For a terrifying second he stared down into the dark water between the pontoons.

Lenny grabbed his arm. "Geez, Nolan."

Guy's breath hitched.

He pulled himself back into the Jeep.

With his butt securely in the seat and his heart pounding, Guy repeated his mantra, "Not today."

Lenny focused on keeping in the tracks, glancing over at Guy.

"I'm okay."

"Don't scare me like that again. I thought sure you were a goner."

Guy shook his head. "Naw."

His white-knuckled grip on the seat relaxed a bit as he consciously forced his breathing into a slow, steady rhythm.

He gazed across the churning water.

Had that been a warning? Was his time running out? Did the end await beyond the water in the heart of Fortress Germany?

Chapter 51

March 30, 1945, Good Friday

Rosemary ducked under the awning at Smitty's Cafe to escape the steady rain. She tightened her scarf, dreading the walk to her grandmother's without an umbrella. At least she hadn't taken off the heavy cardigan she wore underneath her raincoat, despite the stuffiness of the overcrowded bus. It would keep her warm in the cold drizzle that made it feel more like January than late March.

Her small overnight case was only a little larger than the purse slung over her shoulder. She'd packed light. She planned to stay the weekend, just long enough to pay a visit to her in-laws and attend Easter services with her family before heading back to work. The sweater had been a lucky afterthought, which she'd worn so she wouldn't have to try to stuff it into her tiny bag.

Along the way Rosemary thought of her mother's letter saying Grandmother Kerr wanted to gather as much of her family as she could for Easter this year. She hadn't said why. Mother said her cousin, Milton, who'd been badly wounded, might be able to come home. And Frances was iffy. Her sister had rarely come home over the years. Oh, she'd had plenty of legitimate excuses, the farm, the children, but Rosemary believed bad memories kept her away.

She climbed the steps to her grandmother's house, ablaze with lights, and knocked at the door.

Grandmother Kerr answered with a broad smile. "I thought it was about time you were getting here." She waved Rosemary in. "Come into the parlor. I have a surprise for you."

Rosemary shucked her coat and scarf, then hung them on the hall tree, atop several others. She followed her grandmother into the well-lit parlor.

"Rosemary." Her sister, Frances, rushed to greet her.

The two sisters hugged. Tears pricked Rosemary's eyes and her throat tightened as she fought to hold back the tears.

"How long's it been?" Frances asked. "Since before you went off with Jack?"

"Yes. I guess so. That was in early '42, so it's been…two, no, two and a half years."

Frances nodded as she turned and waved for several others to come forward. "You remember my husband, Lee."

Rosemary shook his hand and stared at the vaguely familiar face. He'd both aged and gained weight since she last saw him. "So good to see you again."

He smiled and nodded shyly before backing away.

"And here's Cole, our oldest," Frances continued nudging the younger version of his father forward. He stuck out his hand, so Rosemary shook it as if the ten-ish boy was a grown man.

"And finally, little Nancy Lynn."

Rosemary saw both herself and her sister in the young girl's eager smile. "Aren't you lovely," she commented, which brought a pleased blush to the young face.

"Come sit over here near the fire," Grandmother instructed. "You can dry out while we all get caught up."

"I didn't expect all of you," Rosemary said as she sank into the offered chair. "I don't really know what I expected. A quiet family get-together, I guess."

"That's why I wanted you to come," her mother spoke up. "Frances said she might be able to be here for Easter, and I thought you two ought to see each other."

"You were right," Frances chimed in.

"How did you manage? With the farm and all?"

"Oh, Lee got a neighbor to watch the place. We can only stay until Sunday. We'll have to get back."

"We drove down this mornin'," Lee said. "Took near four hours. The old truck broke down. Luckily there was a station nearby and we got her runnin' again."

"Lee's worried about driving back, so he wants to get an early start right after church on Sunday," Frances said.

"Don't want to take any chances. Not with the children along."

"Well, you're here now, and that's all that counts," Grandmother Kerr concluded.

After a light supper, Rosemary sat and talked with her sister and her mother. They caught up on all the happenings on the Ransom farm and the latest news from their brother, Bobby.

After explaining she had to get up early the next morning, their mother headed back to the boardinghouse and Frances put her children to bed.

Rosemary settled into the side room, exhausted after working a full shift the night before and then traveling what felt like all day by bus.

Nevertheless, she was glad she'd come. The reunion with Frances had meant more to her than she'd expected.

Chapter 52

April 4, 1945

Lt. Jones strode toward the Jeep. "Get in. And follow those tanks."

Lenny jumped into the driver's seat and fired up the Jeep. Guy climbed into the back as the lieutenant got in up front.

They fell in behind the last tank.

"Where we goin'?" Lenny asked.

"To check something out."

Lenny glanced over his shoulder and Guy shrugged.

Apparently, the officer didn't want to say. Lt. Jones got that way sometimes. Refused to share information until he decided it was time.

They'd gone several miles in silence when the officer finally opened up.

"I overheard an interesting radio report at the CP. Seems some of our guys found something. Decided we'd go along to check it out."

"What kind of something?" Guy asked.

"Not real sure. Some kind of camp."

Guy decided against asking more questions. Presumably they would be there soon, and he'd have his answers.

A short time later the tank stopped on the road.

"Pull over there, off the road."

"What about mines?" Lenny asked.

Lt. Jones glared at him.

"Yes, sir," Lenny ground out.

Guy would have climbed out, just to be on the safe side, but Lenny pulled over so fast, Guy was thrown back into his seat.

They drove alongside the whole column of tanks stopped on the road. Some of the tankers had climbed down and were walking.

"Just park it here. We'll walk the rest of the way."

"Should we bring the radio?" Guy asked.

"Just the small one." He caught Guy's gaze. "For now."

They walked up the road, staying close to the tanks.

A large German house sitting back from the road came into view, but the tankers were looking across the road from the villa. A few steps closer and a horrible stench swept over them like a cloud.

Guy pulled out his handkerchief and covered his nose and mouth. "What's that smell?"

Lenny shook his head and coughed.

Guy, Lenny, and Lt. Jones pushed their way through a group of soldiers gaping at something.

"Oh, my God!" Guy couldn't believe his eyes.

"Jesus!" Lt. Jones exclaimed.

A pile of rag-clad corpses, so thin their bones protruded through their skin, were stacked almost head high before them. Bullet holes in their heads told of a violent end.

Guy heard a gag and turned toward the sound, his own stomach clenched tight. Lenny pushed through the other GIs and doubled over vomiting.

Fearing he couldn't keep his own bile down, Guy followed Lenny.

"Who would do such a thing?" Guy asked to no one in particular.

A tanker responded, "Go on back that way. It gets worse."

How could it get worse?

They wandered through a rugged camp. More bodies lay where they'd fallen, yellow Stars of David sewn onto their ragged uniforms, all with gunshot wounds.

Lt. Jones stopped a fellow officer. "What happened here?"

"Seems the guards shot everyone who couldn't make the march back to the main camp." The officer jerked his thumb over his shoulder toward a group of Americans. "They found a few still alive."

"Main camp?"

"Yeah. This is just a small sub-camp of a bigger camp. Much bigger, from what the survivors said. Called Buchenwald."

"Where's that?" Guy asked through the handkerchief he held over his mouth and nose.

"Forty miles up the road."

"What's this place called?" Lt. Jones asked.

"Ohrdruf."

"Are they all Jews?" Lenny asked, wiping his mouth with the back of his hand.

"Yeah. Most of 'em." the officer said. "I gotta get back. We put in a call for medics."

"This needs to go up the chain of command." Lt. Jones' voice cracked with emotion. "They need to know about this and the other camp."

"Don't worry. It already has."

Guy looked around. "This is unreal." He removed the handkerchief long enough to blow his nose. The overwhelming smell reminded him of Normandy, only ten times worse. "How could they let them get in this kind of shape? And then just shoot them because they couldn't walk?"

"I saw something in the *Stars & Stripes* a while back. About concentration camps. But it didn't sound like it was this bad." Tears streamed down Lenny's face. "I mean…how?"

Lt. Jones walked toward a group of Americans a short distance away.

Guy stood motionless. He wished he hadn't come along. Wished he'd never seen this place.

He'd seen plenty of dead soldiers from both sides. He had killed at least two Germans, that he knew for sure. Maybe there were more.

He'd seen the results of the artillery's shelling. Towns reduced to rubble.

Death. Destruction.

But that had all been part of the war, the fighting.

This was different. This was inhumane. These were helpless human beings tortured and murdered.

How could he tell the others? The people back home, even his fellow soldiers, wouldn't believe it.

Chapter 53

The same day Lt. Jones had taken them to see the Ohrdruf camp, the 276th received orders to detach from the 4th Armored Division and move a day's drive south to support the 11th Armored Division. Most of the battalion never saw the horrors Guy had seen. They were lucky.

Spring days flew by. The weather warmed and the landscape turned a luscious green. They rolled from town to town subduing any remnants of the German military. Pockets of resistance continued to appear. No one knew why they continued to fight. They were clearly beat. Yet some refused to surrender.

Rumors flew about Hitler and his henchmen. An article in the *Stars and Stripes* reported that Hitler was dead although nothing could be confirmed.

Ironically, they'd heard on Armed Forces Radio about Roosevelt's death. Like most of the other young men, Guy could barely remember a time when Roosevelt hadn't been President. Now, so near the end of the war in Europe, the leader of the United States had succumbed to a cerebral hemorrhage. A man named Truman succeeded to the Presidency, yet no one seemed to know much about their new President.

If the rumors about Hitler's death were true, then two of the opposing leaders in this long, destructive war had both died before it was over, like so many of their soldiers.

No one wanted to be killed so near the end, so the Americans became cautious. More and more, they used artillery to destroy the enemy rather than risk the lives of GIs unnecessarily.

They headed toward the German-Austrian border toward the city of Linz, Austria, on the banks of the Danube River.

Lt. Jones pointed out their position on his map. "We're here." His finger traced the lines that represented the borders. "This is the Austrian border, and this is the Czechoslovakian border."

Guy studied the map. "So we're still in Germany."

Lt. Jones nodded.

The radio squawked to life. Guy quickly answered.

"Lieutenant, they want us to report back. Seems the Krauts are kicking up a fuss in some town up ahead."

They made their way to the battalion CP where they were quickly briefed on the action. Near a town called Wegscheid, what was left of the German Army had decided to make a stand.

Guy shook his head in disbelief. "What do we have to do to convince them they're beat?"

"Guess we'll have to kill 'em all," Lenny said, with little enthusiasm. "I think I'd rather live."

"Me, too," Guy agreed.

Earlier that day Guy had written a cheerful letter to Rosemary. In it he'd predicted the war would be over by April 30, 1945, less than two weeks away. "It has to be," he'd said. "They don't have anywhere else to run. And there can't be many left who aren't dead or captured."

He wondered if his bold prediction was premature,

especially after they observed the concentration of fire coming from the small town and nearby cemetery. Lt. Jones directed the guns of the 276th to pound away at the relentless enemy.

A firefight broke out near their observation post.

Lt. Jones shouted, "Pull back," as small arms fire zinged around them.

Guy ran for the Jeep, carrying the radio. Lenny followed with the battery.

Amid the noise and confusion, Guy didn't see Lenny get hit. His friend stumbled up behind him and leaned against the Jeep, bright red seeping down the back of his uniform.

Lt. Jones appeared at Guy's elbow. "Get him in the Jeep. We'll take him to the medics."

Guy broke out his first-aid pack as the lieutenant swung the Jeep around. Holding the bandage firm against Lenny's wound, Guy wasn't sure what to say to his friend.

"We've got you. We're almost there," he shouted in Lenny's ear.

Lenny nodded but didn't answer.

Within minutes they'd reached the aid station and handed Lenny over to the medics.

"Will he be all right?" Guy asked.

The medic shrugged and focused on treating Lenny.

"Come on, Nolan." Lt. Jones waved for Guy to get in the Jeep. As they drove back toward the guns, he added, "Hell of a time to get hit, when it's almost over."

Guy just nodded. He had a sinking feeling in his gut, but he fought it. Lenny couldn't die. Not now.

Later, when they drove into the rubble that had

once been a quaint little town, very few German soldiers remained alive. They'd made their final stand with complete disregard for the poor civilians.

Although Guy knew these people had been complicit in starting the war, he couldn't help but feel sorry for them. All their material possessions had been destroyed and their young men were dead because they followed that madman, Hitler.

Lt. Jones spoke with another officer, then approached Guy. "Nolan," he called.

Guy turned around. "Sir. I've almost got everything packed."

The officer had a grim look on his face. "The latest report on casualties just came in. Stavely didn't make it."

"Lenny? But…" The news hit him like a punch to the gut.

"I know. I thought he had a chance." The officer looked away, clearly fighting his own emotions.

"Damn! It's not fair. It's gonna be over any day now."

It seemed so pointless for Lenny to die now, so near the end, for him to have made it through everything, all the misery and destruction, and not see the end. He would never go home.

The battalion continued to move. They crossed into Austria on May 1st. Then, repeating their pattern of being reassigned, orders came down for the 276th to pull back and rejoin the 4th Armored Division in Germany.

With the 4th, they advanced into Czechoslovakia, where the citizens received them as liberating heroes. People lined the roads leading to Strakonice, where the

276th took up positions but did not fire.

Uncertainty ruled the day. Everyone knew the war was almost over, yet they still had orders to liberate Prague.

Guy was in the radio tent when a message came in that the German Army had surrendered. He notified the colonel, who insisted it not be announced until it was official. So when the word "official" came over the airways, Guy jumped up and whooped for joy.

Word spread like wildfire.

All the men left their posts to join in the celebration, sharing grins and hearty handshakes and enthusiastic bear hugs. Stashes of booze emerged from their hiding places and everyone drank toast after toast to "Victory."

Guy finally sank onto the stool by the radio, sipping on some truly awful schnapps someone had poured in his cup. He would have refused the drink on any other day, but this day was special. He had survived, he'd be going home, back to the States, back to Rosemary.

He smiled at the thought of the letter he would write to her. The one telling her that he was alive. The only letter he was supposed to write to her. His promise not to write her had evaporated with her first letter to him. Still this letter was important. It signaled a change in their relationship. At least he hoped it did. He hoped it opened the door for him to court her.

Hell. He hoped it opened the door for him to marry her.

She'd had plenty of time to mourn Jack, to come to terms with his betrayal and his death. No one in that small town of hers could criticize her for moving on with her life. Not now. Not a year and a half later.

She'd have to explain him, of course. How they'd met. Why they'd started writing.

All they had to do was tell the truth. And leave out that one night. The one no one needed to know about but them. Their own private, personal secret that he could never forget. A night he hoped she couldn't forget either.

****

Rosemary's stomach growled. She checked her watch, waiting for her supervisor to signal for her lunch break.

"Okay, Rosemary. You can go now."

She smiled as she hurried past the middle-aged man who'd had infinite patience with her when she'd first wandered into the vast plant unable to find her workstation.

In the cafeteria line she surveyed the day's offerings, looking for something filling that she could afford. She'd overslept this morning and hadn't made her usual sandwich. Thankfully she didn't have to starve.

The loudspeaker blared another announcement. This time, everyone fell silent.

"…effective immediately. I repeat, the German Army has surrendered effective immediately."

Rosemary gasped. Had she heard right?

A spontaneous cheer went up.

Faces around her quickly went from shock to grins and giggles. Someone slapped her on the back. Others shook her hand.

The announcer continued, but Rosemary couldn't focus. Her thoughts raced.

Guy.

It was over. And Guy had survived.

At least he was still alive about two weeks ago, when he wrote his last letter. He'd said they were moving across Germany. He couldn't say exactly where, but she could guess from the newspaper reports.

How soon would he come home?

Her stomach reminded her why she was here. She gobbled down her lunch. Despite all the excitement, no one said they didn't have to go back to work.

No. Whatever they were working on would continue. They were still at war in the Pacific. They still had to beat the Japs.

Would they surrender, too? Would the whole thing be over soon?

Oh, God, she hoped so.

Chapter 54

Solemn-faced, German POWs stared at him from behind the barbed wire fence. Guy avoided eye contact. Not that he feared meeting their gazes. He just preferred to remain aloof. He didn't want any form of personal contact with the defeated men. They were still the enemy and they had to pay the price for the war they'd started. The war they'd lost.

Thankfully, it wasn't up to him what happened to these men. His only responsibility was to stand guard, to ensure that none of them left the enclosure.

Others were responsible for sorting them out, for deciding which ones would cause trouble and which ones were harmless. And that decision would determine which ones went to prison and which ones went to work, rebuilding. At least that's how it had been explained to him, and who was he to question it?

At the end of his watch, Guy made his way back to the eight-man tent he called home where he found a card game in progress.

"Wanna sit in?" Dick asked. "I'm tapped out."

"Naw. Not now," Guy responded. "I just want to rest for a while."

He picked up the letter he'd received the day before, intending to reread it. Amos Campbell had written from a hospital in England. His old buddy said he'd been wounded after they crossed the Roer River but didn't say how bad he'd been hurt. If the Army was sending him back to the States, then it had to have been pretty bad.

Guy stretched out on his cot and read through the short letter wondering if he'd missed something.

After a few minutes Dick left the game and sat on the neighboring cot.

"Is that from your girl?"

Guy looked up. "No. From a friend of mine. Why?"

"You wrote her, didn't you? After the Germans surrendered?"

"Sure. But it hasn't been long enough to hear back yet."

Dick nodded. "I guess." He studied his hands for a minute. "It's just…I haven't heard anything from Amy in a while. And I just wondered if she thinks she doesn't have to write me anymore…now that we're not fighting, I mean."

Guy thought about Dick's concerns. They almost matched his own. Now that he wasn't in danger, now that he'd survived, would Rosemary still write to him?

"It's not like we were engaged, or anything like that," Dick continued. "Still I was hoping…"

Someone stuck his head into the tent. "You guys need to get out here and hear this."

Guy and Dick joined most of the battalion gathered around their commanding officer, who stood in the back of a Jeep.

"You men. Get closer." The colonel held up a paper. "I'll speak loudly so everyone can hear."

"What's going on?" Guy muttered to the soldier next to him.

"Maybe they've changed the points again," the man speculated.

"Hold it down. Hold it down." The colonel waved his arms.

Lt. Jones and another officer stood in front of the colonel's Jeep and helped to quiet the soldiers crowded around.

The senior officer began reading the document. "The 276th Armored Field Artillery Battalion will be relieved of occupation duty effective immediately."

That brought a loud cheer and caused the colonel to stop until they settled down again.

Guy listened intently as the man read on. "…move to another location in Germany to await transportation to the Zone of the Interior."

"Where?"

"What's that?"

"It means the United States."

"We're going home!" someone shouted.

A cheer went up. Everyone laughed and shouted and jumped up and down with glee.

"Hold on, men. Settle down." The officer shouted over the din. "Please settle down so we can finish."

The other officers took their cue and called the men to attention.

"Thank you," the colonel said to his subordinates. "Now I can finish." He looked down at the papers to find his place again. "Yes, here we are. 'Await transportation to the Zone of the Interior where the battalion will commence training in preparation for the invasion of Japan.' "

Shocked silence met his words.

"Japan," Guy whispered. He'd just read an article

in the *Stars & Stripes* about a battle waging over there in a place called Okinawa. Even from the watered-down version the Army put out, he could tell it wasn't going well. The Navy and the Marines, fighting alongside the Army, had been at it since April and the "fanatic" Japanese kept fighting.

Men around him muttered and whispered their displeasure. Guy barely heard the order to dismiss.

The officer drove off, and Guy stood among the disheartened men. No one seemed to know what to do.

"At least we get to go home first," someone nearby said.

"Yeah. Go home and say goodbye…again."

****

In the quiet of her room, Rosemary took out the stack of letters from Guy. On top was the last one, the one he'd written after Germany surrendered. She pulled the single sheet of paper out of its envelope and read it again.

Dear Rosemary,

By now you have heard that the Germans have surrendered. So this is my official letter telling you that I have survived. Remember on the train when you told me I could write to you after it was over to let you know I was still alive? So now you know. I hope you are glad. And I hope you still want to write to me.

No one has told us where we go from here. And I guess now I can tell you where I am. In Czecoslovakia. Hope I spelled that right…

A knock at the front door broke her concentration.

Ida had invited Virgil to supper…again. Not that Rosemary minded. She liked Virgil. But Ida couldn't get it through her head that Rosemary wasn't interested in anything serious.

She folded the letter and slipped it back into its envelope, wondering, "Where do we go from here?"

She'd been thinking about that ever since she got the letter. And she still didn't know. She hadn't written him back because she didn't know what to tell him. But she needed to write him. Maybe she'd just be cheerful and happy that he was still alive and ignore any question about the future.

Someone tapped on her door.

"Yes?"

"Virgil's here. And supper's almost ready." Sweet Ida. She meant well.

"I'll be right there."

****

Guy managed to stay above deck for a good portion of the trip back across the Atlantic. Like many others, he hated being confined in the crowded, stifling conditions below. So when the ship sailed passed the Statue of Liberty into New York harbor, he crawled out from his spot beneath a stairway to gaze at the majestic lady. He hadn't expected to be so emotional, returning home to his own country, to his native soil. Yet he was.

After a year in foreign countries dreaming of this day, it somehow seemed unreal.

"She's a beautiful sight, isn't she?"

Guy turned to see Jacob, a friend from the 276th, beside him at the rail.

"Sure is."

They stood there in silence, the wind swirling around them.

"Hey, Nolan. I've been looking for you."

Guy recognized the voice. Dick Fairchild strode up

and slapped him on the back. "Told you we'd make it home."

"Yep. You sure did." Guy couldn't contain his grin. This must be what happiness feels like.

Dick slid his arm around Guy's shoulders. "You still interested in flying to California?"

"Sure, if you can arrange it." Guy doubted his bragging friend could pull off a flight across the country. Suited him fine if he couldn't. Guy had plans to make a detour to Tennessee on his way home. He'd surprise Rosemary. He ached to see her, to hold her. And he hoped she felt the same.

By afternoon they had disembarked at Piermont, New York, and loaded on trucks for Camp Shanks. Sitting beside him, Dick spouted off about how the 276th had departed from this same place just over a year ago.

"I was with the 30th Division when I went over. February '44. Out of Boston."

"Man, you've been gone five or six months longer than us. I never knew that."

Guy laughed. "Yeah. Seems like a lifetime ago."

The next morning Guy had his thirty-day furlough in hand when Dick caught up with him.

"I got in touch with my cousin, you know, the one I told you about," Dick said.

Guy nodded.

"He says he can get us on a flight to San Francisco. Well, not exactly San Francisco, but close. Anyway, we have to be there in two hours, or we'll miss the flight."

Guy stared at him in disbelief.

"Well, are you interested or not?"

"Sure, I guess." His plans for a side trip to

Tennessee would have to wait for the return journey. “How long will it take to get there?”

“We’ll be in California by tomorrow. Way faster than by train.”

He could go home, see his mother and the rest of the family, and then come back early to see Rosemary before reporting to Ft. Bragg, North Carolina. The flight would save him at least three days’ travel time.

“Okay.” Guy grinned at his friend. “Let’s get going.”

Chapter 55

Guy handed his bag to the porter and followed him to a waiting taxicab. As the returning hero, he would arrive home in style, even though he could easily walk from the station.

He'd sent his mother a telegram to let her know he was coming.

Sitting back in the seat, he imagined his excited mother welcoming him home. His sisters and his nephews and niece would all celebrate his safe return.

He gave the cabby a generous tip. The man thanked him profusely and shook his hand.

Guy strode up the walk, then hesitated. Should he go right in? Or should he knock? Better knock. He'd been gone a long time and almost felt like a stranger.

While he stood on the little porch wondering what to do, a car pulled up and a beautiful young lady got out. As she rounded the hood, he recognized his younger sister, Harriet, all grown up.

"Hi, Sis!"

She hurried up the walk. "Guy. You made it home." She smiled tentatively. "You look…well, different."

Guy grinned. "It's been a long time." He reached out and gave her a little hug, hoping that would warm her up to him.

She stiffened. "Yes. It has."

She turned and opened the front door.

"Mother," she called. "Guess who's here."

Guy followed her inside. The house felt familiar but different somehow. He glanced around, then heard footsteps coming from the back. His mother emerged from the kitchen.

Her face lit up. "Guy."

He didn't wait for her to come to him. He hurried to reach her and wrapped his arms around her, feeling her softness and breathing in her familiar scent of powder and liniment. "Mother," he managed through overwhelming emotions.

She pulled away but kept hold of his hand. "Son…you…you look so…"

"Different," Harriet injected. "That's what I said."

He glanced from his mother to his sister. Both smiled, but not as widely as he'd hoped. He'd imagined more excitement. Instead, his mother swiped at tears.

He squeezed her hand. "I'm okay. More than okay, now."

"Yes, yes. Your telegram. It came late yesterday. I…I didn't expect you so soon."

"Friend of mine got us on a plane. We flew into a field outside of San Francisco. Took the train from there."

Harriet took his arm and led him into the parlor. "Come. Sit down."

He sat on the sofa and eagerly looked around.

New curtains. A new chair. And lamps.

"The place looks nice."

His mother eased into a chair opposite him. "Yes. We've kind of spruced the place up." She clasped her hands together. "How was your trip?"

Harriet plopped down beside him. “Did you fly in one of those big bombers?”

“More like a big transport.” Remembering the long flight sitting on the floor made him want to rub his backside. “Not so comfortable, but it took a lot less time than coming by train.”

“Harriet, go call Lorene.” His mother’s gaze darted from Harriet back to Guy. “Or is she working today?”

“Not today,” Harriet answered. She jumped up and grabbed the telephone sitting on a nearby table. Guy glanced at his mother, who wore her familiar worried look.

She met his gaze. “Oh, I’m sorry. You must be hungry.” She got up. “I’ll see if I can find you something in the kitchen.”

She hurried out.

His eating had been pretty sporadic, what with standing in long lines on the ship for the two meals they served and then hurrying to make the flight. He’d grabbed a sandwich on one of their stops but hadn’t had anything since, except coffee.

He got up to follow his mother to the kitchen when Harriet stopped him.

“Lorene will be over later. She’s feeding the kids.”

“Okay.” He noticed a new picture on the wall. “Looks like Mother’s been fixing the place up.”

“Don’t you think it needed it?”

“Guy,” his mother called from the kitchen, “I’ve got something for you to eat.”

Guy nodded to his sister and made his way down the dim hallway to the kitchen, where his mother had set out some food.

“I just pulled some things out of the icebox. Cold

chicken. Cheese." She set a plate with slices of bread on the table. "Do you want milk to drink?"

"No. Water will be fine." He pulled out the chair and sat down.

His mother hovered nearby, wringing her hands. "I…uh, I was going to fix a big meal…for tonight. That way everybody can come over and eat."

"That sounds swell," he told her as he assembled a make-do sandwich.

"How's Tad?" he asked. When she frowned, he clarified. "Wasn't he sick?"

"Oh, Yes. Tad. He's fine." She looked over at Harriet, who stood in the doorway. "That was last winter when he was sick. I'd almost forgotten."

"Well, glad he's okay." Guy took a big bite. The cold chicken tasted good.

"It's kind of strange, you being here and all." Harriet snitched a piece of cheese.

"Harriet, why don't you take Guy's bag and put it in my room."

"Your room?"

"Yes, well." She wrung her hands again. "You see I made your old room into a sewing room. And it's got so much stacked up in there. I will stay in with Harriet."

Guy looked from his mother to Harriet. "Well…okay."

After Guy finished eating, he lay down for a while. He didn't intend to fall asleep, but he did.

Female voices woke him. He went down to the kitchen.

His mother looked up when he came in. "Oh, did we wake you?"

"It's okay. I didn't mean to fall asleep."

His sister, Lorene, stepped forward and gave him a hug. "Glad to have you home," she said.

He nodded. "Good to be here."

He looked around. "Something smells good."

"That's the chicken. It's all I could get on short notice. I'm baking it with some vegetables. I thought we'd eat supper about six. That'll give Lorene time to round up the children."

"That's all right. I'll just putter around for a while."

"You do that, son."

"Maybe I'll round up ol' Buster and take him for a walk."

"Oh," his mother gasped.

"What?"

"I thought I wrote you. Buster was killed. A few months back. Truck hit him over on the main road."

"What was he doing over there?"

She turned back to the stove. "Don't know. He'd taken to roaming around."

The sweet old dog who'd gotten him through the difficult move from Arkansas had been his only friend when he first came to California.

Guy walked back through the house and out onto the front porch, determined not to let another loss ruin the beautiful day. His first day home. He'd dreamed of this day. Yet it felt strange to be here. Surreal even. Maybe because he'd traveled so far in such a short time.

California hadn't been touched by the war, so unlike Germany and France and England. The whole of Europe was in ruins while everything here appeared to be thriving.

He wandered around the side toward the old

garage. He'd left his ham radio set in the back, all boxed up. For some reason he wanted to see it. Maybe that would bring back some good memories.

****

His mother outdid herself with the supper she served. She kept apologizing and making excuses, but he assured her it was delicious. He couldn't remember his last home-cooked meal.

Lorene's children had grown so much that Guy hardly recognized them. They, on the other hand, stared at him in awe.

Harriet went out and returned with a Marine. The newly minted second lieutenant wore his dress uniform, which put Guy's plain khaki to shame.

Guy saluted the officer upon his arrival, which embarrassed the young man who insisted that they dispense with any formalities.

"You are the one I should be saluting," he stated. "You've been in combat. And survived unscathed."

"Not entirely unscathed," Guy corrected him. "I was wounded last summer. In France."

"I see the Purple Heart amongst all those medals. Quite impressive."

Guy felt himself blushing. "Not really. Just did my job."

"Guy was a radio operator," Harriet said.

"Oh, I see. Then you didn't see much action?"

"Well, some." Guy didn't want to get into discussing his combat experiences. Most he'd rather forget. "I spent some time with our FO."

Harriet frowned.

"Forward observer," the Marine explained. "Interesting," he nodded, looking at Guy with even more respect.

"Have you gotten your orders yet?" Guy asked. He knew not to ask where he might be going.

"I report to Camp Pendleton next week. From there..." The Marine shrugged.

Guy nodded his understanding. Everyone knew the war with Japan had to be won, and now that Hitler had been defeated, all the American resources would be directed toward Japan.

After supper Guy followed Harriet and her Marine out to the car parked in front of the house so he could smoke without disturbing his mother. When the Marine headed for the driver's seat, Guy commented, "Nice car you have here."

The Marine grinned. "Not mine. Harriet's. She's been chauffeuring me around."

Guy glanced at his sister as she climbed into the passenger seat and gave him a little wave.

Warning bells went off. Harriet's car. How could Harriet afford a car? Had she gone to work, and nobody mentioned it?

Back inside, his mother fussed over little Lucy. He turned to Lorene.

"Where's Harriet working these days?"

His question surprised her. "Uh...well, she's not working exactly."

"Harriet's doing volunteer work. With the USO," his mother said from across the room.

"We got a letter from Henry yesterday," Lorene said. "All the way from Australia."

He recognized the quick change of subject but let it go for now. Something was off, and he would get to the bottom of it soon enough.

"How's ol' Henry doing? Recovered from his wounds yet?"

His mother's face lit up at the mention of her favorite son. "Henry's doing fine. He's been out of the hospital for months now. Good as new."

"Yes," Lorene continued. "He says he's stationed near Melbourne helping to train the Australians. Expects to remain over there for a while."

"I know that relieves a lot of your worry." He directed his remark toward his mother. "Is he still seeing that girl?" Guy knew his brother well enough to know he was involved with someone and had probably arranged to stay in Australia to be near the ladies.

His mother's face went red with anger. "That hussy. I told him to get rid of her. Those girls just want to latch on to American boys so they can come over here. That's what she's up to, you mark my word."

Guy fought to contain his smile at his mother's reaction. She'd always loved Henry the most and his girlfriends never gained her approval. None were good enough for her Henry. Some things never changed.

He glanced at Lorene, who gave him a hard look. Apparently, he'd brought up something that she'd rather not talk about.

Guy took his cue and walked over to his two nephews, who were deeply enthralled in a game of cards.

"What are you playing?" he asked.

"Go fish," the oldest one responded without looking up.

"Can I join in?"

That got both their attentions. They didn't expect him to show any interest in them.

"Sure," Tad answered.

As he sat down, Guy noticed the scar on the boy's arm. That must have been from the accident.

"Is that what put you in the hospital?" Guy asked.

Tad looked up. "That? Naw. Broke that arm a couple of years ago." He played a card.

"I thought you'd been in the hospital."

"Oh, that wasn't nothing," Little Ben answered.

Tad poked his brother. "It was not. I was sick. Had a fever and spent the night at the hospital so's they could get it down. That's all it was."

"It's your turn," Little Ben prodded Guy.

"Oh, yeah. Sure." Guy played a card. "Then it wasn't serious. No operation?"

Tad shook his head and frowned. "Ma made it out to be a big deal, but it wasn't. I got over it okay."

"I'm glad you did," Guy smiled at the boy. He wasn't surprised his mother had exaggerated Tad's illness. It made him wonder what else she'd stretched the truth about.

Chapter 56

Guy didn't sleep well. He kept thinking about getting back east to see Rosemary. He debated sending her a telegram but thought better of it. He didn't want to scare her off before he even saw her. Or give her a chance to make some excuse not to see him.

Somewhere along the line he'd decided to ask Rosemary to marry him. Ever since they'd been told they were coming back to the States, he'd thought of nothing but seeing her again. She was all he ever wanted. And if he asked her to marry him, if she agreed, if they were engaged, he'd know she would wait for him.

A ring.

If he had a ring when he proposed to her, maybe, just maybe, she'd accept. He wouldn't push for marriage right away, not unless she wanted to. But if she had a ring, then she'd wait for him. He'd know for sure she'd be waiting. No more of this uncertainty. He couldn't face the Japs not knowing.

As soon as he heard someone up and stirring, Guy got up and dressed. He'd talk to his mother after breakfast. Then he could go to the bank and on to Mr. Cary's jewelry store.

That meant he had to tell his mother about Rosemary. No details. Just keep it simple. But he'd have to tell her something, since he wanted to withdraw so much money. The rest he'd leave with her. While he went overseas…again.

He'd have to tell her about that, too. About his orders to go to Japan. He only had a few days at home. No point in putting off telling her. After all, she was his mother.

In the hallway, Guy noticed the door to Harriet's room standing ajar. He hesitated, knowing he shouldn't, before he pushed it open and stepped inside.

He glanced around. So many clothes. A rod stretched across one end of the room creating a make-shift closet. It hung heavy with all kinds of dresses and blouses and coats and whatever else women hung in closets. Shoe boxes were neatly lined up beneath the hanging clothes. A half-open drawer overflowed with lingerie.

Where did Harriet get so many clothes? Why did she need them?

Then it hit him. How could she afford them? Especially with rationing. The black market had to be expensive.

He stepped further into the room and picked up the dress draped across the foot of the bed. His mother hadn't made this. It was store bought and expensive.

He stumbled on a shoe sticking out from under the unmade, rollaway bed.

Coming to his senses, he hurried out of the room before he got caught snooping. And before he could process the implications of what he'd seen.

Downstairs, Harriet sat at the kitchen table drinking coffee while his mother stood by the stove. Guy didn't usually pay much attention to his younger sister, but this morning he perused her pretty, pale blue dress. It looked brand new.

"There you are. We didn't expect you up so early," his mother commented.

"I didn't sleep well."

"Sorry to hear it," Harriet said as she rose from her chair. "Hate to leave in a rush, but I have an appointment." She brushed close enough for Guy to inhale her expensive-smelling perfume and made her way out saying, "See you later," over her shoulder.

"Go ahead and sit down. I'll fix you some eggs."

Guy did as his mother told him, like he had all his life. Even when he disagreed with her, he'd done what she wanted.

Soon a plate piled high with scrambled eggs and toast sat in front of him. He dug in. The image of Rosemary sitting across from him devouring a similar plate of scrambled eggs made him smile.

His mother ran water into the sink to wash up the breakfast dishes. "Do you know how long you will be able to stay?" she asked.

"No. Not sure." He took another bite and tried to figure out how to tell her about Rosemary. "I have to go all the way back to North Carolina. That's where we have to report after our leave. Ft. Bragg."

"Oh…so you won't be stationed nearby?"

"Nope." He hesitated. Might as well take the plunge. "I want to stop and see someone on my way back. Someone I met on the train…when I left."

She didn't look up from the dishes. "That's nice."

"And I won't be able to fly back. That was just a lucky thing, getting that plane ride. I'll have to take the train back, all the way across the country. Probably take a week."

"Too bad your brothers can't come home."

"Yeah." Typical for his mother to think of them. "It's not likely Henry would be able to get leave to come all the way from Australia."

"Yes, I know. Only I still wish I could see him. Talk some sense into him."

Something told him there was more to the story about Henry, but he didn't ask. "And Wilson?"

"I don't know. His ship is somewhere in the Pacific. Probably out there where they've been fighting."

"Haven't heard from either of them in a long time." He should write to his brothers while he was home. He'd been as remiss as they had.

He finished off his breakfast, gathered up the dishes, and took them to the sink for her to wash.

"Thanks, Mom. That was real good. I've had so many powdered eggs, I'd almost forgotten what fresh ones taste like."

She looked up and smiled, that sweet, rare smile he'd longed for growing up. She'd done her best, he supposed. She just hadn't been very happy.

"I'll finish up here. You go on into the front room."

He had turned away before he remembered what he wanted to ask her. So he turned back to her. "Mom, I need to get my bank book."

The plate slipped from her soapy hands and clunked against the sink. "What?"

"My bank book. I want to go down to the bank and withdraw some money."

She grabbed the dish towel and wiped her hands as she slowly turned to face him. Something was off about her expression; he just couldn't tell what.

"Why do you need money? We've got everything here we need."

"There's something I want to buy."

"Buy?" She paused. "Are you going back to San Francisco?"

"Oh, no. What I want, I can get here in town." He didn't know how to explain to her. Why would he buy a ring for a girl he barely knew? A girl who might or might not accept his proposal.

Her gaze roamed the room as she wrung her hands together. He sensed her unease.

"Go ahead and finish the dishes. I just want to go down to the bank sometime this morning."

"Uh…okay. I…I'll get it directly." She turned back and plunged her hands into the dishwater.

Guy left the room but the feeling that something was wrong gnawed at him. Why did it upset her when he asked for his bank book?

Other things ran through his mind. Harriett's automobile. All those clothes. Tad's exaggerated illness. He needed to ask his mother how much she'd spent during his absence.

In a few minutes his mother came out of the kitchen and headed upstairs, her face in that stony expression he remembered, the one that said she didn't want to do something.

He followed her instead of waiting for her to return. All his instincts told him something was wrong.

He reached her bedroom just as she took something out of her bureau drawer. She held it for a moment, then handed the little book to Guy.

Drawing a deep breath for strength, he took the book and opened it.

He flipped the pages, scanned the entries of deposits and withdrawals. His eyes zeroed in on the running balance that decreased gradually. Several pages in, he saw a larger withdrawal. The date was last year in the fall. Long before Tad's hospitalization.

He looked up and met his mother's stony gaze. No explanation there.

He returned his focus to the bank book, flipping pages until he came to the end…to the current balance. His heart sank.

"What happened to my money? Where did it go?"

"It's expensive to live these days."

"But…" His throat tightened so he couldn't speak, couldn't think what to say.

"With the war, everything costs more. And you were all gone. What did you think Harriet and I were living on? With Ben gone, Lorene was barely getting by. Tad was sick…"

"But all of it?" Anger flared. "I had saved over a thousand dollars before I went into the Army." Breathing raggedly, he couldn't keep still, couldn't look at her.

"I knew you needed money to live on. I didn't mind that. But spending all of it…all the money I sent home while I was overseas and all I'd saved." He spun around to face her.

She wrung her hands and pursed her lips the way she'd done when his father had yelled at her for spending so much all those years ago in Arkansas. A stabbing pain, reminiscent of when his father died, overcame him.

He looked down at the little book again.

He couldn't trust her. Never again could he trust

her about anything.

His mind raced. Take her name off the account. Stop the allotment. Maybe he had enough back pay to get a ring. Not as nice a one as he'd hoped, but maybe…

"You're just like your father," his mother scolded, her voice bitter and angry. "He never wanted us to have anything. Always grubbing and saving for some future pipe dream. Expanding the store. Adding a new line of merchandise. He never thought of me or my needs."

Her face flushed in anger, her voice screeched. "Well, I decided Harriet's going to have more than I did. She's going to dress nice and go places where she can meet a nice young man and marry well. Someone who'll take care of her, support her, buy her anything she wants."

Guy stared at his mother. He hadn't heard her rave like this in years. Oh, she'd complained constantly about not having enough money. About not being able to buy things. But this…this was more, much more.

"What about me? What about my plans?"

"Your plans? What plans do you have? You never cared about anything but your precious radio set. You went off to work in Oakland when I needed someone around here to help me."

"Help you? I gave you money, all the time. And I came on weekends to do all kinds of chores around here. Where were the others? What about them?"

"How dare you talk about your brothers! Henry joined the Marines as soon as the war started. He wanted to defend his country just like his brother. What did you do? You worked in Oakland. So you could make money off the war."

"I joined up, didn't I?"

"After you were shamed into it. You didn't want to go, did you?"

She'd hit a nerve. He hadn't wanted to go. He could have avoided it, used his deferment at the shipyard to stay out. But so many people had treated him like a coward, like he was afraid to go and fight. They'd asked why a healthy young man hadn't joined up. He didn't even have the medical excuse some had.

So he'd done it. He'd joined the Army. And now he had memories he struggled to forget.

Coming home had kept him going. Had it been worth it? Did he really have anything to come home to?

His own pain spurred him to inflict pain on her. "You will be happy to know that I have to go back. To Japan." He stared at her. "That's why I'm home. My outfit is going to invade Japan."

He'd hoped that announcement would upset her, pull her out of her anger and make her remember that he was her son, that he wasn't out of it yet, that he might be killed.

"Good!" Pure hatred flared in her eyes. "Maybe you won't come back this time."

"You'd like that, wouldn't you? Then you could live on my life insurance and wouldn't have to put up with me. Since you obviously don't want me around. You don't want anything from me but money." He shook his head trying to tamp down the hurt. She'd always been shallow and selfish. "Just like you treated Pop." With that memory, a deep sadness enveloped him.

"If that's so, then it's because you're just like him. Never let me forget for a minute what you are doing for me. Like I'm supposed to grovel and be grateful for the least little thing. I deserve better. I worked hard, too. Raised you kids, practically on my own, while he worked in that store around the clock. Always helping others instead of taking care of his own."

"You never did without what you needed."

"What I needed? How do you know what I needed?"

He obviously wasn't going to get anywhere arguing with her. She would never admit she'd done anything wrong.

He shook his head at her. What could he say?

He turned and left the room. Down the stairs and out the front door, his mind racing.

He'd go to the bank. Close the account.

As soon as he got to Ft. Bragg, he'd stop the allotment. It would take a while to stop, so they'd have enough to live on until Harriet could get a job. For that matter, his mother could get a job. For once in her life she'd have to support herself. Because he wasn't going to. Never again.

Chapter 57

The argument with his mother spread a blanket of unease over the remainder of his time in California. Whatever she told Harriet and Lorene made him out the villain. None of them saw his side of it.

She'd spent practically all his money. Money he'd not only planned to use to buy Rosemary a ring but also to start up a business after the war. It was his future. Now he had no future. Nothing to offer Rosemary. Nothing but his love.

After closing his bank account, he went to Cary's Jewelry Store to look at engagement rings. He thought they were a little pricy, but he trusted Mr. Cary more than some jeweler in Oakland or San Francisco.

"I can't afford anything expensive, but I want it to be special."

"I understand." The older man pulled out a tray of rings. Most were tiny diamonds. Some in clusters.

"I don't know." Guy didn't see anything that suited him.

"Are you set on diamonds?"

"I guess. I hadn't really thought of anything else. I mean, isn't that what you normally get for an engagement ring?"

"Well, not always. You said you wanted something special, and for some, that means something different."

Guy thought about Rosemary. She'd already been

married once. And all she'd had was a plain gold band. No fancy diamond. That's what he'd wanted to buy her. A big flashy diamond. But now, that was out of the question.

"What do you have in mind?"

"Well, I have some other stones. A pretty sapphire. An emerald, but that's probably too expensive for you." He turned around and pulled out a drawer from inside his big safe. He placed another velvet tray on the counter.

Guy's gaze roamed the tray.

Mr. Cary pointed to the first row. "Now these should be well within your price range."

"What about that one on the top left?" The pale blue shimmered like Rosemary's eyes.

"Well, that one…" Mr. Cary hesitated. He gently ran his finger over the ring, and then picked it up. He gazed into the soft blue stone accented by darker blue ones on each side. "This is special."

"What is it?"

Mr. Cary held it out and Guy took it. "A lovely aquamarine with sapphire accents."

It was even prettier up close. The way the light caught in the stone sparkling, shining, captivating, just like Rosemary's eyes.

"You like it, don't you?"

"Oh, yes. It's beautiful." Guy hesitated, then handed the ring back to Mr. Cary. "But I'm sure I can't afford it."

"This ring is special for more reasons than one. I bought it at an estate sale. It's older than most of my rings. It was specially made for its owner. A lovely woman." He looked up at Guy. "And it is part of a set. I promised myself that I would only sell it as a set, since they were made together with matching stones."

"What do you mean…a set?"

"There are matching earrings."

"Oh. Then I'm sure I can't afford it."

"What if I sold it to you for exactly what I paid for it?"

"Why would you do that?"

"Like I said, I've had it for years. And no one has expressed interest in it before."

Guy shook his head. "I'd love to have it. But I know I can't afford it."

Mr. Cary named a price for both the ring and earrings. Guy couldn't believe it.

"Are you sure?"

"Yes, I'm sure."

"Will you hold it for me for say…two days?"

"Of course. It'll be right here waiting for you."

"And can it be sized, in case it doesn't fit?"

"Any competent jeweler can size it. If you'll bring the young lady in, I'll be happy to do it myself. No charge."

"Thank you, Mr. Cary. Trouble is, she's all the way across the country."

Guy's brain whizzed through the calculations. How much he needed for train fare, for a place to stay in Tennessee, and extra money to take Rosemary out on the town. He had the back pay he'd gotten when they'd landed and the money from the bank account.

The only thing he owned was his ham radio. Before he went off to the Army, his longtime friend, Mr. Johanski, had offered to buy the radio. Guy hoped the man was still interested.

As it turned out, Guy sold the radio set for more than he expected to get. Enough to cover most of the cost of the ring.

His conscience finally got the best of him. He went to his mother and apologized to her. He gave her a little money out of the back pay. The gesture seemed to placate her a little.

He also fixed the gutter on the back of the house, and after moving his radio set and equipment out, cleaned the garage.

He made a point to go on a drive with Harriet, ironically in the car his money had bought. He told her things were going to change, so she might as well start looking for a job.

"I knew it was too good to last," she commented.

"Then why haven't you gone to work before now?"

"Mother wouldn't have it. She's the one who wanted to buy all that stuff…the clothes, the furniture. Even this car."

Relieved that his sister sounded more practical than he'd expected, it was still hard for him to believe her. No one could buy that many clothes if she didn't want them.

"Is it true? That you've got to go and invade Japan?"

"Yes." He didn't like to think about it.

"I'm so sorry. Marty says the invasion of Japan will be worse than the fight on Okinawa." She glanced at Guy's frowning face. "You remember Marty, the marine lieutenant who came to dinner."

"Sure. I remember." He started not to ask but plunged ahead since he probably wouldn't get another chance. "You serious about him?"

"I don't know…maybe. I like him a lot, but he's leaving. He doesn't know anything official, yet, but he's pretty sure he'll be going to Japan, too."

"Yeah. He's probably right."

"So we'll wait. See what happens."

Guy looked out the window, debating what to say to her. Doubting that she cared much what he did. But something urged him on.

"I don't think I'll be coming back."

She slowed down and pulled into a parking space near their destination.

"Don't talk like that." She pulled up the emergency brake and turned in the seat to face him. "You have to believe that you'll make it." She hesitated. "You've been in combat, so you know what to expect. Yet here you are, safe and sound."

"That's why. I know how much luck has to do with whether one guy lives or dies. And my luck is running out." He swallowed hard. "But that's not what I meant."

He met her gaze and marveled at just how beautiful his little sister had become.

"I met a girl. Before I went overseas." He looked down at his rough hands. "We've been writing."

"And you're going to marry her." She made the statement as if she'd already known.

He looked up into her solemn face. "Yes. If she'll have me."

She didn't smile, just nodded slightly. "And she lives back east somewhere."

"Yes," he nodded.

She turned and stared out the windshield. "You haven't told Mother, I assume." Her voice had changed to haughty and distant.

"No." He waited for her to say more.

Instead she opened the door and got out. "I'll only be a moment," she called over her shoulder.

Guy sat in the car watching his sister go into the store.

So, that was that. Harriet coolly accepted that he wasn't coming back. He knew in his heart that his mother would do the same. She'd silently let him go. No begging him to come back. No saying she needed him. Nothing.

A simple "goodbye" was all he would get from his family. He'd always known he wasn't the favorite. Far from it. But he thought they appreciated what he did for them for all those years. It turned out he was wrong. They didn't care about him at all.

Chapter 58

The MP approached his window.

"Is this Oak Ridge?" Guy asked. He'd been sitting in a line of vehicles leading to what looked like the entrance to a military base, except he had never seen a military base with guard towers manned with armed guards. It was a little unnerving.

"Are you a visitor…Sergeant?"

"I guess you could say that. I came to see a friend of mine. She works here."

"I need to see some identification."

Identification? Wasn't his uniform enough? He glared at his fellow soldier. "What about these?" Guy pointed to the ribbons on his chest.

"Like I said, I need to see your identification."

Guy dug out his wallet for his ID. As he handed it to the MP he quipped, "You wanna see my orders, too?"

Without looking up, the MP said, "That would be helpful."

Before Guy could react, the man took a step back, glanced up at the guard tower and spoke again. "Would you please pull over to the side?" He motioned toward a spot near the guard shack.

Guy glanced up. The guard on the tower stared down at Guy's vehicle. Rather than argue, he pulled over and waited.

The MP approached him, with Guy's ID still in his hand. "Please turn off the vehicle and get out."

"Why?" Guy spoke before he thought.

The MP tensed. Guy sensed the slight movement of his hand toward the pistol holstered at his waist.

Oh, great. All I need is trouble out of this guy.

"Okay, okay. I'm getting out."

Another MP approached.

"Your orders?" the first one said.

Guy pulled the envelope out of his pocket and handed it to the man.

The first MP took the envelope and without opening it turned to the new man who had reached them. A lieutenant.

Guy snapped to attention and saluted.

The officer reached out and the papers were placed in his hand.

"Get back to your duties, Schmidt. I'll take over here."

He looked down at Guy's ID, then back up at Guy, still holding the salute. A casual movement that passed for a return salute signaled Guy to drop his arm.

"At ease, soldier."

Guy drew a breath and relaxed a bit, still wondering what was going on.

"What's your business here, Sergeant Nolan?"

"My friend works here. I came to see her."

"Is she expecting you?"

"Uh, no, not exactly." Guy felt a little sheepish admitting that to the officer. Truth was, he wasn't certain Rosemary wanted to see him.

The officer glared at him.

"You see, she thinks I'm still in Europe."

"In Europe?"

"Yeah. We just got back. Well actually, we got back about two weeks ago. I went home to see my family and then I came here, to see Rosemary."

While Guy blathered on, the lieutenant studied his orders.

"It says here you are to report to Ft. Bragg by August 12th."

"Yes, sir."

"And who is this Rosemary?"

"Rosemary Hopkins. We met before I shipped out, and we've been writing." Guy glanced over at the vehicles inching their way through the gate. "She wrote that she worked here, so I came to see her."

"Who does she work for?"

The question startled Guy. "Uh, I know she said. Let's see…Maybe Clinton Engineering. Yeah, that's it."

After giving him a hard stare, the officer handed the papers back to Guy. "Okay, wait here."

He went back into the shack. Guy could see through the window that he picked up a telephone and talked to someone. After a few minutes he returned.

"One of my men will escort you in. Just follow him and do exactly what you are told."

A Jeep driven by another MP pulled up beside Guy's rented car.

"Take him to the Castle," the lieutenant ordered.

****

Guy continued to pace from one wall to the other. He'd been cooped up in this small room for over two hours and still no sign of Rosemary.

The MP had escorted him to a large building at the

center of a hastily built town. Inside, the soldier led Guy to a woman at a desk. He told the woman who Guy was, and the lady requested his papers. She then escorted him to this small room furnished with only a wooden table and four chairs.

When she left, he noticed another MP posted outside the door. No one had said he was under arrest, but it sure felt like it.

An Army lieutenant came in to talk to him—or rather, to interrogate him. The officer wanted to know more about Rosemary, their relationship, and what he specifically knew about Oak Ridge and Rosemary's work.

He remembered Rosemary saying the place had tight security, but he never dreamed it would be this difficult to see her.

After the interrogation, the officer left him alone. They still had his ID and orders, which bothered Guy. He'd be in trouble at Ft. Bragg if he didn't have his paperwork.

The door opened, and the lieutenant came in. A glance told him the MP still guarded the door.

"Sergeant Nolan, we've looked into your story and you appear to be who you say you are." He handed Guy his ID and orders.

"Of course I am. Who did you think I was?"

"We have to be careful. Normally, visitors have a clearance before they are allowed on the site."

"Okay. Sorry. I didn't know the rules." Guy put his papers back in his pocket. "Can I go now?"

"You may remain here, in this building. We've notified Mrs. Hopkins that you are here."

"Rosemary is coming here?"

"Yes." The officer turned to leave.

"Sir? Does that mean I'll be able to stay? I mean, will I be able to go with Rosemary? Visit with her?"

"No. She will come here to meet you. Then you will have to leave the site until you can get a proper clearance."

"But..."

The officer pinned him with a stare that said, loud and clear, *Don't ask questions.*

****

Security had never picked her up from her workplace, much less escorted her to the Castle. She prayed it didn't have anything to do with Wallace Monroe. She hadn't heard anything about Martha Sue's friend since her cousin told her of a letter she'd gotten from him saying his departure had been a big misunderstanding. Martha Sue may have believed the man, but Rosemary sure didn't.

Rosemary presented herself to a lady sitting behind a desk.

"I'm Rosemary Hopkins. Someone sent for me?"

"Yes, Mrs. Hopkins. You have a visitor. Someone you did not request a visitor pass for."

"A visitor?" Rosemary thought about who might come to see her unannounced. Not her family. Surely not Miranda. How would she know where to find her?

"He's waiting to see you." The woman rose from her seat. "He will not be allowed to stay until he receives the proper clearance."

She indicated that Rosemary should follow her down a hallway. "If you wish for him to visit you on site, you will have to fill out the appropriate request and have it approved."

Rosemary had no idea who would come to Oak Ridge to see her, especially a man, so she wasn't sure what to say.

"How long does it take? To get approval I mean?"

"About two weeks."

"Oh," Rosemary muttered.

The woman opened the door and Rosemary stepped into the room.

She gasped. Her heart almost stopped at the sight before her.

"Guy."

"Rosemary!"

He crossed the small room with two strides, his arms out as if he were about to hug her. Within inches he stopped, a question on his face.

Their gazes locked. Both stood in shock waiting for the other to do or say something. Rosemary's heart pounded.

"I'll just leave you two to talk."

The woman's words broke the spell. Rosemary sucked air into her lungs. Then, before either could speak, she threw herself into his arms.

Burying her face against his shoulder, she pulled his strong body as close as she could. His arms wrapped around her as he rocked her back and forth.

"Oh, Rosemary. I've wanted to do this for so long," he whispered into her hair.

She could only nod, fighting tears that choked back any words.

It felt so good, here in his arms. Her body relaxed into his strong embrace. Like coming home to where she belonged. She wanted to stay here forever.

Finally, she pulled back just enough so she could

look up into his face.

"How?" she asked. "I…I thought you were in Germany."

"I was, a few weeks ago."

"Then how?"

"They shipped us back. I would have been here sooner, but I caught a flight to California. Went to see my mother." A frown crossed his face like a shadow, quickly chased away by a broad smile. "Then I came to see you."

"Just like that. No warning. No nothing."

"Yep." He nodded. "But I didn't expect it to be so difficult. I was just going to pop in and surprise you. I never expected this place to be so hard to crack."

"Yes. It is rather strict." She smiled up at him, still holding tight.

His face went all serious as he leaned down. "Can I kiss you?"

Her throat tightened again. "Yes," she whispered.

His lips quickly covered hers, transporting her back to that last day, that last kiss, on the platform in Chicago. Only now he was back, safe, and hers.

Chapter 59

"Let's go," Guy said. "Somewhere we can talk. Be alone."

"I don't…"

"I've got a car, a room in Knoxville. We can go there."

"But I have to work."

"Can't you take a few days off?" he pleaded. "I haven't seen you in so long."

She took his hand and led him to the table. "Look, they're not going to let you stay here. Not for long." She sank into a chair and he followed her lead. "I'll have to apply for a visitor's pass. That'll take a while."

"I don't understand."

"They won't let you stay on site. You haven't been approved." She hesitated. "If I had known you were coming, I could have requested a pass. But…"

"So you're saying I should have called. Sent you a wire or something?"

She nodded, hating the disappointment on his face.

"Listen, there's a small town near here. Clinton. There's a place there called Mason's BBQ. And a group of us are having a party there tonight. It's Virgil's birthday. That's a friend of mine." She suddenly became aware of her work clothes, of what she must look like to him. "Anyway, you could go there, and I could meet you in a couple of hours."

"A couple of hours?"

"Well, I have to go home and change." She reached up and touched the snood covering her hair. "Maybe I could get there sooner."

She racked her brain trying to figure out how. She didn't know the bus schedule to Clinton. Maybe Ida would let her use their car and she and Steve could come with Virgil.

"I'll just wait for you here."

She could hear the disappointment in his voice.

"I…I guess we could ask."

"Get one of those MPs to take you to get your clothes." He took her hand. "You can pack a bag and after the party we can go to Knoxville. Surely you can miss a day or two."

The pleading in his voice and those soft green eyes pierced her heart. How could she deny him?

"I can ask. After all, you have come all this way."

That brought a smile to his face, and she smiled back.

Suddenly she wanted to be in his arms, wanted him to kiss her again. And again and again.

A light tap on the door sounded before the woman came back into the room.

"Sergeant Nolan, sorry to break this up, but I'm afraid that you will not be allowed to stay on site until you are approved as a visitor."

"Bring us the forms and we'll fill them out before he has to leave," Rosemary said.

"Very well, I'll get the forms." She glanced from one to the other. "But the sergeant will not be able to stay much longer."

"You mean you don't even trust a soldier who's

been over there fighting?" Guy queried.

"It's not that. We mean no disrespect. But this is a high security site and we have very strict rules. Everyone who works here or visits must be thoroughly investigated before gaining access."

"So that means I can't take her to get her clothes?"

Rosemary grabbed his hand before he said any more. "What he means is that I need to go change clothes so I can meet him in Clinton later."

"If you won't let me take her, how about letting her take my car. I can wait here. Fill out your paperwork. And she can go change."

Rosemary's breath caught. She could barely drive. Hadn't even tried in years. Not since Jack tried to teach her.

She looked over at Guy and her heart melted. She'd do her best to drive his car up to the house and back. It wasn't far. Surely she could manage.

"I'll get the forms and ask security about Mrs. Hopkins driving your car."

She left the room, and as soon as the door closed, Guy jumped up and planted a kiss on her cheek.

"See. It'll work out. You go get your clothes." He winked. "We can go to your party, put in an appearance anyway. And then go where we can be alone."

She nodded. "Okay." His giddiness was contagious. In that moment she wanted to do just what he said. Go somewhere so they could be alone.

****

Clinton was a typical small town except for the fact that there were a lot more people than would normally be in such a place.

"Where did all these people come from?" Guy

asked.

"They probably work in one of the plants," Rosemary casually replied.

Guy glanced over at her. Apparently, nothing appeared out of the ordinary to her.

"Turn right at that road up ahead."

After only a short distance more, Rosemary told him to pull into a large parking lot on the right. Back from the road, a long, low building stretched the width of the lot, with big trees behind and on either end. A large sign read, "Mason's BBQ."

"So this is where you're having this party."

"Yes. I've only been here a couple of times. Virgil loves the barbecue, so it made sense to have his party here."

Guy pulled into a parking spot and cut off the engine. "Tell me about this guy, Virgil." He sensed more to their relationship than she had told him.

The way her eyes darted away, and the awkward set of her shoulders told him more about the man in question than she would actually say, yet he hoped she would be honest.

"Well…?" Guy tried to control his impatience.

"He's a friend." She fidgeted with her purse. "I met him soon after I arrived in Oak Ridge."

"You been dating him?"

Her eyes darted to his face and their gazes locked. "I guess you could say that. We've been out a few times. But I've made it clear that I'm not interested in having a relationship with him or anyone else."

"But he keeps coming back."

"Yeah." She looked down then. Fiddled with her nails just like he remembered.

"You in love with him?"

"No." She looked up then. "He's just a friend. Really. And he's friends with Steve and Ida. That's the couple I live with."

He didn't like the sound of that.

"You remember, when I first wrote to you I was living in a dorm?"

"Yeah, I remember. Then you moved into a house with this couple." She'd written about the roommate she didn't like.

"That's right." She nodded. "Minnie, my old roommate, will be here tonight. And some other girls from the dorm."

"And some other guys." She'd steered the conversation away from Virgil. He wondered why.

"Sure. There will be guys. But not couples. At least only the married ones. We have some married friends. And some of the girls from the dorm are married. Either widows like me or their husbands are overseas. We usually go places in a group."

"I'm looking forward to meeting your friends."

She clearly wasn't ready to tell him more about this Virgil fellow. He needed to find out where he stood with her. Maybe if he told her how he felt about her, she would tell him more.

"And I want them to meet you."

"Do they know about me?"

She looked down at her hands again. "Some do. Minnie knows I've been writing you. Ida knows because she saw your letters in the mail. And Steve, too. That's her husband."

"But not Virgil."

She barely shook her head. "He knows I've been

writing to someone, but I haven't really told him about you."

Guy looked out the side window to where another vehicle pulled in and parked nearby. "You didn't want anyone to know about me, did you?"

"I didn't mind…except…well, it's hard to explain how we met." The color that crept up her neck and reached her cheeks told him their relationship embarrassed her.

"What did you tell them?" He couldn't pull his gaze from her blushing face, even as he told himself that his stare furthered her embarrassment.

"That we met in the train station in San Francisco. That we rode the same train from there to Chicago."

He forced himself to look straight ahead, out through the windshield. "Is that what you told your family?"

"The ones who know."

He glanced down at her hands clutched together in her lap. "You didn't tell your mother, did you?"

"No. Well, that's not exactly true. Amos' letter went to Kerrville and she sent it to me. I had to explain who it was from, so I told her it was from a soldier I met on the train."

He held his tongue, unsure what to say, unable to understand why she wanted to keep him a secret. Unless his fears had been correct. That she didn't really want to see him. That thought hurt more than he wanted to admit.

"And my cousin, the one who works here, she knows. But I haven't told anyone in Kerrville."

He nodded.

"You understand, don't you? I explained all that

before."

"Yeah, that your husband had just died, and you couldn't very well tell them about me, how we met or the time we spent together."

"No. I couldn't tell anyone." She reached out and touched his arm. "But that doesn't mean it didn't mean anything to me. That you don't mean anything."

He turned in the seat so that he faced her. "You said in your letters that you cared for me. Do you?"

"Oh, Guy. Of course, I do." She smiled that sweet smile he remembered. "I'm so glad you came."

"Me, too." He scooted closer to her and thankfully she didn't back away. "You're more beautiful than I remembered."

She blushed at his words, lowered her head, still smiling. "You shouldn't say such things."

"Why not? You're the most beautiful woman I've ever met."

"You're just saying that because you want me to go to Knoxville with you."

"I'm saying it because it's true. And I do want you to go with me." He reached out and pulled her close. "Isn't that why you brought your bag?"

Chapter 60

The parking lot began to fill up. Much as she enjoyed necking with Guy, she was painfully aware that it was still daylight and her friends would be here any minute. She didn't want them to see her kissing Guy.

At least that's what she kept telling herself as she fought the temptation to lose herself in the incredible sensations his mouth created. Her body knew what it wanted, even though her mind fought it.

Between kisses she kept an eye out for Steve's familiar black car. When it rolled into the parking lot, she pulled away from Guy. "There's Steve and Ida's car."

Guy frowned but let her straighten up as he glanced over at the newly arrived automobile.

"I left Ida a note saying I was coming with a friend so she wouldn't wonder what happened to me."

Guy met her gaze, disappointment written on his face. The same disappointment she'd seen when she'd left him in Chicago, only deeper. She wanted to soothe it away.

She touched his cheek.

He took her hand and kissed her palm, sending shivers through her body. Then silently he got out and went around to open Rosemary's door.

"I see they picked up Minnie and Drucilla. The others should be here soon." She hoped meeting her friends would lighten his mood.

Rosemary waved, then grabbed Guy's hand and hurried toward the group, joining them just outside the door.

"This is Guy Nolan."

Minnie eyed him. "Ooo. Aren't you handsome."

"That's my old roommate, Minnie. And this is Drucilla."

"Hello." Drucilla smiled and nodded her approval.

"Ladies." Guy nodded to each.

Rosemary felt a gush of pride.

Next, she introduced Steve and Ida. Their subdued reaction conveyed their underlying questions about him, but they nodded politely.

They'd like him once they got to know him, she assured herself.

Another car pulled into the lot and parked. Virgil climbed out of the back seat while Howard came around and opened Dorothy's door.

As they approached, Guy stiffened beside her.

Virgil stopped in front of them. "Hi, Rosemary. Who's this?"

"Sgt. Guy Nolan, sir." Guy sounded very military.

Rosemary turned to face Guy. He stood at attention, his hand at his brow in a stiff salute. Suddenly it dawned on her what was happening. How could she have been so stupid?

Virgil casually returned Guy's salute as did Howard, who said, "At ease, Sergeant."

Rosemary's throat tightened and her entire body tensed as she looked from Guy to Virgil and Howard. "Oh, I'm sorry. I didn't realize."

Everyone's attention focused on her, expecting an

explanation for this awkwardness in their midst. She forced the words out, slowly, deliberately. "Virgil, uh, I mean Lieutenant Virgil Rushing, this is Sergeant Guy Nolan, a friend of mine who has just returned from Europe."

"Sergeant," Virgil nodded his acknowledgement.

"And this is, uh…" Her mind blanked.

"Captain Howard Charleston and my wife, Dorothy."

"Captain, Lieutenant, Mrs. Charleston, it is a pleasure to meet you."

Although Guy had relaxed his stance a bit when Howard had said "at ease," he still looked stiff and uncomfortable. Her heart went out to him.

"I didn't realize there would be this…this difference…"

"Don't worry about a thing," Dorothy said. She glanced from her husband to Virgil. "We're here for a party, not a military event. I'm sure we can relax the rules just a bit, can't we, darling?"

"Certainly, dear," replied her captain husband.

"Good. Now that that's settled, let's go inside and get a table before the rest of the crowd gets here."

Dorothy's kind words, as she took charge of the situation, allowed Rosemary to relax a bit.

The Charlestons led the way into the restaurant. Rosemary touched Guy's arm just enough to signal for him to hang back while the others went ahead.

"I'm sorry. I didn't even think about the Army stuff. I'm not used to all this military protocol or whatever you call it."

"You work at a place crawling with military personnel and you didn't think about it?" Anger tinged his words.

"I know. I should have thought. Only here everybody works together, and there's not much of that military stuff, at least not when I'm around."

"Well, it would have been nice if you'd mentioned your 'friend' is an officer."

His words hurt, but she'd hurt his feelings, too, with her thoughtlessness.

She squeezed his arm. "I'm sorry. It'll be okay. You heard Dorothy. It won't matter."

She hoped they could have a fun evening with her friends. Guy's expression didn't bode well for those hopes.

Inside, the others stood while two waitresses pulled several tables together and arranged the chairs. When they were done, Virgil and Howard and Dorothy took their seats along with Minnie and Drucilla, who were whispering between themselves. Guy pulled out a chair for Rosemary on the opposite end of the table, but Howard spoke up.

"Come, sit closer. I'd like to talk to you, Sgt. Nolan, about your experiences overseas."

Guy shot her a glance as they complied with the senior officer's request.

In all the chaos of other people arriving and introductions, there wasn't much conversation until after the waitress had taken their orders.

"So, Sergeant, what outfit are you with?"

Guy's head jerked up to meet Howard's gaze. "Sir, I'm with the 276th Armored Field Artillery Battalion."

"What division?" Virgil asked.

"We're non-divisional, sir."

"So you were moved around to where you were

needed?" Howard sounded genuinely interested.

"That's right, sir."

"What does Armored Field Artillery mean?" Virgil asked in a tone that Rosemary interpreted as distrustful, which she didn't appreciate one bit.

Before Guy could answer, Howard responded. "They are track mounted. Isn't that right?"

"Yes, sir."

"I read about them. Interesting concept. They mount an artillery gun on a tank chassis for more mobility," Howard stated.

"Yes, sir."

"You said you were in Europe." Virgil sipped from his glass of beer. "My old outfit, the 30th Infantry Division, went into Normandy right after D-Day. They saw some really heavy fighting." Virgil clearly wanted to show he knew a little about the fighting units.

Guy took a drink and nodded.

"My friends wrote me about it," Virgil continued. "About the fighting and the conditions. Real interesting stuff."

"Guy was in the 30th," Rosemary announced proudly. She thought the information would explain to Virgil her connection to Guy. But as soon as she said the words, she realized it was a mistake.

Guy cut his eyes to her and his look told her he didn't appreciate her sharing that information.

Virgil's gaze darted from Rosemary to Guy and back. "So, your battalion was attached to the 30th. When? What engagements?"

"It wasn't like that exactly, sir." Guy apparently didn't want to explain but knew he had to. "I was originally in the 230th Field Artillery," he continued.

"Then after I was wounded, the Army assigned me to the 276th."

The food arrived, and Rosemary hoped they would let Guy eat and stop asking him questions. Of course, they didn't.

"Where were you wounded? What battle?" Howard asked.

"At Mortain."

Virgil froze, a fork-full of barbecue in mid-air. "You were at Mortain?"

Howard glanced at Virgil. "Are you familiar with the action?"

"Sure. That was the German counterattack after Patton's tanks broke through in Normandy." Virgil shifted his attention back to Guy. "The 30th held the high ground. Stopped the attack."

"I see." Howard looked to Guy as if expecting a comment, but Guy continued to eat without replying.

"The artillery would have been back a ways." Virgil wouldn't let it go.

Guy straightened in his chair and drew a deep breath. "Yes, sir. The 230th's guns were behind the lines. But I was with the FO on the hill."

Virgil stared at him. His fork clattered as it struck his plate.

Rosemary wanted to ask what he meant by "FO," but based on Guy's reaction to her last comment, she decided to ask him later.

"How badly were you wounded?" Dorothy asked in her kind, gentle voice.

"Not too bad, ma'am. I had to go back to the hospital for a while, but I recovered."

Rosemary's insides tightened at the memory of

reading Amos' letter saying Guy had been badly wounded. The memory of that fear made her even more grateful that he sat here beside her now, all strong and healthy.

"You must have been out a while for you to be reassigned," Howard said.

"A month or so."

"I thought most wounded men went back to their original unit." Again, Virgil's tone implied Guy had done something wrong.

Guy looked Virgil in the eye. "In combat anything can happen…sir."

"As I recall, a month after that counter-offensive, we'd taken Paris and the Germans had pulled back all the way to Germany," Howard said. "My guess is your unit was all the way across France by then."

"They were in Holland, on the German border," Virgil responded.

"Virgil kept in touch with his buddies in the 30th. That's how I knew where you were." Rosemary wanted Guy to know she'd befriended Virgil to get information about Guy. And again, she understood how bad her remarks sounded when she saw how Virgil and the others reacted.

Their silence spoke volumes.

Guy touched her leg under the table and a thrill zinged through her, something she didn't expect. But then she hadn't expected to feel so excited, so pleased to see him again.

She slid her hand over to cover his. Their gazes met briefly, and her pulse raced.

The fact that he'd come to find her so soon after returning was incredibly flattering. She knew from his letters that he wanted to see her. And she wanted to see him, too, just to prove to herself that he had survived.

Had she been kidding herself? Were her feelings for him much more than she'd allowed herself to believe?

"Hey, Virg. How'd it go with the horses? Did you get to ride?" Harold called from further down the table.

"No. They said no dice. Strictly military use." Virgil smiled.

"Virgil wanted to go horseback riding to celebrate his birthday," Rosemary explained to Guy.

"You can go swimming with us girls on Saturday," Minnie offered. "That pool will feel really nice in this heat."

"Sorry, Minnie. I've got to work."

"Too bad. It's going to be a lot of fun."

"Sounds like a country club. Horseback riding, swimming pool," Guy said. "Pretty nice place to work, I'd say."

"We do have a good variety of recreational opportunities," Steve said. "I think they decided that to keep all of us from going crazy, stuck out here in the middle of nowhere, they needed to give us something to do in our time off."

"The horseback riding is only for military police who parole the perimeter fence, at least that's what the MPs informed me when I asked."

"Too bad." Steve laughed. Then he turned his attention to Guy. "And that swimming pool they're talking about is fed by a stream they diverted into a concrete basin. It works great. Ida and I have been in it several times."

Ida had remained quiet through most of the meal.

Now she nodded to her husband and said, "If you will excuse me for a minute."

She stood to leave. Minnie jumped up to join her.

"I think I'll head to the ladies' room, too." She poked Rosemary in the shoulder. "Come on. Go with us."

Rosemary looked up and met her gaze. Minnie nodded and winked, which told Rosemary that Minnie was dying to ask her about Guy.

"Sure, I'll come." She rose saying, "We won't be long."

As soon as they were out of earshot, Minnie had her by the arm. "All right, girl. You're gonna tell me all about this handsome soldier you've been writing to."

Chapter 61

"So, did you see much action with this mobile artillery outfit?" Lt. Rushing asked after the girls disappeared.

Guy wasn't sure how to take the lieutenant sitting across from him. The man was clearly interested in Rosemary and not at all happy at Guy's sudden appearance.

"Quite a bit," Guy replied. Then he took a sip of the two-percent beer the waitress had just set in front of him.

"You said you were non-divisional," Captain Charleston said. "Were you assigned to an Army or a Corps?"

"Third Army."

"Ah, Patton's outfit."

"Yes, sir."

"Then you were in that push Patton made to close the bulge when the Germans counterattacked." Steve had moved into Ida's seat to get closer to the military men.

"Yes, sir. But it was more than a counterattack. It was a major offensive."

Howard shook his head. "No one expected the Germans to attack in the wintertime. And through that forested terrain. The same way they came at the French in 1940."

“Was it really that cold?” Steve asked.

All Guy could do was nod. He still vividly remembered the long drive on snowy, frozen roads in blackout conditions, in vehicles with no heaters. He’d seen several vehicles slide off the icy roads and down steep hillsides. They hadn’t had time to retrieve them in their mad dash to Luxemburg, and he’d feared for the men who’d had to stay there in the freezing cold, unable to even build fires for fear of alerting the enemy to their presence.

“Hitler thought he could just break through our lines and take Antwerp, but our guys showed him.”

The lieutenant’s bravado sounded like someone who’d never seen combat. Guy wanted to shut him up. The Stateside officer had no idea what the soldiers who had been overrun went through, what it was like to fight for your life, not knowing the outcome, seeing others fall around you.

But Guy held it in, stared down at the table, his fists clenched out of sight. He didn’t want them to see how their talk upset him. Instead, he needed to put it behind him, focus on Rosemary, and stay calm. He wouldn’t be here listening to this crap if not for her.

“Where are you stationed now?” Dorothy’s question cut through Guy’s muddled thoughts.

“Uh, Fort Bragg, ma’am. I’m to report there in a few days.”

“So you stopped here, on your way, to see Rosemary.”

“Yes, ma’am.”

He glanced in the direction the girls had gone, wishing Rosemary would return. He wanted to get her alone, so they could talk.

"You made it back to the States pretty quickly," Lt. Rushing said. "I thought they had some kind of points system going as a way to decide who gets to come home first."

"That's right," the captain agreed. "I read something about that." Both men looked at Guy for an explanation.

"Our battalion will be participating in the invasion of Japan. We're supposed to get some training here in the States before shipping out to the Pacific."

"Oh, my," exclaimed Dorothy. "Then you're not through fighting?"

"No, ma'am." Guy hadn't meant to mention that little bit of information. At least not until he had a chance to explain the situation to Rosemary. Before that he had to get her alone and convince her to marry him.

Taking another drink of beer, he remembered another girlfriend, Julie, and another night out. Julie had thrown him over for a Naval officer with better prospects. Would Rosemary do the same? She seemed happy to see him. But maybe that was just relief that he had made it home. Would she decide that this officer sitting across the table had better prospects? Would she be as money grubbing as his mother and sister, looking only at what he could do for them and not caring how he felt?

He didn't think Rosemary was like that. He prayed he was right.

****

Music drifted in from the next room where couples filled the dance floor.

Rosemary made her way back to the table with Minnie trailing behind. After Ida left the ladies' room, her ex-roommate had pressed her for more information about Guy. Rosemary broke down and admitted that she hadn't expected to be so excited to see him again. She'd fantasized about it, but the reality was so much more. She even admitted to Minnie that he'd kissed her at the Castle and again later in the car. Just talking about it made her pulse race.

"You're in love with him," Minnie had teased her.

Was she? Rosemary wondered. If this was love, it sure felt strange…and wonderful.

"They're dancing in there," Rosemary announced when she made it back to the table where Guy waited. "Care to give it a try?"

Guy's face lit up. "Sure."

"Excuse us," she murmured to the others.

Once they reached the dance floor, Guy drew her into his arms. She melted into his strong embrace, remembering their dance in his friend's apartment.

Too soon, the song ended.

"Let's see what they've got on the jukebox." Guy steered her toward the large, colorful music-maker.

"Are you looking for anything in particular?"

He grinned at her in that kind of lopsided way of his. "Sure. Something special."

Couples jitterbugged to an upbeat tune. Rosemary hoped he picked some slow ones so she could enjoy being close to him.

Nickels rattled down the slot and buttons clicked as Guy made his selections.

"Aren't you going to tell me?"

"Nope. Just wait and see."

The fast number ended, and the smooth sounds of Bing Crosby filled the room. Guy swept her into his arms and out onto the floor. They swayed together to the slow, soothing rhythm.

"How long before you have to report?"

He hesitated. "A few days."

"I asked because it could take two weeks to get your visitor pass approved."

"That place has way too much security. You'd think the Germans or the Japs were just down the road."

"There are spies everywhere."

"You think so?"

She nodded.

"And what's so top secret about that place anyway?"

"I don't know exactly. We aren't told much except not to talk to anybody about the site or what work we do. Not even other workers."

"Nobody? Not even each other? That's crazy."

"Maybe. But it's to keep us all safe."

He snorted. "Not sure it worked."

The song ended and another began. This one she recognized as one of the songs they danced to in California. Memories flooded back. She looked into his soft green eyes crinkled into that sweet smile she loved.

Loved? Was she really thinking that? Is that what this warm, safe feeling was? Like she'd come home.

He held her close, so close he must have felt her heart beating against his chest.

"Remember?"

She nodded.

"I remember everything. Every moment, every kiss, every touch," he whispered.

She shivered as the vivid memories flooded her mind.

The song ended but he didn't release her. She looked up into his face. Was he longing to kiss her as much as she wanted to kiss him?

Another familiar tune began to play. Instead of immediately starting to move again, he glanced around the room as if searching for something. When they started dancing, he steered her across the floor toward one of the exits.

"Let's get some air," he said.

Before she could answer, he led her through the door and out into the dark night.

Within only a few steps, he pulled her close and his mouth descended on hers. Where the kisses they'd shared earlier had been fairly chaste, this one was hungry with desire.

She matched his fervor as if something stored up inside her had been unleashed.

When his mouth finally left hers, allowing her to gasp for air, he trailed kisses down her cheek onto her neck.

"Oh, Guy," she whispered, thrilled by his expert touch.

"Come away with me," he pleaded.

Before she could answer, he found her lips again. All she could think of was how much she wanted this, wanted him, wanted what they had before and more, so much more.

Chapter 62

His desire for her consumed him. He wanted her so. Needed her.

"Come away with me."

He made himself stop. Made himself grab her shoulders and look her in the eye. Maybe it was too soon, but he couldn't wait any longer.

"We'll get married. If you'll have me…" God, he hoped she would.

Shock skittered across her face then transformed into a smile. Hope blossomed in his chest.

She drew a ragged breath. "You're going pretty fast, aren't you?"

He nodded, tried to laugh. "Yeah, I guess. I just can't wait. I've already waited so long."

She touched his cheek, a gentle caress.

"You haven't even met my family. And I haven't met yours."

"It doesn't matter. Nothing matters but you and me. And how we feel about each other."

He saw the hesitation. He had to convince her.

"I love you, Rosemary. I've loved you since…I don't know…since that first day, since I watched you wolfing down a plate of eggs, remember?"

She nodded, smiling.

He had her going now. "Since I offered you a place to stay and you agreed…with your one condition."

He could almost see her blushing in the dark.

"Marry me," he pressed his case. "Please."

"I, uh…"

Before she could answer, before she could even think about saying no, he kissed her again, pouring out his heart in that one fervent kiss.

Cigarette smoke wafted through the breeze.

"Uh-hmm." Someone cleared their throat.

Guy released her lips but still held her close.

They turned together to see who had so rudely interrupted them.

In the dim light of the moon, Guy saw the officer's bars glistening. Lt. Virgil Rushing. Had he come looking for Rosemary?

Guy straightened, resenting the officer's intrusion. Still holding onto Rosemary with his left arm, he managed a salute with his right.

Virgil did not return the salute, leaving Guy to stand in the awkward position waiting.

Captain Charleston stepped out of the shadows and returned Guy's salute. The senior officer's gaze darted from Guy to Virgil and back to Rosemary.

"Sorry for interrupting, Sergeant," Captain Charleston said.

"Yes, sorry," Virgil ground out.

"We were wondering where you two got off to, weren't we, Virgil." The Captain tried to quell his fellow officer's anger.

"I'm sorry, Virgil." Rosemary reached out toward the lieutenant. "It's just that Guy… He's been gone."

"I've asked her to marry me," Guy injected.

"Oh, I see." Virgil looked over to the captain, and then back to Rosemary. "He just swoops in here out of nowhere and thinks you're going to marry him."

"Virgil…" she said, as if she could stop the man's jealousy.

"Did he tell you?" His question hung in the air between them.

"What?"

"That he's going to Japan. That's why he's here, back so soon. His outfit's going to invade Japan."

Rosemary turned to Guy, shock evident on her face.

"I was going to tell you."

"When? After we were married?"

"I…" Did she mean she was going to marry him? "I just hadn't had the chance."

"Too busy kissing her."

"You stay out of this." Guy struggled to control his temper. He didn't want to hit an officer, but this one was pushing it. After fighting for his life, he wouldn't hesitate to fight for Rosemary.

"If you have to go to Japan, then you're not safe. Not yet. You could still be killed."

"Don't think about that. Think about now. We're together now. That's all that matters."

"Is it? Is that all that matters to you?" She stared at him. "What about me? I can't go through that again."

Her dead husband stood between them again. That's why he wanted to get her to agree to marry him, let her get used to the idea before he sprang the Japanese invasion on her.

He reached out to her. "Calm down. It wouldn't be like that."

She jerked away. "Wouldn't it? How do you know?"

"From what I hear, the invasion of Japan will be worse than Okinawa. You think you can survive that?" Lt. Rushing had to stir it up some more.

"What do you know? You've been sitting back here…" Guy lunged toward the arrogant bastard.

Captain Charleston stepped between the two men. "Enough of this. Both of you." He looked from Rosemary to Guy to Lt. Rushing. "Maybe we should all go back inside and have a civil discussion."

"No. There's no need." Rosemary looked at Guy. "I'm sorry. I can't go with you. I can't marry you."

"But Rosemary…"

"I can't bury another husband. Don't you see that?" Tears streamed down her face.

Guy nodded. He couldn't speak. Couldn't breathe, not with a knife in his heart.

"Come on, Rosemary." Lt. Rushing stepped forward. "I'll take you home."

Guy watched her go with him. With the officer. How ironic. Just like Julie.

"Go ahead," he called after her. "Go with the officer. He's a much better bet. Safe job here Stateside, better pay, better future even."

He was just a lowly radio operator, headed for an unknown fate on the shores of Japan. Why would a girl as lovely as Rosemary want anyone like him?

"Sergeant, that's enough."

She looked back over her shoulder. He could see the hurt on her face.

He'd messed up everything.

"Sergeant?"

Guy looked at the captain. "Sorry sir. I, uh…" He shook his head, unable to think where to go, what to do now.

"Come on back inside." The man sounded almost fatherly. But he was Lt. Rushing's friend. They all were. Guy was the one who didn't belong here.

"No. I'd better go." He turned away. "She left some things in my car. Will you make sure she gets them?"

The captain nodded. "Certainly."

****

Rosemary couldn't think. Didn't know what to do.

In one minute, Guy was kissing her and asking her to marry him. In the next he was off to get himself killed.

Much as she wanted to be with him, much as she was tempted to throw caution to the wind…again, she couldn't do it. She couldn't give him her heart and have it broken to bits…again.

Losing Jack had almost destroyed her. Even before he died, her heart had been crushed by his betrayal, his lies. Now Guy had lied to her, or he had lied in effect by not telling her that he had to leave her again and go back to war. He'd tried to trick her into marrying him.

And she'd almost fallen for it. She'd let her desire override her good sense. And what had that gotten her before? A miserable marriage to a man who didn't want to be married, not to her anyway.

Virgil drove in silence.

Good, steady Virgil. Patiently waiting for her to let him in. Maybe she should. Maybe Guy was right. Virgil was safe here at Oak Ridge. And Virgil had a future ahead of him. Ida said so. She and Steve worked in those high-up, secret places where Virgil worked. He had a college degree. He was smart and nice and would make somebody a good husband someday.

Maybe she needed to think about that and forget about Guy. Forget about the temptations. That handsome face and those soft, green eyes had tempted her before, had drawn her in, made her want him. And he'd given her so much.

Her whole body longed for him, for his touch, for his kiss.

No. Stop it. Don't think about that.

Be reasonable, rational. Think about what would be best. Think about somebody steady and reliable. Somebody who's a good prospect.

"Here we are," Virgil said. He parked the car in the driveway.

She sat motionless for a moment, unable to move.

"I'll take you in."

He got out of the car, walked around and opened her door.

She forced herself to get out. "You don't have to."

"I want to."

She looked up into his kind, concerned face. "No. Not tonight."

"Why not? Because of him? What about me?"

Her breath caught. "What?"

"Is that why you've been putting me off? Saying you didn't want a relationship right now? Because of him?" He shook his head and turned away. "It is, isn't it? You've been stringing me along waiting for him to come back."

"It's not like that." She wasn't sure what to say to him.

He faced her. "Then explain it to me."

She tried to think. Tried to make sense of her

feelings. “I can’t.”

“Can’t or won’t?” A hint of anger invaded his voice.

“I don’t know.” She ran her hand through her hair. “I just don’t know.”

“Great. That’s just great,” he ground out through gritted teeth.

Tears pricked her eyes. Her throat tightened. She couldn’t speak, so she shook her head back and forth.

“What am I supposed to do?”

“Leave me alone,” she shouted. Then she turned and ran toward the door. “Just leave me alone.”

Chapter 63

Rosemary sat on her bed, staring into space. She heard the door. Steve and Ida must have come home.

Forcing herself to move, she got up from the bed and sat on the stool in front of her dresser. She pulled her earring from one ear and then reached for the other.

It wasn't there. Her earring was gone.

She looked in the mirror to verify what her fingers told her.

Jack's earrings. The pearls he'd given her.

She whipped around, looked at the bed, the floor. She got up and ran her hands over the bed as if she could feel what she couldn't see. Not finding it, she dropped to her knees and searched the floor. Under the bed, under the throw rug, under the dresser, all around the room.

Someone tapped on the door.

"Rosemary," Ida called. "Are you okay?"

"Ohh," Rosemary moaned. She sat up on her haunches and ran her hands through her hair.

The door pushed open and Ida stuck her head in.

"You left so suddenly…" Ida stared at Rosemary. "What's happened? Are you all right?"

Rosemary held her head and shook it.

Ida gently touched her shoulder. "Now, now. Come on now. Let's get you up."

Realizing she was on the floor, Rosemary got to

her feet. “It’s gone,” she cried.

“What’s gone?”

“My earring.” Her hand shook as she held out the one earring for Ida to see. “I…I must have lost it.” Then it dawned on her. “Oh, God. At Mason’s. I must have lost it at Mason’s.”

“I suppose that’s possible.” Ida didn’t sound encouraging.

“I need to go look for it.”

“Tonight?”

“Uh-huh. Now. Right now.”

“But it’s late. We can go tomorrow if you don’t find it…”

“No. I have to find it. I have to.” Her heart raced. Why didn’t she understand? “Jack…Jack gave them to me. He…He…”

“What’s going on?” Steve appeared in the doorway.

“She lost her earring. Tonight. Maybe at Mason’s. And she’s upset about it.”

“Who is Jack?”

“Her husband. The one who died.”

“Jack gave me these earrings…that first Christmas after we…after we got married.” Tears streamed down her cheeks. “He…he picked them out himself.” He’d said he’d known they were perfect for her as soon as he saw them.

“See,” Ida said as she pulled Rosemary’s hand up to show Steve the remaining one.

“Yes, very nice.”

“I have to find it. You understand, don’t you?” Rosemary pleaded with Ida.

“Why don’t I call Mason’s and have someone there

look for it?" Steve offered. "Somebody may have already found it and turned it in."

Rosemary stared at the treasure in her hand, a larger pearl encircled by small ones, all set in gold. She had been surprised that Jack had selected something so beautiful.

Ida took the earring from her palm. "You know, if you don't find the other one, you could have this one made into a pendant. It would make a really pretty one."

Rosemary snatched it back. "I don't want to make it into a pendant. They're earrings." She squeezed it in her fist.

"Maybe it's in the car." Rosemary jumped to her feet and ran through the door into the hallway. Ida followed.

"You don't have to…"

Rosemary reached the front door and flung it open. She hesitated when the darkness greeted her.

"Thank you very much." Steve's voice cut through her muddled brain.

She whirled around.

He met her gaze. "I'm sorry. No one has found your earring. But they will look," he assured her. "They promised that the cleanup crew will make a thorough search."

"A flashlight. Do you have one? Or a lantern?"

Surprised, he nodded. "Yes. I'll have to look…" He glanced at his wife.

"She wants to search the car."

"The car. Yes, of course." Steve sounded bewildered, but cooperative.

"And Howard's car. Virgil brought me home in it."

"Steve, can you call Howard? Ask him to look in his car?"

"Sure, sure. As soon as I find the flashlight."

He pulled a battery-powered flashlight from a kitchen cabinet and presented it to Rosemary with a sympathetic smile.

"Thanks," she muttered.

She hurried outside and frantically searched Steve's car. Under the seat. In the floorboard. In the back seat. She even ran her hand between the back cushion and seat cushions to make sure it wasn't wedged in there somewhere.

Nothing.

Then she inched her way from the car to the house and back, illuminating every inch with the flashlight.

Nothing.

Ida came out and found her standing by the front door.

"Come on, Rosemary. Come back inside."

"You don't understand," Rosemary said, close to tears. "It can't be lost. It just can't be."

"You're upset. You've had a difficult day. It'll be better tomorrow."

"Yeah, sure. Tomorrow." Rosemary retreated to her room. "I guess I'll go to work. Only I asked to be off. I was going to…" She stopped herself from blurting out that she had planned to go away with Guy. That he'd come back to see her. That he wanted her to marry him. No. She wouldn't tell Ida. She wouldn't tell anyone. She'd made her choice. She wouldn't marry a man who was going to die. She wouldn't go through that again.

Chapter 64

A constant stream of glaring headlights forced him to focus on his driving so he wouldn't end up down the side of a mountain. The heavy traffic on the road back to Knoxville reminded him of a military convoy, only these weren't military vehicles. They were all going to Oak Ridge where Rosemary worked, where she couldn't tell him what they made or even the kind of work she did.

He remembered her surprise when she first saw him, the smile that had bloomed on that beautiful face. He could feel her body against his as they embraced.

A horn blasted him back to reality.

Watch the road. Get this heap back to Knoxville in one piece. Think about her then.

In the darkened lobby of his hotel, he rang the bell to get someone's attention.

The sleepy-eyed night clerk emerged from the back.

"Yeah. What do you want?"

"My key. Nolan. Room 212."

The man eyed him suspiciously. "Kind of late, ain't it? You got any identification?"

Guy fished his military ID out of his pocket. "Sorry. I drove down to Oak Ridge and just got back."

After examining Guy's papers, the night clerk grabbed the key off its hook and handed it to Guy.

"You ever been down there, to Oak Ridge?"

"Nope." The clerk shook his head. "I heard about it, though."

"The traffic surprised me…and the security."

"Yup." A knowing smile enlivened the man's face. "The sayin' around her is that everythin's goin' in and nothin's comin' out."

"What do you mean?"

"All them trucks and trains loaded down go into that place but ain't nothin' ever comes out. No tanks or trucks or bombs or nothin'."

Guy nodded, absorbed in the man's words.

"The gov'ment, they bought up a bunch of land. Like TVA did when they built them dams, only nobody knows what they been building. Got it locked up tighter'n a drum. An' anybody works there got to swear not to talk about it 'cause if they do, they get fired or worse."

"Worse?"

"Yep. Don't let 'em work on any other gov'ment job, no defense plant, nothin'. I've even heard tell that some of 'em that talked got jail time."

"They've got tight security, that's for sure. Tighter than any Army base I've been on."

"Yep. Top secret's what they call it. Built a whole town out there and don't let nobody in unless they work there. Make good money, too. Some of them folks come here to Knoxville and spend lots, buying all kinds o' stuff. Stuff nobody here can afford."

Guy nodded. His thoughts went back to Rosemary…and that lieutenant.

She had a good thing going with him. And she knew it. Both of them making good money in safe, cushy jobs, while he'd been over there getting his ass shot off.

Seemed like everyone here in the States got what they wanted. And they would get everything they could before the war ended. Meanwhile, the Army planned to send him over there to finish it off. And nobody here cared whether he came back or not.

****

Rosemary couldn't sleep. Her mind wouldn't stop.

She thought through every moment she'd spent with Guy, which only made her heart and her body ache. So much had been good between them, but so much hadn't. Life, the war, everything had been against them from the start.

And Virgil. How did she feel about him? Not the incredibly strong attraction she felt for Guy. Virgil was more like the older brother she never had, or one of her cousins, pleasant to be with, fun at times, and serious at other times.

When he got into discussions with his colleagues and she didn't know what they were talking about, she felt so wrong for him. He was educated and she wasn't. Steve and Ida both had college degrees and could carry on conversations for hours about science or history or Shakespeare. Rosemary could only listen and pretend she knew what they were talking about, when in truth she didn't have a clue.

But Virgil would be safe. He wasn't going to go off and get killed. He wasn't reckless like Jack. And he didn't have orders to invade Japan.

When the war first started, she'd worried about Jack, but not about him getting killed, not then. She'd been too naive. No. She'd worried about him coming back all messed up, like her father. She'd feared that Jack would be wounded or that he would go through such horrible experiences that he would be changed, a different person. That's what she'd heard people say about her father, that he'd been a different man when he came back from France. She'd never known him before, so she had no way of knowing. And her mother never talked about it, at least not with Rosemary.

Maybe that was why her mother worried about Bobby. Because of the way their father had been changed by the Great War.

She prayed her brother wouldn't have to invade Japan. Not only would he be killed, it would kill her mother.

And all these mental machinations brought her back to Guy.

She'd been so happy to see him and so pleased that he didn't have any obvious physical or mental injuries. He'd seemed overly anxious to get her alone, to take her away to Knoxville. He wanted to get her in bed. And she was pretty sure she would have gone, both to Knoxville and to bed.

Why did he have to spoil it? Or rather, why did the damn Army have to spoil it? It wasn't Guy's fault his outfit had orders to invade Japan. It wasn't like he had volunteered. He had to follow orders.

He couldn't understand that she'd waited. She'd wanted to be sure he was safe before she made any commitment. She'd held tight to her heart because she didn't want it to be broken again.

And she'd been right.

She hadn't told him she loved him. She hadn't let herself love him.

Maybe, if she'd spent more time with him, and she'd known he was back for good, then maybe she would have let herself fall in love with him.

But she hadn't.

She didn't love him.

She didn't care that he'd left.

She hadn't wanted to hurt him, but she hadn't wanted to get hurt, either.

No. This was better. He went back to the Army and she'd go back to…to work.

And after the war, she'd figure that out, too. She'd find something to do that wasn't in Kerrville.

She'd figure out something.

Someone stirred in the kitchen. Ida must be up.

Rosemary couldn't face going to work. She hadn't slept.

And her earring. She had to find her earring.

She'd go to Clinton herself. Go to Mason's and search, inside and out. It had to be there somewhere.

Otherwise it was in Guy's car. The only place left was the rented car he'd driven back to Knoxville. If it was in that car then…then she'd never see it again. Just like she'd never see Guy again.

Chapter 65

On the bus ride from Knoxville to Fayetteville Guy slept on and off, dreaming of damp foxholes and incoming rounds when he slept and stewing in his hurt and anger when awake.

He surveyed the small town just outside Fort Bragg as the bus wove its way through the narrow streets. It wasn't much. Yet, like in so many other small towns near military bases, soldiers swarmed like flies.

At least the place hadn't been reduced to rubble like the towns in Europe.

In Germany they had pulled up outside a town, sent a messenger in demanding surrender, and then, depending on the answer, they'd either blown it to bits with artillery or driven in to take over.

None of the Germans had been happy, but most accepted their defeat. They had to watch out for the ones who wouldn't give up. All it took was one man, woman, or child with a gun to kill several Americans before they could be silenced.

Now here he stood in a typical American town. The locals went about their business, trying to make a buck. They'd either make it off the government or off the GIs. They didn't care which. The war made them money.

He shook his head trying to erase the cynical thoughts. It was just the natural way of things. It wasn't the cause of his misery.

No. Rosemary and her inability to make a commitment for fear of getting hurt had caused it. And that Lieutenant Rushing, who wanted her for himself, had spoiled everything before Guy had even had a chance.

After the debacle in Oak Ridge, he'd come to the conclusion that Rosemary didn't care about him any more than his mother did. Rosemary had written to him to ease her conscience so she wouldn't feel guilty about sending him off to war. While his mother just cared about his money. Both had betrayed him.

He spotted some other soldiers milling around outside a beer joint. Perfect. He didn't have to report for a few more days. Enough time to get good and drunk. Drink all his troubles into oblivion.

Inside the bar, to his surprise, he saw a familiar face.

"Tony," Guy called. "What the hell are you doing here?"

Corporal Tony Valachi looked up from his beer. "Nolan. Good to see you."

Guy pulled up a chair and sat beside his old friend. "You back from leave early, too?"

Tony shrugged. The way he stared at the beer bottle said a lot. Another broken heart. A kindred spirit.

Guy ordered a beer and looked around. Nothing special, just a typical joint in a post town full of Army uniforms.

"You're from Boston, right?" Guy asked.

"Yeh."

"Did you see your family there?"

"No family to speak of. My parents died years ago.

Saw my aunt and some cousins. Went to a ball game at Fenway Park." He motioned to the bartender for another beer. "It was okay, I guess."

Guy sensed he didn't want to talk about the reason for his long face and early return. That was okay. Guy felt much the same.

"Yeah. I went to California. Saw my mother, sisters." He took a long swig of his beer. "My brothers are in the Pacific."

"In the Navy?"

"One's in the Navy. The other in the Marines."

Tony nodded. "I think you told me that…before…" He then turned up his beer bottle.

They sat in companionable silence, each lost in his own thoughts.

Guy decided not to share his side trip to Oak Ridge. That would only lead to an explanation about Rosemary and why she rejected him. He didn't want to talk about it.

After a while, Tony asked, "What about these orders to Japan?"

Guy looked up, the question pulling him out of his self-induced fog. "I dunno. Kinda sucks."

"That's what I say. We've done our part. Why've they got to send us over there? It ain't fair."

Guy chuckled to himself. "You're right. It's not fair."

He thought of a letter he'd gotten from Henry months back. "Be glad you're fighting the Germans. At least they are civilized," Henry had said. "These yellow bastards won't surrender, even if they're beat. And if they do, they'll try to trick you or get you with a hidden grenade. So we don't take prisoners unless we're ordered to."

"My brother, the one in the Marines, says the Japs won't surrender."

Tony nodded. "I heard that, too." He ordered another beer, then turned back to Guy. "They say on Iwo Jima that the Japs would kill themselves rather than surrender."

Guy nodded. "Sounds crazy."

"Over there in Germany, those guys surrendered by the thousands." Tony nudged Guy with his fist. "Remember them walking down the Autobahn, down the middle, while we drove past."

"Yeah, I remember."

"Ain't gonna be like that in Japan." He shook his head and took a long swig of his fresh beer.

"And we're not going to come back. We're going to invade Japan and go from village to village, city to city, fighting the whole way."

"That Marine brother of yours, he ever write you about the fighting over there?"

"Yeah, some." Guy thought of Henry's strange letters after he'd been wounded. "He said a booby-trap got him. When he was wounded, I mean."

Tony just nodded.

Music blared from the jukebox in the back. Someone must have fed it full of coins. It suited Guy to forget this morbid conversation and just listen to the upbeat music. He might as well enjoy it while he could because he wouldn't be coming back from Japan. He knew it, deep in his soul.

And nobody cared. Not his mother, or his sisters, or even Rosemary.

Chapter 66

The cavernous building swallowed her up in its giant pipes and constant noise. A sense of uncertainty swirled around her as if she were moving into some unknown world.

She stubbornly pulled herself together and found her assigned workplace. She would do her work and block everything else out of her mind.

Two hours later, Rosemary moved her ladder to her next inspection location. She slung her test equipment over her shoulder and started the long climb.

Lack of sleep had her talking to herself to focus her mind on the task at hand. Thoughts of Guy kept intruding, vivid memories of the dream she'd had the night before. The explosions, the blood, the dead bodies, and the screams of the attacking Japanese with Guy standing in the midst of it all, as if waiting to be killed.

A few months back someone had talked her into going to a war movie about the Marines fighting the Japanese on Guadalcanal. Terrified by the battle scenes, she had walked out. In the dream she imagined Guy fighting the Japanese, and she knew in her bones they would kill him.

Rosemary shook her head to dispel the memory of the dream and the fear she'd felt. *It was just a dream, just a stupid dream.*

She made the marks that showed she'd finished inspecting this section and started down so she could move on to the next area.

Move on without Guy.

Her tester slipped from her shoulder.

She grabbed for it.

The ladder wobbled.

The tester hit her leg.

She lunged for it.

Lost her balance.

Stupid. Let it go.

Her hand slipped.

Grab…hold.

Too late.

Her foot slid from the rung.

Oh no.

She grabbed for the ladder.

Catching air as it swayed. Too far.

The pipe above her shifted.

It wasn't moving.

She was.

Falling.

Clanging! Crashing!

The ceiling, far above, blurred.

Then a hard jar…

Her father smiled down on her.

"You'll be all right."

"Papa."

She tried to reach out to him.

But she couldn't move.

Her arm was so heavy.

****

"It's not a bad break. It should heal in a few

weeks."

The doctor smiled, busy applying plaster to her left arm.

"You were lucky. Could have been a lot worse," he continued.

Rosemary's head pounded. She reached up for the hundredth time and felt the bandage wrapped around her head. She couldn't reach the place on her left side that hurt the worst. The same side as the broken arm.

The nurse fitted her arm into a sling and escorted her to the exit where a young man waited to take her home.

"You won't be alone?" the nurse asked again. "You're sure someone will be home?"

"Yes," Rosemary nodded, then regretted moving her head. "Ida will be home from work by now."

"Don't leave her if no one is there," the nurse instructed the young man. "And make sure they get those instructions."

Rosemary sank into the passenger's seat and watched the young man shift gears, hoping he could drive.

Of course, he can drive. Why would they send someone who couldn't drive?

The car stopped and she realized that she must have dozed off. She felt so tired and washed out. Inside she could rest.

"Oh, Rosemary." Ida's voice penetrated the fog as she pulled her from the car. "You poor dear."

"I'm okay," Rosemary heard herself murmur. "Just need to rest."

Steve was there, too, talking to the young man.

"Don't let her sleep too long. Wake her every hour.

Make sure she knows where she is."

Her bed beckoned. So soft. And a warm blanket.

Then sweet oblivion.

"Rosemary. Wake up." Ida's voice echoed through the fog. "They said you had to wake up. Not to let you sleep."

"I'm awake." But the warm cocoon of sleep tugged her back.

"Sit up." Strong hands pulled her up.

"I think we better get her up to walk. So we know she's awake."

"Come on, hon. On your feet."

She walked, supported by Ida on one side and Steve on the other.

"I can walk by myself," she insisted. But, when they loosened their hold, she wobbled and almost fell.

Steve took her good arm. "Come on. Into the kitchen."

She made it to the table and eased into a chair.

"Do you feel like eating something?" Ida asked.

"No," she said, moving her head enough to know not to.

"Can you tell us what happened?" Steve asked.

"I fell."

A glass appeared on the table in front of her. Suddenly thirsty, she picked it up and took a long drink. The cool water brought her mind into focus. She looked into the two anxious faces across from her.

"I was coming down the ladder…and…and…I fell."

"How far?"

"I don't know." She had to remember to hold her head still so it wouldn't feel like something sloshing around inside.

"They said you hit your head. Knocked you out for a while."

"I guess. I don't remember much." Except her father's face, smiling down at her.

"You were too upset. You shouldn't have gone to work." Ida wrung her hands and paced between the sink and the table.

Steve shot her a warning look.

"Why was I upset?"

Both Ida and Steve stared at her, as if they couldn't believe what she'd asked.

"About the…"

Steve touched Ida's arm, silencing her.

"About Guy."

"Yes." Ida nodded.

Rosemary looked away, staring into nothingness. He was gone. The pain stabbed through her heart, worse than the pain in her head or in her arm. Like losing Jack all over again. No. Not exactly. Guy was still alive. At least for now.

****

There was nothing left to do but go home. Home to her mother and her grandmother to recuperate from being stupid.

She didn't have to go. She could sit here in this empty house all alone.

No. She'd go home. Take her medicine and sulk. Wallow in self-pity. Like she'd wanted to when Jack left her. Only she hadn't let herself then. She'd buried herself in work. Now she'd broken her stupid arm and couldn't even work.

She'd have to take the big suitcase. Take enough

clothes for a month. Not work clothes. Clothes for going to the store, to church, to visit relatives. And Dr. Turnbull. To make sure her brain was intact, and her arm was healing.

She pulled the bag from her closet. The little overnight case sat on the floor beside it.

I never unpacked it, did I?

Well, might as well transfer the outfit in there to the big bag.

Setting the small case on the bed, she opened it and scooped out the clothes.

Something clattered as it fell back into the case.

Her pearl earring. The one she'd lost.

She reached in and retrieved it. Squeezing it tight in her fist, she brought it up to her heart.

He must have found it. In the car. He must have put it inside the case.

Her chest tightened.

From force of habit she fought the tears.

Why? She was all alone. It didn't matter. Nobody cared if she cried.

So she let them come.

At first, tears streamed down her cheeks unchecked. Then thoughts of her complete and utter aloneness brought heaving sobs.

Chapter 67

She settled into her grandmother's spare room and tried to make herself useful within her physical limitations.

She couldn't wash dishes one-handed, but she could put them away and set the table. When she offered to help with the cooking, both Miss Nora and her mother quickly turned her away.

She visited her mother-in-law and stayed over for supper, for once glad to have their company.

"You shouldn't be working in such a dangerous place," Dad Hopkins chided her. "Can't they give you something more appropriate? Answering the telephone or typing."

"She can't very well type with a broken arm," Felicia said.

"You know what I mean. Before. She wouldn't have broken her arm if she'd been typing instead of… What is it you were doing, Rosemary?"

She looked up from her plate. "Leak testing." As soon as she said it, she clamped her mouth shut. She wasn't supposed to talk about her work, what she did or where she did it, not to anyone, away from the workplace or not.

"And what is that exactly?" Dad Hopkins stared at her with that same look he used on his high school students, daring them to tell the truth or else.

"I'm not supposed to talk about it," Rosemary stated, using as authoritative a tone as she could muster. "I've already said too much."

"That's preposterous." He put his fork down and looked from Rosemary to his wife and back. "You work in a place that is supposed to be a war plant and yet you cannot tell us what you do there or what they make."

"Loose lips sink ships." Rosemary rattled off the slogan she'd seen plastered on the walls at the shipyard.

"So we have Japanese spies right here in Tennessee, do we?" He pulled his napkin from his lap and placed it on the table. "Well, young lady, the war is over in Europe. The Germans surrendered, in case you haven't heard. And I expect the Japanese will soon do the same. So what does it hurt to share just a little bit of information with your family?"

Rosemary fixed her gaze on her plate. He was right, but that didn't mean she could break the rules. She'd signed those papers swearing she would keep silent.

"I'm sorry. I don't want to lose my job."

"Horace, settle down. She's right. She has to do what she's been told."

"I know. I know. It's just upsetting to see you sitting here with your arm in a sling and stitches in your head. You could have been killed."

That's when it dawned on her how much they worried about her.

She met her father-in-law's gaze and found it filled with anguish. "I'm sorry. I didn't think about how much it would upset you."

Felicia's hand covered Rosemary's. "We do worry about you. You're our daughter. You're all we have left of…of Jack."

Rosemary forced a smile. Something to comfort them. After all, they'd lost a son to this war. And she'd lost a husband.

"It's not so bad, really. The arm is just a fracture. It will heal in a few weeks. And the cut on my head, well, it's almost healed now." She wanted to reach up and scratch the healing stitches but willed her hands to be still.

She drew a deep breath, searching for the words to explain to them.

"I have to go back to work. This war's not over. We still have to defeat Japan, and mounting another invasion, especially on Japan, will…will be difficult." Images of Guy slugging through hordes of Japanese soldiers sent a shiver down her spine. "I have to do something to help."

"Well, right now you have to get well." Felicia patted Rosemary's hand as she spoke.

Rosemary searched her father-in-law's face as he struggled with his own demons.

"Yes. Thousands more will die before this thing's over." His steady gaze met hers. "I envy you."

"Why?" she asked, astonished by his statement.

"Because you are doing something. And here I sit, unable to do anything except watch the youngsters we've raised, tried to teach morals and citizenship, in addition to academics, watch them go off to the military, to the uncertainty of war."

Rosemary got up then and went to him. She wrapped her good arm around him. He was the closest thing to a father that she had. And in that moment, she saw the man beneath the facade, with all his vulnerabilities.

Later, as she left, Felicia said, “Rosemary, you know that we love you and want only the best for you.”

In that moment it seemed immensely important to ask something she hadn’t thought of before. “What if I were interested in someone? Would you mind?”

Astonishment, with a hint of pleasure, colored her mother-in-law’s face. “A young man, you mean?”

Rosemary nodded.

“We’d be pleased. If he made you happy, mind you.”

She hugged the older woman and whispered, “Thank you.”

****

As fate would have it, Rosemary’s older sister Frances, with husband and children in tow, arrived in Kerrville for a weekend visit just days after Rosemary’s accident. So instead of her grandmother’s house being a quiet retreat for her to lick her wounds and recover, it was a madhouse of activity.

Fortunately, Rosemary recognized that she needed to be surrounded by family. The activity, the talk, the warmth made her realize how much she had missed.

After their Saturday midday meal, Frances’ husband, Lee, went to sit on the porch with Grandmother while the children ran and played in the yard. Miss Nora had asked for the afternoon off to visit her family, so Frances and their mother washed up the dishes while Rosemary did what she could to help.

When they’d finished, Frances joined her husband and children, leaving Rosemary alone with her mother.

“Let’s go up to the beehives. I need to check on them, and the climb will work off some of that food.”

"Okay," Rosemary agreed.

They exited through the back door, climbed the rock steps, and made their way around the outbuildings to the well-worn path up the hill.

"I'll need more honey soon," her mother commented over her shoulder. "For the pies."

Rosemary remained silent until they passed by the chicken yard. "I saw Martha Sue before I left. She heard from her husband."

"He's safe then?"

"Yes. And anxious to get home."

"I can't blame him."

"I don't think Martha Sue is looking forward to his return."

At that her mother paused. "They married awfully quickly. I'm not surprised she's having doubts."

Rosemary hadn't expected her mother's words. She didn't think anyone in Kerrville knew of Martha Sue's relationship with Wallace Monroe. Did her mother suspect?

"What do you mean?"

"Just that she's young and they only knew each other a short time. Louise said at the time she wondered if it would last."

"Aunt Louise said that?"

Her mother nodded as they made their way through the garden where summer vegetables waited to be harvested.

"Not to change the subject, but you said you'd moved from the dormitory into a house, with a married couple?" Her mother scrutinized her with that look she used when she wanted to get to the bottom of something but didn't want to ask a direct question.

Rosemary nodded. "It's so much better than in the dorm. I actually have a room to myself."

"Well, I hope it doesn't cost you too much."

Rosemary smiled. Her mother always worried about money. "I'm paying the same amount as before."

The older woman nodded as if satisfied with Rosemary's answer and continued uphill in silence until they reached the one-lane road that marked the upper property line.

Along the eastern portion of the property, downhill a little from the road, sat four beehives enclosed in a wooden, picket fence. Further down, grapevines entwined themselves around the aging arbor her father had built.

"Papa would be pleased," Rosemary said.

"Why?"

"That the bees are still here, that you are still taking care of them and the grapevines he planted."

"I'm glad you remember those things about your father."

"I remember coming up here with him. Watching him steal the honey, with bees swarming around him. And he never got stung."

Her mother smiled, a faraway look on her face.

Rosemary seized the opportunity. "You remember more about him than I do."

"Of course, I do." Her mother smiled, a rare thing these days. "I knew him long before you were born."

"You mean before he went off to war?" The question emerged before she thought about how it sounded. "Grandmother said it changed him," she offered in explanation.

Her mother sighed. "Yes. It did." She didn't add

any more. Instead she opened the gate and went into the beehive compound.

Rosemary moved to the fence, careful to keep a watchful eye out for any bees that might come her way.

"I saw him," Rosemary stated.

"What?" Her mother, busy inspecting the hives, did not look around.

"Papa. He came to me. When I fell. Told me I'd be okay."

Her mother turned around then. She stared at Rosemary for long enough to make her uncomfortable.

"Do you mean you saw him in a dream?"

"It didn't seem like a dream. He was just there, leaning over me and smiling."

Her mother left the bees and came to her side, touching her gently on the shoulder. "Haven't I always said that he would watch over you?"

Rosemary nodded.

"I'm sure that's it. He was looking down from Heaven. Watching over you." She glanced back at the beehives. "They're fine for now. I'll come back another day." She slipped her arm around Rosemary's good one. "We should get back."

A few steps brought them to the grape arbor. Fearing she'd never get another chance to talk to her mother like this, Rosemary ventured to ask the question that had been burning in her for years.

"Do you remember the day he died?"

Chapter 68

Her mother hesitated before answering. "Yes. I remember." Deep sadness coated her words.

Rosemary rushed to continue before her mother ended the conversation. "He sent me away that day. I wanted to go with him, to his workroom, but he sent me away."

"He probably wanted to be alone." Mother faced Rosemary. "He wasn't well."

Rosemary nodded, and then, took a deep breath. "But I came back."

A question flittered across her mother's face. Before she could speak, Rosemary plunged on. "The door was open. You and Frances…and the doctor were in there with him." She swiped at a tear. "You were hovering over him, crying and muttering something. 'Why?' I think you said."

"That's right." Her mother took a step closer. "Frances and I came running when Ol' Mose called. He said your father was down. That he was sick." She looked away shaking her head as if to clear her vision. "I sent him for the doctor, and we went to the workroom."

"Why did the doctor pump his stomach?"

"What?"

"I saw him. He put a tube down Papa's throat, and he tried to pump out his stomach." Rosemary's voice shook, but she couldn't seem to stop. "He told you that he had to get it out of him." She stared at her mother's disbelieving face. "He took poison, didn't he?"

Her mother grabbed her by the shoulders. "No." She squeezed while shaking her head. "No. He didn't take poison. He took too much of his medicine."

Rosemary heard her mother's ragged breath and tried to turn away, but her mother pulled her into an embrace.

"They said…at school…that he killed himself… that he…"

"He didn't mean to," her mother assured her.

Rosemary felt the tears choking in her throat. "But I saw…"

"You were a child. You didn't know what you were seeing. And I didn't know you were there. If I had known, I would have explained it to you."

"But you didn't. You wouldn't even talk to me about it."

"I thought it best. We all did. You adored Papa and he you. I wanted to spare you."

"I wanted to go with him. To cheer him up." Rosemary pulled away. "I could always make him smile." She nodded. "So I came back. But he'd sent me away so he could leave me. Leave us all."

"He didn't want to leave us. He was just in so much pain." Tears were streaming down her mother's face, too. "Oh, Rosemary. My dearest. I'm so sorry you saw all that. So sorry you didn't understand."

"Did you understand?"

"Not for a while. Dr. Turnbull talked to me several times. He explained about the medicine, how he'd warned Marion about its effects." She led Rosemary to a rough wooden bench almost hidden within the arbor and they sat down together.

"The war had affected him deeply. Not just his wounds but in his mind." She grasped Rosemary's good hand and squeezed it. "There were times when he was in so much pain. Not so much physical pain as a mental pain. He couldn't forget what he saw over there." She swiped at the tears streaming down her face. "I tried to get him to talk about it…but he wouldn't. He said he didn't want me to know."

Rosemary thought of Guy. What had he seen and done? Had the war changed him, too? Would he ever be able to put it behind him?

Her mother drew a deep breath and then stood. "I think we should get back to the house."

"Now?" Rosemary had never been able to broach the subject with her mother, so she feared they would never speak of it again.

"Yes, now. I have work to do." The frown told Rosemary her mother wanted to end the painful conversation.

Rosemary jumped up and touched her mother's arm to stop her. "Would you do it again? Marry him? If you had known what would happen?"

Her mother's frown deepened. "What?"

"Was it worth it?"

"Of course it was." She faced Rosemary and took her hand again. "I loved him. And he loved me."

"But…the pain…the suffering?" She met her mother's gaze. "Then he left us."

"It wasn't all bad. He was a wonderful man who loved us all." She squeezed Rosemary's hand to emphasize her words. "He loved you. You gave him so much joy. That's what I remember. It's what you should remember."

Rosemary nodded, tears streamed down her face.

"I didn't want him to leave me."

"I know. I didn't either. But that's how life is, sometimes. So we have to love while we can. Treasure every moment together, knowing the future is never certain."

Chapter 69

After Frances and her family left, the silence in her grandmother's house was deafening.

Rosemary roamed the rooms trying to sort out her feelings.

She'd been so thrilled to see Guy, to hold him in her arms and feel his strength. To see for herself that he was not just alive but whole.

She'd been on the verge of chucking her job and everything else to go with him to Knoxville, maybe even to marry him. Then Virgil had intervened with that little tidbit of information.

Fear had taken over. Fear for Guy's safety, the fear she'd lived with for so long. Fear of going through what she'd gone through with Jack, with her father. That paralyzing fear of having to bury a loved one…again.

But her mother's words kept coming back to her. Treasure every moment. Love while you can.

The realization came to her like a bolt of lightning. She wanted to be with Guy…for every minute, every second…until he had to go away again.

They could be together, now, and not worry about later. That's what he'd wanted. To marry her. To spend whatever time they had together.

And she'd so stupidly sent him away.

"There you are," her grandmother said as she entered the parlor.

Rosemary looked up and smiled.

"I'm glad to see something has cheered you up."

Rosemary stood and ran to her dear, sweet grandmother.

"What would you think if I told you I am going to get married?"

"What? Married? To who?"

"A soldier."

"Someone you met where you work?"

"No." She felt herself grinning from ear to ear. "His name is Guy. I met him on the train, last year. I've been writing to him."

"I don't understand. Where is he?"

"He's…" Rosemary stopped to think where he said he was going. "North Carolina. He had to report to a camp there."

"But…"

"He's been in Europe. He just got back, and he came to see me at Oak Ridge." She slipped her arm around her grandmother's plump waist and squeezed. "And he asked me to marry him."

"And you said yes." Her grandmother smiled.

Rosemary hesitated. How could she fix what she'd done?

****

August 5, 1945

The bus pulled into Fayetteville, North Carolina, after dark. With suitcase in tow, Rosemary fought off her exhaustion from the long bus ride and walked from the bus station to a local hotel recommended by the man behind the ticket counter.

"Do you have a room I can rent?" Rosemary asked the older lady behind the small wooden registration desk.

The woman looked Rosemary up and down before asking, "You alone?"

"Yes." The woman's frown deepened, so Rosemary offered more information. "I'm going out to Ft. Bragg to find my…"

"This is a respectable hotel. If your husband shows up, he'll have to be registered, too." The woman interrupted. "I'll put you down for a double."

She produced a book for Rosemary to sign.

Debating with herself whether to correct the woman, Rosemary signed.

"All right." The woman turned the book so she could read the name. "Missus Hopkins. That'll be two dollars. In advance."

Rosemary took the money from her purse and handed it over. "I don't know how long I'll be here."

"Oh, that's all right. You can let me know." She hesitated. "Course you have to pay each day."

"Of course."

As she placed a single key in Rosemary's hand, the woman said, "Up the stairs, end of the hall on the right."

"Thank you."

Rosemary clutched the key, picked up her suitcase, and climbed the stairs, thinking about the woman's words. She just assumed Rosemary was here to see her husband. Probably because Rosemary still wore Jack's ring.

Collapsing on the bed in the sparse room, Rosemary wondered what it would be like to be married to Guy. Her thoughts drifted back to that night. The one night they'd spent together in California. It seemed so long ago, yet every moment remained vivid.

She would never understand why she'd done it. Why she'd been so brazen. Perhaps the anonymity of the big city convinced her that she could do anything, could give in to the temptation of a handsome man in uniform.

Would that handsome man still want her after she'd pushed him away? After she'd refused his proposal? She could still see the hurt on his face.

Maybe he wouldn't see her. Maybe she'd hurt him so bad he didn't want anything to do with her.

A wicked idea swirled in her head. What if she said she was his wife?

It had worked at the train station…except they'd only implied the relationship. They hadn't told an out-and-out lie.

The lady at the desk had assumed she was married. Maybe she could make the Army think so, too.

Chapter 70

Guy, Tony, and several others kept busy inventorying equipment in the warehouse after its arrival from overseas.

"Hey, Nolan. Look at this." Tony handed him what looked like a box of radio parts.

"Where'd you find it?"

"Over there." Tony pointed to an area stacked with boxes of M-7 spare parts. "Didn't look like it belonged."

Guy examined the items. "Well…" He shook his head. "I'm not sure. These may be parts for the onboard radio."

He took the box over to a worktable where he had been sorting out the radio equipment.

Tony followed.

"Much as you know about all this…" He waved his hand to include all the electronics. "You ought to go to school. Get a good job after this is over."

"Yeah, well…" Guy hated to talk about future plans. "There was a time when I was going to start up a business, working on radios, selling them. That kind of thing."

"Not a bad idea."

"Yeah, except it takes money. Which I don't have." His gut twisted with disgust every time he thought about all the money he could have had, and what he could have done with it, if his mother hadn't spent it all.

"Woodson over there says he's going to go to college. Says the government will pay for us GIs to go."

"You thinking about it?"

"Maybe." Tony looked up toward the ceiling, lost in thought. "Wouldn't mind studying law."

"Law?" Tony surprised Guy. His friend was plenty smart, Guy just didn't expect such ambition from him.

"Yeah. The way I look at it, if Uncle Sam will pay us to go to college, maybe I should do it."

"Sure, sure. But why law?"

"Oh. There was this lawyer in our neighborhood. He helped folks when somebody got in trouble. Helped me take care of things when my folks got killed." He paused. "Everybody liked him, looked up to him."

"I think it's a fine idea." Guy smiled at his friend.

"You ought to think about it, too."

Guy nodded. Maybe he should. Maybe he could look into it. Maybe study engineering. Learn to design things, build better radios, better communications equipment. Could be interesting.

Except all that depended on him living through this war. With a trip to Japan on the agenda, he doubted he'd be going to any school after the war. No, he'd be pushing up daisies in some graveyard.

"Hey, Nolan."

Guy looked around. The sergeant stood near the doorway motioning for Guy to join him.

"Someone wants to see you."

"Who?" Guy asked, puzzled.

"Don't know. Just know they want you to report to the battalion commander's office."

****

Rosemary's stomach churned. They told her she had to wait, so here she sat, her hands clasped together as best she could without picking at the ragged nails on the hand awkwardly sticking out of her plaster-encased arm.

Despite her determination to sit quietly and wait, panic threatened to overcome her.

What was it about Guy that brought out the brazenness in her?

She'd arrived at Ft. Bragg on the early morning bus, and she'd managed to bully her way in to see the battalion commander. Brazenly flaunting her wedding ring, which wasn't easy with her left arm in a sling, she'd demanded to see Sergeant Guy Nolan. She'd carefully avoided calling him her husband. Instead, she'd expounded about her outrage at him leaving her.

The colonel had listened and looked her over. Then he'd asked if Guy had caused her injuries.

She hadn't expected that. It never occurred to her that the Army might think Guy had hurt her in any way except emotionally.

She'd felt the hot stain on her face when she'd said, "No. I fell. Off a ladder."

The look on his face said he didn't quite believe her, but he'd summoned Guy. And he'd told her to sit and wait.

So there she sat, waiting and shaking in her best pumps.

She almost jumped out of her skin when the door opened.

But it wasn't Guy.

The sergeant from before glanced her way, then knocked on the colonel's door. Seconds later he disappeared into the inner office.

Rosemary stared at the closed door and drew a deep breath to calm herself.

Not yet. He wasn't here yet.

Would he be mad? Would he deny the whole ruse and tell the colonel that it had been her who'd sent him away?

Would he tell her to leave? That he didn't want to see her again?

Tears welled up in her eyes. She quickly blinked them away. She wouldn't cry. No matter what, she wouldn't cry.

The door opened again, and a young private came in. She looked away, fearing he would gawk at her.

"Rosemary!"

She turned. Guy stood in the doorway.

She jumped up, but before she could take a step, he stood in front of her, that beautiful smile spread across his face.

"What are you doing here? And what happened to you?"

Her heart thudded. Her throat constricted. She couldn't speak. He touched her shoulder, and she finally blurted out, "I fell."

He slipped his arm around her good shoulder.

Relief washed over her as she leaned into his warm embrace. She'd found him, and he was glad to see her.

She couldn't stop the tears now.

Someone behind them cleared his throat, loudly.

They turned in unison to find the colonel standing there, with the sergeant and private peering over his shoulder.

Guy snapped to attention and saluted.

The colonel returned his salute. “At ease, soldier.”

The older man’s sharp gaze went from Guy to Rosemary and back. “Your wife here tells me you went off and left her.”

Rosemary stood so close she could feel Guy’s body stiffen. What would he say?

“Sir…” He hesitated, then turned to meet Rosemary’s gaze. “Well, sir…we had a sort of…a disagreement.”

“I see.” The officer took a step closer. “She says that these…” He waved his hand toward Rosemary. “…injuries were not caused by you but by a fall. Is that true?”

“Yes, sir. Well, I guess so. If that’s what she says.” He met her gaze again. “She was fine the last time I saw her.”

“I…I fell off a ladder…at work. I was upset, after you left, so I guess I wasn’t being careful.”

Guy smiled at her, and she knew it was all right.

“Sergeant, get Nolan here a three-day pass. He’ll need to go into town and get his wife situated.”

Rosemary’s heart raced.

“Thank you, sir,” Guy said. “I’ll take good care of her.”

“See that you do.”

The colonel returned to his office, and the sergeant directed them to follow him.

Guy grasped her hand and led her through the building, following the sergeant. Then they waited in silence for the pass to be typed up.

She didn’t know how she was going to explain to him why she’d come, but judging from his firm grip, she didn’t think she had to worry too much.

Finally, they exited the building, still holding hands. Guy led her around the corner, pulled her into his arms, and kissed her, an all-consuming kiss, filled with passion and longing.

All she could do was kiss him back. And enjoy every minute of it.

Chapter 71

Finally, seated on the bus headed into town, Guy turned to face her. “Are you going to explain now?”

She looked down, unable to meet his gaze.

“Well?”

She drew in a deep breath. Then she raised her head and faced him. “I thought about what you said. What you asked me…and I changed my mind. My answer is yes.”

His neutral expression softened into a smile. “Does that mean you’ll marry me?”

She nodded. “Yes.”

“Even though I may be killed?”

“Yes.” She reached out and placed her hand on his leg. “I want us to spend whatever time we have together. You and me. Together.”

“Even if it’s only a short time, maybe a month, before I have to leave?”

“Yes. Even if it’s only a few days. I want to spend them with you.”

“Oh, Rosemary.” He leaned in and softly touched his lips to hers.

“Uhumph.”

They jerked apart.

“Sorry,” Guy said over his shoulder to the man sitting behind them.

Rosemary and Guy both grinned at each other.

"I guess we'd better figure out how we're going to get married...since the colonel thinks we already are."

"About that..."

"I wondered when you'd get around to explaining." His light, joking tone let her know he wasn't mad.

She fingered her wedding ring. "Remember the train station in Oakland? When you bought our tickets?"

"And the ticket agent thought we were married?"

"Yes. But we didn't actually say we were married."

"So that's what you did with the colonel?"

"Pretty much. I waved my ring around and went on about how you went off and left me."

"So that's why he thought I'd beaten you up."

"I didn't really mean for him to think that."

Guy laughed. So Rosemary laughed with him.

He slipped his arm around her and pulled her close, while looking over his shoulder at the man behind them.

He leaned down and whispered in her ear. "We'll just have to find a preacher or a Justice of the Peace to make an honest woman of you."

Rosemary nodded, her heart bursting with joy.

****

Guy steered Rosemary into a cafe on the street between the bus stop and her hotel. "Maybe somebody in here will know where we can go to get married."

They slid into a booth near the front and waited for the waitress. "Do you think they'll make us wait? Some places make you wait."

"I don't know. All I know is that I'm gonna marry you before you get a chance to change your mind."

Rosemary smiled across the table. "I'm not going

to change my mind. I've taken too long as it is."

"I'm not arguing with that." He grabbed a menu from behind the napkin holder and studied it. "Might as well eat while we're here."

The waitress came over with glasses of water. Before she could ask for their order, someone called to her from behind the counter.

"Hey, listen up. We've dropped a bomb on Japan."

"So what?"

"Shut up and listen. They're readin' the President's statement."

"Turn it up."

"What'd he say?"

"Pipe down. I can't hear."

The volume suddenly increased so everyone in the place could hear the announcer's voice.

"...With this bomb we have now added a new and revolutionary increase in destruction to supplement the growing power of our armed forces. In their present form these bombs are now in production and even more powerful forms are in development.

It is an atomic bomb. It is a harnessing of the basic power of the universe. The force from which the sun draws its power has been loosed against those who brought war to the Far East."

Guy looked at Rosemary. She whispered, "What does it mean?"

He shrugged, a frown furrowing his brow. He jerked his head in the direction of the radio.

"...We knew that the Germans were working feverishly to find a way to add atomic energy to the other engines of war with which they hoped to enslave the world. But they failed. We may be grateful to

Providence that the Germans got the V-1s and V-2s late and in limited quantities and even more grateful that they did not get the atomic bomb at all.

The battle of the laboratories held fateful risks for us as well as the battles of the air, land, and sea, and we have now won the battle of the laboratories as we have won the other battles."

"Yeah, but at what cost," Guy muttered.

Rosemary remained quiet.

Guy's gaze roamed the cafe. Everyone was spellbound by the man on the radio reading President Truman's statement. All of them were wondering how it would affect them and the outcome of the war, just like him.

"But the greatest marvel is not the size of the enterprise, its secrecy, nor its cost, but the achievement of the scientific brains in putting together infinitely complex pieces of knowledge held by many men in different fields of science into a workable plan. And hardly less marvelous has been the capacity of industry to design, and of labor to operate, the machines and methods to do things never done before so that the brainchild of many minds came forth in physical shape and performed as it was supposed to do. Both science and industry worked under the direction of the United States Army, which achieved a unique success in managing so diverse a problem in the advancement of knowledge in an amazingly short time. It is doubtful if such another combination could be got together in the world. What has been done is the greatest achievement of organized science in history. It was done under high pressure and without failure."

Rosemary touched Guy's arm. Her eyes were wide

as she whispered, "I wonder…" Then she clamped her hand over her mouth.

"We shall completely destroy Japan's power to make war," the announcer continued.

"It was to spare the Japanese people from utter destruction that the ultimatum of July 26 was issued from Potsdam. Their leaders promptly rejected that ultimatum. If they do not now accept our terms, they may expect a rain of ruin from the air, the like of which has never been seen on this earth."

The whole cafe cheered.

"Behind this air attack will follow sea and land forces in such numbers and power as they have not yet seen and with the fighting skill of which they are already well aware."

"I guess he means us," Guy muttered bitterly. It didn't sound like he would be off the hook. "On to Japan."

Rosemary frowned at him.

"The Secretary of War, who has kept in personal touch with all phases of the project, will immediately make public a statement giving further details."

"His statement will give the facts concerning the sites at Oak Ridge near Knoxville, Tennessee…"

Rosemary gasped and covered her mouth, her eyes wide. Guy stared at her.

"…and at Richland near Pasco, Washington, and an installation near Santa Fe, New Mexico. Although workers at the sites have been making materials to be used in producing the greatest destructive force in history, they have not themselves been in danger beyond that of many other occupations, for the utmost care has been taken for their safety."

"I guess that answers what you've been making at Oak Ridge. And why there's all that security."

She grinned. "It's incredible." She looked around at the others still listening intently to the announcer. "I wonder if it means I can talk about it?"

"If the President can talk about it on the radio, I guess you can."

"Shush!"

"Under present circumstances it is not intended to divulge the technical processes of production or all the military applications, pending further examination of possible methods of protecting us and the rest of the world from the danger of sudden destruction."

"Golly," she whispered. "Maybe I'd better call somebody before I say anything. I sure don't want to get into any trouble."

The announcer completed the statement and everyone in the place started talking at once.

"What do we do now?" she asked.

"We get married. We can worry about all this later."

Chapter 72

Rosemary hurried to keep up with Guy's long strides.

"Are we going to a fire?"

"What?" He slowed and glanced at her. "Oh, sorry. I guess I'm kind of anxious."

"Me too."

It hadn't taken many inquiries to learn that all they had to do to get married was go to the court house, get a license, and get a judge to marry them. It sounded simple enough, but it was already past midday.

"After we get married, we can stay in your hotel room tonight." He'd resumed walking at a more reasonable pace. "Then tomorrow we can find someplace more permanent for you to live."

"Okay."

He slowed a little more and looked over at her. "You sure you don't want to change clothes or go buy something new to wear? I could go back to the base and get my dress uniform."

"What happened to the guy who was in a hurry? Aren't you afraid they'll close for the day before we get back?"

"Oh, I don't know." He pressed his lips together in that frustrated look of his. "I just want you to be happy. I don't want to rush you into something you'll regret."

"Regret? Here I've come chasing after you, all the

way from Kerrville, and you think I'm not sure."

"Well, are you?"

Rosemary gulped at his direct question. Was she? What if she was making another mistake?

No. Don't think like that. You've been over all this and you know in your heart it's what you want.

"I'm sure," she said firmly.

He let out a big sigh and grinned at her. "Then come on." He grabbed her hand and practically pulled her down the sidewalk.

"Truman sounded pretty tough. Maybe with this atomic bomb thing we can scare the Japs into surrendering."

"I hope so." Her heart ached every time she thought of him having to invade Japan.

"I still might have to go over there. Serve as occupation forces, like we thought we'd be doing in Germany."

"At least they wouldn't be shooting at you."

The huge stone building loomed ahead.

"Well, that's it." He sounded nervous.

"Yes," she nodded and squeezed his hand.

"Getting married. Starting a new life together. Settling down and starting a family. That's what I want. I'm not sure exactly what I'll do, how I'll support you, but I'll figure out something."

A family. Rosemary hadn't even thought of that. Of course, she wanted a family, she just wasn't sure…

He started up the steps. She pulled on his hand to stop him.

"Guy. There's something I should tell you." She couldn't let him marry her not knowing.

"What is it?"

"When…when I was married to Jack, well, you see…I…I was pregnant." Her eyes darted to his face to gauge his reaction.

"Okay?"

He dragged the word out like he wasn't sure he wanted to hear what she had to say. So she plunged ahead to get it over with.

"I lost the baby."

He nodded. His odd expression made her wonder what he was thinking.

Say something.

Finally, he spoke. "What happened?"

"I don't know. The doctor didn't say. Just to wait and try again."

"Did you want the baby?"

A man walked by close enough to hear them. She felt the heat rising to her face. Anyone could see her obvious embarrassment.

"Well?"

"I guess. I don't know." She wrung her hands despite the awkward cast. "We didn't plan it. It just kind of happened."

"Did he want it?"

"No." She said it too quick. "I don't know. He was getting used to it. I think after he thought about it, he said he wanted a child, but then…"

After a moment Guy slipped his arm around her. "That's all in the past. We're starting new. Isn't that what we said?"

She nodded, blinking back tears. Was it that easy?

They climbed a few steps toward the entrance.

"What if…what if I can't…"

"We'll cross that bridge when we come to it."

"But you want a family."

"Don't you?"

She nodded.

He pulled her into his arms. "Then we'll have a family. One way or another."

A sense of relief washed over her and lifted a weight off her that she hadn't even realized she'd been carrying. She saw it so clearly now. Her fears. Not just losing Guy, like she'd lost Jack and her father. She was afraid of losing another baby, too. But Guy wasn't the least bit worried. That, and his love, would get her through anything.

Soon they were filling out paperwork and signing on the dotted line.

"I'll send someone to tell the judge not to leave," the clerk said. "Sometimes he sneaks out early and goes fishin'."

Rosemary looked up in time to catch his broad smile.

In a few minutes, the clerk ushered them into the judge's chambers.

"Here they are, Judge. Another young couple wanting to get married before he ships out."

"Not exactly," Guy spoke up. "I already shipped out and shipped back."

The judge perked up. "Is that so? Where've you been?"

"Europe, sir. Spent almost a year and a half fighting Germans."

"And now he's got orders to go to Japan."

"Japan, eh? Well, maybe not. Not after this big bomb. Surely they'll give up now."

"I hope so, sir."

The judge nodded. “Well, let’s get this taken care of.” He looked around. “Harold. You round us up some witnesses.”

“Yes, sir, Judge.”

The clerk disappeared, and the judge took their paperwork to look it over.

“Do you have a ring?”

Guy nodded and fished a cloth pouch out of his pocket. He poured the contents out into his palm. A ring and earrings.

“You have a ring?” Rosemary exclaimed. She’d expected to use the gold band she wore. “And earrings!” She flashed Guy an excited smile.

“Go ahead.” He nodded and held them closer. “Try them on.”

“Why earrings? How did you know?” She fumbled to take off her pearls, Jack’s pearls. She didn’t remember ever telling Guy about Jack giving her the pearl earrings. It didn’t matter now.

“They came with the ring. Mr. Cary would only sell them as a set.” Guy handed her the earrings.

“And you bought them for me.”

He grinned. “They match your eyes.”

She fought back tears as she put the pale blue earrings on her earlobes.

“How do they look?”

“Gorgeous. Just like you.”

Holding his ring out for her to see, he glanced up and their gazes met. “I bought them in California. I was going to give it to you…well…”

Her gaze shifted to the pale blue stone flanked by darker blue ones. “It’s beautiful.”

“It’s an aquamarine with sapphires. Like I said, the

color reminded me of your eyes."

"Oh." She blinked but failed to keep the tears from slipping down her cheeks. "That's so sweet."

"I…I hope you like it."

"I love it. I absolutely love it."

"Good." He grinned.

Just then, Harold returned with two middle-aged women and an older man. One of the ladies handed Rosemary a bunch of homegrown roses with a damp handkerchief wrapped around the stems.

"You have to have a bouquet," she said.

Rosemary smiled and nodded. "Thank you."

Before the judge began the ceremony, Guy slipped Jack's ring from her finger and she put it in her purse, along with the pearl earrings.

The judge quickly reached the point where he instructed Guy to place the ring on her finger. "Repeat after me. With this ring, I thee wed."

Guy slipped the aquamarine ring on her finger. "With this ring, I thee wed."

"By the power vested in me by the State of North Carolina, I pronounce you man and wife."

Rosemary locked gazes with Guy. Her grin must have been as big as his.

"Go ahead. Kiss her." One of the ladies prompted.

Guy pulled her close and captured her mouth. And with that kiss both poured out all their love for each other. Her whole being told her she'd done the right thing, for herself and for Guy.

As they broke the kiss, she whispered, "I love you."

"I love you, too, Mrs. Nolan."

Amid congratulations from all present, the happy

couple hurried from the court house, out into the world and the rest of their lives—however long that might be.

A word about the author...

Barbara Whitaker writes historical romances with a focus on the World War II era. Originally from a small town in Tennessee, she currently calls Florida home. You can visit Barbara's website at:

http://www.barbarawhitaker.com/

Thank you for purchasing
this publication of The Wild Rose Press, Inc.

For questions or more information
contact us at
info@thewildrosepress.com.

The Wild Rose Press, Inc.
www.thewildrosepress.com